D1524255

UNGUARDED EDGE

Part 2 in "The Dutchville Series"
Large Print Edition

❖

HADLEY HOOVER'S NOVELS

❖

Preview chapters: www.hadleyhoover.com

UNGUARDED EDGE

Happy Reading!
Hadley Hoover

Hadley Hoover

Large Print Edition

ISBN: 978-1-387-21870-7

DEDICATION

Kendall: Like Lena, I found love on "the edge of the world." Thanks for loving me so long, so much, and so well.

My sisters, Ann and Mary Gail, inspire, amuse, support, and amaze me; I treasure our friendship.

I'm grateful to the late Marion Dunbar whose personal horse-and-buggy stories entertained and enlightened me.

❖

ACKNOWLEDGEMENTS

Rough Terrain's avid readers let me know *they* weren't done with the story, even if *I* was; they won! Stanley & Lorna Olson and my Mom shared personal stories of one-room schools. Thank you, one and all.

❖

1929–1930 Dutch Valley School Roster

Battjes **Katrien** ~ 3rd grade
Parents: Caspar & Cokkie

Beekman **Lucas** ~ 5th grade
Liesbeth ~ 1st grade
Parents: Filip & Helena

Bleecker **Maas** ~ 3rd grade
Parents: Piet & Klaartje

de Boer **Antje** ~ 2nd grade
Maartje ~ 1st grade
Parent: Cornelis {*Juanita; deceased*}

De Groot **Janneken** ~ 5th grade
Parents: Frans & Betje

De Jong **Jaap** ~ 6th grade
Parents: Joris & Magda

De Jong **Adda** ~ 3rd grade
Parents: Ruben & Agnes

Hazenbroek **Elsje** ~ 8th grade
Parents Gerolt & Martina

Ten Broek **Giertje** ~ 3rd grade
Parents: Leendert & Sytje

Vande Veer **Raimund & Bartel** ~ 4th grade
Parents: Teunis & Mirjam

Van der Voort **Sterre** ~ 2nd grade
Parents: Ruud & Geesje

Van Leuven **Saartje** ~ 8th grade
Parents: Jillis & Dirkje

Wynkoop **Wim** ~ 1st grade
Parents: Dries & Hilde

Part One

Monday, September 9, 1929 ♦ A final task remained: distribute new chalk and erasers along the blackboard tray. With that done, Lena wrote *Miss Stryker* in decisive strokes on the clean board.

First-Day-of-School tradition required that the teacher's name be displayed in proper cursive letters, even if it was no surprise to the students sitting in polished wooden desks. Seeing her name would remind them to call her the proper name for the teacher in this one-room school—not Tante Lena as much of Dutchville did.

She added *Welcome to Dutch Valley School! Today is Monday, September 9, 1929* below her name. "My fourth year!"

Despite the gap between her initial training for the classroom in 1900 and the delayed beginning of her teaching career in 1925, she truly was a teacher, at last, with three years' experience to her credit.

During the years since 1900, the borders of Lena's life rarely extended beyond the realm of the parsonage that stood in the Dutchville Reformed Church's shadow. At her brother-in-law Dominie Gustave Ter Hoorn's behest, Lena had rushed to aid her sister Hanna when Brigetta was born.

As the welcomed and revered Tante in the Dutch minister's family, Lena had cooked, cleaned, soothed wounded pride, bandaged scratched elbows, gardened, and laundered throughout the years of her niece's childhood. When Brigetta had married Bram de Boer, the essence of Lena's responsibilities (though she never considered helping to raise Brigetta to be a burden) subtly shifted, freeing her to pursue the long-dormant dream of becoming a teacher.

Lena knew the power of words. All it had taken to bring her cross-country on the train to Northwest Iowa in 1900 was a telegram:

Come immediately? Hanna ill, baby healthy. Gustave

Back then, she promptly set aside her personal desires and plans, and never looked back. Now, her name—written in flowing Palmer-style strokes on gleaming slate—set her on a different journey in this, her fourth decade of life. Now, chalked words confirmed who was in charge.

Being in charge was not fearsome to Lena, not after all she had survived. What could be more terrifying than arriving, as a seventeen-year-old girl, in a strange town with little time to make new friends her own age? Or being handed custody of a busy household? Or finding her sister floundering in the seas of depression? Or learning, day-to-day, how to mother Brigetta without negating Hanna's role as the actual mother?

Yes, those were fearsome things, but Lena had weathered them all. Preparing a full range of lesson plans across the spectrum of grades could seem overwhelming. Now she faced this from the bedrock of confidence that had formed over previous years of meeting each successive challenge with courage and increasing insight.

Soon, she would walk out the doorway of Dutch Valley School to greet the arriving children. As if to remind her of approaching duties, the Royalton clock on the wall struck the three-quarter hour.

With shrieks and trills of children's voices gaining volume and number in the schoolyard, Lena gave the potted ivy a half-rotation on the teacher's desk. She then quickly scanned the room with pride:

. . . fourteen desks bolted to tracks in three rows of five-four-five, with the pot-bellied stove squatting like a chubby uncle at the back of the middle row,

. . . the water cooler, a thin glaze of moisture already coating its pearly porcelain curves, with the dipper hooked over one edge ready for thirsty lips,

. . . narrow windows, four on each side wall, half-curtained to allow circulation but minimize distraction from long-division, geography, or spelling,

. . . the pull-down United States map concealing vocabulary words on the blackboard, and the smooth-faced globe on the table by the dictionary stand.

Satisfied that all was in order, Lena stepped out onto the stoop she'd swept in dawn's first light. She blinked in the day-bright sunshine and moved back into the overhanging roof's shade.

Her *klompen* bumped a basket; she shifted it to one side. At her feet were an assortment of tin syrup pails, lard cans, drawstring knapsacks, and one cloth-lined basket—all containing lunches and school supplies that the students would reclaim when the bell rang. Lena's lunch was in a tin bucket in the teacherage.

Teacherage. Even thinking that word made Lena happy. Years back, a single male teacher coming from Michigan balked at boarding with strangers, so a storage area had been converted to private quarters, never to be returned to its original purpose.

To be hired to teach at Dutch Valley School held a measure of prestige for each successive teacher. The teacherage meant they did not need to impose on (or endure) school families for room and board.

Small and primitive, the room was Lena's abode from Sunday evenings through Friday afternoons during the school year. Weekends and the evenings when her monthly Sewing Circle met, she returned to the parsonage in Dutchville and slept again in the familiar bed in her room there.

Hardly a week went by without Hanna fussing, "I don't know why you insist on living in such Spartan conditions when you could be at home with us!"

Though she would never tell her sister this, months before Lena had first applied for the teaching position she'd begun to feel life's pinch like an accordion squeezing the joy of living right out of her. She was a mature woman who had never had her own home, never been kissed by a man in a passionate manner, and never had her own child.

But when she applied and the school board offered Lena this teaching position, it was as if *Hemel's* angels turned life's pinches into life's music. She had felt her soul expand as if its bellows would burst, so wide was her bliss.

Spartan conditions? By some standards, yes, but it was home. She may not own it, but the room at the back of the school, despite its inadequacies, satisfied a profound desire.

As for passion? Perhaps in the past she'd longed for a man who possessed such deep feelings for Lena Stryker that he was unable to express them in any manner other than pressing his lips against hers. But, at age forty-six, she suspected her future, like her past and present, would require only a single bed. She had baked her share of Dutch Letter cookies for Dutchville brides, including Brigetta, but she doubted she'd ever offer a groom an **S** pastry to signify their marriage.

As for children? Although Brigetta came close to satisfying most maternal instincts, Lena was always aware she was the Tante, never the mother. But now! Children of all shapes and sizes, ages and abilities filled her days and populated her dreams.

They, in turn, basked in her love and flourished under her creativity. Her zeal made even a lesson on fractions fairly hum. The way she explained the correct use of semi-colons gave punctuation a spin and sizzle. Under Lena's tutelage, every student in Dutch Valley School felt they had been part of Christopher Columbus' discovery of America when the history curriculum reached those lessons.

Two of three longings had been granted; to expect more would be greedy, Lena reminded herself. *I have two places to feel at home, plus a respectable and exciting career that fills my life with children. What blessings God has bestowed on me!*

A faint clanging above the din of excited voices caught her attention. She easily identified it as metallic echoes from an empty swing's chains. A sullen boy pushed the painted wooden seat away each time it returned to him; he did so with no visible enjoyment and even less purpose.

"Good morning, Maas!" Lena called across the playground, though not expecting an answer. If Maas held true to form; it would be Thanksgiving before more than a grudging smile reshaped his tight lips.

Third grade was the largest class this year and consisted of three girls—Katrien, Adda, and Giertje— and one disgruntled boy: Maas, the swing-pusher. In a few years, the unbalanced male-female ratio of his grade would not bother the lad, but his carry-over impression of school from first and second grades was clearly unchanged on this, his first day of third grade.

"Miss Stryker!" An excited voice drew Lena's attention to the opposite corner of the yard. "We're teaching Freek to drink from the pump instead of puddles!"

"Freek is a mighty smart puppy, Wim," she responded with a smile, noting the third-grade girls formed a rapt audience for boy and dog. Each girl longed for a pet—not just the family's farm dog. Possessing Freek gave Wim hero-status in their eyes. Lena sighed at the contrast between the always-cloudy Maas and the predictably-sunny Willem who was called Wim by all who knew him. She let her mind drift on this sunny September morning . . .

Although just a first-grader, Wim walked a winding mile from his house to school nearly every weekday throughout August "to show Freek where I'll be all day," he explained to Lena, sticking his head in the open schoolhouse door on the first such morning.

Setting aside her lesson preparations for the moment, Lena had joined Wim on the low stoop (while a panting Freek sprawled in ungainly fashion on the ground between them) to discuss just how this dog-boy relationship would work, once school began.

"Could Freek come inside and sit by my desk?" Wim had asked hopefully.

Smiling, Lena shook her head. "No, he wouldn't like that very much. He needs to chase squirrels and find rabbit holes, and you need to learn to read and write. But a smart dog like Freek could learn something very important."

"He can? I mean, sure he can . . . uh, what, exactly, can he learn?" He was stuck between doubt and hope.

"Freek appears to be a dog that could learn what time you must wake up to get to school on time . . ."

"Oh, he already knows that, and he can tell time," Wim boasted. "He sleeps by my bed and sticks his nose in my face right before Mother calls me."

"That's good. He will learn to find his way home when you begin school. And then Freek can learn what time school is dismissed and he'll be waiting on the playground for you to walk through the door. That part you can teach him, and you will always have a friend along for the walk home."

Freek flailed his ear with a paw to discourage a fly, but suddenly straightened to stare at a spot on the horizon that offered none of the action of Hendrik Wielenga's mule team that was pulling a wagon in the field across the road. Just as Lena had begun to wonder if she had misjudged the dog's abilities, pride squared Wim's chin. "Freek's awfully smart."

"I'm glad. Today, on your way home, you say, 'Go home, Freek,' and lead him home. Take the same path you want him to follow. If he wanders off, get him back beside you and repeat, 'Go home, Freek.' If you do this every day, on the first day of school all you will need to say is 'Go home, Freek,' and off he'll go," Lena said with bold confidence.

The boy studied his dog thoughtfully. His fingers scratched around one golden-haired floppy ear until Freek moaned with joy. "But how will he know when to come get me?" Wim had asked, suddenly suspicious.

"First, you teach him what home and school mean. Beginning tomorrow, after breakfast and your morning chores, you say, 'Time to go to school, Freek,' and bring him directly here. You could ask your mother to tell him, 'Go to school, Freek,' every afternoon."

Lena imagined Hilde Wynkoop rolling her eyes when Wim told of this plan, but could a mother deny such a simple request from a trusting lad? *Time will tell* was the only self-assurance Lena could muster.

Throughout August, Wim approached his task with a diligence Lena hoped extended to his education. Each day, she bicycled to the school and worked on lesson plans to the accompaniment of Wim's chatter with his dog. "This is school, Freek. You take a nap, I'll swing, then we'll get a drink at the pump, and then we'll go home. Home is where we live."

Now, the true test of Lena's daring promise would come at the end of the day: Would Freek be waiting for Wim?

"One can only hope," Lena murmured. "With fourteen students spread across eight grades, I have no time to worry about what a dog has learned!"

From the stoop, she continued her head-count. Leaning against the fence, deep in conversation, were this year's oldest students: Elsje and Saartje. The girls lived at opposite ends of the township, but were best friends. Elsje's two older brothers attended high school in Dutchville, and Saartje was the only child still at home in her family.

Aware that the girls had summer tales to tell, Lena made a mental note to monitor their whispers and inevitable note-passing until they slipped back into the groove of proper school behavior.

Lena's review skipped seventh grade since no one occupied that position this year. Jaap, the lone sixth-grader, tossed a ball to Lucas, a fifth grader. Each boy had shot up several inches over the summer and would likely outgrow their new pants and shirts by spring.

Janneken (who to Lucas' disgust was his sole fifth-grade classmate) wandered the playground contentedly, tugging at the blouse whose strategic tucks hinted at blossoming womanhood on her horizon. Like Maas,

Janneken was a loner, but unlike Maas who stewed in a cauldron of glum thoughts, Janneken was a dreamer—fully content to be alone. Lena knew getting and keeping Janneken's attention would remain the challenge it had been the previous four years.

Fourth grade was next on the visual tally. *Where are the Vande Veer twins?* Lena's eyes automatically turned east. Most students rode bicycles, or walked, or had older siblings who dropped them off at the country school on their way to high school in town.

Raimund and Bartel came the greatest distance. On nice days, the twins rode a horse and tied it behind the school to graze on field grasses throughout the day; in harsh weather, they arrived in a buggy that offered the boys some protection. As if summoned by her thoughts, two riders and a horse crested the road's gentle rise and soon cantered through the gate.

"Good morning, boys," Lena called. "I see you're riding a different horse this year!"

"Our pony got strong enough to work, so Father says we have to ride Midnight because he's too old to pull a plow anymore," Bartel tossed over his shoulder.

His brother tugged the rope tied to the bridle and guided the aging horse behind the schoolhouse where hitching post and watering trough awaited. Lena knew their afternoon trip home would find Bartel holding the reins because the twins employed a precise system of fairness between themselves.

With the third graders fully occupied at the pump and swings, Lena continued her visual journey around the schoolyard until she reached the corner of the fence. Crowded like lambs in a stall, Liesbeth (Wim's fellow first grader) linked arms with Sterre who— though in second grade—was small for her age, and as fragile as the fine China doll her doting parents believed her to be.

Each time the older boys' ball bounced near them, the girls squealed and clung to each other. Protected by the perceived security of distance, they observed the activity by the pump, both obviously enchanted by the scene, but clearly terrified of something.

Freek has them scared silly, Lena decided. She privately believed that Sterre's parents not only spoiled her shamelessly (proof being the fancy lunch basket on the stoop) but overly protected her from anything they deemed upsetting. Liesbeth had suffered a goat's nip the previous summer—all of which meant neither child had pleasant experiences with friendly animals.

The two girls noticed Lena and, after a whispered exchange, held hands, plotted a course that gave the pump wide berth, and ran toward her. But before they could reach the stoop, Freek spotted their little legs moving like greased lightning and took off in pursuit.

Squeals became screams and the two frightened lambs, clad in new cotton dresses with crisp Dutch collars and snow-white bibs, veered away from Lena and headed straight towards the ash pile—a mound that seemed certain safety to their frantic minds.

Unfortunately, the ash heap was hardly a stable retreat. At best, it was dirty; at worst, it was wet with dew.   In one ear-piercing chorus, three children alternately sobbed and howled: two little girls from terror of dog and loathing of dirt, and one little boy from fear of retaliation against his beloved dog.

Remembering too late his mother's morning instructions to "Watch out for your sister, Lucas," Liesbeth's brother appeared on the scene and blended scolding with comfort—an odd mix, with neither being effective.

Meanwhile, Freek bounded around the circle of children, making frequent trips across the rapidly disintegrating pile of ashes, and leaving charred footprints on trousers and skirts while Wim chased him. Mayhem ruled until the teacher was forced to bellow, "Children! Stand still and be quiet!"

Sobs sputtered into silence upon the disheartening situation. Lena gathered the girls around her and glanced at the fringe of gawking students.

"Janneken, hurry inside and get rags from the bag in the cloakroom, and wet them at the pump. Elsje and Saartje, take Liesbeth and Sterre to the swings and clean them with the wet rags."

Next, she turned to Wim. "Call Freek; then go wash his paws and your hands at the pump. When you're both cleaned up, take Freek over by the gate and hold him there until I come."

Puppy and boy connected, at last, as Wim latched hold of Freek's collar. Gulping final sobs, the little girls accepted the older girls' proffered hands. Lena turned her attention to the other children.

"Jaap, there's a hoe in the horse shed; try to get the ashes back in one heap without getting yourself mussed. Lucas, get the gunnysack from the fence and wet it in the horse trough; when Jaap finishes, put it carefully on top. The rest of you may play until opening ceremonies."

Grimly, Lena looked at her ash-smeared dress and sighed. She crossed the yard to where Wim and Freek presented a solemn picture of dejection. Today, Lena completely identified with The Old Woman Who Lived in a Shoe. In less than ten minutes, what should have been a happy day had crumbled into a regrettable beginning to a school year.

Over by the swings, the older girls' ministrations had calmed the younger girls. Wim, however, closely resembled a prisoner banished to a dark dungeon with no hope of release. Lena set aside her own frustrations and knelt on the grass beside the boy and dog. Freek's tail thumped a steady beat against a fence post; Wim's bottom lip quivered.

"I tried to 'splain to Freek what he did wrong, Miss Stryker, but I don't know, either . . ." Wim's uneven voice faded altogether; he blinked rapidly. He rubbed his forearm across his eyes, leaving an ashy trail.

Lena pulled a handkerchief from her pocket and rubbed at the raccoon-eye pattern dirt and tears had painted on Wim's face.

Such loving attention weakened his shaky hold on maturity. He threw himself on Lena, sobbing into the folds of her skirt, "I hate school! I'm going home!"

"Shhh. School isn't usually like this." He pulled back, only to look in horror at the dark circles he had left on Lena's dress. "Don't worry, Wim. It will all come out in the wash. Listen to me! Freek was just being a dog. Dogs like to run and chase things, and he saw the girls as something fun to chase, and one thing led to another. Some people are afraid of dogs."

"Afraid of Freek?" He was stunned. "Why, he's the best dog in the world! He ain't nothing to be scared of. Not like bulls or lions or . . ."

Lena gently cut short what promised to be a lengthy listing of every terrorizing thing a six-year-old lad could name. "We will try to help Liesbeth and Sterre learn what a wonderful dog Freek is, but now it is time for school to start, and time for Freek to go home."

Wim looked wistfully down the long road. "Could I should walk him a little ways toward home?"

"No, because then you would be tardy for school."

Two skinny sun-bronzed arms hugged the dog's neck. "Okay, Freek; this is it. You know what to do," he said tremulously. "Go home, Freek." He pointed down the road. "Go home," he repeated.

"You know, Wim," Lena said casually, "first graders have an important job on the first day of school."

"We do? What?" Curiosity wrested his attention away from his four-legged meandering friend.

"First-grade boys are bell-ringers and the girls are flag-raisers every year on the first day of school."

Awed, Wim tucked his hand into hers. At the stoop, he halted. "I can't look. Is Freek going home?"

Lena glanced over her shoulder. "He's thinking about it. I guess he wants to be sure you are inside," she admitted, realizing belatedly the dog's summer's training had never included the crucial step of actually leaving the young master at school. "When you and I come back outside after ringing the bell, Freek will be on his way home."

The bell-pull nearly lifted Wim off the floor but, with Lena's help, he got sound from the old belfry. With melodious notes riding the breeze across the fields and along the creek bed, the thirteen other students gathered around the flagpole.

To Lena's relief, Freek was out of sight when she and Wim emerged from the building. The school-year's initial flag-raiser looked bedraggled, wetted down considerably more than necessary, but at least Liesbeth's tears had ceased.

Lena ruefully hoped no one on the nearby farms was setting clocks by the school bell this first day. *Mercy! It must be a quarter-past-eight by now!*

She mentally adjusted the day's schedule to accommodate the late start even as she said cheerfully, "Good morning, students!" and slipped into the familiar rituals without further delay.

"Good morning, Miss Stryker," a chorus of voices responded.

"Woof!" Freek's happy voice sounded in the distance. A plume of dust, visible only to Lena, rose from the road as the dog put feet to his exuberant response to the children's greetings. Rows of tall corn had hidden him, but he now loped back to the gate as if propelled by his wagging tail.

Two little girls froze in the ranks, one little boy gulped, and one teacher's spirits sank.

Lena said firmly, "We will not give Freek the slightest indication that we notice him. He has been taught to go home after he walks with Wim to school, and that is what he must do now. Liesbeth, will you help me raise the flag?"

Lena threaded the forty-eight–star flag onto its lead and placed the chain in Liesbeth's damp and shaking hands. With her glance alternating between Old Glory rising to the sky and Freek pacing on the road, the little girl somehow managed her task.

Right hands covered hearts while fifteen voices recited the Pledge of Allegiance, the youngest students chiming in sporadically as familiar sections came around. Then all marched around the flagpole, singing, "My Country, 'tis of Thee" in loud, yet melodious tones. The 1929 school year had officially begun in the freshly painted building rising proudly midst Iowa's cornfields.

"Please line up by grades and follow me. When you reach the doorway, pick up your lunch and wait there until I call your name. One-by-one, I will direct you to your assigned seat." Lifting her ankle-length skirt, Lena crossed the stoop.

Excited whispers and resonating nonhuman sounds behind her alerted Lena that their uninvited canine guest was no longer outside the gate. Battling frustration, Lena turned. "Jaap, since you're the boy nearest the back of the line, please ensure that Freek remains outside the building."

"Yes, Miss Stryker." The shy sixth grader strutted a bit as he moved into place to execute his duty.

Wim crept ahead of Liesbeth in line and tugged on Lena's skirt. "Miss Stryker, I better take Freek and go home now."

"No; I prepared many things for you to do today. You don't want my work to be wasted, do you, Wim?"

He frowned, released a deep sigh, and ducked down to see past his schoolmates' legs to where Jaap held a struggling dog by the collar. "Go home, Freek; don't get us in any more trouble. Go home," he pleaded, blinking fast against the threat of returning tears.

Slowly, he rose. "Okay, Miss Stryker; I will stay."

"I knew I could count on you," she said solemnly. "Now, first grade students, follow me." Soon, each student sat in the appointed seat.

"Take a few minutes to arrange your supplies inside your desk. Today, I'll dismiss you, row-by-row, to take your lunches to the cloakroom. On future mornings, you will visit the cloakroom before taking your seats. Elsje, please lead the way and remain in the cloakroom to help the first graders find the hooks I assigned to them."

With that accomplished, Lena walked to the blackboard, picked up her pointer, and used its rubber tip to underscore her name. "I am Miss Stryker. As you know, my given name is Lena, and though you may hear others call me Tante Lena, I expect you to call me Miss Stryker. All rise and we will sing the first *Psalmen* on this, the first day of a new school year."

Even the youngest were familiar with the Dutch language, having heard it since infancy from parents and grandparents. Living in the lap of all-things-Dutch, and having been rocked to sleep with Old-Country lullabies, and raised to know and revere the Holy Scriptures, the children sang enthusiastically:

> "*Welgelukzalig is de man, die niet wandelt in de raad der goddelozen, noch staat op den weg der zondaren, noch zit in het gestoelte der spotters . . .*"

As the song ended, Lena thought she heard a sound outside, but rather than break the regained flow of the morning, she ignored it.

"You may be seated. We begin this first day of lessons with a speaking exercise. We will concentrate on following instructions. As I call names, you will stand and clearly say your name and grade in school, and tell the others something about your summer. Elsje, you may be the first."

Lena walked toward her desk. Since it was positioned at an angle in the corner opposite the door, her back was turned when the door creaked open. Irrational though it was, her first thought was *Freek?*

She pivoted on her heel and was startled to see two little girls tottering on the threshold as the closing door bumped them from behind. *Did I miscount my students? No, of course not—these are strangers.* Lena's pleasant greeting revealed none of her confusion. "Good morning, girls. Come in!"

"Father is getting our lunches," the younger one blurted, her eyes as shiny as coal beneath a head capped by dark tumbling ringlets. "We forgot them by the gate when we picked thistles off our leggings." A gap in her front teeth accounted for her sweet lisp. The girls looked enough alike to be twins, but the difference in size indicated a gap of one or two years between their ages.

A shuffle from behind distracted the girls from their furtive glances around the room. They looked up with evident relief into the hat-shadowed face of the man whose impressive bulk filled the doorway. He handed a cloth bag over each girl's shoulder and bent to kiss her cheek as she accepted it.

He rose to his full height, tucked his hat under his arm, and let his hands rest on the girls' heads. "These are my daughters. We arrived two days ago; I initially planned to return to Chicago after a short visit, but decided to remain here for the school year."

The other children gaped at this unknown person so unlike their own fathers who—though toughened by the grueling taskmaster of farming—had none of this man's presence or persona. *Charm,* Lena thought. *The man possesses a rough-hewn charm, made all the more enticing by his physical appearance.*

A blush heated up her cheeks; she quickly looked away from the muscles that stretched the man's shirt and vest. But diverting her eyes didn't erase the memory of a trim waist at odds with his obvious strength. *What is wrong with me, acting like a schoolgirl?*

Schoolgirls! Disapproval firmed her jaw as she saw each girl lean forward, like tides following the moon.

It required no special skills to read Bartel's lips whispering to Raimund: *"He's like Charles Atlas!"*

Each boy heard the magic name and, like a sponge, absorbed first-hand what he had previously witnessed only in comic books. Their expressions trumpeted their wild hopes: *"Will he flex his muscles? Or lift Miss Stryker's desk right off the floor? Golly-gee-whizzicles, that'd be something!"*

Lena sighed. *Familiar voice?* she mused, scanning the stranger's face for a clue to his identity. *Something about him rings a bell, but what? "Chicago," he says?*

His eyes drifted across Lena's maltreated dress, but he seemed unconcerned that the teacher's dress resembled a dirty dust rag. He cleared his throat.

He's nervous, Lena noted with surprise.

He smoothed the older girl's hair. "This is Annie, I mean, Antje; she's in second grade."

He repeated the action on the other girl's head. "This is Mary, that is, Maartje; she will be first grade." He shuffled, clearly wanting to leave.

Lena's attention drifted from the father to the children, all three of whom seemed weighed down beneath a melancholy mantle. *Not fear of something new,* she mused, *but sadness.* The syncopated rhythm of her *klompen* on the varnished floor matched her heartbeat as she walked over and knelt by the sisters.

They clutched their lunches as if to prevent anyone from snatching the bags, pulling back even from Lena. The older girl visibly trembled and the younger child's earlier burst of confidence had waned.

"Welcome to Dutch Valley School, Antje and Maartje," Lena said gently. "Or do you prefer to be called by your English names?"

Both girls looked up questioningly at their restless father.

"What is your other name?" Lena asked gently.

Antje whispered, "de Boer."

Her sister said, "I'm Maartje de Boer; I'm five. Annie . . . I mean, Antje's seven."

Sought-for hints emerged as facts, scorching Lena's mind, sucking her breath away like a fire consuming a prairie. Slowly, she rose to her feet and let her eyes take the measure of the man. Gentleness flattened into a neutral tone. "Cornelis. Cornelis de Boer."

His eyes met hers fleetingly as he dropped his hands protectively to his daughters' shoulders. "Yes, that's who I am, Tante Lena."

Like an echo in a cave, Wim's stage whisper reached Lena's ears. "He called her Tante Lena, not Miss Stryker like she said we're s'posed to do!"

A flood of memories crested a dam. "I will have desks ready for you tomorrow, but for today . . ." Lena turned numbly to students who soaked up the scene like towels left on a clothesline in a summer rain. "Let's see . . . Sterre, you may share Liesbeth's desk so Maartje and Antje can sit together in your seat today."

Clear, concise instructions surfaced from a churning pool of thoughts that had little to do with seating arrangements. *So; I'm to teach Cornelis de Boer's children?*

"It's my fault they're late today," he said. "I walked with them to show them the way, but it took longer than I recalled, even cutting through Aalberts' field."

His daughters snuggled against him. He swept them both off the floor in an embrace and nuzzled their cheeks with his nose. With a whispered word intended only for their ears, he lowered them and left.

The room stilled as if a persistent hum had finally been silenced. Each person breathed deeply for the first time since the door had opened. *"He loves them."* The inner voice said only three words, but they saturated her subconscience like melting snow seeping into the Floyd River's banks after a thaw.

Two little girls watched the door close, separating them from all that was familiar in their lives. All other eyes shifted from an unblinking focus on the closed door to the curly-headed children.

Antje put her arm around her sister and the girls blinked back tears, looking gravely at Lena. Although each desk was of adequate size for two children to share, the sisters sat so close to each other there was sufficient room for a third child on their seat.

Lena's voice seemed as loud as a bugle. "We were preparing to have the students tell us something about their summer, Maartje and Antje. This activity will help you get to know your classmates. Elsje, you were to be the first."

Lena wanted nothing more than to lower her head to her desktop and wait until the world steadied around her—no, actually, she wished the day were over. But *Miss Stryker* on the blackboard meant she was in charge. Even if her world had turned topsy-turvy, she must not only maintain her dignity and model self-discipline, but launch fourteen students— *No, now there are sixteen*—on the year's voyage.

A penetrating question surfaced before she forced her attention back to the classroom: *How did I not realize Cornelis de Boer was back?*

She tried to remember when she had last spoken to Hans and Rebecca. Whenever it had been, she was certain not one word about Cornelis had crossed his parents' lips. And she wouldn't have heard from Bram and Brigetta about Bram's renegade brother—that topic was off-limits among the three of them.

"My name is Elsje Hazenbroek and I'm in eighth grade, which means next year I go to school in town!'"

Elsje's clear voice cut through the murky waters in Lena's mind; she dragged her sodden thoughts to the churning surface and gave herself a mental shake.

"This summer," the girl continued, "I won a blue ribbon at the County Fair for my strawberry jam, and white ribbons for mittens and a scarf I knitted."

"Thank you, Elsje. Congratulations!" Lena said a little too brightly. "Saartje, you may speak next."

"I'm Saartje Van Leuven and I'm in eighth grade. This summer I went to Sioux City for two whole weeks. We ate at a diner once and I ordered chicken-fried steak for fifteen cents, and mashed potatoes and buttered corn that each cost four cents. And I got a whole bottle of Nehi soda for a nickel, and pie for seven cents. My *Grootvader's* meal cost forty-four cents!" she boasted, scanning the rows to judge the impact of such excesses.

Lena cleared her throat, but before she could end this bragging spree, Saartje barreled on:

"And I rode in a streetcar, and my cousin gave me a nearly new pair of leather shoes she outgrew, but I can only wear them to church in nice weather or they'll be ruined," she ended, ignoring the fact her feet, like her classmates', were lodged in sensible wooden shoes, despite her high-and-mighty airs.

"Such interesting experiences, Saartje," Lena said. *If my own thoughts were not so tangled, I would have halted her bragging early on.* "Jaap, what can you tell us?"

"I'm in sixth grade so I only have two more years after this one when I'm the only kid in my class because in high school I get to be with the town kids. Oh, my name is Jaap De Jong. All I did this summer was pull weeds."

"I saw you participating in the watermelon-eating contest on the Fourth of July, so you had at least one day when you didn't pull weeds!" Lena teased gently. "Janneken, you are next."

Each move measured and dispensed gracefully, the girl rose to her feet like a bird taking flight. Lena entertained a moment's wonder at how stout Frans and clumsy Betje could have produced such a lithe being. "My name is Janneken De Groot. I'm in fifth grade. This summer I read a book every week, and wrote a four-line poem every Sunday afternoon, and painted with watercolors, and collected butterflies."

"What a pleasant summer you had, Janneken! Lucas? You're next," Lena said, interrupting the boy's eye-rolling behind his classmate's back.

Lucas stumbled to his feet and mumbled, "Uh, I'm in fifth grade. Uh, my name is Lucas Beekman. Uh, I didn't read books or write poems or kill butterflies. I, uh, helped my father with milking and, uh, planting."

The fact Lena allowed Lucas' habitual *uh*'s to pass without comment only illustrated the sorry state of her mind. "You had a very busy summer, Lucas!" The remaining children stood, when called upon, and presented their pieces:

"I'm Raimund Vande Veer and this is my twin, Bartel. We're in fourth grade. We went swimming in the river almost every day this summer and I caught a snake and it bit me and our mother had to cut my leg with a razor blade—can I show my scar?"

"That isn't necessary," Lena said hastily.

"Okay, but if anyone wants to see it at recess, just ask. Oh, and Mama sucked out all the poison, and I kept the snake in a bucket for two days, but it got away."

"Your turn, Bartel." Lena braced herself for more of the same.

"I'm Bartel Vande Veer and this is my twin, Raimund. We're in fourth grade and we swam every day if there weren't no lightning because then we would-a died, right in the river, and our heads would-a exploded and all anyone would-a found was pieces no bigger than our fingernails."

Several girls flinched; Lena closed her eyes briefly. *Oh, my; this could be a very long year.*

Looking nauseous after the twins' graphic descriptions, Katrien stood by her desk and averted her eyes from the offending boys. "I'm Katrien Battjes," she announced pompously, sounding so much like her mother (who lorded it over Lena's Sewing Circle) that Lena half-expected to see Cokkie standing in Katrien's place. "Adda and Giertje," she swept her arm dramatically toward them, "are my best friends and we are all in the third grade. This summer I invited them over to my house four times and once they stayed overnight and we had *vet and stroop* for breakfast, just like it was Christmas!"

The third-grade standard was set; Adda's path was prescribed. "My name is Adda De Jong and this summer I invited Katrien and Giertje over to my house three times and they stayed overnight once and in the morning," she inhaled rapidly, "we had breakfast outside just like a picnic! Oh, I'm in third grade." Still the focus of attention, she grasped this opportunity to inform the new girls, apropos of nothing, "Jaap is *not* my brother; he's my cousin," before she sat down.

Giertje would rather die than break with tradition. Little unique remained to report, but she added her special brand of breathless chatter. "I'm Giertje Ten

Broek and Katrien, Adda, and I stayed up all night once at my house and we walked outside and saw bats so we screamed and ran back inside and told ghost stories and in the morning, we didn't wake up until ten o'clock so we didn't have breakfast, just tea with milk and rusks," she said, now shamed by such a blatant lack of hospitality. "But next summer, we'll have *vet and stroop* outside like a picnic—five times," she ended, beaming over her impromptu solution to the vexing dilemma one-upmanship always poses.

"The third-grade girls had a very busy summer," Lena said. "Maas, you are next."

"Maas Bleecker. Third grade. Shot ten rabbits. Learned how to skin them."

Praise, not criticism today! "You must be a good shot. Skinning rabbits is a useful skill. Sterre, it's your turn."

"I'm Sterre; I'm named for stars in the heavens," she trilled for the benefit of the new students who seemed more bewildered than impressed. "My last name is Van der Voort. *Three* words, not two," she added proudly, as if personally responsible for such bounty. "I passed first grade with *very* good grades. They were *such* good grades that Father gave me a new doll. Now I'm in second grade and I can't *imagine* what I'll get when I pass again! This summer I practiced my piano lessons *every* day and learned a *very* hard piece *by heart*. Oh, and my *Grootmoeder* taught me how to crochet. She says I do very well." She lowered her eyelids modestly, a virtue undone when she added smugly, ". . . *very* well."

Making a mental note to keep Saartje and Sterre apart lest they infect each other with new strains of conceit, Lena simply said, "Perhaps you can bring something you made to show for our first exhibit day, Sterre. Now, Liesbeth, what about you?"

With knees visibly shaking, the little girl stood beside her desk. "I'm Liesbeth Beekman and I'm in first grade. I don't remember what I did this summer," all came out with a quivering lisp.

Lena masked her amusement. *Freek scared every thought out of your pretty little head!*

With a shudder that exploded into wails, Liesbeth plunged across the room from her desk and landed against Lena like a stone leaving a slingshot.

When it became obvious the girl had no intention of loosening her grip around her teacher's neck, Lena lifted Liesbeth onto her lap and smoothed her braids. "Thank you, Liesbeth. Perhaps another day you can share some memories of your summer."

Liesbeth's denial bumped against Lena's shoulder.

"Wim, it's your turn," Lena said, rocking in place.

He sucked in air and words rushed out, riding his exhaled breath like a jockey in the saddle. "Freek an' me played every day an' I taught him stuff an' he leaned against fresh paint on the barn an' got red paint all over him an' had-ta have a kerosene bath an' he didn't like it one bit an' neither did I because he stunk an' couldn't sleep in the house for two nights."

He gulped, glanced at the new girls, and suddenly remembered the instructions. "My name is Willem

Dries Wynkoop but everybody calls me Wim because that's a name, too, an' I'm in first grade."

"Thank you, Wim." A smile lit Lena's eyes. *If I allowed favorites, Wim would head my list!* "Antje, please tell us about your summer."

Slowly, the older girl rose from the desk. Still clutching her sister's hand, she said in a quaking voice, "My name is Annie . . . I mean, Antje . . . de Boer. I'm in second grade." She squeezed her eyes tightly shut— much like someone diving into a pit prefers temporary blindness rather than witnessing the downward trip that lacks a positive outcome. "This summer I got to name kitties on my grandparents' farm." She tugged her sister out of the seat and they stood together, arms circling each other's waists.

"Thank you, Antje. Maybe this year you can write a story about the kittens. Maartje, we would all like to hear from you now."

"My name is Mary, I mean, Maartje de Boer. Father says I get to be in first grade." She shot a questioning glance at her sister and, in an act of defiance against whatever unspoken warning passed swiftly from elder to younger, blurted, "We live at our grandparents' farm now because our mother died this summer."

Silence engulfed the room like a heavy fog.

Oh! Only when Liesbeth squirmed in her lap did Lena realize she clutched the girl tightly enough to cause physical distress. The clock's ticking was a steadying sound, muffled only by the strident call of a crow in the elm tree that shaded the building.

As Liesbeth slipped off her lap, Lena addressed the group, "Thank you all."

I should respond to what Maartje said, if for no other reason than to offer comfort, but what can I say? What is appropriate, in front of all the others?

She ignored the inner voice, option to say instead, "You all did a good job of speaking extemporaneously. That long word means speaking without time to prepare beforehand, which is what I required you to do. Say the word with me."

"*You are babbling, Lena,*" her inner voice chided.

Mutely agreeing, she walked to the blackboard and pronounced each syllable while writing it, "Ex-tem-por-an-e-ous-ly. Extemporaneously."

The children look to me for how to respond to shocking news, and I turn it into a vocabulary drill? Lena gave great care to replacing the chalk in the tray and dusting off her fingers. "We will take an early recess since you have all been sitting still for so long. After recess, we will begin our lessons."

Noting two lunch bags next to Antje, Lena selected the student least likely to increase the de Boer girls' private miseries. "Janneken, will you please show Antje and Maartje where they can put their lunch bags until it's time for noon recess?"

Klompen on a wooden floor was a familiar sound as the children moved out the door. Lena filled the dipper at the water cooler and then drifted to the window, slowly sipping as she stared at the world outside. A world where the summer of 1929 had been a time when some sweet young children lost mothers while others played with snakes or butterflies. A world where one father rewarded his daughter with a doll . . . and another buried horrid secrets as he returned to Dutchville to create a new life.

Shadows flitted as clouds passed before the sun and then drifted away like wisps from white-headed dandelions. Only when Lena tipped the dipper and found it empty did she glance at the clock. *Mercy! Today's schedule is a shamble!* Quickly, she lifted a ribbon from inside the neckline of her dress and leaned out the window to blow one sharp blast on the whistle.

Somehow, she survived the morning. Midst the lessons, the students took turns selecting their first reading choices of the year. Lena allowed quiet conversation by the bookshelf, knowing how a classmate's recommendation encouraged a reluctant reader to choose a challenging book. To stock the shelves with different books each year, Lena scoured the bookshelves in Brigetta's childhood bedroom and often borrowed from Dutchville citizens to provide a rich selection to supplement previous years' favorites.

"Around the World in Eighty Days" and "Peter Pan" and "Treasure Island" and "The Merry Adventures of Robin Hood;" and "The Adventures of Tom Sawyer" and "The Jungle Book" and "The Adventures of Pinocchio"—all shared shelves with other boy-pleasing tales.

"Alice's Adventures in Wonderland" and "The Secret Garden" and "The Wind in the Willows" and

"Hans Christian Anderson's Tales" and "Heidi" and "Little Women" and "Anne of Green Gables" and "Black Beauty" and "The Wonderful Wizard of Oz"— promoted virtues amid fine stories for girls.

Also included were familiar nursery rhymes and fairy tales for the youngest readers. Lena was pleased when Maartje and Antje returned to their seat with "Raggedy Ann" and "Raggedy Andy"—as comforting as a silk-edged blanket. Some illustrated books offered abridged versions of more difficult stories.

Older students often read books to the younger children. The vocabulary in some books prompted students to consult the dictionary, much to Lena's delight. Seeing them act out stories during recesses made her nod approvingly.

In a pattern of working together that would become second nature, Elsje showed the first graders how to write on the blackboard without squeaking, and helped them trace alphabet letters. Lena introduced the twins to history lessons. When she was ready to work with the first graders, Elsje joined Janneken and Saartje in reading Longfellow's "The Village Blacksmith.". Following their reading, they would choose a dozen words for which they could provide antonyms.

Meanwhile, the third graders began on a grammar assignment that introduced punctuation. Jaap, doing his own long-division assignment, sat between the second-grade girls, ready to assist with their social studies lesson. Geography and reading worksheets filled out the morning for the remaining students.

Soon it was lunchtime. "Since it is such a pleasant day," Lena said, "we will take our lunches outside. You may select a rug from the pile beneath the bell-pull. All rise, and we will sing our lunchtime prayer together before going outside."

The children burst from the building like bees from a hive. Lena recognized Rebecca's soft ginger cookies when the de Boer girls unwrapped their lunches. *Of course, without a mother in the picture, Rebecca would assume care of her granddaughters—including making their lunches.* As Lena pondered the living arrangements at the de Boer farm, the students finished eating and most of them wandered off to play a rowdy game of Squat Tag.

Lena sank down in relative comfort in the shade of the schoolhouse. Usually, she would have joined in a game or chatted with students choosing less rowdy activities, but this was not a usual day. Between the rocky start with Freek's antics and Cornelis' abrupt reappearance in her life, Lena considered the day as fraught with tension as a loose tooth connected to a doorknob by a strand of thread.

As she monitored, Lena's gaze often returned to the de Boer girls who watched activities from a distance. Given the situation, Lena didn't force involvement in any type of play, though there was an empty teeter-totter. Today carried enough punch for Antje and Maartje; tomorrow was soon enough to help them form new friendships.

During the afternoon, the sun heated the room and wilted the children's enthusiasm for learning. Even the flies outside the window seemed to circle more languidly. After recess, Lena pushed curtains aside to allow the best movement of air, warm though it was. The cycle of lessons continued: history for some, penmanship for others, then a science experiment for the older students while the younger ones worked together to color the life cycle of a tree on a six-foot length of butcher paper tacked on the wall.

Then it was Music Class for all grades until the clock struck three-thirty which meant Storytime. This was the students' favorite half-hour of the day.

Lena pulled a stool into place, as happy as any student to have reached this point. "Our first story this year is titled 'The Enchanted Castle' by Edith Nesbit. The main characters are children who seek adventure in the woods and find a magic ring." She opened the book and began reading, "There were three of them: Jerry, Jimmy, and Kathleen . . ."

A collective groan rolled through the room when the clock struck four. School was over for the day—and while that delighted them, they regretted needing to wait twenty-four hours to hear more of the story. "That's a good story, Miss Stryker," Raimund said.

She smiled. "I'm glad you like it."

She noted with amusement how Wim's circuitous route from the cloakroom to his desk took him past the window closest to the pump. There he saw something that made him quiver with excitement. He pounded his fists like castanets in a surge of uncontrolled bliss.

Lena knew why without asking: *A thirsty Freek awaits his young master!*

Midst the flurry of children gathering their lunch tins and returning to their desks for an orderly dismissal, a loud horn sounded outside. Everyone, including Lena, craned to see out the window that offered a view of the road. "It's the new girls' father," Maas announced, awestruck.

Sure enough, Lena noted grimly. A car spun into the schoolyard and parked parallel to the side of the building. *It's Cornelis, driving a shiny Model-A Ford Tudor Sedan. Is it the one from Baumgartner Motors' lot?* Students fidgeted while she watched Cornelis swing open the driver's door and position himself against the side of the car, as if aware he was being observed. *Such is doubtless the case wherever he goes*, she fumed.

She struggled to reign in her frustration. *My instinct is to withhold his audience and see how long it takes Cornelis to realize we're not falling over ourselves to sing his praises—but why punish the children?* "You are dismissed." Sixteen students flew like iron filings responding to a magnet. Her feet dragging, Lena stood clutching the doorpost so tightly it made her knuckles ache.

Cornelis called out jauntily, "Come along, girls, we are going home to celebrate! Your father got a job today in Dutchville selling these beauties! This one has only been on the lot for four days, and it's ours now!" He patted the bonnet of the automobile while his daughters paused long enough to wave shy farewells to their new teacher before climbing into the back seat.

After allowing time for the students to feast their eyes on shining metal, reflective chrome and spot-free glass, Cornelis set his cap at a jaunty angle and tooted the horn at the boys racing after his cloud of dust.

Some of the fizz went out of the day, pricked by Cornelis' unabashed boasting. What Saartje's report on her extravagant summer had failed to do, Cornelis' flaunting of wealth accomplished.

This new-model, boxy, russet-colored vehicle made anything their families owned look second-rate in the eyes of fourteen students who now realized that, though the Dutchville Bank's easy credit plan allowed families to borrow and buy beyond their means, nothing could transform their stodgy fathers into a mesmerizing man like Cornelis de Boer. He didn't think twice about buying a showy new automobile instead of a sensible farm truck.

Lena wondered what Hans and Rebecca would think when Cornelis drove up in one of the finer automobiles around town. While they scrimped and saved to keep the farm afloat, apparently their prodigal son had been accumulating riches. *Did it ever occur to him to offer that money to his parents, rather than selfishly spend it on his own pleasures?*

The playground emptied slowly, leaving Lena alone on the stoop. "So much for his claim the girls would walk!" She aimed a stone at a fence post . . . and missed it.

"First, he comes late this morning, more intent on making a scene than concerned that his daughters could have a tardy against them." Another stone missed its mark.

"Then he returns like a conquering hero this afternoon for that same purpose, roaring up in that fancy-schmantzy automobile of his." A third stone careened off the post and startled something hidden in the grasses below. Field grass parted like the Red Sea before Moses when an unseen animal scurried to a safe place where frustrated maiden ladies didn't throw rocks. "Between Freek and Cornelis, today is a travesty." Lowering the flag brought early morning to her mind: *To think I believed the messy beginning to the day was the worst that could happen.*

Washing the blackboards, Lena sloshed so much water it required mopping, lest the water ruin the floor. As she imagined Cornelis' grinning face looking back at her from a puddle, she gave so much elbow grease toward removing his image that she splashed water straight up her arm, leaving her with a drenched sleeve.

Sopping up the spill, she scrubbed the floor hard enough to loosen a splinter that wedged itself beneath her thumbnail, forming a blood blister. Tears sprouted as she plucked it out with her teeth.

It didn't improve her mood in the slightest degree when she plopped down to conduct a good pity-party—right in the middle of another puddle. Rising, she stepped on her hem and before she could lift her heel, she heard a distinct *r-r-r-i-i-i-ppp!*

While rinsing out the buckets, vigorous action at the pump ripped the wet sleeve loose at the seam. "That does it." She stormed inside to change clothes—something she normally would have done promptly after the students left: another strike against Cornelis. All this toil and trouble amounted to more blots on his record as tasks ignited Lena's grumpiness until it sizzled like a Fourth of July firecracker.

Scowling, she dragged two desks from the storage closet and loosened bolts connecting the desks already in place. Twice, she cracked her head on a desk as she backed out. She shoved the three rows into four with four desks per row. Now, the stove held court at the back of a wider central aisle. "It looked so nice the other way," she grumbled as she gathered supplies to scrub and polish the two additional desks.

Her hair had long since escaped its dignified braided loop around her head. It now followed wandering paths. Tendrils clung to her forehead and drooped along her collar. Her face glistened from her exertions; her lips formed a tight angry slit in a flushed face. She was too tired to even think about cooking, despite hunger gnawing at her innards. "I'll open a half-pint of stewed tomatoes and eat right out of the jar," she decided around a jaw-cracking yawn.

With a nod to propriety, she spooned the cold supper into a bowl, but ate it at her desk with papers spread all around while she reviewed the next day's lessons. One thought stubbornly refused to fall into place, however: the answer to her unvoiced questions. *When a wayward son returns home, can all be forgotten? Must all be forgiven?*

❀ ❀ ❀

Monday Evening, September 9 ◆ For the past three years, the first day of school had left Lena too excited to sleep. Each year, she worked far too late into the evening, reliving the day's exhilarating events and humorous moments, preparing the next day down to the smallest detail. Even after she sternly sent herself to bed, she stayed awake making mental lists.

But not the evening of September 9, 1929. Though it was only seven o'clock, Lena was so exhausted she considered going to bed without grading papers, or adjusting the grade-level lesson plans to accommodate two new students. *And how will I find time tomorrow to assess if Antje truly is at the second-grade level?* she wondered. Even a normal day required much of her. There simply were no spare minutes in a one-room schoolteacher's day.

The image of a juggler being bombarded by balls filled her mind and she winced, knowing who would be hit first by plans gone astray. Not that Antje's grade level made much difference in the day-to-day workings of the school. Grade divisions could blur, with each child working at a comfortable level in any given subject until ready to move on.

But the danger of taking Cornelis' word about his elder daughter's abilities was that Antje may not be at a second-grade level. She could suffer a set-back if she were assigned work too advanced for her abilities. Children could destroy a sense of confidence with a taunt, and Antje's self-confidence already floundered.

It was up to Lena to prevent this, even if Cornelis had said matter-of-factly, "second grade" in the hearing of the very ones who could paralyze Antje with smirks if Lena assigned her first-grade work. One more offense against Cornelis, and they were adding up.

She dragged the spoon around her empty supper dish, making senseless lines in the remaining splats of broth—lines that disappeared when she moved the spoon. If only her thoughts could recover as quickly after each anxiety dragged through her mind. Over-and-over she stirred, sinking lower-and-lower in the chair until her head sagged against her arm on the desktop. Worries rolled like tumbleweeds across the wind-swept prairie of her mind:

It all began ten years ago with my chance visit to Brigetta's home. Why was Cornelis trapped in a closet with Bram's wife, rather than working out in the field? Why was I the one who had to find the knob on the floor outside the closet door?

Then Cornelis suddenly left home . . . and our sweet Brigetta, sunlight personified, became a shadowy shell. A wall sprang up between Brigetta and me . . . actually, Brigetta built a wall that kept everyone at a distance.

Lena shivered in the warm night. *Out of the blue, Bram and Brigetta moved to Rochester. Something dreadful happened in Minnesota—I know it, though I have never named it to another human being. I place all the blame at Cornelis' feet. He is a wolf in sheep's clothing—or maybe just a wolf.*

"Why are you sitting here in the dark, Lena?" A shadow in the doorway spoke with bemusement and gained shape and identity as it moved into view.

Lena's spoon flew from her hand and skittered across the floor, stopped by the track holding the second row of desks. Flustered, she sat upright and erupted from her chair as if retrieving the spoon were of utmost importance. "Oh! Hello, Hanna!" Bending over sent blood rushing to her face and muffled her voice. "And Gustave, too, of course! My, it's getting dark already! How did I not hear you drive up? I was eating supper, and time got away from me. I am just tired, I guess."

She clamped her lips too late to stem the hysterical laugh powering the nervous rush of words. When arched her back, she winced when seemingly every muscle cramped in protest.

"You? Tired?" Gustave joked and lit the lamp on Lena's desk with a match from his pocket. "On the first day of school, you're usually soaring high above Hanna and me—like a kite escaping earth's gravity!"

Lena smiled distractedly at him. They watched Hanna flit around the room—adjusting, touching, inhaling school smells as if they were perfume—while still holding a basket. The classroom never ceased to fascinate Hanna. "Tell your sister what we brought for her supper since we know, first-day-of-school, she forgets to eat!" Gustave said, laughing.

Hanna paused to look in the forgotten basket. "Eggs and such," she said dreamily. She resumed spinning the globe, straightening reading-circle chairs, and strumming fingers along the spines of a row of books before drifting to the front of the room.

Balancing her wire-rimmed glasses on the tip of her nose, she danced the tip of Lena's pointer around Iowa's borders on the canvas map, and intoned, "Class, what is the major export of this state?"

Lena's dish diverted her. "You already ate? My, goodness—that's different for the first day! What did you have?" Hanna strode across the room, picked up the bowl, and sniffed it. "Stewed tomatoes? You call that supper?" Her eyebrows rose in mock incredulity. "No wonder you're as thin as a willow-whip! Here." She handed Lena an apple from the basket.

"Stewed tomatoes was a quick and filling choice. I had saltines, too," Lena defended herself weakly. Setting the apple aside, she brushed telltale cracker crumbs onto her hand and showed Hanna.

"Ahhh, that changes everything—no need to worry, Gustave," Hanna teased. "She had tomatoes and saltines. I feel much better, knowing crackers will hold my sister's skin and bones together! A new tradition!"

Lena offered a feeble smile in response to their laughter. "It was all I wanted after a disturbing day." She was not ready to speak Cornelis' name aloud, so offered a humorous account of the Freek incident. Though Hanna and Gustave had enjoyed her stories throughout August of Freek's education, Lena's retelling of today's tale lacked her usual flair.

"Poor Liesbeth!" Hanna said, peeking into student desks. "She'll probably have bad dreams, and Freek is hardly the substance of nightmares. The flowers on this tablet are exquisite! Whose desk is this?"

"Janneken's."

"Don't be surprised if Ruud and Geesje accompany Sterre to school tomorrow," Gustave cautioned with a grin as he watched Hanna's pilgrimage around the schoolroom.

He knew she would have loved to teach, just like her sister. *But God in His wisdom* . . . Gustave refused to let doubt lodge in his heart, but at times like this, even he wondered at God's ways that permitted his beloved wife to flounder for many years in the dark cave of depression.

Lena groaned. "You're likely right. As if I did not have enough to worry about, without needing to reassure Mama and Papa Van der Voort their daughter is safe in my care."

Catching Hanna's signal, Gustave asked casually, "Did something else go wrong, Lena? You seem troubled. How can we help?"

Lena's brow furrowed. This time, she caught the worried look passing between her sister and brother-in-law. She raised her hand in a sweeping gesture that took in all four rows of desks. "Notice any changes?"

Both studied the room. Gustave's eyes widened. "At the end of our work day, we had cleaned and positioned fourteen desks, but now there are sixteen?"

No answer from Lena; pursed lips from Hanna.

"What happened?" he persisted. "Did you have help to rearrange all the desks, which I now notice are in four rows, now three? No, of course. you didn't! Oh, Lena, no wonder you're so tired!"

She shrugged. "It felt good to do something physical; it took my mind off why I even need more desks." Her hollow laugh bounced off the painted tin ceiling. "All summer, I planned for fourteen students—not sixteen. I prepared daily lessons, practice exercises, tests in the correct number for each grade level. It was a good division: seven younger, seven older. Today, plans blew out the window when two new students appeared; a first grader and a second grader if their father is to be believed," she sniffed.

Hanna clicked her tongue sympathetically as she adjusted the lamp's wick. "Poor dear, you're in a tizzy! I know how hard you worked, but think how wonderful it is that Sterre has a classmate, and how much more fun Wim and Liesbeth will have with another child in first grade."

Lena refused to be comforted by practical wisdom. She stared moodily at the curved tips of her *klompen*.

Like lamplight seeks dark corners, Gustave's words strove to dispel her gloom by injecting reasonable thoughts: "Adding more students at the lower grades guarantees the district will not close your school."

"Not that we don't understand why you are upset," Hanna added quickly.

"So!" Gustave slapped the desk in emphasis. "Put us to work. We can help prepare tomorrow's lessons for the new students, at least." He paused, then chuckled. "Hanna, your sister has distracted us from an important detail! We have yet to learn who the new students are. Or are we expected to guess?"

Hanna played along, sensing Gustave's motive was to lure Lena back to her cheerful self. "Hmm . . . the Voorhees' farm is the only one for sale. Rumor has it the old man will deed it to Koenraadt Ostrander who has been more like a son than a hired man, but he is unmarried. I give up: Who are they?"

Lena pushed back her chair and crossed to the water cooler. While Hannashot questioning glances at Gustave and fidgeted in silence, Lena slowly drank her fill from the dipper. In a seeming non-sequitur. she asked, "Did you know Cornelis de Boer has returned to Dutchville . . . expecting to live here, again?"

At this startling news, Hanna clasped her hands and exclaimed, "No, we didn't! Oh, Hans and Rebecca must be thrilled! How long has it been, Gustave?"

Before Gustave finished calculating, Lena supplied the answer in a lusterless tone. "Ten years. It has been ten years since he disappeared."

"That's right," he mused. "Bram and Brigetta had been married about a year, which makes it 1919. Quite soon after Cornelis left, they moved to Rochester."

Lena's grimace hardly matched their pleasure in hearing the news. "The two new students are Antje and Maartje—his daughters."

Gustave's jaw dropped. "Cornelis has children . . . and plans to live here?"

"Apparently. The girls' mother . . . Cornelis was married; his wife died this past summer. I suspect he needs help raising the girls, so *now* he thinks of his family, *now* he remembers his roots."

Her brittle tone startled Hanna, but Gustave's hand on his wife's shoulder halted words from gushing out.

For an awkward moment, no one spoke. Lena's pacing footsteps echoed like the rhythm of a distant drum. Finally, she perched on the edge of her desk and let her *klompen* dangle off her toes. The shoes fell to the floor in two dull wood-striking-wood thuds.

"Not every young man wants to live in Dutchville," Hanna gently reminded Lena. "Even Bram moved on to improve his skills, which, as we know, proved to be a marvelous opportunity for him. Granted, Cornelis' disappearance was abrupt, but he followed his dreams."

Lena rolled her eyes.

"He could have left with more consideration for his family," Hanna said quickly "but he was young and impulsive. But that is water under the bridge and Hans and Rebecca have two *kleindochter* here to spoil!" she said, revealing none of the loss she felt in being so far from her own granddaughter, Sanna.

Gustave said, "Having experienced such a recent and tragic loss, Cornelis and his daughters need our comfort and understanding. I will call on him soon."

"Save yourself a trip," Lena said darkly. "He'll be in town every day, selling automobiles. He'll be easy to find. Go to Baumgartner Motors, or follow any cloud of dust. In the middle of it, you'll find Cornelis terrifying people and horses everywhere."

"Gracious, Lena, you certainly are in a dither over this!" Hanna scolded.

Lena said, "Sorry; don't mind me. Gustave, you're the de Boer family's Dominie; they'll appreciate a visit. Cornelis and the girls need comfort, prayers, and wisdom. I'm cranky; I just need a good night's sleep."

Hanna hugged her. ""Of course. Cornelis' girls will love you. I can't think of anyone better able to help them in this difficult time. When I think of all you did for our family . . ." She fumbled for a hanky.

"Oh, Hanna, don't get weepy."

Sensing their fragile hold on emotions, Gustave said gently, "Let's focus on the present, not our past. We have a returned and grieving son with his two young children, and a teacher who is too exhausted to see the obvious in a trying situation. As the girls' teacher, Lena, you will be so *belandrijk* to them. Your kind and loving spirit will greatly help them. They must feel the bottom has dropped out of their world."

Lena sighed. "I will hardly be important, as you claim, to anyone if I can't even quit being so . . . upset . . . over their arrival. My 'kind and loving spirit,' as you deem it, is sorely in need of a boost." She swept straggling curls up off her neck and secured them in place, once again, with pins.

"You've worked hard for too many days, getting ready for the school year. What you need is rest," Hanna said firmly. "We'll leave now so you can go to bed and wake up refreshed. Come, Gustave."

"Wait, Hanna; my offer to help Lena still stands." Gustave contorted his body. "The desks shrink more every year; it simply cannot be that my girth increases!"

Lena yawned without apology. "I do need to copy a vocabulary worksheet for Antje. And two cards for our penmanship exercise in which children write notes to say *danken* to those who cleaned and painted the school this summer."

Gustave said, "Hanna, you prepare the note cards; I'll write out Antje's worksheet. It will be like when I helped Brigetta with her vocabulary lessons."

Lena laughed. "I'd better not find make-believe words on Antje's list like you added to Brigetta's!"

They all began their tasks. Eventually, Hanna asked, "Who do the girls resemble?" Positioning a pattern to trace, she didn't pause for an answer. "Strange to think of Cornelis being married all the years he was gone—at least many of them, if Antje's in second grade. Yet, we never met his wife . . ."

The easy-going conversation released Lena's tension enough that she could discuss the de Boer girls with better control. She began to write the third graders' science assignment on the blackboard.

"It is odd," she agreed, then answered the earlier question. "The girls' eyelashes are long and beautiful. Their hair is dark, not straight like Hans and Bram's. At first, I thought it was a deeper red than Cornelis and Rebecca's hair, but their hair turns black and reveals hidden chestnut tones in sunlight. Overall, the girls' hair is all curls and wildness."

Gustave tapped his pencil on the desktop. "Remember how Cornelis always seemed so restless to escape Dutchville? It's wonderful that he returned just when Yzaak Baumgartner needed someone. That boy loved automobiles as much as he hated the farm. Better that his daughters' hair be unruly than their spirits, hmm? Or is that not the case, Lena?"

She responded slowly, "They seem subdued, actually. Perhaps their mother possessed a more . . . restrained nature than their father does."

"Or, it could reflect their shock over her death. Even a rambunctious child would be expected to change after such a tragedy," Gustave said.

Hanna frowned. "I hope one of them has spunk. With both Liesbeth and Sterre so timid, you need someone in the lower grades to keep up with Wim!"

"Maartje, the younger girl, speaks up. But don't forget, there's always Katrien, the chatterbox of Dutch Valley, to add spice to the lower grades."

Hanna laughed. "Caspar and Cokkie unwittingly released an unending stream of conversation when they taught Katrien to speak!"

"I hope she has the sense to keep her nose where it belongs. She's likely to corner the girls and worm details out of them before they're ready to handle her. She either doesn't realize, or doesn't care, that her curiosity borders on snoopy. "Katrien can be hurtful."

Following Lena's instructions, Hanna made stacks of note cards and envelopes and added sheets of assorted colored papers from which the students would cut decorations for the thank-you cards. Then she filled two jars from Lena's larger container of flour paste and sealed them tightly.

Lena placed the prior year's Sears-Roebuck catalog beside Gustave. "Do you have your pocket knife?"

He patted his trouser pocket and nodded.

"Good; then if you would slit the spine on this catalog to make about a dozen smaller sections, it would be easier to remove individual pages without ripping them."

"Ah, yes—your inventive uses for the catalog!" he chuckled. "What is tomorrow's assignment?"

"It's arithmetic in the guise of shopping! I hope to ease the shock of sums and multiplication after a summer off with the allure of an exciting catalog."

While Gustave applied blade to binding, the women finished their tasks and moved to the open window. Lena leaned across the sill to inhale the evening air. "The schoolroom will cool down nicely overnight." She turned to Gustave. "You were right: many hands made light work. Thank you both for helping me."

"Well, at supper we enjoyed beets that you pickled from the garden, so it only seems fair that we lend you a hand," Gustave said.

They walked outside together. While Gustave pumped a pail of water and took it to the teacherage, then readied Storm and turned the buggy around, the sisters linked arms and moved toward the gate. "Why don't you come into town for dinner tomorrow night?" Hanna suggested casually. "Gustave can time a country visit to pick you up on his way home."

Lena shook her head, but kissed Hanna's cheek to soften the nonverbal refusal. "I know I worried you with my crossness, but the invitation is not necessary. I'll see you Friday evening, as always. How about fixing a pork roast with autumn vegetables that night?"

"It sounds perfect, and Gustave's already drooling!" Hanna smiled up at her husband who waited to help her into the buggy.

After lingering by the road until the buggy disappeared around a curve, Lena walked slowly across the playground. To the accompaniment of night songs from critters in fields, ditches, and trees, she lowered her tired body onto the board-and-chain swing. Leaving her *klompen* in the hollow formed by many feet, she pumped herself into a high arc. The swing followed the curve of a quarter-moon in the night sky.

A hairpin flew loose and her hair brushed across her face with each backward thrust; her muscles firmed with each forward lunge. She extended her arms and leaned back in the swing. The breeze kissed her face and rustled her hair as the swing's steady movements erased the day's troubles.

Finally, she hooked her shoes with her toes on a forward pass, and came to a complete stop with one foot planted on the ground. After a trip to the outhouse. she closed the bottom sections of the classroom windows, and used a long pole to open the top sections. Taking a moment to straighten her desk enough to be presentable, she picked up her supper dish and the lamp and walked to the back of the room.

There, a partition stopped at the eaves to allow air circulation. At a right angle to the partition, another wall formed two smaller rooms, each with a window on the back wall. The room on the left was the cloakroom with its utilitarian décor: hooks with a shelf above, and a storage area blocked from view by a stiff canvas curtain. On the right was the teacherage.

She entered and whispered, "This is my sanctuary."

Left of the door leading into Lena's quarters was a low bookcase. A covered lunch tin (she would repack it in the morning) sat between two framed pictures: one, Hanna's and her parents; the other, Bram and Brigetta's wedding. Opposite the door, a three-foot bar, extending between the shared and outer walls, formed a triangular closet shielded by a curtain.

Lena loosened curtains' tiebacks, placed the lamp on her bedside table, and drifted to the room's center. Her gaze traveled to a sturdy cot with a handmade quilt. On the curved top of a trunk at the bed's foot, an afghan awaited nights when chills would do battle with the classroom stove's heat. Beside the bed, a fringed rag rug met the curved legs of a low stand on which were a lamp, her Bible and *Psalter*.

A four-drawer dresser between the window and bed contained the basics. An oval wall-hung mirror reflected the lamp's soothing glow. In the corner opposite the cot, a chair faced a sturdy drop-leaf table.

On the wall against the classroom, a sewing rocker sat in front of a heating grate, flanked by a sewing basket and an upholstered footstool. Next to the rocker were two treasures Lena had purchased with her first-year-of-teaching salary: her prized Singer sewing machine with its wooden cabinet and cast-iron foot pedal, and the table-model Airline radio she kept on top when not sewing. These occupied either mind or fingers on snowy nights when cold winds blew.

Pleasant memories engulfed the kitchen hutch that stood between the closet and the window. Until four summers ago, it had been stored for years in the Dominie's buggy barn. Lena and Hanna scrubbed, scraped, and varnished it. Gustave replaced drawer-pulls, hinges, and the door's window-glass, and diligently refurbished the tin countertop.

Though she knew the precise placement of each object, Lena reviewed the contents of the hutch as if for the first time. A four-place setting of hope-chest China and other dishes filled the top shelf. The second shelf held food grown, gleaned, and preserved from the parsonage vegetable garden's bounty.

In the hutch's lower section, she kept a dishpan and washbasin, cookware, and a cast-iron frying pan. When used, all fit beside the pipe on the claw-footed and kerosene stoves—both out in the classroom. Since she required nowhere near the amount of flour that the pullout bin could hold, it held other staples.

On the tin counter, Lena kept a cookie jar and also the covered water bucket Gustave had refilled. To these, she added Hanna's basket, finding several carrots in addition to eggs and apples within it. The counter doubled as her boudoir, so a towel and washcloth hung off hooks on the left, with embroidered kitchen linens on the right side.

She poured water from the bucket into a blue-speckled white enamel bowl, loosened the buttons on her dress, and slipped it off for a sponge bath. Calmed at last, Lena pushed aside the window curtain and brushed her hair, watching the horizon swallow the last wisps of daylight. Her faint smile mirrored the bend where earth met sky beyond the silhouetted trees.

✹ ✹ ✹

Tuesday, September 10 ◆ Did Cornelis always require grand entrances? For the second day in a row, he arrived with his daughters just in time for opening exercises. Wim was tossing sticks for Freek to retrieve, but sounded the alert. "The new girls' father is here in that fancy automobile again!"

Moments later, with Katrien sitting beside her, Cokkie Battjes swung her buggy to face the road right when Lena reached the schoolhouse door. Both women witnessed the fourteen students' complete capitulation to Cornelis' magnetism.

Yesterday, the students had floated on Cornelis' ethereal charms. Today they plunged into the deepest currents, instantly swept away by the sheer force of his personality. Forgetting games, they circled the car, drawn by glitter and Cornelis' buoyant patter. *If I rang the bell, I doubt anyone would hear it.* Lena's heart sank when Cornelis threw back his head and laughed at something Bartel said.

His lack of character is appalling—hardly a suitable hero for impressionable youth. She turned away in disgust. "Good morning, Cokkie," she said neutrally.

"Hello, Lena. I imagine that is Cornelis de Boer? I heard he's back in town. Oh, are those his daughters?"

Lena nodded curtly, biting her tongue lest she blurt, *"As if you didn't hear Katrien's full report yesterday!"*

"I'm not sure I can get out behind his fancy automobile—he paid cash for it, you know. Isn't it something how a young man could have that much money? Even though it's my brother-in-law who owns Baumgartner Motors, I drive this old buggy and am very glad to do so, despite the fact we own a very respectable automobile."

"Oh, Cokkie!" Lena interrupted, caring little about manners at the moment, especially when she saw Cokkie's eyes fasten on Antje and Maartje. "There's sufficient room for you to go around him. I know you must be busy today."

Regretfully, Cokkie took the hint. "I'm on my way to Circle Meeting, which is why I brought Katrien. Goodbye, Lena." But she couldn't depart without a final jab. "The new girls have quite dark complexions for *full-blooded* Dutchmen, don't they?" With a crack of her buggy whip and a toss of her head, she was off, leaving Lena to grit her teeth against a hiss.

During the women's brief exchange, Freek lost interest in chasing his tail and circled the automobile in a frenzy. As he passed the driver's side for the third time, he bounded through the door Cornelis had left open so Saartje and Elsje could admire the upholstered seats. Freek parked himself on the front seat, much to the children's giddy amusement. Cornelis halted his air-boxing match with Jaap long enough to ask, "Whose dog is this?"

"Mine." Wim's eyes heralded his fear of a scolding.

"What's your name, son?"

"Wim. Willem Dries Wynkoop."

"And what is this dog's name?"

"He's Freek."

"Looks to me like Freek understands a good thing when he sees it!" Cornelis reached into the car to scratch the dog's head while all the gaping children wished they had been as brave as Freek.

Midst the commotion, the de Boer girls collected lunches and hugs from their father while Raimund and Bartel joked about learning to drive, and Giertje hinted a ride to school would not be difficult since they lived along the same road. Even Sterre and Liesbeth left fingerprints on the high-gloss paint in evidence of their longing.

Cornelis easily slipped into the role of salesman. He distributed small cards to each child with instructions to ". . . tuck these in a safe place now. Just think: your families could soon own a vehicle like this one! There's money to borrow from the Dutchville Bank for just such purposes."

Wim moved closer to the automobile and hissed, "Freek, come here, boy! Mister de Boer has to leave now." Freek stared into space as if deaf. "Freek! Get out of there," Wim pleaded, not daring even to touch the vehicle, though his dog had taken much more serious liberties. "Oh, we are in trouble, Freek, and it's all your fault" he moaned as the dog lifted his right front paw, which landed right on the steering wheel.

Lucas' voice rose above the ensuing ruckus: "Freek thinks he can drive!"

Cornelis answered Maas' question about tires in time to hear Wim's last attempts to dislodge his dog. "Say, Wim, is your father Dries Wynkoop?" he asked casually.

"Yessir." Wim swallowed hard, contemplating the punishment awaiting him if Cornelis visited his father.

"You know," Cornelis said off-handedly, "I drive right by your family's farm on my way to town. What would you say if I take Freek home? He seems to like the view from the front seat!"

Wim's jaw dropped. "You'll give Freek a ride in your automobile?"

"If that's all right with you, it's all right with me."

Whereas Freek had been nothing but trouble the day before, today he was King of the Hill, riding away in splendor on Cornelis' lap where he had an unobstructed view of the road. His master strutted to the flagpole—a hero in his own right, though he had done nothing more than bring his dog to school. "Ain't that something what them new girls' father did, huh?" he kept saying. "Them two new girls is sure lucky to have him for a father, huh?"

Lena steeled herself against scolding a boy for things beyond his control. Considering her mood, she didn't even trust herself to correct Wim's grammar. Lena wished Cornelis could witness his disruptive effect on the lad who should be learning, not staring at the sky through the window, daydreaming about his dog seeing the world from the driver's seat of a Model-A Ford Tudor Sedan.

Cornelis had not strayed from the schoolyard during his brief morning visit, but his presence filled the schoolhouse all day as surely as if he had squished himself into a desk beside his daughters. Maas and Jaap hid their doodling, but not before Lena noticed shapes looking suspiciously like headlights and fenders.

From morning exercises (when Lena discovered the de Boer girls knew little Dutch, rendering the *Psalmen* meaningless) until afternoon recess, Lena had a sense of trudging uphill through mud. Once all were playing, she slipped inside to prepare for the rest of the day. "Day Two is no better than Day One," she moaned. "Forget Cornelis; focus on the students."

But, when an automobile horn ended the day's section in "The Enchanted Castle," Lena stiffened; the de Boer girls perked up; others trembled, eager to flee the schoolhouse. "You're dismissed." She waved them out the door. She was still sitting on the Storytime stool when Cornelis sounded the horn again.

Freek barked joyously. The children chirped, "Goodbye, Mister de Boer!" as if Cornelis truly were someone worthy of adoration. Shouts and laughter faded, the children heading home to tell tales of the knight in a shining automobile, the prince who rode a mechanical horse, or the strong man capable of trouncing Charles Atlas.

Lena sagged beneath the weight of every one of her forty-six years. Lackadaisically, she corrected papers—not even smiling over childish errors or misconceptions she usually would have committed to memory to share with Hanna and Gustave. Grimly, she realized she had neglected the traditional second-day activity of writing thank-you cards. "Unless I talk to Cornelis, I may as well toss any hope of having a schedule out the window," she fumed.

As she resumed working, she imagined how such a conversation with Cornelis could occur. Proper options for a privacy were limited. Perhaps, if she asked him to come after the children had left for the day, they could talk outside in full view of the road. *Even that provides fuel for gossip if the wrong person sees it.*

For her to suddenly appear at the de Boer farm to speak privately with Cornelis would raise Hans and Rebecca's curiosity. She wasn't ready to speak to them yet, though it would be necessary, once truth came out.

Would it be a chance encounter with Cornelis in Dutchville or on a country road? She did not like the mental picture: Lena on her bicycle, Cornelis at the wheel of that confounded automobile; her glaring, him laughing while the whole world witnessed the encounter, each person adding a detail here-and-there until the resulting full-blown rumor would surely end her career.

Lena's opportunity to ask an all-important question of Cornelis seemed as unlikely as the event ten years earlier that made such a question even necessary.

✱ ✱ ✱

Wednesday, September 11 ◆ Wednesday morning, Lena refused to join what was quickly becoming a society of Cornelis de Boer admirers. She heard him arrive (*Only the deaf or dead could miss that exasperating horn*) and knew by the students' glee precisely when Freek, once again, rode home in style.

"*Oh, he's a smart dog, all right, Wim,*" Lena thought.

Rising above the cheerful clamor as students spread out around the playground, one officious voice wafted through the open windows. "Follow me, girls. Everyone hold hands. Antje and Maartje, you stand in the middle of the circle. Now, I will ask you some questions. Why does your father call you 'Annie' and 'Mary' instead of your given Dutch names?"

The crack of a bat, resulting shouts and pounding feet carried childhood's joys, but the dominant voice from the playground pierced Lena's consciousness and sent other thoughts spiraling. Katrien's unmistakable voice left no doubt as to her identity; the questions she posed confirmed whom she addressed and her intent. "Did your mother die before she could make you proper Dutch dresses for school? Your frocks are something foreigners wear."

Lena reacted so violently, she upset the inkbottle. While she daubed frantically with papers to absorb the spilled ink, she listened in mounting dismay as Katrien demanded, "Are you ashamed of being Dutch? Oh! Maybe your mother wasn't Dutch!" Gasps rose from her audience. "*Not Dutch? Unthinkable!*"

It wasn't so much the rudeness of the questions that made Lena's teeth clench. It was the inquisitor's tone—a bubbling layer of taunting seeking a crack through which to spew forth.

Lena clomped to the window, pushed aside the curtain, and fastened her unflinching gaze on the cluster of seven little girls. "Katrien," she called in a voice that brooked no discussion.

Seven heads swiveled toward the window. Seven faces looked frightened, but one chin jutted defiantly.

"Come inside, Katrien. I need your help."

Katrien rolled her eyes for the benefit of her captive audience, but responded in a singsong voice, "Yes, Miss Stryker," and slowly left a hole in the gaggle of girls that held Maartje and Antje captive at its center.

"I'm waiting, Katrien," Lena said sharply.

Katrien's actions complied with Lena's demand, but she was reluctant to lose the ground so recently gained. "If you are truly Dutch, why don't you wear *klompen?* My mother says wearing leather shoes for everyday is wasteful," she tossed over her shoulder as she ambled toward the schoolhouse stoop.

Lena sucked in a lungful of air and expelled it in a hiss through clenched teeth. Only when her lungs emptied was she calm enough to say, "Katrien will be busy until morning exercises, so go play until then." Six girls dispersed like feathers in the wind. Lena spun around and faced the doorway, hardly able to breathe past the erratic pulse in her throat.

The door inched open, then slid shut, inched open again and threatened to close once more, stretching Lena to the limits of her patience. "For heaven's sake, just pull it, Katrien! Your father oiled the hinges this summer so it would be easy for even the youngest child to open."

The door slid open as smoothly as butter rolling off a hot knife. "Here I am, Miss Stryker. What would you like me to do?" Katrien asked innocently, though Lena noted that she plucked nervously at her skirt.

Good question. Lena quickly glanced at her desk and picked up the sections of the catalog Gustave had prepared. "Give each third- and fourth-grader four parts from a variety of sections. Work quickly."

I should confront her, but what I need to say requires careful thought on my part. What I really want to do is shake her until her teeth rattle!

"Yes, Miss Stryker." Katrien blithely set about her task with a light-hearted air that gave no clue she had so recently feared reprimand. "I suppose you chose me to help because I am so dependable."

"Yes, you are dependable," she said, but thought, "*I can depend on you to stick your nose where it does not belong!*"

"I don't know what to think of the new girls," Katrien chattered on, ignoring Lena's steely gaze. "Mother says she doubts if they've been raised Dutch." Her eyebrows arched, perfectly imitating her mother's easily recognizable look of condescension. The impudent mimic expected Lena to agree with her inflammatory remarks.

Lena bristled. *Caspar and Cokkie lack the common sense of a goat!* Cokkie's judgmental attitude and Caspar's oft-touted negative viewpoints resounded in Katrien's words. Like her daughter, Cokkie seldom hesitated to share her pointed opinions with anyone, regardless of whom was within the sound of her caustic voice. Even Lena's none-too-subtle hint last year that humility was a virtue to pursue had brought no change, either in the child's behavior, or the parental example.

"Being Dutch is a matter of heredity," Lena said stiffly. "The de Boer girls are at least half Dutch, and it is none . . ." She bit back the sarcasm boiling inside her. "Katrien, I am going to ask you to do something difficult."

Katrien halted expectantly by Maas' desk, her smile dimming when she realized her teacher was not smiling in return.

"Let's make a secret pact, you and I, that we will not ask the de Boer girls any questions about their life before we met them. If we hear others doing so, you and I must step in and change the subject."

"But that's rude . . . why, it's interrupting!" Katrien protested.

"No, 'rude' is asking personal questions about a subject someone obviously does not want to discuss. What if . . ." Lena struggled for a suitable example. "What if some day you came to school wearing a dirty, ripped dress?"

Katrien gasped. "That would never happen," she insisted, only to be stilled by Lena's raised hand.

"Probably not, but what if it did? I think you'd be embarrassed and hope no one mentioned your dress to you or to the other children. Am I right?"

"Well, yes . . ." Katrien admitted.

"Imagine how frightening the past few days have been for two little girls who have had something far worse happen to them than a dirty dress. They have moved to a new place, and come to a new school that has different ways of doing things. Think what it would feel like if it were you who had made such a move. How would you make friends when everything is so strange?"

"My mother says I am a very friendly person," Katrien said airily, but doubt shaded her confidence.

Lena refused to give a stamp of approval to Katrien or Cokkie's definition of friendly. "I need your help in preventing anyone from asking Antje or Maartje about things that are not our business."

Katrien frowned. She had enjoyed this conversation much more when the talk had centered on happy things, like dependability. "I'm not sure I could get someone like Liesbeth, for instance, not to ask how their mother died, or keep Wim from asking, 'Did you see your mother die?' without being rude to them."

Lena nearly snorted. *Wim and Liesbeth, indeed!* "If you put your mind to it, you can be a positive influence; it's a matter of choice, whether to say a kind word or to pry. For instance, you can help the de Boer girls learn how to play games that are new to them."

From her expression, Lena knew Katrien basked in the perceived privilege of befriending the new girls. Even so, she attempted a negation when Lena's suggested activity fell short of her desires. "But they must have such interesting stories to tell. Wouldn't it be better to let them tell . . . I mean, it could be . . . educational for us to learn about their family."

Lena shook her head firmly. "No, Katrien. Our most important task is to make them feel welcome. That means no meddling questions."

She heaved a pained sigh. "What if they never-ever want to tell about their life before they came here?"

"We will respect their wishes. I will not tolerate anyone making them feel uncomfortable or unwelcome. Do you understand what I'm saying?" She waited for a responding nod that was slow in coming. "Good. Now, quickly distribute the catalog pages. It is almost time for morning exercises."

While Katrien sullenly fulfilled her tasks, Lena headed outside. A subdued Katrien joined the others belatedly around the flagpole. All through the Pledge, singing, and scripture reading (verses chosen today were from the English Bible's Gospels out of deference to the newest students) dismal thoughts shared space in Lena's mind with rote words. *Surely, there's a way to undo any damage Katrien has already done. But what is it?*

As the students took their seats, Bartel aimed a pencil at the ridge on his desk where it should lodge, but it missed and rolled off to the floor. The slight noise was enough to startle Lena out of her reverie. An idea took shape from her disjointed thoughts. *It's worth a try.* She scanned the room as if taking attendance. Her eyes slowed at Jaap's desk, and returned twice to Sterre's desk as she contemplatively pressed fingertips against her lips.

Well, it's now or never. She cleared her throat. "Katherine has distributed catalog pages to the third- and fourth-grade students. You may work in two groups, the girls at Adeline's desk and the boys at Bartholomew's desk."

Students glanced furtively around the room. Then, Saartje uttered the question that hovered like fog. "Miss Stryker, who are you talking about?"

"That's a very good question, Sarah!" She walked quickly to the blackboard and drew a long vertical line. "For the rest of the day, we will use only English names as part of our language lessons. Who knows your English name?" In the hush that followed, she wrote *Dutch* above the left side of the chalk line and *English* above the right side, filling in the names she had already covered:

Katrien . . . Katherine
Adda . . . Adeline
Bartel . . . Bartholomew
Saartje . . . Sarah

When Lena turned around, one hand was raised. She smiled. "Yes?"

"My English name is Mary."

Nodding, Lena wrote:

Maartje . . . Mary

From the seat next to Maartje came a whispered, "Mine is Annie."

"Very good! Our newest students are putting the others to shame!" Lena said as she added:

Antje . . . Annie

"I don't have an English name," Sterre blurted, sounding close to tears.

Lena laughed lightly. "Oh, you do! You mentioned it yesterday when you told us about your summer," she said. Turning back to the board, she wrote:

Sterre . . . Star

"My English name is Star? Yesterday, I said my name means star. How can my English name be the same as my Dutch name?"

"I cannot explain it, but it's true. Come, come! I should be seeing hands raised all over the room. Surely you know your English names!"

"Why do we need to?" Lucas dared to ask.

Before Lena could respond, Katrien's hand waved furiously and she spoke without being called upon: "Miss Stryker, I don't want an English name!" Her tone was laden with desperation.

"After your little playground speech, I am sure you don't!" Lena thought, but answered Lucas, instead. "Your name is part of your identity. When we meet people, what we usually ask first is, 'What's your name?' Let's pretend a Dutch boy moved to Chicago and a neighbor asked him that question. The neighbor may never have heard a Dutch name before and would be

embarrassed to try to pronounce it. But if the Dutch boy could give his English name, no one would have any trouble. In your case, Lucas, your English name is very close to the Dutch. Can you guess what it is?"

"No," the boy admitted sheepishly.

Lena wrote:

Lucas . . . Luke

"It's Luke. Your English name sounds like the first syllable of your Dutch name; the spellings are similar."

"Well, I am never going to leave here, so I don't need to know my English name," Jaap blurted.

"Perhaps you will stay close to home as you grow older, but Dutchville will be changing over time, Jaap." Lena said, adding to the growing columns:

Jaap . . . James

"Your English name can be either James or Jacob. We'll use James for this exercise."

Wim waved his hand, blurting before called upon, "Miss Stryker, I think my English name is Wim."

Lena smiled. "Actually, Wim is a shorter name for Willem; both are Dutch names. Like Jaap, you have more than one English name." She wrote:

Willem . . . William

"Your English name, William, is very close to Dutch in sound, and has several short names. You can be Will, or Bill, or Billy! How about that?"

He gaped as he pondered the profusion of names.

"I don't see the point," Saartje protested. "I mean, we're Dutch—not English. I know we live in America, but our names are who we are!"

Lena said, "That's true, but we all have different names in many languages. For this lesson, we'll learn your names in English, the most common language in our country. Someday, even people who never move away will speak English more frequently than Dutch here. Someday, we might eat food from Italy, Spain, Sweden, and Mexico—not just Holland and America. You might have a neighbor who has never tasted *nieuwjaarskoekjes*." A collective gasp quickly turned to scoffing.

Midst the hubbub, Antje raised her hand timidly. "What are *nieuw*—uh, those things, Miss Stryker?"

"Who would like to answer Annie's question?" Lena asked. "How about you, Katherine?"

Torn between discomfort at being called by her English name and a chance to show off, Katrien opted for the latter. "At New Years, we eat cookies shaped like the number eight. We call them *nieuwjaarskoekjes*."

"Thank you. The word *nieuwjaarskoekjes* means New Year's cookies in English. Yes, William?"

"Does Freek have an English name?"

"Indeed, he does. It's Fred." Lena added both names to the growing list:

Freek . . . Fred

Lucas jeered, "No wonder Freek doesn't obey you, Wim! He probably answers only to his English name!"

"He does not! He's a Dutch dog if there ever was one," Wim protested and turned pleading eyes to Lena. "I don't think he'll like his English name. Can't we just call him Freek?"

"Of course. I'm not saying everyone must always use English names after today. I merely want you to be aware you have more than a Dutch name. Wouldn't it be fun to learn our names in different languages, like Spanish or Russian?"

Silence ensued. Lena finished the list, pronouncing each name she wrote:

Liesbeth . . . Elizabeth
Maas . . . Thomas
Giertje . . . Margaret

She paused, chalk poised against the slate. "Raimund is very close in sound to Raymond, with just two letters different in the spelling." The list came to an end with:

Janneken . . . Joan
Elsje . . . Alice

Lena surveyed the list of names for sixteen students and one dog. "Another day we'll cover the meanings of your last names. For the rest of today, we will use only English names. I'll leave this list on the board so you can call each other by the correct name. Older students can help those who can't read. Remember to write your English name on your papers. I'll print the first-graders' English names for them to copy."

Maartje and Antje shared a worried glance. "We know how to write our English names, Miss Stryker," Antje said, "and I know how to spell my Dutch name, but Mary is just learning hers."

"Good!" Lena looked up from Liesbeth's desk where she was writing *ELIZABETH* in block letters. As she wrote WILLIAM on the top of his tablet, she addressed the other students. "While I explain the third and fourth graders' arithmetic lesson, second graders may go to the bookshelf and select a book to read. Older students, you have geography. I will ask Alice to write your assignments on the blackboard."

Maybe as *Elsje* the girl could have functioned, but as *Alice* she stumbled to the front of the room. From the first word she copied off Lena's paper, she suffered through a recital of chalk-squeaks. Scattered snickers turned her cheeks a furious red and she finished her task hastily, rushing back to her seat where she wrote her name on her paper . . . only to erase it and sneak a peek at the board to check how to spell *Alice*.

Elsje's changed demeanor made Lena's heart skipped a beat. *I would rather have Elsje less dour and more accepting of something new, but now she is embarrassed.*

Passing nearby, she overheard a smattering of Elsje's furtive whispers to Saartje, "*. . . my father . . . school board . . . trouble . . .*"

Lena asked, "Is your assignment complete, Alice?"

Elsje's response was a lifeless, "No, Miss Stryker." She lowered her head until her hair drooped over her face, effectively blocking Lena's presence.

In three years of teaching, Lena had never sensed the subtle tremor of what felt like mutiny. The idea nearly paralyzed her. She had given an assignment—fully within her rights as a teacher—but it was as if fourteen of her sixteen students rebelled inwardly, while cooperating outwardly.

Everything ties back to Cornelis. If his daughters were not here, the issue of English names would not have come up. But she knew it was more than English names. If her foul attitude hadn't intruded on the abrupt assignment, the students would have accepted it enthusiastically.

She shifted over one aisle to address the third and fourth graders. *It would be so much easier to go back to using Dutch names, but I've made my decision and will stick by it in hopes their good humor returns soon.*

"You each have a set of catalog pages. Katherine, Adeline, and Raymond, you will use even-numbered pages; the others will use the odd-numbered pages. List each item on your pages in one column and the price in a second column. Make a list of the prices on each page and add them to get a subtotal. Then, add the four subtotals to get a total for all the pages."

Despite the fact this assignment was far more exciting than the predictable pages in their arithmetic books, no one showed visible interest.

She continued, "Raymond and Bartholomew, since you are in fourth grade, you are to order three of each item, so make an extra column for the times-three prices." She anticipated grimaces from the twins—and was not disappointed.

By lunchtime, Lena was so tired she would have gladly fallen into bed and pulled the covers over her head until morning, but the irritability brewing deep inside her would have prevented sleep.

During penmanship, Lucas griped, "We write these notes every year to the same people. It's boring!"

Lena snapped, "You did not find it boring when you were easily able to find your ball on the mowed grass this noon. Nor do you appear to mind having a freshly varnished desk with well-oiled hinges so you can sneak licorice drops when you think I am not looking. Don't you suppose those who kindly performed these tasks for us got bored doing them?"

Lucas mumbled, "Yes, Miss Stryker," licked a tell-tale licorice stain off his lips, and picked up his pencil.

Lena regretted her tone, but refused to back down. She distributed flannel-backed alphabet letters to the first graders and set a flannel board on an easel, then she got Wim, Liesbeth, and Maartje busy finding letters to spell words on an illustrated list. She asked Giertje to help them, as needed, and moved along to the students who were already in the reading circle.

Her crankiness lingered, but she controlled it—that is, until Cornelis tooted his horn before Storytime ended. The Royalton clock showed three minutes remained until four o'clock. Irritability stiffened her spine. She strode out the door, letting it bang shut behind her (though she'd have reprimanded a student who did so) and headed straight toward the offending driver of the lustrous automobile.

She shook a stiff index finger at Cornelis' surprised face and announced in clipped tones, "If you truly want your daughters to fit in, you'd let them walk like everyone else." She dropped her hand to her side, bemoaning the flush rising from her collar. *Well, not all of them do—but that's beside the point.*

At that moment, Midnight, whinnied. Cornelis chuckled. "Would you like it better if my daughters rode a horse? Would that make you happy, Lena?"

"You know precisely what I mean, Cornelis," Lena retorted. "You are showing off, which does nothing to help your girls fit in."

"If that's true—and it's a big *if*—I'll be glad to have them walk. What about rainy days or snowstorms?" Exaggerated earnestness furrowed his brow. "Will their friends desert them if I drive them those days?" His laugh ignited her smoldering fury.

"When you make light of serious counsel, you do so to your daughters' detriment."

"No, you are not offering counsel. For some unknown reason, you expect me to fall in line with your silly rules. I'm not one of your students."

"An 'unknown reason'? Yes," she said caustically, "I can see that's how you have boxed up the mess you created and left here a decade ago. As for 'silly rules'? That type of thinking is what got you in trouble. You disgust me and bring shame to your family."

Cornelis' lips formed a tight red slash in his now serious face. A controlled sigh barely lifted his chest, but his hands clenched the steering wheel in a white-knuckled grip. "When you are ready to release your captives, I'll beg your indulgence for one more day and take my daughters home." He met her unflinching gaze with stone-cold eyes.

A retort sprang to Lena's lips, but Cornelis' words registered: *Students!* She tumbled up the steps, flung open the door and waited for her breath to stabilize enough for her to say, "School is dismissed."

Shame overwhelmed her in the emptied classroom when she noticed the curtains fluttering at the windows. *Suppose our voices carried inside? What was I thinking? I behaved in a manner unseemly for a teacher. This . . . this chaos must cease or the year will be unsalvageable.*

She glanced outside and saw no one. "Of course; there's no one left on the playground; they're all racing home to tell their families about crazy Miss Stryker! I've given them three days of pathetic behavior on which to report."

She fled to the teacherage and used her last ounces of self-control to prevent landing on the cot in a flying leap. Humiliation rained down in hot tears that began as rivulets but soon gushed until her pillow was as saturated as a dry field after a gully washer.

And still she cried. When her tears were spent, she rolled onto her back and stared at the ceiling. "I didn't know what to do about Cornelis ten years ago," she whispered in the still room, "and I don't know now."

She plunged into a dreamless sleep, awakening in response to a bird-call, shocked to see the last shards of sunlight dancing crazily off the mirror above her dresser. Even then she could rouse neither energy nor desire to arise. She lingered, her forearm slung across her eyes until the sun had completely vacated the sky, giving way to the moon.

Hunger accomplished what willpower failed to do. She boiled two eggs and a potato on the kerosene stove, mashed them with butter, and carried the plate to her desk. As she worked long into the night, only a moth flirting with the lamplight kept her company.

The catalog/arithmetic assignments made her sigh.

WINTER COAT = $28. WOMEN'S ROBE = $1. LEATHER BAG = $2.25.

Adda's total was $254; Maas had missed her error.

Re-do. Remember decimal points, she wrote at the top of Adda' page, and flipped to Bartel's paper:

SLED = $3.95 X 3 = $11.85

DOLL = $1.95

$1.95 X 3 = $5.85

All would have been perfect on Bartel's assignment had he not also multiplied each subtotal by three for an alarming total approaching the price of Cornelis' automobile. On and on it went.

Raimund hadn't corrected his brother's errors, since each boy believed the sun rose and set on his twin. Holding her pen over the account of Bartel's excessive spending spree, Lena finally wrote: *Re-do; only multiply each item by three—not the subtotals.*

The confusion evident in this assignment, alone, exemplified the impact of her distractedness on the students' performance. Education at the Dutch Valley School was disintegrating at an alarming rate. Teacher and students were sinking in quicksand.

The plaintive calls of an owl echoed Lena's troubled thoughts: *Who? Who? Who will make things right?*

✹ ✹ ✹

Thursday, September 12 ◆ "Miss Stryker?" The voice was a curious blend of timidity and challenge.

Startled, Lena looked up from her desk and glanced at the clock. *Seven-twenty.* "You're early today, Elsje!"

"So, you are willing to call her 'Elsje' now?" Gerolt Hazenbroek's voice cut the morning air as sharply as the pungent aroma of tobacco announced his presence. "What was that nonsense about, yesterday?"

Shuffling reminded him that his daughter stood by him. "Go outside, Elsje, can talk with the teacher," he commanded. The girl fled, but not before Lena noted that fear marred her usually happy face.

Lena kept her tone even. "Good morning, Gerolt."

He chewed his pipe stem so vigorously Lena expected sparks to land on his vest. "We hired you—believing you to be a good Dutch woman—to teach our children. We didn't hire some floozy who would spread her wild ways."

His words failed to even extend a backwards compliment, but she said, "Thank you," nonetheless.

"I meant no commendation. We're not paying you to corrupt our children, Lena." His voice rose in pitch and volume with each clipped word.

She forced herself to square her shoulders and meet his eyes. "If you do not lower your voice, Gerolt, we might as well invite Elsje back inside to witness this exchange. She is surely able to hear us."

Startled, he complied. "Your job is to teach our children reading, writing, sums—the subjects children have always learned in school."

"Perhaps you would like to stay for the morning's classes. The lessons are already prepared. There will be no time for me to change a single thing merely to impress you, if that were my intent."

"Yesterday is when someone should've been here."

"I've yet to hear what I'm accused of doing that brings you here—and the reason for your hot temper."

His shaggy eyebrows met over his broad nose. "We expect you to teach them to be God-fearing Dutchmen, follow Dutch ways and keep our families strong." He tipped his head to glare past his smudged eyeglasses. "None of that includes demanding the children learn their English names," he trumpeted. "What came over you?"

She cleared her throat and instantly regretted allowing any sign of weakness. She met his gaze without blinking. "I fail to see how a lesson on English names undermines our heritage." Her voice held steady, but when she reached out to smooth a paper on her desk, it stuck to her hand that was damp from nervousness.

"You insisted they use their English names, even on their papers." He dug a folded tablet page from his pocket and he moved closer, waving the evidence. "Elsje was shaking like a leaf when she got home— that's how afraid she was that you would punish her if she forgot and called another child by their God-given Dutch name."

Shaking? If so, Elsje is a better actor than her performance at last year's Christmas play indicated. "The assignment extended for the remainder of the day. Repetition is key to learning. To reinforce a lesson, I frequently incorporate it into other parts of the curriculum."

"Hardly the same, I would say, as forcing the use of foreign names. Do not let it happen again or I will bring the matter before the school board."

Her jaw dropped. "As the teacher, I have discretion in what I teach, do I not? It's not as if I were throwing out the McGuffey Readers! I teach in English and the children's textbooks are in English, but that does not change their heritage, any more than learning their English names does."

He snorted. "As you know, I have never been in favor of the English textbooks. There is no need!"

"Present your complaint to the school board; it was their decision, based on a state directive," she said mildly, though her pulse pounded. "As a parent, you can supplement the teaching at home with whatever Dutch materials you wish. These children, Gerolt, will see a different world than either you or I—a world in which they may be the only Dutch person in their circle of friends."

"Highly unlikely," Gerolt said, "unless you also encourage them to desert their families. What's next? Morning devotions from the English Bible?"

She counted to ten before she asked, "Tell me, Gerolt: Do you know your English name?"

Shrugging, he said nothing, although his color heightened to a deeper hue of red than his fury had achieved.

"It is Gerald. G-E-R-A-L-D. Not all English and Dutch names are so different in sound or spelling."

"This is foolishness—not something worth wasting valuable school time on. I strongly suggest you go back to teaching the way you have for the past three years. That is, if you wish to continue here."

"Are you threatening to release me, just because I taught children their English names?" Lena asked incredulously.

Hearing it put that way, he backtracked: "Calm down; there will be no need for anyone to petition the school board if you obey the rules."

"I see," she said stiffly. "In that case, I will require a more specific listing of all the rules I am expected to follow so I do not unwittingly stray."

He cleared his throat. "Common sense. That's what I am talking about. You are a mature woman, Lena; just use better sense. You should not require every little detail written down."

The bristles of an inappropriate retort rose in Lena's throat. "If that is all, I have several things to accomplish before my students arrive. Good day."

Gerolt blinked, hearing what could only be a direct dismissal. Somehow, he did not feel victorious in his endeavor. He had come, fully expecting Lena to back down—maybe even beg and sniffle. He was leaving with nothing. She hadn't denied his accusation, but neither had she repented or promised not to repeat the offense. He assembled his features into the stern look his family knew well. But Lena never looked up.

He opened the door, stepped out and pulled it shut with a resounding *thump*. Leaning against its solid surface, he wondered how the tables had turned so quickly. *Martina didn't want me to come; she was afraid I'd be too harsh. Now I know I wasn't direct enough. How dare Lena dismiss me as if I were a student?*

"What did she say?" Elsje asked eagerly, rising from the stoop.

"That is not your concern."

Inside the school, Lena trembled. She rushed to the teacherage and gripped the edges of her dresser. The mirror reflected the turmoil raging within her.

She pressed her hands against flaming cheeks. When she lifted them, white pressure points lingered. "Oh, how I envy Hanna the quiet, predictable world of the parsonage kitchen today!"

She sank down onto her rocker and forced herself to sit quietly for a full minute. The steady creaking of the rocker on the wood floor soothed her troubled spirit, but she could not hide in her private room all day. Students would soon gather—students whose families assumed she would teach, inspire, encourage, and befriend their children.

Teach—not merely inform. Inspire—not thwart through poorly executed lesson plans. Encourage—not stifle with harsh words. Befriend—not alienate by letting my emotions rule. We are fast setting the course the year will follow.

An all-too-familiar horn sounded and, like a bull ready to charge, Lena leaped up before she remembered her new resolve. "Lena, stop letting others' actions govern your reactions." She returned to the classroom. "This problem can be resolved in a civilized manner with a note I will send home this afternoon with the girls."

Retrieving her fountain pen from the floor, she opened her tablet and wrote:

> *Cornelis, You correctly said that you are a parent and, as such, have the right to make decisions regarding your daughters. However, is it necessary for you to use the horn? Mornings, it serves no purpose other than disrupting the children's play and incite jealousy; afternoons, I dismiss school at 4 o'clock—not in response to a horn. Henceforth, kindly cease this practice. Lena*

She reviewed it, nodded, crossed a t, and blew over it to dry the ink. When she looked up, a stony-faced Cornelis stood in the doorway, braced with both hands held at shoulder's height against the frame.

A dull ache that had begun as a pinprick in her right temple during Gerolt's tirade flared like dry kindling lit by a spark until it engulfed her whole head.

"Are you ignoring me?" Cornelis asked sarcastically.

He looked like Samson in Brigetta's childhood book of Old Testament stories. *If he pushes, the schoolhouse will tumble.*

Lena ripped the note she'd just finished into four pieces. She followed the aisle to the stove, dropped the scraps into the cold box and closed the door, recoiling as the metallic clang joined her inner cacophony. Suddenly dizzy, she groped for a desk to steady herself and stood looking at the blur she knew was Cornelis. She blinked until he came into focus.

"Just because I do not leap in the air when you signal your arrival so blatantly is hardly cause for an insolent tone of voice," she replied. "There must be no more horn-honking outside the school. It is rude, disruptive, unnecessary, and ineffective."

She moved to within ten feet of him and stood quietly, a model of good posture and proper teacher demeanor.

A sneer shaded his eyes and curled his lips. Words gushed out like a stampeding herd ramming the gate. "You and your cockeyed ideas embarrassed my daughters yesterday."

Her lips formed shapes, but no sound emerged.

His voice shook with rage. "I move my girls here in hopes they'll learn their Dutch heritage, and what do you do? Undermine everything by dragging out English names—and not just them, but everyone else, even a dog! Now, there's a brilliant example of fine teaching. Don't you understand how desperately Maartje and Antje want to fit in?"

"That is precisely—"

He silenced her with a snort. "Don't worry; I heard your speech yesterday. If not for your thoughtless actions, they would've walked today—even though, being raised in the city, they're terrified of cows and other things along the way. But if their *teacher*"—the word dripped with derision—"thinks walking is so important, I'll make them walk and let you deal with their terror when they arrive. What I want to know is why did you force all the attention on them?"

"But—"

He didn't intend to let her speak until he finished ranting. "Maartje says the other students were upset about being required to use English names. My daughters suffered doubly for your poor judgment."

He pounded the doorframe with both fists.

Her blinks were in sync with each wallop.

"I warn you, Lena, anyone who messes with my girls will deal with me."

Somehow, she had reached her desk. She sank to her chair, limp as a rag doll, and stared at her accuser. *He is more enraged beast than loving father.*

He crossed the threshold, becoming even more ominous as he entered the room. "If you can't justify your actions, perhaps you are not a fit teacher for this or any school. I should approach the school board and offer my services. Once they hear my reasons, they'll jump at the chance to hire me in your place."

"Have you taught school, Cornelis? Back in Chicago?" Of all she had imagined Cornelis doing in the past ten years, teaching was not on the list.

His laugh mocked. "I'd do no worse than you."

Those words set a boulder loose inside Lena. She exploded from her chair, causing it to totter in place. Placing both palms flat on the desktop, she leaned forward and squinted fiercely at Cornelis. Her voice rode a steel rail, each word raising sparks. "I have served this school well for three years. Go ahead— approach the school board! But remember one thing: In this community, the name Cornelis de Boer carries a taint of suspicion."

"Nonsense. My family is held in high regard."

"Your family, yes; but you?" She sniffed disdainfully. "There are people who still wonder why you took off ten years ago. I kept silent, Cornelis, but remember this one thing: I witnessed your shame. You need to deal with that before your threats against me hold any water. If your name ever stands on a slate of teachers, I will be forced to tell what I know."

For an agonizing moment, Cornelis de Boer and Lena Stryker glared at each other, unflinching and ominously silent—just as they had one fine day in 1919 when life plunged over an unguarded edge.

He moved closer.

She steeled herself against signs of visible fear.

"I'm not here to discuss ancient history," he said in a chilling voice. "I'm here as the father of two of your students. We are talking about your cruel lesson plans yesterday."

"*Plans? Lesson plans flew out the window when you first appeared in the doorway.*" She tossed her head. "My students all receive a good education under my instruction."

He eyed her with disdainful amusement. "I get the feeling if you never saw me again, you'd be happy."

"It's true," she spat out. "If your daughters did not deserve their grandparents' comfort, I would wish you had stayed in Chicago."

He muttered something; his tone made her glad she missed it. His hands clenched into fists. "I have as much right as anyone to be here. What is in question is whether you're a competent teacher for my girls."

Blood roared in her temples like snowmelt cascading into the Floyd River. "You have the option of enrolling your daughters in the town school. But be aware that any student who transfers between schools is usually viewed as incorrigible. Is that the reputation you want your daughters to carry? Also, you will be expected to explain the reasons for the transfer. Surely you do not want to unearth—what did you call it? 'Ancient history'?"

Lena heard his teeth grind as Cornelis left. Her pulse pounded like an army on the move. The clock struck eight. Outside, the Tudor Sedan roared to life, the sound fading as Cornelis put distance between them. Only children's voices broke the eerie stillness:

"Goodbye, Mister de Boer!"

"Goodbye, Freek!"

"See you tonight, Mister de Boer!"

"Goodbye, Father!"

Lena sagged like a hundred-pound potato sack tumbling off a wagon—not a teacher who faced sixteen students requiring all she had to give. It was time to begin the school day, but she wanted to cry, or quit, or slap something senseless. *Not something—a specific someone.* Instead, she willed herself to swallow her bilious anger and went to help Sterre ring the bell.

Every smile she gave was a lie; every sliver of caring was a sham. Older children knew the rituals and moved morning exercises along. "Do you have the pitch-pipe, Miss Stryker?" Janneken prompted.

"Hmm? Oh, yes, of course," Lena said, belatedly sounding the note.

". . . sweet land of liberty . . ." they sang.

Cornelis is at liberty to say what he wishes—but I am equally at liberty to reply as I did.

". . . land where our fathers died . . ."

And mothers . . . what will be better, in the long run, for Maartje and Antje? If, every time I look at them, all I can see is a guilty Cornelis standing in the doorway of a dark closet, he is right to wonder if I can truly be an impartial teacher.

". . . long may our land be bright . . ."

Those little girls face enough darkness without their teacher being at odds with their father.

". . . protect us by Thy might, great God, our King!"

As God is my witness, I am afraid. Ten years of silence has wound fear so tightly inside me that I can scarcely breathe, and now I am afraid of what lies ahead.

For the fourth day in a row, Lena struggled to keep her mind focused. The morning *Psalmen* was startlingly close to her own heart's cry. "*O Heere! Hoe zijn mijn tegenpartijders vermenigvuldigd; velen staan tegen mij op.*"

The Psalmist David was not the only one with foes on every side. Seeing the de Boer girls' dark eyes staring blankly as she read the Dutch words of the third Psalm—in a language they couldn't understand—lunged her into despair, despite the uplifting closing verses.

Best intentions aside, Lena's aggravation grew as the day progressed. Her frustration with the students' lack of concentration made her snap at them. Her cross words pushed them into dark corners where she could not reach them. "Your purpose in being here, Lucas, is not to stare out the window. I'm sorry if school is not as entertaining as summertime. Your poor work requires you to redo this assignment during recess."

She chose to ignore Lucas' responding mutter and turned her attention to the first graders who awaited her like frightened sparrows trapped in the reading circle. "We'll begin with your copies of the alphabet."

Three sets of puzzled eyes blinked at her.

"The alphabet. You were to bring your copies of the alphabet to the reading circle."

"Excuse me, Miss Stryker," Elsje interrupted nervously. "It's my fault. I forgot to tell them. They are working on their alphabets, but have only finished half their capital letters."

"If you are going to be a good helper, Elsje, you'll have to learn to follow instructions," Lena said sharply. All around the room, children stiffened as if fearing a physical blow. Lena instantly regretted her words and tone. *Don't take out the anger you feel toward Gerolt on Elsje.*

"I'm sorry, Miss Stryker." Elsje ducked her head over her geography lesson, but not before Lena noticed her trembling lip and rapid blinking.

Elsje is one of my best helpers, yet I've treated her as if she is a problem—only because I'm furious with her father. And now the first graders are afraid of me. "I'm sorry, children; I'm not upset with you," Lena said. "We'll review your letters tomorrow so you can complete them. Let's go to the blackboard instead."

Lena distributed chalk and drew a large square for each child. She then wrote *CAT* in the box closest to Maartje. "These letters—c-a-t—spell cat. Can you draw a cat beside the word?"

In Wim's box, she wrote *DOG*. "D-o-g spells dog. You may draw a picture of Freek next to this word."

"Miss Stryker?" Looking close to tears, Wim tugged her skirt. "Freek climbed in that automobile again, but the new girls' father didn't say he was gonna take him home. Maybe he took Freek to town instead. Freek can't find his way home from town!"

"I'm sure Mister de Boer took Freek to your farm, Wim. We'll have to remind Freek that he can walk home, won't we?"

Wim nodded, but a flicker of disappointment showed his heart as he drew the line that would become Freek's head. "I guess so . . ."

In Liesbeth's box, Lena spoke as she wrote, "S-u-n spells sun. Draw a sun shining on the cat and dog."

She stood behind them while they worked. Three hands gripped chalk and painstakingly made lines and curves to form their assigned drawings. Each first grader looked at Lena and breathed a happy sigh at her approving nods.

"Nicely done. Now, trace my letters. Good; now write the word again below."

Chalk squeaked. Each child switched places twice and repeated the exercise until each had written all three words. Wim's letters trudged uphill, Liesbeth's curved downward, and Maartje's letters were so close together that they nearly blurred, but it was an exercise completed without mistakes.

"What nice letters you have made!" Lena turned. "Elsje, would you please come forward?"

The room became eerily still as Elsje obeyed. Lena placed her hand lightly on the girl's shoulder and felt a tremor. "I apologize for being cross with you, Elsje. See how fine the first graders' letters are? That shows your good work in helping them."

Sighing audibly, Elsje met Lena's eyes. "Thank you, Miss Stryker. I'm sorry I didn't listen to instructions."

"I'm not sure you missed anything. I likely didn't mention it."

The return of Lena's goodwill strummed a responsive chord in each student. Even Maas ventured a smile. Lena studied each face. Except for Wim, Liesbeth, and the de Boer girls, she had taught each student before. Students and teacher knew each other well and like each other. Never before had days been as strained and volatile as this year.

"Elsje, please bring out the cookie jar from the teacherage. I think we should begin morning recess with a special treat. Does anyone else think that is a good idea?"

"Yes!" sixteen voices chorused.

"Maybe two cookies?" Raimund suggested impishly.

"You drive a hard bargain, young man! Okay, two cookies each, it is."

As day's end, the children cocked their ears when Lena closed "The Enchanted Castle." But no horn sounded; no Tudor Sedan appeared. Gradually, the students left for home. Lena looked at Antje and Maartje who wore worried expressions as they sat primly on the stoop, lunch bags on their laps.

"Your father is a bit late, but he'll come." She searched her options for a distraction. "Would you like to see where I live at school? We'll be able to hear your father when he arrives."

The girls consulted each other with a wordless glance, and then both nodded. Lena led the way to the teacherage; the muted sound of four button-top shoes trailing behind her kept time with the steady pace of her *klompen*. She opened the door and stepped aside.

Maartje clapped happily. "It's like a playhouse!"

"A sweet little playhouse!" Antje echoed. "Here is your bed," her fingers tiptoed over the quilt's bright squares before she spun away, "and your table and chair . . ."

". . . and your rocker," Maartje enthused and plopped down to test it, only to bounce up again, ". . . and a dresser—oh, and a radio! When I grow up, I'll be a teacher and live in a house exactly like this."

Lena laughed. "Such high praise for my humble abode! Oh, listen—is that an automobile I hear?"

The girls shot past Lena. "Father came!" Antje's voice rose above the sounds of four pounding feet.

"I did!" Cornelis was saying when Lena reached the doorway. The girls danced around him, but something in his voice put Lena on full alert. Cornelis-the-winsome-charmer was missing; only the shell of his usual exuberance remained. His raised hand kept them from climbing into the backseat, "I need to talk to your teacher. You can go swing until I call you."

Well, now; I wanted to talk to Cornelis, but on my terms, not his. Lena watched Antje and Maartje skip away. Noting the set of Cornelis' jaw, Lena wished she could join the girls, rather than talk to their father.

With his daughters beyond the range of hearing, Cornelis spun on his heel and leveled his gaze on Lena. Time stood still as his long legs ate up the distance between them. Gone was the smooth-talking salesman. In his place was a gun-slinging cowboy facing his nemesis in a smoky saloon. All that was missing in the silent-movie drama playing out on the Iowa countryside was a pianist banging out a discordant warning that signaled *"Trouble ahead!"*

Cornelis reached the stoop and dropped his right foot there with a thud. His eyes were like a hammer setting a nail; Lena was the nail. "I have just one thing to say to you: Before you go spreading more nasty lies about me, you'd better realize—"

Lena's glare would have paralyzed her students, but it left Cornelis unfazed. "How dare you accuse me? I have said nothing about you to anyone."

His lips curled. "If—and I say *if*—that were true, why would Yzaak . . ."

For once, Lena cared little about interrupting: "You doubt my word and insult my character?" She reached for the doorknob. "Antje . . . Maartje," she called, one foot on the threshold, "your father is ready to leave."

"No, not yet." His voice rose above hers. He waved the girls back to the swings. "Wait," he snapped at Lena with the confidence of a person who is unaccustomed to being ignored.

An irresistible force had just rammed an immovable object.

"Okay, okay." Hand motions matched his placating voice. "Maybe I jumped to conclusions," he hedged. "If not you, who is spreading rumors about me?"

"Yes, *who*?" she asked sarcastically.

Looking at here again, he saw she was remarkably unchanged, despite the years since their last encounter. *I don't recall her being such a spitfire, but she was always Brigetta's Tante Lena. She's slender, almost thin—but not gaunt, and certainly not fragile.* He cocked his head. *A good-looking woman, though she must be in her forties by now.*

The feisty woman he examined was simultaneously searching for the boy she remembered within the man confronting her. *Were it not for all I know, it would be difficult to remain immune to his infectious charms, regardless of the difference in our ages. Sadly, he has not matured beyond the discontent, feral youth I once knew.*

As if reading her thoughts, that scalawag set aside his appraisal of the woman a mere five steps away, which had become an assessment at definite odds with his intentions for this encounter. "I've changed."

"The proof, as they say, is in the pudding."

"Exactly. That is what I hope to do: prove myself. It's hard enough to break into new sales territory without battling rumors about my wife's heritage— things that have no bearing whatsoever on my ability to do the job. All I need is a chance. But someone," he eyes bored into Lena, "made Yzaak Baumgartner nervous about having hired me."

"Because of that, you blame me?" she snorted. "I don't speak of things I do not know—and I know nothing about your wife. Nor do I speak of *all* the things I do know," she continued pointedly. "Yzaak is an upright man. If he formed unsavory opinions, that's not my doing. You became your own worst enemy one sunny day ten years ago."

"In my defense, I was not much more than a boy."

"If that is your defense, then the years may have made you an adult, but you are still not a man." The flagpole's chain clanged like a cymbal.

Disbelief rolled across Cornelis' face, changing pale intensity to flaming shock. "What do you think you witnessed that day?" he asked hoarsely.

"I'm not on trial, Cornelis. It is not I who allowed a terrible secret to eat away at four hearts for ten years."

His brow furrowed. "Four . . . ?"

Her hand became an abacus to tick off names. Index finger: "I know what it has done to me." Middle finger: "I watched Brigetta change from a vibrant bride into someone living beneath a cloud of sorrow." Ring finger: "I sensed Bram's heart hardening against his brother." With index finger poised above the little finger, she paused. "But, perhaps, it is only three ... Have you escaped unscathed, Cornelis?" Cynicism tainted the question.

His jaw tightened. He thrust a hand into a pocket and brought out a jackknife.

She gulped. *Does he plan to stab me?*

But no; he merely flicked open the knife's blade and extended the fingers of one hand.

She listened with growing irritation to the *Scritch!* of the knife cleaning beneath each fingernail and the *vwoop-vwoop* as he wiped the blade against his pants leg after each swipe. By the time he switched hands, she was ready to seize the knife and hurl it away.

He paused, squinting at the horizon marked by swaying stalks of corn. Lena's eyes moved from the knife to the chiseled mask of his face to the silent cornfield and back to the knife. *Scritch! Vwoop-vwoop!*

He snapped the blade shut. His rock-hard gaze belied his deceptively calm voice. "I was nineteen, with barely enough clothing to keep warm, and no money after two scant meals. Bram had wounded me, so as I rode in a boxcar to Chicago I was bleeding, bruised, and had a broken nose and ribs. Someone stole my spare shirt as I slept my first night there. 'Unscathed'? No ..."

"That's superficial; it reflects your self-indulgence. Cold, hungry, wounded? Good. Stolen possessions?

Good. You robbed *others* of innocence and trust, but *you* suffered only discomfort and inconvenience."

"What do you want me to say, Lena? That I cried every night? That I feared Bram would hunt me down to kill me? That I missed my family and would've given anything to be home, but I was afraid that you, Bram, or Brigetta had told what you knew, and made up lies to make the story more interesting? That I feared my family would disown me? Is *that* what you want me to say?"

Each word was like steel against flint, each strike exposing another layer of pain in two hearts.

"It'd be a start to show you have a heart, Cornelis, that you care at all about the mayhem you left behind."

"Watch us, Father!" Maartje called with unfettered joy. "We're holding hands while we swing!"

The incongruent interruption startled both adults. "I see that, Mary," Cornelis responded vaguely without even glancing at them. "Mayhem?"

"Yes, mayhem. After all these years, Cornelis, the truth deserves to be heard."

"And why are you the one who deserves to hear it?" he challenged.

She dipped her head in acquiescence. "Perhaps I'm not. But have you made things right with Bram and Brigetta? Are you being honest with your parents? Or with Gustave and Hanna?"

His voice took on a defensive tone: "I've seen Bram and Brigetta."

Lena steadied herself on the stoop's post. "When?"

"Several years ago," he admitted. "Mary was still a baby. I'd been to California for business, and stopped off here to see my parents. I was alone, so they never met my wife and daughters."

"Hans and Rebecca have never mentioned it."

He flushed. "It wasn't a good visit. I asked for a loan and they turned me down."

"I'm not surprised; with both sons gone, they struggle to keep the farm. Money does not grow on trees for your parents, Cornelis." She looked pointedly at the glaring metallic evidence of his excesses parked near the stoop.

"I sell automobiles, Lena," he snapped. "It's the tool of my trade, like a carpenter's hammer."

"Based on the showy 'tool' you chose to buy, I suspect you'd use only a jewel-studded hammer if you were a carpenter, Cornelis," she said curtly.

Sitting on the step, he stretched out and crossed his ankles.

Leather shoes, Lena noted. *No wooden shoes for Mister Hot-shot.* She sank down on the stoop's bench and tucked her skirts around her ankles, leaving the tips of her *klompen* exposed as a subtle, albeit futile, rebuke.

"I didn't know Bram had left here, not until my visit home. I wrote to my family, but didn't give them my address; they had no way to communicate with me. I wouldn't have asked for money if I'd known they were strapped."

She refused to offer words or gestures that could be misinterpreted as approval. "*You get no pardon from me.*"

"Father told me if I wanted money or his help to secure a bank loan, which was my alternate request, I'd have to return home."

"Why was that not an option?"

Cornelis sprang off the stoop like an over-wound top. Control returned slowly. "I'd met Juanita and fathered a child with her. She was beautiful, olive-skinned—a vision. We married a few months before Antje's birth." He rubbed an invisible smudge on his trousers with his thumb. "I suppose you'll add that damning detail to your list of grievances against me."

It required no giant leap for Lena to imagine the pointed stares, cool reception, whispered comments, and not-so-subtle barbs—all of which a woman named Juanita would receive from some in the Dutchville community. Although there were few small-minded individuals, their unbridled scorn and prejudice could spread like skunk spray. *As for the timing of Antje's birth … ?* "No, it does not concern me," she said tersely, adding to herself, *But, it does give credence to what I've suspected all these years about Cornelis and Brigetta.*

Like a whisk creating froth of cream, Cornelis' mention of rumors whipped facts into sharp and jagged peaks in Lena's mind. *Cokkie Battjes is not only Katrien's mother, she's also Josina Baumgartner's sister: Josina, the wife of Yzaak who—surprise, surprise—suddenly has second thoughts about his new employee's reputation.*

Sounds of him sitting again yanked her attention back to the stoop. "One thing I gained from visiting my parents was I learned where Bram moved."

Lena eyed him shrewdly. "Surely, you didn't expect your brother to give you money?"

"No, I wanted to see him; I missed him. I thought he'd be on the farm and we could meet again without violence, but that was not to be." He interlocked his fingers around one knee. "On the train heading back to Chicago, I spotted the station sign for Rochester. I had second thoughts . . . but I got off."

Silence enveloped them as he remembered and she envisioned the encounter. "So, you saw them," she prompted when he failed to elaborate.

"I ate with them, stayed overnight at their house, and Bram took me to catch the train."

Lena realized how high her heart had leaped only when she felt it plummet. "But you said nothing, did you? You had a chance, but offered nothing that could lead to reconciliation."

Cornelis rose and slowly walked to his automobile. He leaned against the front fender and ran his fingers through his hair, which left it looking like a prairie fire. "I did not speak of . . . certain things, but they seemed to know what was in my heart. We did not come to blows." Distractedly, he smoothed his hair with both hands and then crossed his arms; his fingers plucked his shirtsleeves without purpose.

"That is to their credit, not yours, Cornelis. Granted, it took courage for you to appear on their doorstep, but it would have shown true strength of character if you had confessed to wrongdoing," she said bitterly.

He rested his weight on hands splayed across the metal curves of his automobile. "Why do you hate me? Of all involved, you're the least affected. As you said, it's been ten years—a long time to harbor hate."

She pressed fingers against her lips, but whether to prevent them from trembling or to stem an outburst, he couldn't discern. She may not have known, either.

When she finally spoke, her voice was brittle. "I'm angry with you for the death of dreams. I despise your lack of caring about those you hurt so deeply. I loathe the ease with which you built a new life away from your accusers. You say you have changed? Ha!" The final word exploded in a mirthless blast.

His voice grated like a rusty hinge. "Exactly what is it you think happened in the closet, Lena?"

A blush tinted her cheeks. "Bram and Brigetta didn't leave Dutchville because Bram wanted to better himself." Looking away, she shook her head so slowly the movement was imperceptible, had not Cornelis' eyes been fastened upon her. "They hoped to spare their families the shame your actions brought about." Her cheeks blazed; her voice faltered.

Three strides brought him close enough to tower over her. "What shame? Blame the closet doorknob, not me," he said with attempted levity.

The girls jumped off the teeter-totter and headed toward the outhouse. Midway, Maartje performed a somersault. Not to be outdone, Antje turned a leap into a cartwheel. Lost in thoughts too painful to utter, Lena and Cornelis watched their carefree antics.

When the outhouse door closed, he pushed against the post, setting muscles rippling as he arched his back. "If you've said nothing, then what's behind Yzaak's grievances against me?"

"Did you know Yzaak's wife is the Tante of a third grader? Perhaps if you had not been so consumed with impressing the students; you'd have seen Cokkie Battjes—who is Yzaak's sister-in-law—driving her buggy here on the second day of school."

He flushed as comprehension hit. "Perhaps I've misjudged you, and others," he admitted woodenly.

"You'd be wise to face the Ghosts of Years Past. Until you do, you will continue to see shadows that are not there and hear voices that do not speak. Do the honorable thing. Tell the truth about the closet."

The girls returned, skipping and singing the song Lena had taught the first graders—"A-B-C-D-E-F-G . . ."—to the tune of "Twinkle, Twinkle, Little Star."

"Come, girls," Cornelis called. He did not look at Lena again, even when Antje and Maartje detoured on their way to the automobile to hug their teacher.

There was no jubilant horn sounding as Cornelis left the schoolyard and no euphoric feeling of elation on Lena's part. Like Scrooge in Dickens' tale, she knew the past and, with the acrid taste of the present filling her mouth, she feared the future.

Words and images blurred: *Yzaak . . . A-B-C-D-E-F-G . . . a pocketknife . . . a wife named Juanita . . . face the Ghosts . . .* Every segment was replayed with blinding accuracy and blaring clarity.

There was no escaping the tension, no denying the unsettling realization nothing had improved.

"Will Cornelis make things right?" she asked a crow on the fence and flinched when he flapped his wings in a flurry of movement without leaving his post. Settling down again, he opened his mouth widely around a "*Caw!*" as if to say, "*What will you do if he doesn't?*"

Finally, mosquitoes chased her inside. She passed through the shadowy classroom, paused long enough to wave off the pile of papers on her desk as if they had audibly called to her, and crawled into bed without undressing or eating. Her evening prayers were only scattered whispers in the darkness.

✸ ✸ ✸

Friday, September 13 ◆ Friday afternoon was never the best time for history lessons, especially for two who dreaded them as much as Saartje and Elsje did, so Lena lingered longer than usual with her oldest students in hopes of infusing tolerance, if not pleasure into their misery. Neither girl enjoyed war stories and tended to rush through those sections in anticipation of the more pleasing biographies.

They needed to understand the efforts of famous Generals held a place in history. They alternately read paragraphs aloud, with Lena listening, and correcting pronunciation when necessary, and inserting questions and comments to stimulate discussion.

To the girls' evident relief, Lena finally sent them in search of the atlas on the bookshelf. Each would draw a map on which to mark the battles of the Civil War.

Puzzled to return and find Lena still holding the McGuffey Reader, Elsje asked, "Do we still have more to read, Miss Stryker?"

"No; I was lost in thought. Begin your maps."

The confrontation with Cornelis had become a filter for every word and action. She saw his face no matter whose innocent eyes looked at her. She heard his voice louder than each recitation. She felt the bite of his scorn, despite the sweet laughter of children at play. She flinched from the heat of his anger, even with a cool breeze caressing her face at recess.

Perhaps it was in the context of her own struggles throughout the week, but something had made words leap off the page when Elsje read of an army that seemed alternately to be fools and willful rebels, or desperate cowards and disciplined men. Lena tapped her finger on one word: leaders. Images of Cornelis finally faded as she belatedly joined the fifth graders for geography.

At four o'clock, she closed "The Enchanted Castle" and smiled. "That ends today's reading and the first week of school. I'm proud to be the teacher of such good students. You are dismissed."

The students emerged from the cloakroom in spurts. Without exception, they halted when they saw Lena by the door, but she merely offered pleasant farewells. Alone at last, she stretched toward the ceiling, but cocked her head at a sound.

"Hello?" she called and watched a subdued girl walk out from the cloakroom. "Katrien! You startled me!

I didn't realize anyone was still here, but I'm glad you are because I meant to thank you for the nice job you did of straightening the bookshelf this morning."

"You're welcome, Miss Stryker." Impulsively, she flung her arms around Lena's waist. "I'm trying very hard to keep our pact."

"I know' I appreciate that." Lena hugged her and lingered on the stoop to watch her skip away. Chatterbox or not, Katrien possessed characteristics that could shape her into a woman whose inquisitive mind could change her world for the better. Katrien waved from the road; Lena waved back. *It's about leadership. Each day, I mold my little army.*

Cornelis arrived without fanfare. For the first time that week, he helped Maartje and Antje get settled and took off with only perfunctory acknowledgement of the other students, much to their surprise and dismay, but to Lena's relief. *The students' fascination with Cornelis is a flash in the pan; what I teach them will last.* She strolled the playground, relaxed enough to appreciate late-afternoon sounds of nature.

Pausing to untwist two tangled swings, she wondered if Yzaak Baumgartner could withstand his wife's meddling and keep Cornelis in his employ. There was no denying the job was a perfect match for Cornelis' interests. *Cornelis' life has been entangled with mine, but we can go our separate ways, just like these swings.*

She reached for the wooden seats and propelled each swing into a sweeping arc with a flick of her wrists. The empty swings collided and shuddered back to her, exhibiting none of the ease with which they had left her hands. "I hope that is not an omen for Cornelis and me," she laughed nervously.

On that sun-spackled quiet September afternoon, she lined up the first-graders' papers on her desk. Smiling, she read CAT HAT DOG LOG SUN FUN in uneven lettering. She gave each one an A.

Working steadily, she graded other assignments and finally chose a maxim for the upper grades to use in a theme for Monday's writing lesson. "Better late than never," she read aloud, writing those words on the board. "True, so very true."

Her stomach growled. She looked up, amazed to see it was already six o'clock. Gustave would soon pick her up for the weekend. Quickly, she finished grading Lucas' arithmetic quiz and loaded the remaining schoolwork into a basket. She was waiting on the stoop when Gustave arrived.

"Oh-oh, am I late?" He swung her laundry bag over his shoulder and scooped up the basket.

"Not at all." She locked the schoolhouse door. "I could have corrected papers until you arrived, but I am eager to put this week behind me."

"A bad week?"

"The worst," she admitted, grimacing, "but it's over. I survived, and I plan to enjoy the next two days and come back ready to face a new week."

"Hear that, Storm? Giddy up! Time's a-wasting!" Gustave whistled merrily on the trip to town, and Lena's frustrations flew away on the wings of song.

But midway home, she startled the music right out of Gustave when she abruptly asked, "Did you ever think that whether Civil War soldiers were led by McClellan or Stuart or Grant, or if they fought against armies led by Jackson or Lee, the men were essentially the same?"

A final note left his puckered lips like a lingering drip from a pump's spout. "Can't say I've given it much thought. Obviously, you have!" he teased.

As if not hearing him, she said, "It wasn't a shifting line of soldiers with different feet filling different boots." She shook her head firmly, though he had neither disagreed nor commented. How could he? He was too befuddled by the unprompted, unusual conversation to formulate more than vague responses.

Lena resumed even more passionately: "The soldiers did not change." She peered into his face, waiting to catch his *"Ah-ha!"* at her revelation.

But there was no *"Ah-ha!"* on Gustave's part. He had a quick mind and a yen for knowledge, yet Lena had left him in her dust on this one.

She held up her hands in a signal of acquiescence to some flash of brilliance she perceived coming from him, and Gustave sincerely wished he knew what that might be. Lena's intensity nearly lifted her off the buggy seat. "It was the leaders—those Generals of contrasting strengths—who shaped the men under their command into fools or rebels, cowards or conquerors." She eyed him shrewdly, watching for any sign of comprehension.

"Interesting idea." Gustave cleared his throat. "The leaders, you say?"

"It's beyond interesting; it's a staggering reminder, as I'm sure you were wisely about to say."

I was? Gustave's brow furrowed. *I'm so lost here, I have nothing wise to say!*

"One thing I seemed to forget amid all the ups-and-downs of the past week is that I am the leader of my students. I can either send them to defeat or shape them into victors."

"I see . . ." Gustave said, though in reality he saw only a sister-in-law who expected more than he could muster. "I'll give your ideas some thought," he hedged, greatly relieved when Lena settled back so he could resume whistling.

Gustave had heard only words, but Lena's thoughts mined for gold beneath the surface. Her newfound knowledge robbed the uncertain outcome of her encounter with Cornelis of power. *Cornelis must face his past if he hopes to find peace. I must do what's expected of me: teach and teach well.* She sighed with such passion, that Gustave glanced sideways.

As behooves a wise man, he said nothing.

Arriving at the parsonage, she raced into the kitchen and flung her arms around Hanna. "What smells so good?"

Startled, Hanna replied, "Why, it's a pork roast. Wasn't that what you suggested?"

"Marvelous! Oh, how I love you!" she tossed over her shoulder.

"For making pork roast?" Hanna exclaimed, waiting for an explanation that never came.

Having lingered in the buggy barn as long as possible, Gustave appeared in the doorway. "A word of caution, my dear," he said, after he determined Hanna was alone. "If Lena starts talking about Stonewall Jackson, just nod and let her ramble."

Hanna looked at him with the same bewilderment he had experienced in the buggy. "She didn't already give you a Civil War quiz, did she?" he asked.

"No, we only talked about pork roast." Hanna wiped perspiration from her face with her apron.

"Consider yourself lucky," he muttered, heading to wash for dinner.

"Why can't I talk about Stonewall Jackson?" Hanna called after him, but got no answer. Returning her attention to the potatoes, she sighed. "I need a house cat; it'd be someone to talk to who won't walk away."

Throughout supper, Lena spun stories of life as a schoolteacher. On the surface, it was just like every other weekend when she came home to the parsonage.

Hanna and Gustave shared bewildered glances when she told of Janneken's report on one of her summer-reading books in which a "swave and de-boner" hero rescued a maiden in distress.

"What on earth does 'swave and de-boner' mean?" he asked.

After a moment, Hanna chortled. "Suave and debonair! For her next lesson, Janneken needs to learn to use the dictionary's pronunciation guide!"

If Lena seemed overly enthusiastic about gravy, or got teary-eyed over Hanna's report of a bird's nest falling from the pine tree, Hanna credited it to changes occurring in women of a certain age.

If she laughed longer than usual over Gustave's antics, he marveled at what must be his untapped skills in entertaining the women . . . had to be either that or Hanna's pork roast.

It was a different story at the de Boer farm outside Dutchville. In her kitchen, Rebecca replenished the breadbasket and kept milk glasses and soup dishes filled around her table while Hans carried on a lively conversation with their two granddaughters. Cornelis stared at his bowl as if the *erwten soep* it held were the most interesting thing in the world.

Rebecca touched his arm and teased, "It's pea soup, Cornelis! Split peas, cold water, and meaty ham bones. Add potatoes, celery, carrots, leeks, and onions and you've made *erwten soep!*" Four puzzled faces looked her way. "Cornelis seemed puzzled by the ingredients, so I helped him out."

Cornelis smiled ruefully. "Sorry, Mother. I guess I'm distracted. It is very good soup."

"The longer it simmers, the better the flavor. This pot was on the stove almost all afternoon," Rebecca said, ladling more of the rich Dutch favorite into their bowls.

But Cornelis was not contemplating recipes. He heard only a voice saying scornfully, *"The years may have made you an adult, but you are still not a man."*

Back in the parsonage kitchen, no one stared moodily at the dinner Hanna had prepared. Laughter reigned. Hanna and Gustave exchanged secret glances, with Hanna asking wordless questions, and Gustave shrugging wordless answers.

"Whatever was wrong with Lena . . . and whatever it was that troubled her," Hanna prayed silently, *"please, God, let it be over."*

Part Two

Saturday, September 14 ♦ Gustave rolled over in bed and sniffed the air. "Hanna . . ." He twisted curls falling over her face around his finger, loving her nearness.

"Hmm?" She burrowed deeper into her pillow.

"I smell apple *pannekoeken*." He pushed himself up on one elbow and inhaled deeply. "Yes, definitely *pannekoeken*, and hopefully apple. Lena has our coffee ready, too . . . Do you plan to sleep all day?" he teased.

Hanna lifted her head and gave her husband the look only a wife can manufacture. "Gustave, what time is it?" Her tone showing no interest in his answer—a detail substantiated by the fact she flopped back on the pillow.

He shifted to reach his pocket watch on the bedside table. "Already, it is a few minutes past five o'clock."

"A 'few minutes' hardly makes me a sluggard." Hanna pulled the sheet over her face. A minute passed in silence while Gustave resumed his curl-twisting. She lowered the sheet enough to reveal one opened eye. "You have no plans to sleep any longer, do you?"

Gustave shrugged, saying only: "Apple *pannekoeken*, Hanna!"

"Lena spoils us," she admitted, yawning. "Or maybe she torments us. First, she keeps us up late with her stories; then, she wakes us—you, that is. I can't blame Lena for your crime of waking me before the chickens. The smell is temping, however." She stuck one foot out from beneath the covers. "Brrrr! It feels like a frost-on-the-pumpkin kind of morning."

He dangled a tempting tidbit. "The kitchen will be quite warm from the *pannekoeken* baking."

Hanna groaned. "If you bring me my robe and slippers, I will forsake my wanton habits of sleeping past sunrise to see if your prophecies are true."

Gustave and Hanna stood in the kitchen doorway and watched Lena work. The room was warm and inviting with aromas of rich coffee, Dutch pancakes in the oven, and the heady spices Lena was blending together for molasses cookies.

When she paused to sip from her coffee cup, she noticed her visitors. "Wonderful! I was afraid I'd need to pound a drum to rouse you this morning—and, as you are aware, we have no drum!"

"As your sister has so pointedly reminded me, even the chickens are not yet up, Lena!" Gustave protested with a chuckle. "What time did you get up?"

"Oh, a bit ago," she said vaguely, although the evidence in the kitchen told otherwise. "I couldn't sleep, so decided to make coffee, but then I got to thinking about *pannekoeken*, and remembered my cookie jar at the school needs refilling—as does yours—and one thing led to another."

She reached for the coffeepot. "As long as you're up, sit. Have some coffee while I roll this cookie dough in waxed paper to chill."

Words ebbed and flowed as caffeine edged sleepiness aside. Lena checked the oven and pronounced the *pannekoeken* done and deftly slid the three baked pancakes from their pans to warmed plates.

After Hanna poured milk, Gustave offered the prayer of thanks. "What will you women do today?" he asked, halfway through breakfast.

Lena and Hanna shared secretive, hopeful glances. Gustave grinned at the two women who had sat across the table from him for so many years. He could almost read their minds: *There's preparation for Sunday dinner, and we should make applesauce—but what if Gustave has something more exciting to offer?*

"The usual," Hanna said airily. "Why do you ask?"

Gustave shrugged. As if such a thought had just crossed his mind, he tossed out a casual question: "Would you join me for a visit to the de Boer's farm this afternoon? I want to talk privately with Cornelis but, not knowing if Rebecca will be available, could you come to be with the girls?"

Hanna's enthusiastic "Of course!" collided head-on with Lena's loud and firm "Sorry; not me; I am so busy." Lena read mystification in Hanna's eyes, while Hanna found hidden emotions on Lena's face.

In the awkwardness that followed, Lena spoke first. "Today is not a good time. This afternoon we will be hot from working in the kitchen," she said and sank down in her chair, only to pop up like a Jack-in-the-Box. "And I need to make banana cupcakes for

Katrien's birthday next week; she would be disappointed if I broke the tradition I began my first year. And, then there's—"

"Don't be silly, Lena!" Hanna scolded, her voice halting Lena's protests. "Hans and Rebecca are practically family. Besides, how long can a batch of cupcakes take? A quick sponge bath and a change of work dresses will make us presentable. I must say, I welcome this opportunity to see, close-up, what I hear around town is a *swave and de-boner* man! I'm interested in seeing how the gangly youngster we knew managed to turn out looking like . . . what's that fellow's name who people are comparing him to, Gustave?"

"The truly *swave and de-boner* Charles Atlas!" Gustave replied with a rolling laugh. "Since no one has seen Cornelis in a number of years, it should be expected he has matured. I hear he has become a fine specimen of God's handiwork."

Lena released a scornful *"Pffffft"* and sprang up. "More coffee, anyone?" Her voice was as bright and dangerous as thin ice on the Floyd River. Without waiting for affirmation, she filled cups and landed again on her chair and looked up, at last, into two troubled faces.

"Gustave, just because I don't want to go doesn't mean you can't see Cornelis while Rebecca and Hanna visit. While the cupcakes cool enough to frost, I'll wash my hair earlier than usual which gives me time trim the ends. Between ragged hair and mussed clothes, I am a fright!"

Gustave studied her thoughtfully. "As you wish; but Hans and Rebecca have seen us in our garden clothes, and even worse. As for Cornelis, how we look is the least of his concerns. He has a lot on his mind these days, what with his wife's death, caring for his daughters, taking a new job, and who knows what else."

Lena gripped her coffee cup until her knuckles whitened. "Yes, who knows what else? He certainly is all wrapped up in himself."

Hanna dropped her coffee cup to the table with a thud and peered into her sister's face. "Oh, my goodness!" She covered her lips with her fingers as her eyes opened wide. She leaned forward. "Has the *swave and de-boner* Cornelis de Boer seduced my sensible sister?" she teased in a singsong voice.

"Hanna!" Lena gasped. Coffee sloshed, unheeded, from her cup to the tabletop. "Enough with this 'swave and de-boner' talk! I assure you that is not the problem!" She choked on a sob. "I wish I'd never told you about what Janneken said!" The room spun around her as the implications of what Hanna suggested rendered her speechless.

Hanna batted her eyelashes. "Hmm! With such strong feelings roused, I wonder . . . is what you feel for Cornelis forbidden love, or secret longing? By all reports, he is a striking man, and he is now a widower—while you, dear sister, are both attractive and available! My goodness, the school board would hate to lose you to marriage." Gustave and Lena's eyes followed her as she wet the dishrag at the sink and mopped up Lena's spilled coffee.

Lena gagged; her stomach roiled like the washing machine when something was stuck in its agitator.

So evident was Lena's discomfort that Hanna took pity on her sister. "If you truly like Cornelis, I will quit teasing. You know I love you and want only the best for you. I would never say anything against someone you . . ."

A sound erupted from Lena and she clapped her hands over her ears. "Stop it! Romance is the farthest thing from my mind—especially with him."

"There is quite an age span, but it won't be a problem if—"

Lena shot off her chair, thrusting her plate aside. "Stop this crazy talk!"

By then, Gustave was baffled. His eyes roamed from his wife to his sister-in-law—two women facing each other across what may well have been the Grand Canyon, so great was the distance he sensed between their spirits. *Just when I think I understand women . . .*

Lena grimaced as she dropped to her chair. "Forgive me; I don't mean to be rude." She reached out blindly and patted whatever part of Hanna she could reach, which turned out to be her hip. Moaning, she lowered her head until her forehead rested on the table's edge. Abruptly, she swung her legs out from beneath the table. "Has anyone dug potatoes lately?"

Hanna blinked. *Potatoes?* She looked at Gustave. Both shook their heads.

"No? I will get enough for potato soup for our supper. The bone from last night's pork roast will add nice flavor." Without another word, she pulled a sweater off a hook and left the kitchen.

Hanna and Gustave stared at the door. Hanna finally said, "It's quite dark. I don't know how she expects to tell a potato from a clump of dirt."

Gustave reached for her hand and examined it, knuckle by knuckle. "Since when does she start potato soup so early in the day? It'll be stuck to the pan by supper! No, our Lena isn't searching for potatoes." They fell silent. "Do you honestly believe Lena harbors amorous feelings for Cornelis?"

She studied his face. "Who knows? I've always wished she could have what you and I share, but I offended her. I expected her to swat me and we would laugh and . . ." She sighed. "Aren't we Stryker girls something?" She shook her head ruefully. "Dear Gustave, living under the same roof with both of us all these years. First, you endured me and my problems, and now Lena is, well, she's not the Lena we know."

"You Stryker girls are something . . . which I admire. As for all those years? They made me love you more than life itself, and to thank God for the blessing He gave us in Lena. Now, she is battling a nameless giant. But this, too, shall pass, Hanna; this, too, shall pass. We'll wait for her to come to us."

Hanna drifted off her chair. She peered out the window, seeing only her troubled reflection staring back at her in the glass. She came back to stand behind Gustave. She dropped her arms around his shoulders and rested her face against his head as she stroked his sideburns. "I love you, Gustave. What did I do to deserve such a wonderful man?" She kissed his cheek. When she straightened, her hands lingered on his shoulders. "I don't understand how men are so blind, they can't see Lena would be a perfect mate."

Gustave caressed her hand. "Maybe you were on the right track with your question—Lena's denial of any romantic interest in Cornelis may fit Shakespeare's line, 'The lady doth protest too much, methinks.' To our knowledge, she has never expressed any interest in a man before, but—"

Hanna interrupted impatiently, "I saw Cornelis briefly when I passed by Baumgartner Motors on my way to the store yesterday. He is a charmer; he had Geertruyd Kortrecht practically eating out of his hand while she and Evert looked at new automobiles." Lost in thought, she began to clear the table.

Gustave rose to help. "Are we agreed to let Lena speak of things in her own time and her own way?"

"Of course, but what about this afternoon? Lena doesn't want to go along, but I would love to entertain two little girls and give you an opportunity to talk with Cornelis privately."

"Let's see how the day progresses. Lena may change her mind."

After a restless morning during which Gustave studied, Lena baked, and Hanna began preparations for Sunday's dinner, they all gathered for lunch.

Conversation was desultory until Lena said woodenly, "I would like to go along this afternoon to get to know Maartje and Antje better."

Gustave chewed a mouthful of bread before answering, as if her capitulation were no major accomplishment. "A fine idea, Lena. Your interest in your students is what makes you a good teacher."

Lena smiled faintly in mute response to his praise.

At one-thirty, Gustave signaled Storm to halt by the hitching post at the de Boer's gate. Gustave helped Hanna down first and, as she headed to the Big House in search of Rebecca, he then offered Lena a hand.

She looked back at the buggy as if contemplating an escape. "Would you please tell the girls I'll be out by the swings? If they wish, they can join me. If not, holler out the back door and I'll walk over to the Big House and chat with Hanna and Rebecca."

Gustave nodded and watched her leave before he followed the short path to what had long been called the Little House. It had been Bram and Brigetta's first home, and now housed Cornelis and his daughters.

He lifted his hand to knock and held it motionless for a moment as a flood of memories and longings filled his heart. "A wise poet once said, 'For of all sad words of tongue or pen, the saddest are these: It might have been.' It's a true saying, indeed." His knuckles struck a rhythmic cadence on the door.

Cornelis seemed shocked to see Gustave. He looked past the Dominie's shoulder to where the buggy was parked. His Adam's apple bobbed furiously. A nervous tic flicked his cheek; he grew sullen as if the reflex had pulled a string. *This young man is the talk of the town? He may have the physique of a Greek god, but his mercurial demeanor hardly seems to match.*

Holding a wet dishrag and sudsy bowl in his hands, Cornelis opened the door with his foot. "Come in!" he invited belatedly—and with false heartiness. He stepped to one side. "The girls and I are just finishing our lunch dishes." He looked at the dish and cloth in his hands sheepishly. "I guess I could have left these things in the kitchen—it's just that you are the first to knock on my door, and it startled me!"

Gustave smiled. "I apologize for no forewarning!"

Cornelis peered past him. "You still drive a buggy? Come by Baumgartner's; I'll show you a new Ford."

"Oh, I have a Ford, but Hanna, Lena and I all love a buggy ride on such a pleasant day as this is."

"Th-th-they are here?"

Why does hearing that fluster him? "No need to worry about female visitors today, though the place looks fine," he said reassuringly, noting the sparse, utilitarian furnishings that showed a lack of feminine flair. "I didn't know if I'd find you here, or at the Big House."

In a far corner of the parlor, a screen provided privacy for a single bed, telling a sad story of a lonely man whose daughters likely shared the cottage's only bedroom.

"I try to be at our house when the girls and I have time together. Mother and Father help so much with them that I don't want to impose more than necessary.

Besides, I am trying to create a home for the girls and me." His face grew more flushed the longer he talked.

What would make a young man so uneasy, words blow out of him like feathers from a pillow? Grief, I could understand, but nervousness puzzles me. He chose his words wisely. "I'm sure Rebecca and Hans don't consider time spent with granddaughters an imposition."

"No," he admitted, "they'd like us there more often. We eat supper at the Big House if I've worked all day. And Mother takes care of the girls while I helped Father, as I did this morning . . ." Cornelis ceased speaking as they entered the kitchen where his daughters were drying dishes. "Girls, this is Dominie Ter Hoorn. Dominie means he is a minister."

He turned back to Gustave. "This is Antje; she is seven. And Maartje, who is five."

"Hello, Antje and Maartje!" Gustave's smile pulled its match from two somber faces. "There's a surprise waiting for you by the swings! May I dry the rest of these dishes so you can go see what it is?"

Four pleading eyes flew to Cornelis. "Go ahead," he said. As they skipped off, he turned to Gustave with x raised eyebrows. "If your surprise has four legs and a tail, we will have to send it back home with you. My girls clamor for a puppy after seeing Freek every day. I tell them barn cats are all the pets we need."

Gustave chuckled, "Well, you can breathe easier! The surprise is Lena. Hanna looked forward to a visit with Rebecca, so Lena decided to take advantage of an opportunity to get to know your daughters better."

The younger man refocused on his task, dipping a handful of silverware into the rinse water. "Well, well, well. I wondered what her approach would be."

Gustave said nothing, just dried three cups, and hung them on hooks in the cupboard. "And I came to talk with you, Cornelis, as your Dominie."

"Yes, I am sure you have much to say to me," Cornelis said sardonically.

Gustave tilted his head in surprise. *What is going on here?* "Lena told me you've had a recent bereavement. Losing a wife is always hard, but to lose a spouse when you are so young must be doubly so. What was your wife's name?"

Cornelis turned to meet Gustave's eyes. "Lena told you of my wife's death, but did not tell you her name?"

"No. Or, if she did, I have forgotten."

Cornelis stared out the window. He puckered his lips, then flattened them against his teeth. *In-out, in-out.*

Gustave watched in silence broken only by the jingling silverware he dried.

"Juanita." Cornelis' voice remained neutral though his eyes revealed inner anguish. "She was as beautiful as her name. I might as well tell you since I'm sure you'll eventually hear it around town," he said with a flash of bitterness, "Juanita was Spanish." His jaw quivered, but quickly grew firm again. "Both girls look so much like her," he added softly.

"Then I know she was a beautiful woman, Cornelis. The girls' dark eyes and hair are striking, even with their childish features."

"Seeing them . . . well, sometimes it is like a sword piercing my heart."

"You shared life and true love with Juanita."

To Gustave's surprise, Cornelis flushed. "Yes," he said simply and began to scrub a plate so hard, Gustave wondered if the china's pattern would fade.

Cornelis finally rinsed it and handed it to Gustave. "I don't know what . . . anyone . . . has told you, but my wild misspent youth was relatively short-lived. I was a good husband, a good worker, and try to be a good father."

Good to know—though certainly not an answer to my unvoiced questions. Gustave nodded, choosing a neutral question based on Cornelis' outburst. "What type of work did you do in Chicago?"

Cornelis visibly relaxed, much to Gustave's relief. "I worked for Henry Ford . . . well, not directly for the man, but in his company. It was a dream job for me. I started out making parts and assembling automobiles, but my skills are in sales."

"Knowing what goes into the production of an auto must make you a better salesman."

Cornelis looked pleased. "I like to think so."

"I saw your advertisement in the newspaper. You have a good head for business, Cornelis, to come up with the idea of giving free driving lessons to anyone who buys an automobile."

Cornelis shrugged. "It is not original with me and I didn't try to pass it off as such, but it has never been tried here. Mister Baumgartner liked the idea, so I managed to get the ad to the paper just hours before the deadline. We will see how many sales result. Meanwhile, I told him I would pay for the ad."

Gustave chuckled. "That may prove to be the best example of your sales abilities because Yzaak Baumgartner pinches every penny until it squeaks! It sounds like you are working well together. You'll bring some much-needed life to his business. He still thinks like the bicycle repairman he was before venturing into automobiles—which means he sees no need to advertise. That may work for bicycles, but not with automobiles, as you well know."

Cornelis carried the dishpan to the kitchen door. The screen door slammed shut behind him as he flung soapy water out across the porch floor.

"May I carry out the rinse water for you?" Gustave called after him.

"Sure, if you don't mind." Accepting the pan from Gustave, Cornelis placed it on the wide railing. He used a broom to swish the dishwater over the wooden slats until he was satisfied the porch was clean, and then used the rinse water to chase suds through the cracks to the ground below.

"My, this brings back memories!" Gustave leaned against the kitchen's doorframe beyond the path of the broom. "I can almost see Brigetta washing this porch! She never wanted to discourage the birds from building their nests up there," he nodded at the gingerbread latticework overhead, "because she loved hearing them sing. She figured having to scrub the porch each day was a fair exchange for the enjoyment the birds brought." The broom's steady *whoosh* faltered. "She and Bram lived here when they were first married, you recall."

"Yes," Cornelis said tersely, "I remember." Abruptly, he collected both pans and brushed past Gustave into the kitchen, letting the screen door slam against his heels.

Standing to one side, Gustave watched Cornelis take an inordinate amount of time wiping off the table, putting away the remaining dishes, and drying the dishpans before hanging them on nails beneath the sink. "Do you mind if we sit on the porch?" Gustave finally asked to break the lengthening silence. "I brought extra tobacco if you'd like to fill a pipe and join me."

The Dominie knew the way to get a Dutchman to talk were to join him in his chores, or to put a pipe in his hand. Since Cornelis' kitchen duties were completed, Gustave was counting on a pipe's allure; he wanted to talk to Cornelis without Hans around.

They settled into chairs overlooking the clotheslines and the field beyond. The squeak of swings and the girls' laughter and Lena's low voice punctuated the lazy afternoon. Cornelis propped his work boots on the porch railing, and accepted the tobacco pouch from Gustave.

"So, you helped Hans in the barn this morning?" At Cornelis' curious expression, Gustave chuckled. "The straw caught in your shoe gives you away."

He grinned sheepishly and rose to scrap his feet on a step's edge. "I was rushed, coming in from the barn to make lunch. I help with chores since we live in the house a hired man would have."

"It must make for very long days for you," Gustave sympathized.

"Long days are good; they make the nights shorter."

Gustave nodded slowly, remembering the bed in the parlor. He sneaked another look at the troubled man with whom he shared the porch.

Out by the swings, Lena caught whiffs of pipe smoke. She alternately pushed each girl's swing. Maartje giggled or poked a toe at Lena each time the swing's arc brought her close, but Antje faced the house as if to keep her father within her line of vision.

The steady rhythm of pushing swings calmed Lena; the girls' idle chatter was like a salve to her aching spirit. Finally, they tired of swinging. Lena suggested that they walk over to the barn to see the kitties Antje had mentioned on the first day of school.

With kittens tumbling all around the dozing Mama cat, Lena climbed up on a bale of hay and patted spots on either side of her. "If we sit here, I'm sure the kitties will let their Mama sleep and come see us. Cats are very curious!"

Maartje and Antje willingly nestled close to Lena and all waited. Almost immediately, first one, then another, and finally all the kittens scrambled over the loose hay to investigate their visitors. Just watching their antics in the hay prompted spontaneous giggles from the girls. Lena soon learned that Maartje's favorite was called Cat and Antje's was suitably named Pretty Kitty.

"What's this little fellow's name?" Lena asked, reaching behind to retrieve the kitten making a trip across her shoulder and down her back.

Collapsing in giggles, the girls replied in unison, "Mister Nosey!"

Lena laughed, too. "What a fitting name! How about this one?" She bent to pick up one that was chewing on her shoelace.

"I call him Boy," Maartje said.

"But his name—I named him, you know," Antje reminded her sister loftily, "is really Tiger because he has stripes like in Grandmother's animal book."

"But if we call him Tiger, he'll be mean like a tiger!"

Antje—in a refreshing display of typical seven-year-old behavior—rolled her eyes at Maartje. Lena settled Boy/Tiger on her lap and drew both girls closer in a one-armed-hug for each. "Do you have a ball of yarn at your house?" Two headshakes. "Cats chase things that roll, they love to play with the little tails of yarn coming off the balls. I have a few balls in my knitting basket I'll give you on Monday."

Antje dropped her eyes first, but not before Lena noticed how quickly the joy disappeared.

"We don't like school," Maartje said matter-of-factly, "but Grandmother says we must go. Unless we have a stomachache," she added. Her eyes darted away. "We might be, uh, sick on Monday."

Antje jabbed her sister behind Lena's back. "In Chicago, each grade had a room." Antje obviously hoped to divert Lena's attention from her sister's unfortunate revelation. "I don't like having everybody in one room. The big kids are noisy and bossy."

Tiger tumbled onto Maartje's lap and pushed his brother aside. Mister Nosey took it in stride and moved to Lena's vacant lap. She stroked his back and scratched his ears and scoured her mind for words to say. "Back in Chicago, Antje would have been in the second-grade room and Maartje in the first-grade room. You probably would've had recess at different times, too. At Dutch Valley School, you get to sit in desks next to each other every day, and play together outside. That part is nice, isn't it?"

Maartje's eyed widened and she leaned forward to inform her sister, "I wouldn't want to be in a different room, away from you, Annie."

Antje nodded pensively. "Me, neither. I like sitting by Maartje," she admitted. "But I miss my friends. And I hate wooden shoes! They're noisy."

"I'm sure your friends miss you, too. How would you like to write letters to your class back in Chicago for your penmanship exercise next week, Antje? I have some pretty cards to copy the final letters on, and I'm sure your father knows the school's address."

The kittens gradually tired and either fell asleep on laps, or returned to curl up beside their mother. When Pretty Kitty nudged her nose beneath Mama Cat's front leg and burrowed in to snuggle, Antje sighed.

Noting the path Antje's eyes had followed, Lena risked a serious topic, hoping Katrien never learned of her blatant disregard for their pact. "When I was seventeen, I left my mother and came across the country to live here. I didn't see her again for a long time. I missed her so much that sometimes I'd cry at night when everyone else was asleep."

Furtive glance passing between the sisters told Lena she was on-target. "Something I did helped me not to be so sad whenever I thought about my mother."

Lena could read the message in their startled gazes as clearly as if charcoal had scrawled the words on a clean white sheet: *"Think about our mother? I thought we were supposed to forget her!"*

"What did you do?" Maartje asked bluntly.

"I made a scrapbook," Lena said nonchalantly. "In it, I wrote or drew pictures of things that I wished I could tell or show my mother. It was a very private book; I didn't show it to anyone." She paused to allow this idea to take root. "Maybe next week everyone could make scrapbooks in Art Class. Do you think that is a good idea?"

"Yes!" Antje said fervently.

Maartje's nod came more slowly.

"It doesn't always need to be writing in a scrapbook," Lena said, correctly interpreting the concern shading Maartje's face. "Sometimes, I pressed a pretty flower, or drew a picture of a new dress, or sketched something that reminded me of a song I had learned. Until you learn to read and spell more words, you could do that, Maartje, so the scrapbook would still be private."

Maartje nodded, visibly relaxing. She petted two cats at once and their purring grew audible. "Are you a mother, Miss Stryker?" she asked abruptly. A streak of dust curved on her pink cheek; a stiff straw poked out of her curls.

"No, I never married, but I love children." Lena removed the straw. "Some people call me Tante Lena because many years ago, a little girl named Brigetta was born in Dutchville. I moved here to live with her family and help raise her. You meet Dominie Ter Hoorn before you came outside; he's Brigetta's father. Her mother is my sister, so that makes me Brigetta's aunt and she is my niece. I miss Brigetta very much."

"Where does she live?" Maartje asked.

"She's grown up, now, and twenty-nine years old, like your father. In fact, she married your father's brother; his name is Bram. Do you know your Uncle Bram?" Belatedly, she wondered if she had opened a can of worms better left undisturbed.

Antje nodded seriously. "He lives too far away for us to see him." It was an obvious quote.

So . . . that's the story Cornelis told his daughters; well, it's not my place to say otherwise. With words that pressed against her heart, she explained slowly, "Bram and Brigetta live in Rochester, Minnesota. Chicago is in Illinois. We live in Iowa. Minnesota is a state, and so are Illinois and Iowa. Your Uncle Bram and Aunt Brigetta have lived there a long time. They have a little girl named Sanna, who is two years old. Sanna is your cousin. Do you have other cousins?"

Antje looked puzzled. "I don't think so. How do you get them?"

"Did your mother have brothers or sisters?"

"I don't know," Antje said. "She never told us."

"The way to get cousins is if your parents have brothers or sisters who have children. Those children are called your cousins."

"Are cousins nicer than the children at school?" Antje asked hopefully. "Because if they are, I want some cousins."

"Me, too," Maartje echoed.

"They can be nicer. Remember when Adda told about her summer on the first day of school? She mentioned that Jaap is her cousin. That's because their fathers are brothers, just like your father and Sanna's father are brothers. That makes Adda and Jaap cousins."

"I just want cousins who are girls, and who aren't big and mean," Antje said firmly.

"Me, too," Maartje said solemnly.

"Cousins are like everyone else—some are girls, some are boys, some are nice, some are bullies. Sometimes a cousin makes a good friend, and sometimes a schoolmate makes as good a friend as a cousin. Do you know what I would like? I would like to have more nieces."

"We could be your nieces!" Excitement glowed in Maartje's eyes.

"No, we couldn't," Antje countered, "because our mother . . ." She floundered, though whether at the mention of her mother or with confusion over how the aunt-niece relationship worked, Lena could not tell.

"We could pretend I'm your Tante. Then I would have two more nieces. And here's a secret: If you are my pretend nieces, you could call me Tante Lena, just like Brigetta does and like Sanna will when she learns to talk more. I know you would remember to call me Miss Stryker at school."

Both girls stared at her face as if memorizing it, then cast a furtive glance at each other, exchanged a secretive signal, and nodded solemnly.

"You don't need to call me Tante Lena if you'd rather not. It's up to you."

"If we can't have friends here," Antje said resignedly, "at least you could be our Tante Lena."

"You've only been at Dutch Valley School for one week. That's not much time to make friends. But next week? Ah, that's a good week to make friends. You'll see," she promised boldly against the backdrop of their skepticism. "Let's go up to the Big House and talk to your grandmother about a fun idea. If you give each student a big smile along with one of your grandmother's cookies, I suspect you'll discover friends living inside those big noisy bodies!"

Coming up to the porch, Lena glanced through the kitchen window and saw Hanna and Rebecca deep in conversation in the kitchen over cups of coffee. An untouched plate of cookies waited between them.

Before the women noticed they had company, Lena overheard Rebecca's worried voice say "... nightmares ..." Lena purposely stomped her feet on the steps as if to remove clods of mud from her shoes and encouraged the girls in a louder voice than necessary to do the same.

"Hello, girls!" Rebecca shot Lena a grateful glance. "How about a glass of milk and some cookies? Coffee, Lena?" she asked, reaching into the cupboard.

"Hello, Rebecca. We were just talking about your cookies." Lena accepted the proffered cup. "But first, girls, I want to introduce you to my sister, Hanna. Hanna, this is Antje and Maartje." She matched each girl to her name with a light hand placed on the appropriate shoulder.

Hanna smile. "I'm glad to meet you, Antje and Maartje!" The girls were polite, but kept a safe distance, choosing chairs opposite Hanna.

Lena pulled a chair into place between the girls. "Hanna is your cousin Sanna's grandmother, just like Rebecca is your grandmother," she explained.

Rebecca and Hanna shared a startled glance. Hearing Lena mention Sanna, left them wondering how that topic had come up in what was apparently now a continuation of Lena's earlier conversation with the girls.

"Maartje and Antje aren't certain if they have other cousins besides Sanna," Lena said casually, as if the topic were normal on a September afternoon. "Do you know if they do, Rebecca?"

"I believe we're the only family on either side," was the guarded reply.

Lena smiled into two upturned faces. "It seems you don't need to worry about nasty boy-cousins! Sanna is a sweet little girl."

"I wish she could go to school here with us," Maartje said. "She could be our cousin and a friend."

"She's too little for school yet, but I wish she lived here, too," Hanna responded with an audible sigh.

"Now, I want to know something," Rebecca said with mock sternness. "Who was talking about my cookies, and were they saying nice things?"

"We were," Maartje giggled, "and we said lots of good things! Our Tante Lena says . . ." Covering her mouth with both hands, she looked at her sister's ashen face. "I'm sorry, Miss Stryker."

"No need to worry, girls," Lena said. She explained to Hanna and Rebecca, "I invited Antje and Maartje to call me Tante Lena in private, though I'll still be 'Miss Stryker' at school." She addressed the girls again: "Sometimes private means only between two people, or even a person keeping a secret to herself. I can be Tante Lena anywhere but at school, okay? Now, your grandmother is waiting for an answer to her question about her cookies!"

Relieved, Maartje said, "May we bring a special treat to share at school next week, Grandmother?"

"Yes! And I know what will be perfect," Rebecca said. "We will bake lots of *Banket Gebak!*" Seeing her granddaughters' confusion, she quickly added, "That means Pastry Letters. They were your father's favorite cookies when he was little. We will make a big batch of almond pastry dough, and roll it and cut it into letters and sprinkle them with sugar . . . but who will help me make the letters? Let's see . . ." She picked up the tablecloth and peered under the table.

"Here we are—we'll help you!" Antje's wild giggle made three women smile.

Maartje ducked under the table and erupted from the opposite side, coming up in front of Rebecca's knees. "Pick me! I'm learning my letters!"

"Mercy!" Rebecca planted a kiss on Maartje's nose. "Two helpers are exactly what I need! We will give your classmates one *Banket Gebak* for their first name and another for the last part of their last name if it has more than one word. Since your teacher is here, let's make a list so we don't miss anyone." Rising, she found paper and pencil on a kitchen shelf.

Lena leaned back. "Starting at the beginning of the alphabet with last names, since that's how everyone's listed in my grade book. First is Katrien Battjes, Lucas and Liesbeth Beekman, Maas Bleecker, and do not forget Antje and Maartje de Boer! Then come Janneken De Groot, Adda and Jaap De Jong . . ."

"They are cousins," Antje interjected with a frown, "and Jaap's a boy."

Maartje wrinkled her nose. "Boy cousins are no good," she pronounced to Rebecca and Hanna's amusement.

Lena winked over the girls' heads and resumed. "Elsje Hazenbroek, Giertje Ten Broek, Raimund and Bartel Vande Veer, Sterre Van der Voort, Saartje Van Leaven, and Wim Wynkoop. That should be sixteen."

Rebecca tapped her pencil along the names on her list, silently counting. "Sixteen, indeed. Is Wednesday a good day for a special treat?"

"Perfect!" Lena said.

"Tante Lena says if we put cookies inside those big kids, friends will come out," Maartje said, wide-eyed.

Rebecca smiled. "Your Tante is very wise. And you are very lucky girls. Not all students get a special visit from their teacher."

Footsteps and voices sounded from the back porch and within minutes the door opened. Cornelis, Gustave, and Hans filed into the kitchen. "Hey, who's eating all the cookies?" Hans rumbled. He tousled the little girls' curls and growled into their ears, making them giggle when his beard tickled their cheeks.

Hans smiled at Rebecca. Lena had to look away, so private was their joy at the sound of little girls' laughter. Against her will, her eyes were drawn to Cornelis. The look on his face pricked her heart. It was a bittersweet moment. *"Because of you, Cornelis, Gustave and Hanna miss the same opportunities with Sanna."* Despite the brief poignancy of Cornelis' expression, she reminded herself, *He is the enemy.*

"Care for coffee, men?" Rebecca asked. "Bring an extra chair or two from the dining room, Cornelis, and I'll refill the cookie plate."

"We shouldn't stay," Gustave said, "since my sermon requires last-minute preparation, but how can I turn down a cookie? And what's a cookie without a cup of coffee?" He joined the laughter and sat next to Hans. "Will we see you and the girls at church with your folks, Cornelis?" he asked, assuming nothing as he shifted his chair closer to the table.

Cornelis avoided his parents' eyes. "Church hasn't been a habit for my family, but I want my girls to know their Dutch heritage, and church is a big part of it. This week, we'll begin new habits."

Not recalling seeing either Cornelis or the girls the previous Sunday, Lena quickly responded to the look of panic on the girls' faces. "I'll meet you at church tomorrow with a surprise, after which I'll introduce you to your Sunday School teacher."

"Is church like school?" Antje asked, aghast.

"Your Sunday School is only girls your ages. The first- and second-grade girls meet in one room, and the boys from those grades meet in another. For church, you sit with your family. I imagine your Grandfather Hans will have a tablet and pencil in his pocket for each of you, maybe even wrapped mints!"

Hans said, "I'll put them in my pocket tonight." The look he shot at Cornelis made him squirm. Obviously, the previous lack of church attendance, while suspected, had not been discussed between father and son in the brief time Cornelis had been home. Hans' firm jawline expressed his disapproval of Cornelis' laxity without a word required.

Moments later everyone walked out to the Dominie's buggy. Storm tossed his head in a welcoming whinny. Gustave chuckled. "Cornelis, if I were not so fond of Storm, I'd be ashamed to call on you in anything but a fine new automobile—purchased from you! To be honest, I've yet to find a vehicle that welcomes my return with Storm's gusto! The Ford I own does little for my spirits, so I park it in the buggy-barn to take up space and gather dust. Washing an automobile is less satisfying than currying a horse!"

"Thankfully, not all horses are as satisfactory to their owners as Storm," Cornelis responded graciously, "or no one could be enticed to own an automobile. If that happened, my job would fizzle like soap suds!"

During the rituals of leaving, Rebecca whispered to Lena, "Your visit with the girls worked wonders"

Lena nodded. Cornelis was in her direct line of vision. She couldn't take her eyes off him. He shook hands with Gustave and, responding to Maartje's tug, picked her up and drew her sister close to his hip. Time stalled as all watched the tender interaction between the young father and his daughters.

Maartje kissed her father's cheek noisily and giggled before whispering in his ear. His mood visibly changed as he let her slide off him to the ground.

The sisters skipped over to Lena. It was Cornelis' turn to observe his daughters' tender farewell with their teacher.

Relieved to be diverted from studying Cornelis, Lena gave her undivided attention to the girls, bending to hug them close. Antje's right arm curled around Lena's neck while her left hand crept up to smooth her hair and Maartje curled herself into a tiny ball that fit perfectly into the crook of Lena's arm.

Cornelis blinked fast. Only he knew that Antje had always played with Juanita's hair, and that Maartje's special style of hugging had always been reserved for her mother.

He pulled his eyes away from his daughters and focused on Lena. The look of utter contentment on her face stunned him. But it turned cool and distant when she rose and their eyes met. Without a word passing between them, he heard her heart say, "*I love your daughters, but my feelings toward you are unchanged.*"

Something deep inside him—a beast that had lifted its feeble head during his talk with Gustave—sagged again, leaving him feeling alone and lonely.

It was a quiet ride to Dutchville. Each person in the buggy had much to contemplate, for each person had heard private conversations that dovetailed in emotion and content, but remained the hearer's secret.

❋ ❋ ❋

Sunday, September 15 ✦ Lena was talking with Rebecca when Cornelis arrived. Conversations around the churchyard slowed as participants watched him park under a tree some distance from the horses tethered in the shade of the Dutchville Reformed Church. A mix of automobiles, farm trucks and buggies formed lines along the street, but no vehicle was as fine as Cornelis' new Tudor Sedan.

Noting the inexplicable shift from light-to-dark across Lena's face, Rebecca said, "Cornelis brought the girls over this morning for me to fix their hair. He does fine with braids, but not curls! He says last night was the first time the girls slept through the night without bad dreams since Juanita died. He claims it was the fresh air, but I know it was your visit. I could see a change in them when they walked into my kitchen with you yesterday afternoon."

"You have made the true difference, Rebecca. They are lucky little girls to have a grandmother like you."

"But you are part of their days, much more so than I am. You have a way about you that makes children love you. I am sure Cornelis will express his gratitude when he realizes the important place you fill in his girls' lives."

The man under discussion opened the back door of his polished Tudor Sedan. The girls, in matching dresses, stepped first onto the running board, then hopped to the ground. Cornelis said something, motioned to the church and they looked up. Spotting the two women, they flew across the lawn, their ringlets bouncing with each step.

"Hello, Grandmother!" they caroled and flung their arms around Rebecca.

She tottered at the exuberance of the greeting, but held her ground and hugged them close. "Hello, my little chickadees! Say 'good morning' to your teacher."

"Good morning," Maartje said, and beckoned Lena with one finger. Curious, Lena bent down. The girls giggled and whispered, "Tante Lena!" in Lena's ears and each planted a kiss on the cheek closest to her.

Something with velvet wings soared through Lena, leaving her giddy with joy. "Good morning to you, too!" She tapped each upturned nose with her index finger. "Shall we go find your Sunday School teacher? Oh, wait! I nearly forgot my surprise for you!"

She opened her pocketbook and pulled out two small beaded purses: one pink, and one lavender. "Unless your Grandmother Rebecca has something else for you, these can be your Sunday purses."

"I've never gotten anything so beautiful in my whole life," Antje said, awestruck. "Thank you!"

"It is my best surprise ever! Thank you," her sister echoed fervently.

"You're welcome. Those purses have been in a drawer for too long. It's time they were put to good use," Lena said. *Especially since it is becoming increasingly unlikely I will ever require token gifts for bridesmaids, which is why I so impulsively purchased them, long ago.*

She extended her hands and the girls latched on, each clinging to Lena with one hand and waving to Rebecca with the other. Outside a basement room, Lena knocked on the doorframe of the open door.

There were no other children in the room yet, but the teacher hummed and arranged Bible-story pictures on a flannelgraph board. "Hello, Hilde! May I introduce you to two new children?"

Hilde Wynkoop spun around. "Of course, Lena! Well, hello, girls!"

"This is Antje and Maartje de Boer." Lena nodded to each respectively. "Their father is Cornelis. They live on Hans and Rebecca's farm, which means they are my students. Girls, this is Mrs. Wynkoop. She is Wim's mother."

Maartje said bluntly, "Your boy's dog rides home every day in our father's automobile. Freek always leaves dust and dog hair behind."

Although startled, Hilde still managed to smile. "Yes, Wim has told his father and me all about, uh, Freek's adventures. I will personally thank your father today for being so nice to Freek. May I tell you a secret?" she asked, leaning down to the girls' level.

Two heads bobbed agreement.

"Wim was afraid to go to school until he realized Freek could walk him to-and-from school every day. But poor Freek gets awfully tired because he really is still just a puppy. Walking Wim to and from school means he makes twice as many trips as Wim! When your father gives Freek a ride home, he isn't so tired."

"That's good," Maartje said with a dazzling smile.

"My, they are pretty little girls, aren't they?" Hilde murmured to Lena.

"Yes, and I think you will also find them to be very bright. They'll be somewhat shy today, perhaps, but once they get to know you and their classmates, they'll be two of your best pupils."

"Such rich complexions, just like Cokkie Battjes said. It's a striking contrast to our Dutch blandness," Hilde ended lamely when she realized Lena was not about to discuss the de Boer girls' non-Dutch characteristics.

Other children arrived and Lena lingered long enough to introduce each girl from the town school. When Liesbeth arrived, Lena surreptitiously arranged to seat that gentle child nearest the sisters. The three girls were soon comparing purses, so Lena nodded at Hilde and slipped away to Adult Bible Class.

During church, Lena sat in her usual seat beside the extremely deaf Huitink sisters. Years ago, in the convoluted ways that habits form, she'd begun sitting beside the great-aunts of Brigetta's childhood friend, Mary. At times, they still discussed Mary and Brigetta, but more often than not, the elderly spinsters directed their attention to their immediate surroundings—a situation that often guaranteed embarrassment for some and (though hidden) amusement for still others.

Well into their nineties, Floris and Femmetje Huitink viewed Lena as their special charge. They would have sent Doc Draayer to check on her had she failed to appear in their pew at the appointed time.

Today, she dreaded sitting anywhere near them and wished, belatedly, she'd thought to drop by their house Saturday afternoon to forestall the inevitable conversation. Both women assumed they whispered, but nearly every word spoken reached the rafters.

No sooner did Lena slide into place than Floris said, "Your collar is rumpled, dear." *That would be Maartje's doing.* Lena smiled faint thanks and attempted to adjust the offending collar well enough to pass muster.

Within seconds, Femmetje leaned across her sister and hissed, "Who is the young man next to Hans de Boer? The one beside the frowzy-haired girls?"

I should be so lucky as to expect only comments on my attire. "Cornelis de Boer," Lena mouthed back, grateful that at least her voice would not be heard. The sisters' deafness rarely required audible speech from others— only crisp enunciation to aid their limited lip-reading abilities. Lena repeated her response with even more exaggerated lip-movement. "Cornelis de Boer." Still no flicker of comprehension.

Oh, for crying out loud! Lena fumbled for the tablet she always carried in her Sunday pocketbook for this very purpose. Motioning for silence from the elderly women, she quickly wrote *Cornelis de Boer. The girls are his daughters* and quickly handed the tablet to Floris.

Floris read it and passed the tablet to her sister. Femmetje tilted sideways and peered at the back of Cornelis' head. "Cornelis de Boer? Didn't he run off, nigh unto twenty years ago? Where is his wife?"

Heads turned, some to shoot remonstrative looks at the sisters, others to toss pleading looks at Lena as if she had any control over the situation. Still others craned for a look at Cornelis. His ears turned red.

Lena wished she could crawl into a hole. Bemoaning her habit of sitting next to these two busybodies, she motioned for the return of her tablet and wrote *He lived in Chicago for 10 years. His wife recently died and he moved back.*

This time, Femmetje grabbed the tablet to read the message. "Died?" Her shocked question rose beyond stage-whisper level. "Floris, Lena says those are his children, and his wife died."

Both women waited expectantly.

Lena shrugged the universal symbol for "*I know nothing more.*"

"Did he kill her? That happens in big cities, you know," Floris suggested.

"Could have used a gun, or poison," her sister agreed, warming to the topic.

More people glared at the Huitink sisters and Lena.

Lena tapped her lips to no avail. Only the first notes from the pipe organ rescued the situation. Thankfully, the spinsters gave music far more respect than the silence that should precede a worship service. The music sought out the farthest corners of the sanctuary, penetrating the Huitink sisters' deafness.

During the sermon, a thought crowded all else aside in Lena's mind: *I don't suspect murder, but do I know with certainty that Cornelis isn't running from the law?*

She looked sideways at Floris who, in an effort to imply she could hear, leaned forward staring intently at the pulpit. Femmetje made no such pretense and soon drifted into head-nodding slumber beside her. An occasional snort erupted from her own lips and awakened her, but never for long.

Don't be silly. Lena forced herself to concentrate on the sermon. But attention is a slippery thing; she soon lost her grip. As she waited for the return of normal pulse and respiration, questions loomed: *If he had nothing to hide, why wait so long to come back? Did it take Juanita's death to spur his return?*

Lena gained little from Gustave's sermon. Even the *Psalmen* didn't burrow into her soul as it usually did. All she saw were three heads: one russet, two with lovely auburn highlights mid the black. *How does Cornelis feel, listening to the revered man speak . . . the father whose daughter left home and family because of his evil deeds?*

The Scales of Justice were erected inside Lena during Sunday's service. On one side sat two little girls who had captured her heart. On the other side, a bundle—with Cornelis' name on the label—filled with hatred, anger and despair.

Lena easily imagined herself as the blindfolded Lady Justice, holding the scales . . . *Does Lady Justice ever lean to add weight to the side she wants to win?*

Late that afternoon, Gustave hooked Storm to the buggy and drove Lena back to the schoolhouse. Holding a box of baked goods on her lap, she asked, "Gustave, may I speak to you as my Dominie, rather than my brother-in-law?"

He nodded, keeping his eyes on Storm's strong back. He remembered only one such conversation during the many years of Lena living in the parsonage, that being a philosophical conversation on Reformed doctrine relating to justification by faith. "Whatever you say will remain between us."

"I have a question that troubles me."

Gustave hoped it wasn't about generals and leaders.

It wasn't.

Rather, Lena's voice held tears and fears. "Can a person ever truly change?"

Having been conducting a quick review of theology in Lena's silence, the question caught Gustave off-guard. Realizing he possessed all the details he was likely to get, he said, "If you mean 'change' as in 'Can a leopard change his spots?'—I leave it to philosophers. If you mean 'change his ways,' there are Biblical accounts of those God changed from the inside out."

Seeing a nod, he said, "Knowing fallen creatures in a fallen world *can* change gives us hope. King David committed a grievous sin, yet was called 'a man after God's own heart.' Unless *God* changes us, we may try to change, but we remain leopards under our skin."

"How I wish I could talk to those who were damaged, but changed! Surely David's family suffered because of his actions. I wonder if his family also changed enough to forgive him, or if they went through life still so angry at David, it devoured them."

Gustave spent his words as carefully as if they were gold coins: "Vexing human situations change us. The perpetrator of evil may become more wicked when he gets away with something once. Or he changes for the good when he is caught. Even if the wicked person does not confess, the person who was wronged can learn to forgive. That requires enormous change—a transformation, even—of heart."

"If a wronged person, or someone close to him or her, cannot forgive . . . then what? The evildoer lives happily-ever-after, while the unforgiving person lives with memories?" She sounded sad and upset.

"It is a hard way to live, when memories haunt.".

Resentment crept in. "Even harder to see evildoers going about their lives with no thought for those they harmed."

While talking, they had arrived at school. Gustave tossed Storm's reins around the hitching post by the stoop while he reached for her satchel. "I recall a little ditty that goes something like this: 'The rain falls both on Just and Unjust fellows, but mainly on the Just because the Unjust stole the Just's umbrella!' Do you catch the implication?"

She smiled ruefully. "I do, but to extend the saying's hard truth, I want my umbrella back—and I intend to get it! Anyone who forgives without trying to get an umbrella back is a fool."

He rode home in the gathering dusk pondering their conversation. Puzzled by Lena's question, he was even more perplexed by her reaction to his quote. "I'm not sure who stole Lena's umbrella, but I hope that poor soul has the sense to hand it over!" It was unsettling to think of thoughtful, humorous, gentle Lena having such ominous, vindictive thoughts.

❋ ❋ ❋

Monday, September 16 ◆ Lena was outside shivering a little in the cool morning air when the first students arrived. It was part of her plan to regain the ground lost during the first week of school. She was back in charge.

Liesbeth and Lucas arrived first, walking on opposite sides of the road, whacking stones with big sticks for no apparent reason other than they'd found a stick and stones were in abundance. Lucas tossed his lunch bucket on the stoop, leaned his stick against the building, grabbed a bat and ball from inside, and headed to the mown section of the yard devoted to ballgames. While he awaited the arrival of anyone, besides his sister, who'd toss a ball, he practiced throwing the ball high in the air and catching it before it hit the ground.

Liesbeth carefully righted her brother's bucket and placed her lunch pail beside it. Looking like a gap-toothed shepherd with her stick held like a staff, she grumbled, "The only thing my brother wants to do is play ball. I hate playing ball."

She tucked her tongue into the vacant spot between two teeth. "I lost a tooth when I ate a drumstick yesterday," she confided proudly. One finger marked the spot for Lena's benefit. "The Tooth Fairy left me a penny under my pillow!" She dug in her pocket and extracted a shiny penny, no doubt saved by Helena Beekman for just such an occasion. "See?"

"I do, and that is the shiniest penny I have ever seen. You'll have to be sure you don't lose it today. Maybe keep it in your desk during recess." Lena examined the hole worthy of such a reward.

Blue eyes as wide as the horizon, Liesbeth solemnly nodded. "I'd rather keep it in my sweater . . . except when I show it at recess," she hedged. Reluctantly, she wrapped it in a hanky and put it in the sweater's small pocket.

"Miss Stryker?" Sterre edged into Lena's line of vision. "I brought my piano book in case anyone wants to see how difficult the pieces are." She patted the canvas bag slung over her shoulder.

Oh, my; I hope I don't regret this. "It is always good to have the music close at hand. You might want to put it on the piano when you play in case you need to remind yourself of a note that comes next."

Sterre said haughtily, "I memorized them perfectly."

"*Hear this: Pride goes before a fall, little girl,*" was what she thought. "Fine," was what she crisply said.

As Mondays go, the day started out well and went downhill in subtle meanderings. Cornelis delivered his daughters with no more fanfare than usual. Freek managed to escort his master to school and chase a few tossed sticks before he caught a ride home with his personal chauffeur.

"*Go and speak truth, Cornelis,*" Lena thought as the automobile disappeared.

After reading the morning *Psalmen*, Lena said, "This morning, Sterre and I have planned a special occasion in honor of her birthday. She will play two piano pieces for us from her summer recital. Are you ready, Sterre?"

"Yes, Miss Stryker." The girl strutted to the piano. After twirling the piano stool to the correct height, she sat down and then spun around to face her schoolmates.

"The first one is called 'The Juggler.' It is from the 'John Thompson Course for the Piano' book. In piano lessons, I am in fourth grade," she added, tossing Lena a look that clearly implied, "*Perhaps you should promote me in school, too?*" She shifted her attention to her already fidgety audience. "When I finish, you may clap."

"*Just play, Sterre!*" Lena empathized fully with Lucas whose facial expression shouted, "*Help! I'm a prisoner!*"

True to her nature, Sterre cared nothing about her classmates' none-too-subtle signs of boredom as evidenced by their delayed and lackadaisical applause at the song's end.

"Next is 'The Nocturne' and it is the song my teacher says I play better than any student she has ever had. It is very, very difficult. I know you will want to clap after that song, too," she said airily as she spun on the stool to face the piano again.

Sterre poised her hands dramatically over the keys, then swung around. "Miss Stryker, could we turn the piano a little bit? Then everyone can see my hands. My piano teacher says I have perfect form."

"Perhaps another time, Sterre. For now, we'll settle for listening. Please proceed."

Sterre lifted her hands above the keyboard and theatrically dropped them into place. Within one measure, it became evident something was amiss. The bewildered performer recoiled from the keyboard, much as if it had transformed into a friendly cat that had suddenly arched his back, hissed and attacked her.

Sniggers between the upper-level boys rolled like marbles on a slanting floor. ". . . perfect form . . ." someone mimicked.

"That's enough," Lena admonished sharply. "Start over, Sterre. Your hands were probably one key off from where they should be."

This time, there was much less drama—and complete success. If the young girl's piano teacher had been present, she may have admonished against racing through the easy parts and dragging the more complicated bars, but the audience merely applauded, as instructed by the now more-subdued virtuoso.

"Thank you, Sterre," Lena said. "Please bring out the hatbox you'll find on the table in the teacherage."

Still flustered from her mishap, the girl scurried off, glad to be out of the spotlight she'd craved. When Sterre returned, Lena immediately knew she'd peeked. Beaming, she handed Lena the box. "Do I smell banana cupcakes with brown-sugar frosting?" she asked coyly. "Are they for my birthday, or my recital?"

"They are for both," Lena said, noting one cupcake had a suspicious dent, hence the supposedly correct guess. "Would you like to share them with the audience at your first private recital?"

The hatbox made the rounds, providing much more enthusiasm than "The Juggler" or "Nocturne" had generated—but Sterre basked in the moment. It is hard to be too concerned about any perceived or actual lack of appreciation for talent when holding a banana cupcake with brown-sugar frosting.

At morning recess, Lena overheard the Vande Veer twins beguiling Wim with tales of how they were going to be "stronger than Charles Atlas!"

Appropriately impressed, Wim gasped, "You mean, stronger than the new girls' father? Why, he's so strong, he could lift his car right off the ground with one arm tied behind his back! Lucas said so! You're gonna be that strong?"

"Maybe stronger—all us boys will be. If you want, you can practice with us," Raimund offered grandly.

He frowned. "What do I gotta practice?"

"Why, getting strong, of course!" Bartel chimed in.

"How do you do that?" Wim persisted.

"We won't know until we get our Professor Charles Atlas' 'Secrets of Muscular Power and Beauty' book." Raimund rattled off the title with exaggerated patience. "It tells 'xactly how to do it. It costs a whole dime and everybody's putting in two cents, but me and Bartel can only do three cents together. Say, now, Wim," he paused, with the surprised air of one who has just thought of something amazing, "if you put in a penny, then you can use the book, too."

"*Why, you little minx!*" Lena hoped Wim would stand firm against such blatant manipulation.

"So, what about it, huh?" Bartel asked. "Should we count you in? Or do you want to be a ninety-eight–pound weakling who cries like a girl?"

"Sure, I'll do it." Forty-pound Wim sounded so far west of *sure* it made Lena marvel that his feet weren't wet from Pacific Ocean waves.

"Bring your penny tomorrow. Jaap's mother has a dime she'll trade him for ten pennies and then we can mail the order. It's a grand book—here's the advertisement." Raimund underscored the words with a grimy index finger: "It's 'full of actual photographs,' and 'in beautiful color'—it says so, right here!" He whistled and exclaimed, "Look at this one!"

Wim studied the paper . . . well, the *pictures*; one week of school had not made a reader of him quite yet.

"What's wrong with that guy? Why's he crying?"

"What're you talking about?" Bartel demanded. "That's Charles Atlas with the world on his back! He don't cry—he's the 'King of Human Per . . . per-fec-tion,' see? Says so." He jabbed his finger on the page.

"Looks like somebody threw the world at him and it landed on his back and knocked him down and now he's crying—otherwise, why's he got his hand over his face like he don't want nobody to see him cry?"

"He's 'The World's Most Perfect Man!' It says so!" Raimund swatted Wim's head with the paper and bellowed, "He's thinking, that's what he's doing. He don't cry! Aw, shucks—forget it! You're just a dumb little kid. You couldn't get strong even if you learned every exercise by heart and did them every hour of every day for a hundred years!" He stalked away with his nervous henchman, Bartel, three steps behind.

"Looks to me like he's crying," Wim repeated, bewildered. "B'sides, I don't want no stupid globe on my back when I ain't got no clothes on," he yelled at the twins.

Lena groaned, "Give me back the days when I found students' fascination with Charles Lindbergh's flight across the Atlantic tiresome! I never dreamed I'd long to see doodled airplanes on math papers, or hear little boys' lips making airplane-engine noises. Instead, I endure unrelenting talk about strong men and muscles!" Fueled by irritation, she blew her whistle especially loud.

Near the end of the morning when everyone always seemed restless, Lena presented the scrapbook project. She had scoured the parsonage storage closet on Saturday evening, coming up with sufficient wallpaper remnants to make covers and enough butcher paper to provide one dozen sheets per book.

Lucas' lip curled. "Who needs a stupid scrapbook?"

"Some of you may decide to make one and take it home to record private thoughts, like a diary. Others may want to write a poem for each month of the year."

Janneken nodded, liking that idea.

Lena said, "Some could keep track of the weather every day: windy, snowing, sunny, raining, what the temperature is, or how much is in the rain gauge."

This intrigued Lucas more than recording thoughts.

Lena strolled the room, offering encouragement or advice while the students punched holes through which yarn would bind the books, or decorated the covers. She sighed when she noticed Raimund and Bartel's beginnings to their scrapbooks. The first page held as large a drawing of Charles Atlas and his back-mounted globe as margins allowed.

It all seemed harmless enough until, during noon recess, she noticed all six boys clustered around the Vande Veer twins' horse. She reached them in time to prevent their attempt to lift Midnight off the ground, three boys on each side, ready to employ the principles espoused by the famed Mister Atlas.

"Boys, there are better ways to get strong muscles than trying to lift a creature whose four powerful legs could kick you senseless!" She parked her hands on her hips and waited for the boys to disperse.

When the third-grade girls asked the younger girls to play a game of Simon-Says with them, the de Boer girls joined in and caught on quickly. After recess, Lena was pleased to notice Janneken spent extra time helping Antje with her reading assignment.

At the end of the day, Lena took advantage of a cool breeze and invited everyone to select a rug and join her in the shade of the largest elm tree for the day's section from "The Enchanted Castle."

"Ouch!" Maas yelped, turned, and slugged Sterre.

"Maas! Apologize to Sterre!"

"Why should I apologize? She pinched me; I barely even tapped her!"

"It was more than a tap, Maas. Now, why did you pinch Maas, Sterre?" Lena asked wearily.

Eyes boring into Maas' back, Sterre spat out, "He's the onliest one who didn't tell me he liked my recital."

"I told her it would've been more interesting if she'd rolled the stool too high and when she reached up to jab them high notes, the stool fell apart," Maas protested. "That's lots better than just saying, 'I like how you played, Sterre,' like the other kids did."

"A simple 'Thank you for playing, Sterre,' would have saved you from getting pinched, Maas. And a truly gracious person, Sterre, does not pinch people who do not appreciate the same things they do."

While Maas exaggeratedly nursed his abused forearm and Sterre entertained dark thoughts, Lena began to read. The students eventually forgot the warring duo and listened intently. Some sat cross-legged, others lolled on their backs watching clouds.

When they heard the clock strike four through the open window, Lena said, "That's all, children. Don't forget your lunch pails."

Minutes passed before Cornelis appeared. Lena couldn't bring herself to acknowledge him with a wave or vocal greeting, but she embraced the girls before they ran off to meet their father. Straightening up, she met his unreadable gaze. After sweeping his daughters off the ground in a bear hug, he turned to see six boys eyeing him with mute but avid interest.

Jaap said with studied casualness, "You're pretty strong, huh?"

"I suppose so." Cornelis shrugged diffidently.

"Strong enough to lift a thousand pounds?"

"Not that strong. If something weighing a thousand pounds needs lifting, I'd ask for help!"

The boys looked disappointed at this nonchalant attitude. "But you're as strong as Charles Atlas, right?" Lucas asked hopefully.

Cornelis laughed, "No, but even if I were, I'd hesitate to say so, because Charles Atlas could hear that I said so, come find me, lift me up and toss me out of the country! No, boys—the thing I'm strong enough to do is lift my girls up and squeeze their bones!" He did so again, eliciting giggles from them.

As Cornelis continued to talk to Jaap and Lucas, Lena groaned inwardly when she heard Raimund speculate, "I bet we could lift those two girls up in the air!" She had visions of the de Boer girls screaming above the heads of six panting boys, just before they dropped to the ground in a heap of broken bones. *Tomorrow, I put an end to all this Charles Atlas nonsense!*

The day ended with a crisis: Liesbeth had lost her penny. "I took it out when Bartel wanted to see it, and I know I put it right here—in my sweater's pocket," she sobbed.

Lena watched Bartel grow more uncomfortable the harder Liesbeth sobbed; she immediately remembered the financial discussion between Raimund and Wim. If Raimund and Bartel had one more penny, they wouldn't need weakling Wim in their Charles Atlas club.

"Bartel, may I see you for a moment?" she asked in a voice that didn't allow refusal. While Bartel dragged his way to her side, she sent Liesbeth to the pump to wash her tear-stained face.

"Yes, Miss Stryker?" Bartel said.

"Have you seen Liesbeth's penny?" Lena asked, careful to keep accusation from her tone.

"No, Miss Stryker." He stared into space.

"Are you sure? Maybe after she showed it to you, you noticed something shiny on the ground."

"No, Miss Stryker."

"Would you be willing to help Liesbeth look around the school yard?"

"Yeah . . . guess I could help her look . . ."

"Good. And I'm sure you can help Liesbeth actually find her penny, can't you, Bartel?"

He scratched his head. "Well, it's real hard to say . . ." He looked longingly toward the other boys clustered about Cornelis.

"Bartel, look at me." His eyes met hers . . . slowly. "I heard Raimund say the two of you can only come up with three pennies to buy the Charles Atlas book. Are you sure you didn't see Liesbeth's penny on the playground and think, maybe, it could be the fourth penny you and Raimund need?"

He saw a verbal gap and leaped into it. "Oh, no, Miss Stryker. I didn't find a penny on the ground. May I go help Liesbeth look now so we can go home? We help with chores, you know," Bartel said piously.

"Go start looking." Wearily Lena waved him off.

He made great show of lifting fallen branches near the fence—an area into which Liesbeth would never venture for dread of snakes. He scraped his foot along the loose gravel around the teeter-totter, saying loudly for Lena's benefit, "Probably lost it here when you were stuck up in the air," though Liesbeth shunned the teeter-totters due to her fear of that very possibility.

At last, even sadly penniless Liesbeth wearied of searching and, at her brother's insistence, headed for home. Bartel dramatically shrugged, for Lena's benefit, as if to say, *"Well, I sure tried!"*

❋ ❋ ❋

Tuesday, September 17 ◆ It was no surprise Bartel's grand search of the playground failed to resurrect Liesbeth's lost penny. Lena grimaced when she overheard Jaap tell the boys he had exchanged ten pennies for a dime, and his mother had contributed a stamp and envelope.

"Bartel lied; I should have made him empty his pockets," she muttered ominously.

The boys' interest in the strongest man in the world took a literary turn. The Vande Veer twins produced a stack of comics from a canvas bag. For once, the boys' recess activities consisted of reading aloud to each other about the amazing feats of strength to which Charles Atlas laid claim.

That led to boasting how they, too, would match him, deed for deed. Sometimes the content of their reading overpowered them and all leaped up to engage in rough-and-tumble wrestling or other rambunctious activities that approximated the living-color pictures.

Raimund described how to act-out the illustrations: "Hold your hands behind your head like you got an itch, but you're really holding one hand with the other." The other boys twisted and turned themselves into human pretzels, touching elbows to opposite knees, and bending and stretching into contortions that looked both painful and humorous when demonstrated on such underdeveloped bodies.

"Well, they're reading," Lena conceded, turning to watch lower-grade girls map out rooms to a house on the playground. Because leaves formed room borders, and sticks marked the outer corners, the quest for supplies ranged far. Lena helped puncture the hard ground enough to hold the sticks in place.

During afternoon recess, the boys elected to "play in the field," they told Lena as they held barbed wire for each other to crawl over or under the fence.

"No snakes in your pockets when you come back to the classroom," she warned.

Liesbeth and Maartje were appointed to go behind the school in search of more supplies for the leaf-house walls. Hearing a screech, Lena ran around the schoolhouse and skidded to a stop at the corner.

On the edge of the cornfield, six boys—all in the buff—posed like Charles Atlas with their skinny little elbows poised on skinny little knees. Raimund, equally nude, ran from boy-to-boy, balancing purloined ears of corn, in lieu of globes, on each boy's back.

"Boys!" Lena thundered, covering Liesbeth and Maartje's eyes as she spun them around and shielded them against her body. "What are you doing?"

"We're being Charles Atlas—The World's Most Handsome Man," Bartel stammered as each juvenile specimen scrambled to find and don his clothes.

"Well, I beg to differ, but you are six boys who are naked as jaybirds behind a schoolhouse—I don't see

anything handsome about that," Lena snapped.
"There will be no recess for any of you tomorrow, and
if this Charles Atlas nonsense does not stop, it will be a
long time before you play ball again. Is that clear?"

"Yes, Miss Stryker," six voices chanted as the boys
pulled on underwear and socks, trousers and shirts and
clamored to sort out the jumble of *klompen*.

The remainder of the afternoon was eerily quiet.
Two little girls had witnessed things that even Lena
had never seen: six naked (albeit, young) male bodies
in one sighting. Eight other girls wished they'd been
the ones to go around the corner so they' know what
caused the commotion. *A strong urge for the forbidden
lurks even in the purest of young Dutch hearts,* Lena mused.

Bartel seemed distracted, Lena noted, during the
time he and Raimund usually applied themselves
diligently to their science lessons. Before she began
the second graders' word drill, he intercepted her.
"Miss Stryker," he whispered, "I wonder if, well,
maybe you've got some job I could do to earn money."

Like a penny, I imagine? "No; as you know, the tasks
the students do are shared. No one gets paid."

Panic flashed across his face. "But, isn't there
something that no one wants to do—something I
could do just once, maybe, and get . . . a penny?"

Lena looked at Liesbeth, one penny short for no
fault of her own—and back at Bartel, uneasy under the
weight of guilt.

"Well . . . if someone were to take a basket out to
the pine tree back by the outhouses and fill it with

pinecones, it would help start fires more quickly. But it's a prickly job and the branches are low to the ground and there are spiders, so I don't know that I could ask a student to do that, but it would be nice to have pinecones. That's worth a penny to me."

A shudder rolled through Bartel, but he stood tall and met her eye. "I could do that job, Miss Stryker. I'll do it right now. I'm almost done with my assignment," he said earnestly.

"And knowing your debt will be paid is likely to help your concentration, isn't it?" She pointed at the cloakroom. "Get the basket from the storage closet and go ahead."

Half an hour later, a subdued Bartel exchanged meaningful glances with Raimund, and presented the bushel basket. "It's full—I picked the best and biggest pinecones and shook off all the bugs, Miss Stryker."

"I can see that. You may put the basket in the entryway." She selected the shiniest penny of the coins in her desk she used to teach how to make change. "Here is your pay, Bartel."

He examined it carefully. "Uh . . . Miss Stryker, is it okay if I, uh, go put my jacket back in the cloakroom?"

Lena read remorse in each molecule of his being. "You may, and then return to your seat and finish your lessons for the day." Shucking off his jacket, Bartel sped off—unaware the most important lesson was already learned: ill-gotten gain is difficult to enjoy.

Lena listened to the cloakroom's floorboards squeak. *He's pausing at his hook, now he's tiptoeing down the line to where a certain sweater hangs.* Moments later, Bartel reappeared, slid into his seat, opened his geography book, and expelled a long sigh.

Watching from the front of the room, Lena glanced at Liesbeth—so blissfully unaware that in the last thirty minutes one boy had worked hard to make things right again for her, and to regain his own peace of mind.

Four o'clock came and sixteen students collected their coats and lunch buckets and pounded off the stoop. Within seconds, one shrill cry went up from around the corner of the schoolhouse.

Everyone halted. As others flew to a distraught Adda's side, a full choir of mournful wails from the lower-grade girls alerted Lena to how much disaster one small dog could create.

Coming to meet Wim, Freek was distracted by all the delicious smells unleashed from the moldering leaves the girls had collected from along the fence-line and between the rows of corn in the adjacent field. The dog had wandered from his customary spot by the door to the fragile boundaries of the new-formed house, leaving havoc in his wake as he frolicked.

Even now, with the girls' howls of protest and shouts of dismay filling the air, he continued to burrow his nose into particularly redolent piles. He flung them skyward with his nose, emitted delighted yelps as the leaves fluttered around him.

As Lena sought to comfort the girls, Lucas upset them further with his practical wisdom that all it would take is "one gust of wind and that stupid house would've been destroyed anyway."

Wim took advantage of the girls' disgust with Lucas to retrieve Freek and head toward home as fast as their six legs could carry them. Lena turned her attention to the girls in time to hear Giertje lash out at Lucas: "You are a wicked and cruel boy to say such mean things about our beautiful house!" she said fiercely.

"Wicked! Cruel!" echoed her entourage, all sobbing over their combined losses. Lena was so delighted to see the de Boer girls identifying with their newfound friends that she allowed the cluster of girls to flounce off without insisting on an apology from either side.

Cornelis arrived minutes later than Lena had come to expect. Both adults seemed surprised that Cornelis' daughters were too busy commiserating with the other girls to notice him immediately.

Bartel lingered near the scene of Freek's destructive act, his eyes never straying from Liesbeth. Clearly, he was torn between wanting her to discover a penny in her pocket, and the fear of the unknown if she should suspect his part in such a miracle.

Lena took pity on him and called, "Is something sticking out of your pocket, Liesbeth?"

The girl paused, pulled out a folded scrap of notebook paper and exclaimed, "My penny's back! Oh, there's a little note. What's it say, Miss Stryker?"

Yes, what does it say? Lena accepted the missive and smoothed the creases. "It says, 'This isn't the same penny, but you can have it. Your secret friend.' Isn't that nice, Liesbeth? Someone replaced your penny!"

"Who did that?" the girl asked, wide-eyed.

"If your secret friend wanted their name known, they'd have signed the note. We'll assume they feel badly about how you lost your penny."

"Thank you, secret friend!" Liesbeth yelled.

The sound of Midnight's pounding hooves gave cadence to her words as he carried the twins home.

Cornelis waved to Jaap and Lucas as they set off for home and when he turned, his eyes met Lena's. For a moment, she wished she could share an adult moment with him, chuckling over the vagaries of childhood.

No. That would suggest friendliness or camaraderie or acceptance—none of which cohabited in the portions of Lena's heart where thoughts of Cornelis lived. When she had evidence that he had owned up to his disgraces and apologized to those he had wronged, *then* she would feel more charitable toward him—but not a minute before.

Until Cornelis had returned to Dutchville, she doubted Bartel would ever have lusted after a penny enough to steal it. The overall impact Cornelis had on impressionable children was frightening enough, but that it could lead—indeed, already had—to outright theft, and subsequent lying, was appalling.

✹ ✹ ✹

Wednesday, September 18 ◆ Refusing her father's help, Antje carefully carried a box from the automobile into the schoolhouse, with Maartje offering her services as opener of doors and dispenser of broad hints such as, "You're all gonna love what's in this box!" and "It's not cake and everyone gets two!"

The string-tied box held center stage on Lena's desk. By noon, there would've been an ambush had the de Boer girls not carried out their promise.

Smugly, they conferred by the box, and finally settled on Antje carrying the box from desk to desk, with Maartje preceding her to distribute a square of waxed paper to each student. "Tell them what to do, Miss Stryker," Antje whispered. "It would be dreadful if they took the wrong letters!"

Lena instructed everyone to select two cookies to match their initials. It required much self-control to wait until all had been served—which Lena insisted was good manners, but also prevented mix-ups about letters. With delivery completed, students and their teacher blissfully bit into *Banket Gebak*.

Elsje started the "Thank-you" chain to which each student added another link. By the time of Raimund's exuberant, "You can bring treats like this every week!" the girls were nearly too excited to eat the cookies.

Before racing out the door at the end of the day, Antje pulled Lena down to whisper, "You were right, Miss Stryker!" Her breath was soft against Lena's ear: "We found nice friends hiding inside the big kids!"

✾ ✾ ✾

Friday, September 27 ✦ Throughout the day, the teacher and her students eyed the clock. All shared one frustration: *"Time must be standing still!"*

Lena kept the pace moving along, varying the order of the classes in an effort to regain drifting attention, but it was nearly a lost cause. She looked forward to day's end as much as any of the students because today was the September picnic.

Instituted her first year, the event gained increasing interest each year. The students worked hard to prepare for the last Friday of September.

That was designated as the day the parents arrived at three o'clock with loaded picnic baskets and extra bats and balls for the much-anticipated ballgame. It was also the parents' chance to view the children's lessons and artwork, thus far—much of which was displayed around the classroom.

All day, the wondrous smell of roasted pork wafted through the windows, intensifying hourly from the deep pit Leendert Ten Broek had dug the precious evening. The burlap-wrapped pig (purchased by the School Board) sizzled on a fire Jaap and Lucas willing tended throughout the day.

They returned each time with unchanging reports: "Smells awfully good out there!" During afternoon recess, the boys did a last-minute cleaning of the school ground (with loud sniffing and idle threats to "steal a chunk of that hog!" Meanwhile, the girls polished the schoolroom to a shine.

Finally, everyone cheered as sounds of buggies and automobiles hit their ears. "You all know what your assigned tasks are, so you are dismissed!" Lena glanced quickly around the room and, pleased with what she saw, followed the students outside.

The excited hum outside the building rivaled any beehive. Students' fathers took boards and sawhorses off wagons and assembled long tables over which the mothers shook lengths of rippling muslin. Boys and their older brothers rolled precisely sawn sturdy logs into place, placing planks on them to form benches.

Schoolgirls and older female siblings took charge of entertaining younger children so their mothers could visit while emptying the loaded baskets. Covered plates of late-garden vegetables and towel-wrapped pots of baked beans and potatoes lined the center of the table like arrows pointing to the precise and fragrant spot where a carving knife and fork awaited the slab of roasted pork ready for eager mouths.

Lena spread dishtowels over the array of breads and desserts that filled the table Lucas and Jaap had carried out from the teacherage. "Jaap," she called when she spotted the boy, "come see what I made for you!"

Curious, Jaap approached the dessert table. Lena lifted one corner of the towel. "Chocolate cookies!" Jaap exclaimed. "With nuts?" he asked hopefully.

"Yes—walnuts. Between today's ballgame and nuts in what you said is your favorite treat, I hope you think you have a worthy birthday treat!"

"I like chocolate cookies almost as much as I like to play ball," he said fervently. "Thanks, Miss Stryker!"

"You're welcome. By the way, I put a couple cookies in a secret place in case the plate is empty before you get through the line." His grin was all the reward a teacher could desire.

That's when Hanna and Gustave arrived. While Gustave unloaded a block of sawdust-packed Floyd

River ice that would chill the cold drinks, Hanna and Lena each grabbed the handles on a bushel basket that held apples from the parsonage tree. "Looks like a good crowd." Hanna said with sparkling eyes. "I'm happy that the teacher's family gets invited!"

"Well, I'm glad, too—mostly because you can witness for yourself things you otherwise would expect me to report in great detail!" Lena teased. "Oh, look—Hans and Rebecca are here." She waved and added in a lowered voice, "I invited them to fill the gap Antje and Maartje might feel when seeing the other children with their mothers."

Hanna squeezed Lena's hand. "Very kind of you."

At four o'clock, a *"Woof!"* sounded from the road. Dries laughed. "Looks like Freek escaped the barn!"

Freek bounded through the gate like a racehorse approaching the finish line—the recipient of cheers as rowdy as any equine winner could desire. If dogs' faces have expressions, Freek's said, *"Whoa! Who are all these people?"* Cautious at first, he skirted the crowd until he found Wim and they shared a joyous reunion.

Soon, many hands reached out to pet the dog whose antics had become well-known in every student's home. "Hey, pup! Adda says you're the dog who rides home in style every morning!" Ruben De Jong said as he scratched Freek behind the ears.

Wim's chest expanded to twice its normal size and he set about escorting Freek from one cluster of adults to the next, each time telling the same earnest tale: ". . . and before I knew it, he jumped in the front seat of

Mister de Boer's automobile . . . same thing, every day
. . . that Mister de Boer—he's sumpthin else, ho-boy.
He don't care one little bit if Freek . . ."

Through it all, Lena monitored the time. At half-
past four, she stood on the stoop, blew her whistle and
announced that the children would now escort their
families into the schoolhouse to see their work.

She lingered behind, increasingly upset that Cornelis
was the only parent who had not yet arrived. *It's a busy
time of year for everyone, but doesn't he know how important
this is to the children?* Lena fumed, forcefully exhaling a
gust of pent-up air after the last family walked through
the door. *If I had not invited Hans and Rebecca, Antje and
Maartje would have no one here.*

Lena lingered outside for a moment, ostensibly to
ensure that Freek was safely tied to the hitching post
to keep him out of trouble with the fire pit and tables.
Actually, she was waiting for her frustration to slow
from full-boil to a simmer.

Children guided adults to show off a tidy desk, or a
favorite book, continuing around the room where
spelling papers or arithmetic assignments or artwork
representing each student were displayed on the walls.

Palpable excitement energized the children because
something new was added to this September's picnic.
Guiding their grandparents around the room, Antje
and Maartje kept eyeing the door. Lena knew why.

Cornelis had better show up soon, she thought grimly
and turned to explain to Magda De Jong how Jaap was
able to use flash cards, being the only one in his grade.

With the casual timing of the person who assumes the world waits for him, Cornelis swung open the door at precisely the moment Lena needed to begin the program. She wavered between relief at his appearance and disgust with the charisma that allowed him to roll through life unencumbered by moss.

Cornelis' girls flew to him; he swept them off their feet midst exclamations of three-part joy. Everyone in the room was mesmerized by the father spinning his daughters around, their heads flung back with shining ringlets flying as they crowed, "Father, you're just in time for our special surprise!" On the floor again, each girl grabbed a hand and dragged Cornelis across the room to sit in Antje's desk. Giggling, they headed to the cloakroom where other students already waited.

Lena forced a smile. She gave a prearranged signal with her pitch pipe. The students marched out of the cloakroom, singing in two-part harmony, "O beautiful for spacious skies, for amber waves of grain, for purple mountain majesties above the fruited plain . . ."

As eight students in the back row lifted hand-drawn flags, they switched to unison for ". . . and crown thy good with brotherhood from sea to shining sea." It was so beautiful, goose bumps formed on Lena's arms.

The boys stepped aside, and a choir of ten girls sang in soaring voices: "O beautiful for pilgrim feet . . ."

Then it was the boys' turn. Standing three on each side of the girls in stair-step formation, their boyish soprano voices rang out. "O beautiful for heroes proved in liberating strife . . ."

Without missing a beat, Antje and Maartje stepped forward and sang in voices so sweet, a hush fell across the room, "O beautiful for patriot dream . . ."

Humming accompanied the de Boer girls when they reached the lines, "America! America! God shed his grace on thee . . ." Humming ceased as all joined a reprise of the refrain. Enthusiastic applause erupted when the children bowed. The students waited without fidgeting until the cheering faded.

Lena moved to the piano. Following several measures of introduction, the full choir launched into a spirited rendition of "Mine eyes have seen the glory of the coming of the Lord . . ."

From the piano, Lena motioned for the audience to add their voices, which they did in four-parts. Boys marked the beat by clapping sandpaper-covered sticks in lieu of drums: ". . . glory, glory, hallelujah . . . His truth is marching on!"

Saartje and Elsje sang a duet on the next verse while Lena played softly: "I have seen Him in the watchfires of a hundred circling camps . . ."

Then to the families' amazement, Lena stepped away from the piano and each student pulled a tonette from sleeve or pocket, placed the mouthpiece between their lips and played the notes for the chorus.

The boys sang the next verse: ". . . Oh, be swift, my soul, to answer Him; be jubilant, my feet . . ."

With the older students ready to step in if needed, the lower-grade students sang in unison: "In the beauty of the lilies Christ was born across the sea . . ."

At Lena's signal, every voice in the room rose to the rafters for the final chorus, while the students led the way outside, with the audience following and singing: ". . . His truth is marching on."

The students formed a circle around the flagpole where Old Glory still waved. Family members gathered behind their children as Lena placed her hand on her heart and waited. A random breeze lifted the flag so quickly that, had every eye not been on it, the motion could have been merely imagined.

"I Pledge of Allegiance to the flag . . ." rang out. Authoritative father-voices, gentle mother-voices, the lilting youthful-voices, and the less robust voices of grandparents all blended together.

Gustave's words echoed in the hearts of all gathered in his prayer of thanks for the meal, "Almighty God, we thank you for this land of liberty . . ."

At last it was time to eat. But even food seemed to take second place for a few moments. Not one child went without praise for the fine program, each parent circling to offer sincere words of appreciation to each student and their teacher.

Compliments wafted through the crowd:

"You sure surprised us with that fine music!"

"No one missed a single cue!"

"You've all worked very hard!"

"You have learned a lot in a short time!"

Plates and places at the table filled. Between bites, the students eagerly told the secrets to their success:

"We practiced every day!"

"We wrote the words for the songs in Penmanship Class to help us memorize them!"

"When we couldn't go outside for recess because it rained, we learned how to play tonettes! Miss Stryker bought them for us from the catalog!"

"We made the flags for Art Class!"

The two de Boer girls beamed more with each successive compliment for their duet until Lena knew their cheeks must ache from smiling. Based on their performance today, she knew they would have a similar role in the next big event on the school calendar: the Christmas program.

With few exceptions, Art, Music, and Speech Classes between October and December would be devoted to preparing for that program. With every student cast in the performance, would assemble this same audience, plus others who loved a good show.

Lena's eyes scanned the crowd. *But it's not Christmas yet, and certainly no seasonal joy fills Cornelis' heart*, she mused as her eyes lit on the strangely quiet man.

He had parked on the fringe of vehicles filling the yard, seemingly content to leave his life as salesman behind in favor of his role as father. For once, he seemed unaffected by the fascination he generated in young and old.

Lena heard bits of conversation between him and several fathers, confirming that their topic of choice was automobiles. Frans De Groot, it was revealed, had taken possession several days earlier of a fine automobile; he and Cornelis talked for several minutes.

For a man with such a recent acquisition, Frans seemed a bit nervous, but Lena chalked it up to the discomfort of a stocky, plain sort of fellow being in Cornelis' presence.

Although Cornelis emerged from his cocoon just enough to be considered sociable, answering Frans' questions and trying to put him at ease, he was not his usual affable self. Even so, he seemed to shed shards of light like sparks from the fire pit as he moved along, filling his plate.

Hans had offered to carve so fathers could sit with their families. Those reaching the end of the table forgot everything but the mouth-watering meat leaving the tip of Hans' carving knife for waiting plates.

Vast quantities of food disappeared; bowls showed their bottoms. Desserts remained covered til later—as was custom at this picnic—but almost everyone lifted the towels for a peek at what awaited them.

Then, it was time for the ballgame. In a system devised for fairness, the red-bandana team was the first- and second graders and the sixth- and eighth graders, and all their fathers. The remaining eight students and their fathers donned blue bandanas. Older siblings were divided equally between the teams.

Men reassembled the benches as seating near the ball diamond. Cornelis was elected pitcher by popular vote when Dries Wynkoop begged off his normal duties due to a pulled shoulder muscle. Hans donned a red bandana so Cornelis could pitch for both teams without upsetting the balance of numbers.

Not one woman in the crowd—even happily married mothers, or properly prim Lena—could keep from gaping at Cornelis when he reared back and wound his pitching arm in several practice swings. Cornelis was the Pied Piper and no woman present could not deny she was, well . . . a willing *rat*.

Cornelis halted to roll his sleeves above his elbows, revealing muscular forearms glistening with russet hair. Even freckles looked appealing when splashed across well-toned skin. He removed the collar on his crisp shirt and stuck it in a back pocket, and lowered his suspenders to free his shoulders.

The black straps bounced against his slim hips, keeping time with each confident stride, when he walked over to give Rebecca his pocket watch for safekeeping. He tweaked her cheek playfully and headed back to the mound. Unlike the other men's utilitarian black pants or sturdy overalls, Cornelis' brown tweed trousers followed the lines of his body like honey coating a spoon.

Every voice stilled, but lips stayed open, ready to exclaim each time Cornelis moved. Lena gritted her teeth. *What fools! Can't all these women see how shallow his appeal is? If only his conscience matched his body's strength.*

He repositioned his fawn-hued fedora, scuffed the dirt around the pitcher's mound with his leather boot's toe, and picked up the ball. A collective feminine sigh wafted over the spectators when he released the first stunning pitch of the game in a move that displayed each tendon or muscle and every visible inch of skin.

Lena shifted on the bench. *Dries Wynkoop pitched many games without raising a feminine eyebrow. Cornelis tosses one ball in the air, and mature women instantly turn to putty?* Her uncharitable thoughts were confirmed as women quickly averted their attention to the players as if Lena had actually voiced her opinion.

"Go, Jaap!"

"Watch the ball, Janneken!"

"Good job, Filip!"

"Behind you, Giertje!"

Lena cheered for both teams, praising everything from near-misses to outright slammers. The only feats she let slide by without comment were Cornelis' pitches—but no one noticed in the ruckus. Just when it seemed the game would end in a tie, Teunis Vande Veer hit a homerun, much to the twins' wild glee, which put the blue-bandana team in the winning place.

According to September-picnic tradition, this meant the red-bandana team went through the dessert line first so it was hard to get too upset about losing. Some men dissembled the tables and benches, and others formed a chain that ferried buckets of water from the pump to extinguish the fire-pit while the women divided the leftover meat into family portions.

Finally, the work was done and families mixed their sincere thanks to Lena with farewells to friends and neighbors. Before the de Boer girls would agree to leave, they insisted Cornelis take the tour of the schoolroom that he had missed. "Come inside with us, Miss Stryker," Antje called.

It would have created more of a scene to refuse than Lena was willing to provide for those lingering to ensure the fire was extinguished, so she followed the de Boer threesome inside. Chattering nonstop, Maartje dragged Cornelis around the room by one hand. Cornelis made appropriate comments, and gave equal time to admire all the objects Antje showed him.

At the girls' insistence, he showed he could write his name on the blackboard without squeaking the chalk. He knelt, flanked by his daughters, and said, "Pick up your chalk! One, two, three . . . go!"

Amid giggles, three names appeared, the final letters of Maartje's running uphill to avoid touching the first letter of Cornelis' name. He pulled the girls against him; three heads touched like obsidian bookends supporting a russet tome.

"Very nice handwriting, girls," he praised.

Antje said softly, "Write Mother's name, too, Father. Please?"

A floorboard creaked. Cornelis picked up the chalk and slowly wrote *Juanita* beneath his name.

"You're squeaking the chalk, Father!" Antje teased.

"That's a J." Maartje pointed to the first letter after he finished. "Miss Stryker says a J sounds like 'jam.' Mother's name didn't start with that sound."

"It can sound like jam," he said in a strangled voice, "but in Juanita, it sounds like a Y." He rose from his crouch, picked up the eraser, and swiped it across the line of names. *Juanita* remained for a second until he swiped it into chalky dust. "Time to go home."

"One more thing—we want to show you our names by our hooks in the cloakroom," Antje insisted.

The trio passed right by Lena but Cornelis looked straight ahead and Lena gazed at the floor. She listened to the girls' excited voices and Cornelis' near-monotone responses.

Leaving the cloakroom, Maartje flew to Lena, pulling her down to whisper, "May We show Father where you live?"

"I don't think he's interested," Lena said quickly, pulling back unconsciously, from the girl's grasp.

"Please?" Maartje begged softly, her eyelashes like wisps of black lace against her skin.

Obviously, this had been discussed earlier because Antje joined in, nodding earnestly. "It won't take long, Miss Stryker!"

"What won't take long?" Cornelis asked.

"They want to show you the teacherage." Lena rued the blush rising from her collar to her cheeks.

He looked down at the girls. "When did you see the teacherage?"

"That day when you were late and we played on the swings while you and Miss Stryker talked." Antje's eyes darted between her father and her teacher.

That day!

Cornelis met Lena's eyes as they unwillingly shared a disturbing memory.

"May we, Miss Stryker?" Maartje asked sweetly.

There was no good reason to say no—at least none Lena wished to defend in the children's presence—and

Cornelis did not argue the suggestion. Rather than voice an invitation, she waved vaguely toward the closed door. Giddily, the girls propelled Cornelis into the one room that, until now, had been Lena's sanctuary until this moment.

Lena numbly watched the guided tour:

". . . sweet little bed! Miss Stryker made this quilt, Father!" and

". . . this chair rocks so quietly. Go ahead; sit down and try it!" and

". . . isn't this a pretty curtain for her closet?"

Closet. The word ended the impromptu tour.

Cornelis said, "We mustn't keep your teacher. The Dominie and Hanna are waiting to go back to town."

"If they left already, we can give her a ride, can't we, Father? I'll give up my turn to sit in the front seat so she can be by you," Antje suggested guilelessly.

A firm and frantic "No!" erupted from Lena's lips. "I mean, that's why Gustave and Hanna are waiting outside—to give me a ride."

"Another time we could, right?" she persisted.

"We'll see." Regardless of his words, Cornelis' expression said, "*Not on your life, kid!*" He herded his daughters out the door and across the room.

Pausing at the door, good manners won over his desperate desire to flee the scene. "Did you thank your teacher for the nice picnic?"

Footfalls on the wooden floor pounded like Lena's heartbeat when the girls raced to give hugs and say "Thank you, Miss Stryker!".

Alone in the schoolroom, Lena sagged, knocking Jaap's displayed arithmetic quiz off the wall. The paper fluttered to the floor and Lena watched it land. Numbly, she picked it up and searched for the tack. Returning the paper to its place in the row, she pressed her thumb against the tack with unnecessary force, and then spun on her heel.

When she opened the door, Cornelis' automobile was cresting the hill; only Hanna and Gustave remained.

"Would you both please help me with something inside?" she called.

"Of course!" Hanna was already heading her way. "Lena, we heard nothing but compliments about the program and the picnic!"

"The students performed well. I can hardly take credit for the picnic; Dutch women know how to cook! Wasn't the pork delicious? And the ballgame— what fun!" It was all forced gaiety that soon deflated.

"How can we help, Lena?" Hanna asked.

"I want to rearrange some furniture."

"Tonight?" Gustave protested. "Can't it wait until some evening next week?"

"No," Lena insisted, "it won't take long. Now . . ." She crossed her arms and surveyed the room. "I think the table should go where the bed is, and the bed can go where the rocker and sewing machine are . . ."

"I refuse to move the hutch," Gustave said firmly. "If you ever quit teaching here, that back-breaker stays in the schoolhouse!"

Lena pursed her lips, ready to argue, but yielded on that point.

Over the next half-hour every piece of furniture (except the hutch) in her quarters moved once; several made two moves. Finally, a red-cheeked Hanna flung herself dramatically across the cot in its new location. "Enough! My muscles tell me they won't recover for a week!"

Lena surveyed the room from the vantage point of the doorway. *Good. Maybe now I can live in this room without seeing Cornelis.* She walked to the spot he had marked indelibly in her mind and adjusted the cloth on the table that now occupied center stage. "Much better; thank you. Now we can leave."

Later that evening, as they stared at the moon-traced shadows on their bedroom wall, Gustave said, "Hanna, is Lena experiencing womanly changes?"

"It could be. She has certainly been acting strangely lately. She'll be tripping over that table in the center of that tiny room all the time! I don't know what she's thinking. Thank you for being so nice to Lena when I know you were tired from a long week and wanted more than anything to come home tonight, not move furniture! You are so very dear."

At first soft, then teasing, and finally intense kisses led to much more as the moon moved across the sky that September night. With Hanna's breath warm against his chest, Gustave knew he'd move furniture over hill and dale to please this woman who had been his one and only love, even during dark times.

"Hmm . . . so very dear . . ." she murmured before falling asleep in his arms. Gustave smiled and stroked her cheek as the house creaked its midnight song.

In her parsonage bedroom, Lena listened to the clock strike midnight. Bushes tapped the window. Tired, but too restless to sleep, she sat up, leaned against the headboard, and hugged her knees. *"Please, God, keep me focused on teaching, and being an example to my students of what is important."*

At the de Boer farm, lying in his single bed behind the screen set up in the parlor, Cornelis laced his hands behind his head. *This cottage is too laden with memories for peace of mind.* His daughters' voices echoed as if still singing: *". . . and crown thy good with brotherhood from sea to shining sea . . ."*

Unheeded tears rolled—some into his ears, some to the pillow. *Brotherhood—what a mockery the word is! Even if I came completely clean with Bram about what happened, he'd hate me. Coming home was the worst idea, but I had no choice. Not with Juanita dying and me needing help with the girls.*

Restless, he moved to the hallway where he stood in the doorway to the room where his girls slept. A dark shadow drew his eyes: *The closet door. How would I feel if someday a fellow I'd trusted for many years, as Gustave trusted me, accosted Maartje or Antje as I did Brigetta in that closet?*

Bile gagged him. *Given the chance, I'd kill him. That's what Lena doesn't understand when she says I must confess. I must squash rumors, prove myself a good worker, keep my mouth shut about ten years ago, and hope Lena does the same.*

❋ ❋ ❋

Saturday, September 28 ◆ Saturday was filled to overflowing with household tasks and preparations for Sunday that the sisters shared. "You do my laundry for me every week, and even all my ironing," Lena argued when Hanna protested about her running the carpet sweeper.

"We are not going to shift laundry day, just so you can help," Hanna said with a laugh. "Think of the amount of laundry you have done for our family!"

"I often had Brigetta to help me. You do it alone."

"But don't I, now, have a better washing machine than you did, then?" Hanna countered, leaving Lena no rebuttal.

"Mail call!" Gustave came in, waving an envelope. "News from the North!"

"Must be from Brigetta! Let's read it over coffee!" Hanna said.

Gustave adjusted his glasses and extracted a single sheet of stationery from its envelope. "My daughter is getting extravagant; spending postage for such a short letter." He flipped over the paper. "And she used only one side?"

Dear Mama, Papa, & Tante Lena,

Wait until you see Sanna! She is the smartest, happiest 2-year-old we know. She loves to have us read her storybooks; often, after we finish she grabs the book and "reads" an even better story to us!

But now for the best part of this letter. You will see Sanna! We'll be home for Christmas! We will leave here on the evening train, December 22, and arrive in Dutchville the following day. We will stay through the 27th. I don't care if I don't get a single present—this is the best gift of all!

Love, Brigetta, Bram, & Sanna!

Hanna bounced off her chair and flew around to Gustave's waiting arms.

Lena frowned. *Does Brigetta realize Cornelis is back? Probably not, or she'd never consider a trip home the best gift.*

Hanna looked at her sister. "You're solemn, considering Gustave just read incredibly good news!"

Lena forced a smile. "It's . . . what did she call it? 'The best gift of all.' Won't it be fun to have Sanna here on Christmas morning? The only better time would be for the *Sinterklaas* parade, or December 5th when we could fill her *klompen*, but she is still young— another year she will understand more. Now, shall I bring up the cabbage from the cellar to grate for sauerkraut? This afternoon we'll pack it in crocks."

"From *Sinterklaas* to sauerkraut," Gustave teased. "Your mental agility is quite impressive, Lena!"

"I would much rather think about *Sinterklaas*, Lena! How can you even think about sauerkraut when our Brigetta is coming home?" Hanna teased, wrinkling her nose. "I can't imagine a less appealing way to spend a Saturday, though I know we should." She sighed. "There are a few cabbages in the garden. I left them there to grow more, but now I worry about frost."

"I know my role," Gustave said. "Get cabbages from the garden, get the kraut cutter down from the top pantry shelf, and then leave you women to your work while I retreat to my study. But I must add my voice to Hanna's question, Lena: How can you think of sauerkraut at a time like this?"

Lena shrugged. "Maybe it's because I know Bram loves our sauerkraut." She plucked a sweater off a hook and left the kitchen. *And maybe it is because if I don't occupy my hands with a routine task while my mind is spinning, I'm likely to waste the whole day. Must every joy in life have its accompanying heartache?*

She returned with a full bushel basket from the cellar to find that Hanna had cleaned the kraut cutter and set out bowls and knifes. While Hanna dunked just-picked heads of cabbage in water to clean off the garden soil, Lena tested the knife blade with her thumb and then sharpened it against the stove's edge before wielding it against the first dripping cabbage. Knife in hand, she froze as the memory of Cornelis holding his jackknife exploded in her head.

"What is it, Lena? Did you cut yourself?" Hanna asked, bringing a dishpan full of cabbages to the table.

"What? Oh, it's nothing. My, aren't these fine cabbages?" she asked brightly. While Hanna shot guarded glances in Lena's direction, the women settled into their established roles. Lena discarded damaged leaves, divided the heads into pieces, and set aside the outer leaves for stuffed cabbage—their traditional supper on what Brigetta had named "Sauerkraut Day."

"Do you still have the remnant of red velvet, Lena, from the dress you made Brigetta after our Rochester visit? Is there enough for a dress for Sanna?"

"It's packed in the sewing room trunk, and there should be enough; I'll check. If there is, I'll cut it out and, between the two of us, we get it sewn."

"I have an idea! Since the children will not be here for the *Sinterklaas* parade, we could reenact it for them! It shouldn't take much to talk Hans into donning his *Sinterklaas* cape again. Oh, Lena, this will be such fun! We'll invite Antje and Maartje and have all three girls all bundled up out on the porch when Hans comes riding up in his sleigh. Cornelis and Bram can be Piet, again, just like old times. Remember how they played Piet when Hans was Dutchville's *Sinterklaas*?"

Lena smiled weakly. "Gustave should be here to hear you rambling. He said I have 'impressive mental agility'? Well, his wife outshines me like our dining room chandelier outshines an oil lamp!"

Blithely ignoring her, Hanna continued, "I'd planned to send them a box of goodies, but now that isn't necessary. After our private *Sinterklaas* parade, we will have everyone in for special treats. We can let the little girls find presents in their *klompen* again—surely having presents twice in the same year will not spoil them just this once!"

What we'll be doing, Lena thought, *is forever linking what's been a happy tradition with a new memory: seeing Cornelis back in the family circle. In 1919, Cornelis violated much more than Brigetta's purity; he ruined holidays and traditions for years to come.*

"It will be good to bake for a crowd," Lena said with hollow enthusiasm.

She grated chunks of cabbage against the sharp openings on the kraut cutter, creating mounds. A steady *scritch* of vegetable-meeting-metal filled their ears. Piles grew in size and number, making a trail around the table as Lena shifted the grater. There would plenty for winter eating and sharing.

They stopped to prepare lunch, covering the mounds of cabbage with dishtowels while buttermilk soup and meat croquettes heated. Gustave returned to the kitchen, rubbing his eyes after a morning of reading fine print. Predictably (though Lena would have preferred otherwise) the conversation over lunch at the dining room table centered on Brigetta's news.

Despite his teasing, Gustave willingly added his suggestions to more activities than could possibly fit into four days and nights. "I suppose we must allow the de Boer family to share in their visit," he chuckled. "We could give them the hours between midnight and three in the morning on December 26!" he suggested playfully.

Hanna pretended to consider this. "No, Sanna needs her sleep. We'll just have to let the de Boers come to everything we plan!" She laughed with such joy that Lena could not help but smile. But fears loomed large: *Will Christmas of 1929 be remembered for even more grief than what two families suffered ten years ago?*

Deciding to delay washing dishes until the sauerkraut project was completed, the sisters resumed their labors. After liberally sprinkling salt between layers of cabbage in huge pottery crocks, Hanna fit a saucer on top of the seasoned cabbage, weighting it in place with a cloth-wrapped clean rock. With Gustave's aid, the women lugged the crocks out to the back porch, around the house to the cellar door, and down into the basement.

"*Oomph!* Thank you, Gustave," Lena called after him. She arched her back. "That's a job I'm most glad when it's done! We'll check next weekend to see how it's fermenting."

Hanna led the way up the steep basement steps into the light. "We'll serve it at Christmas, but remind me to send several jars home with Brigetta. I love canning vegetables but, not for your help, Lena, I couldn't face the tediousness of doing sauerkraut alone," she admitted. "Though I must say, today the task was more pleasant because of Brigetta's letter."

Like beauty, pleasant is in the mind of the beholder, Lena thought dourly, lowering the cellar door onto its nearly horizontal frame. "I don't mind this task. It's pickles that I dread making. But, since we work together on both, we enjoy sauerkraut and several types of pickles all year." Out of nowhere came a memory of a Sunday School picnic years ago: *young Cornelis . . . tasting her watermelon pickles . . . running away from the sawhorse table with the jar tucked under his arm.*

Something in her sad, strained smile caught Hanna's attention. "Are you happy with your life, Lena?" Hanna asked abruptly.

Lena pursed her lips. She bent to free a blade of grass trapped in the cellar door. When she rose, she met Hanna's eyes. "Some parts delight me; some parts don't. Which is all quite similar to how you feel, I'm sure."

They linked arms for their slow return to face dirty dishes. "Are the parts that delight enough to make you happy?" Hanna asked, rinsing the kraut cutter.

"Before school began, I'd have said yes. But it's been a rough start. Don't worry; each day is better. As you know, the chasm between happy-once and happy-again can be quite deep."

While Lena stirred up a batch of currant pudding, Hanna rinsed the dishtowels that had covered the grated cabbage, then hung them out on the clothesline.

"How well I understand deep chasms, dear Lena," she murmured as she pegged each towel in place. "What I wish I understood better is the hollow cave I see in your eyes lately. Dark and worried and heavy-laden—lately you're nothing like the sister I've loved since the day you were born."

❋ ❋ ❋

Sunday, September 29 ◆ Sunday afternoon in the lull between the inevitable dinner guests and evening vespers, Hanna and Gustave napped and Lena puttered in the kitchen, packing food to take to the teacherage.

Thinking she would search Brigetta's bedroom for books to take to school, she instead halted on the steps and pivoted to sit in the quiet permeating the house. She idly ran fingers along molding that continued from the hallway, along the stairs, to the upper story.

In this hallway, she mused, *Brigetta and Bram's life together officially began.* Within the narrow space between the stairway and the wall, on which hung a gallery of family photos, Bram declared his intentions.

If that day had never happened, Cornelis would've been free to pursue Brigetta. We still would've lost Brigetta because Cornelis was never interested in staying here, but the distance wouldn't have seemed as great without hidden sorrows' burden.

Books forgotten, she walked downstairs, entered the parlor, and lit the lamp on Hanna's writing desk. A stack of pretty paper with matching envelopes on a narrow shelf drew her attention like a magnet.

She had opened the desk with a precise plan in mind, but now balanced precariously on the sharp edge of indecision. *Do I tell Brigetta about Cornelis being here?* She filled a pen with ink and recapped the bottle. Selecting one sheet of stationery, she began to write:

> Dear Brigetta,
> How wonderful to get your news of a Christmas visit! We are all very excited and have already begun to plan every minute of your time with us. It will be wonderful to see you and Bram, but especially exciting to see Sanna before she grows much bigger and smarter!

Tapping the table, she pondered how to continue.

> Perhaps you've already heard from Hans and Rebecca that Cornelis' wife died recently. He and his daughters (Antje, 7; Maartje, 5) are living

She gripped the pen so tightly, her fingers hurt. Breathing felt risky, each inhale sharp, each exhale hot. She wouldn't pen the words that would bring specific pain: . . . *in the Little House where you and Bram once lived.* Instead, she ended the sentence vaguely,

on the farm. Both girls are my students, and they are delightful children.

I've told Antje and Maartje about Sanna, so they are eager to meet her. They say she is their only cousin. I will write more later, but I just wanted you to know how things are here and that your parents, in-laws (I presume they received the news in their own letter?) and I are impatiently counting the days until December 23.

Love to all, Tante Lena

It was a letter laden with poignant memories and harsh realities, with only faint hope all could be well. Lena addressed and stamped the envelope, quietly left the house, and walked purposefully to the Post Office.

Since it was Sunday, there would have been more than adequate time—and thriftier—to let Hanna add a note before the mailbag was sealed and tossed on Monday's train. But Lena knew that an unsealed letter lying around would tempt her to rip it up. Only when she lifted the metal flap and sent the letter beyond her reach into the secure box outside the Post Office did she relax.

✸ ✸ ✸

Monday, September 30 ◆ All day, Lena imagined the letter passing from hand to hand, from box to bag, from train to platform, finally reaching the mailbox that Bram opened each day and found news and fliers and letters—letters that, until this one, had never lifted the veil from a dark time in four people's lives. The letter Lena mailed shouted, *"Read between the lines!"*

The last act of Lena's day had been to rip the September page off the calendar on the schoolroom wall. "Good riddance," she muttered, as she cut it into scrap paper that she added to the stack in her desk. "I doubt there has ever been a September as troubled as this one. I'm ready for a new month."

Lips tight and jaw firm, she wrote, *Today is Tuesday, October 1, 1929* on the blackboard in anticipation of the new day dawning. After a day filled with reminiscences of the well-received picnic and, thus, an easily distracted group of students, it was an exhausted Lena who slowly released her hair from its braid, collecting hairpins in her lap as she sat on the edge of her bed.

Even in the quiet teacherage, she knew sleep would be evasive, so she spun the radio dial in search of distraction. It was mostly static, and any voices that came through clearly spoke of things of little interest. She dusted, refolded undergarments, and tested buttons on every garment, finding nothing even as simple as mending to distract her.

Finally, she crawled into bed. Counting sheep reminded her of arithmetic assignments; hearing night sounds proved worse than static. Even the bedclothes seemed too constraining.

Lena thrust one foot from under the sheets, resting it on the quilt. *"Miss Stryker made this quilt, Father!"*

She scolded herself, "This is ridiculous." Fumbling for slippers and eyeglasses, she donned both and walked out to the classroom. Like a beacon guiding sailors home, a moonbeam illuminated the very space on the blackboard where four names of the once-complete Cornelis de Boer family had been written.

Childish scrawls surrounding Cornelis' confident letters were so imprinted on her memory, she pressed her hands against her temples. Images sprang to mind—like pages opened at random in a photograph album: a mishmash of Cornelis, past and present:

. . . leaning against his automobile, his head thrown back as he laughed at what Lucas said,

. . . driving away, Freek sitting proudly on his lap,

. . . staring back at her from a shallow closet,

. . . holding his fork inches from his lips, a look of bliss softening his face as he savored Mirjam Vande Veer's custard pie at the picnic,

. . . in the schoolhouse doorway, calming his frightened daughters with a gentle kiss,

. . . eyes like steel, and jaw to match—spewing his anger right at her, as if trying to clear something nasty right his throat,

. . . marking her sanctuary—the teacherage—like a dog expanding his borders to warn the competition, or make it difficult to forget he'd been there.

Hopeless sobs escaped. "Why did I give in to the girls' pleas? There's no place to avoid his presence; he has invaded every corner of my life."

She headed for the piano, lifting the first piece from the pile of sheet music stacked neatly on top. It was too dark to read music, but there was sufficient moonlight that she could tell from the cover she knew it well. Her fingers searched and plucked out the melody line for "Shine on, Harvest Moon."

She sang storytelling verses of a boy pleading with the moon to shine on him and his gal. Each time she reached the plaintive words, "I ain't had no loving since January, February, June, or July, " she choked.

Heavyhearted, she slid the sheet music under the pile where it could hide for many weeks. "Foolish to think such a song is appropriate for a morose single lady," she rebuked herself. "I would do better to sing *Psalmen* than such drivel." With little regard for good intentions, a memory rose within her with startling clarity. *"Shine on, Harvest Moon" is what Hans and Rebecca and their young sons sang at a Dutchville talent show long ago.*

She crossed her arms on the piano's music rack and rested her head on them. Inches from her nose were ivory keys on which a musician could strike up a song to make couples dance until dawn, or accompany a hymn to comfort mourners or encourage saints.

Tonight, those eighty-eight keys caused a lonely teacher to struggle to stand firm when a father kept mowing down her defenses like weeds in a scythe's path. The Cornelis she had despised so long bore no resemblance to the man who could set a crowd on its ear with his confident stride and arresting good looks.

The Cornelis who had sparked her fury was not the devoted father she saw nearly every day—sometimes twice—or the grieving young widower she glimpsed within the façade he presented to the world.

Unbidden, one finger repeated the three notes for *"no loving . . . no loving . . . no loving"* until Lena could no longer tell if she heard or imagined them. She slapped both hands across the expanse of several octaves. The resulting cacophony drowned out the haunting sounds and shocked sense into her.

She spun around on the stool and faced the empty desks, planting her feet firmly on the floor and rising to her full height.

"Lena Stryker," she scolded in a no-nonsense voice that would have sent her students scurrying to follow her command, "At the ripe old age of forty-six, you have developed a most unappealing talent to make things more than they ought to be. Get your nose back where it belongs, keep your opinions to yourself, and do the job you were hired to do."

Back in bed, she added one more command. "Go to sleep, or you'll look like an old hag in the morning." Apparently when Miss Stryker's voice spoke, it carried enough authority that even Tante Lena listened because she slept straight through the night.

※ ※ ※

Sunday, October 20 ♦ By mid-October, Jack Frost had perfected the delicate edges he painted around the edges of the schoolroom windows. By January, Lena would be less enchanted by the lacy designs, but in October they still captured her fancy.

When Hanna and Gustave drove Lena back to the schoolhouse on Sunday evening, they noticed a stack of split wood between the boys' and girls' outhouses. "It appears Ruud Van der Voort has been busy this weekend," Gustave commented, following the women inside, each carrying something.

"He has, indeed. I'll send a thank-you note home with Sterre tomorrow. I was beginning to see the ground beneath last year's woodpile, so I figured he'd deliver soon. Fires feel pretty good most evenings and on frosty mornings. His timing is perfect; we will soon need to keep a fire going all day."

The Ford was already out of sight when Lena noticed Hanna's pocketbook on Sterre's desk. "They'll return for it soon, if I know my sister!" In the time it took to check the box holding the chocolate layer cake for Saartje's birthday, she heard the unmistakable sounds of an engine and a door slamming, followed by rapid footsteps. She hurried to the door and flung it open, calling out, "I knew you'd miss your— Oh, it's Cornelis!" Her voice cracked.

Grim-faced, he jerked the door away. "Yes, it's Cornelis. Not as happy to see me as whoever it is you expected, are you, Lena?" he goaded her.

"What do you want, Cornelis? It is not proper—"

Cornelis interrupted with a snort. "Is it *proper* to shun me and look down your nose at me? Is it *proper* the Huitink sisters accuse me of murder and you do nothing to stop them?"

"That was weeks ago, and hardly my fault!"

"Everyone knows you answer their questions on a tablet. After church that day, two people who were this close," his thumb and index finger marked a scant inch, "to buying an automobile suddenly wouldn't look me in the eye when we passed on the street."

"You must have imagined it."

He leaned toward her ominously. "Do you know what time does to a rumor, Lena? It enflames it. One person tells another who tells another, and a rumor grows and explodes into a wildfire."

Feeling nauseous, Lena said crisply, "Tell me what brings you here, and then be on your way.

"The final straw is what brings me here: my own mother asks me what I have done to offend 'sweet Lena, who doesn't have a mean bone in her body.' *Ha!* If she knew only the damage you have done. When Mother asks that question, it shows me the destruction is widespread." The ferocity in his eyes sent a chill down Lena's spine that had nothing to do with dropping temperatures.

Rebecca! A momentary twinge in Lena's conscience riled her. "That she needs to ask is only because you have failed to tell the truth," she said loftily.

As if she hadn't spoken, Cornelis' tirade continued, each word pounding like a sledgehammer. "I have had more than enough of your snippiness and tight-lipped disapproval. People notice how you treat me as if I were a leper. When will you let your grievance die? Or have you replaced your secret grudge with outright slander? Is that why you allowed the Huitink sisters to go unchallenged?"

They saw you and the girls sitting in the church pew. They asked who you were and, when I told them, they had a logical question: where was your wife?" Indignation may have blurred Lena's vision, but it knit steel into her words. "It's always 'poor Cornelis' with you, isn't it? Once again, instead of setting things right about the closet, you lash out at someone else. If you had done what I assumed you would do after our last conversation, your mother would have no need to ask upsetting questions."

"And it's always 'remember the closet' with you, isn't it?" he snapped. "I can't undo what happened. The doorknob fell off, Brigetta panicked, you showed up. It's history. I wish I'd kicked the blasted door off its hinges before you came. What I'm talking about has serious ramifications for the future—but your mind is stuck in the past! Just because your niece flew out when you opened the door, and told you tales, doesn't give you the right to treat me like dirt now."

Lena shook her head so forcefully, hairpins flew. "If only the doorknob coming off were all that happened that day." The corridor spun around her like a child's top. Words, fettered for years, broke loose. "Forget about the whispers and think about this: I suspect, with good reason, Brigetta gave birth to a child after you attacked her in the closet."

None of the freedom or relief Lena had long imagined accompanied the telling. Instead, something withered inside her and sank like a rock dropped into a well. In early moonlight, filtering through the hole for the bell's rope, she saw Cornelis' face blanch.

He staggered back a pace as if physically shoved. "And you suspect—no, you actually believe this . . . this mythical child is mine?" he rasped.

"Mythical?" Bitterness raised her voice's pitch and volume. "Oh, that's priceless! Didn't you tell me Antje's conception preceded your marriage? It's not as if you're a man of scruples, Cornelis."

He scowled. "I knew I would regret telling you that damning detail. The circumstances of Antje's birth hardly prove what you suggest."

His failure to counter the accusations intensified her conviction that what she suspected was true: *It was more than a kiss that day.*

"We visited Bram and Brigetta a year after their move to Rochester. I fitted Brigetta for a dress." Discomfiture heated Lena's face. "I may not ever have married, but I recognize the effects of childbirth on a woman's body."

"But, for you to believe that I—"

Her retort stunned him with their venom. "You well knew, then and now, that before Brigetta and Bram's wedding, Doc Draayer had told Bram of . . . his condition."

"Impotence. You won't let that word pass your lips, but you say nothing when 'murderer' is linked to me?" He slammed fist and palm together. "Why is Bram always cast as the saint and I am the rogue?"

"If the shoe fits . . ." she taunted.

A jerky Adam's apple was the only visible chink in his armor. "If what you say is true, where is the child now? Here's a bigger question: Do you blame me for fathering Sanna, too?" he asked with a mocking laugh.

"How dare you joke about such a thing? Perhaps Brigetta miscarried, or the baby died . . ."

"Sanna's existence poses a problem, hmm? Even for a maiden lady who's afraid to say 'impotence.' You can't have it both ways, Lena. Either my brother is impotent, or he's capable of fathering both children, which means you hate me without cause."

"That's what you want to believe, isn't it?" Lena challenged, though doubts niggled at the edges of her mind—doubts that had loomed throughout many a sleepless night.

He expelled a tight-lipped blast of air. "Nothing I can say or do will change any of what you accuse me of doing."

"If that's true, what's the purpose of an apology?" she retorted. "Honoring marriage vows goes beyond the two people in a marriage."

"For an unmarried woman, you certainly have sweeping opinions about things outside the realm of your experience," he scoffed.

"You violated Bram's marriage vows when you lusted after your brother's wife. You killed something in their marriage."

"What happened is something only Brigetta and I know. Just because you suspect something does not make it true."

"It's appalling how easily you shirk responsibility. You are a fool to think you can run from this again."

"I'm not running, Lena. I returned. Does that look like the actions of a guilty man? Bram and Brigetta are the ones who are still gone. Doesn't that seem odd? Maybe they are hiding something far worse than what you accuse me of doing."

Revulsion rose like sea foam from the undercurrents between the two combatants. "Leave. Now," she ordered. "You should be grateful I have kept silent all these years. At least have the courtesy not to sully my reputation by being here alone with me."

"Oh, you're Little Miss Pure-and-Blameless, right? No scandals, no raised eyebrows about Prim-and-Proper Miss Stryker! If your worst sin is entertaining a man at the schoolhouse, your reputation is so pristine that I'm sure it will survive." Sarcasm dripped off each word. "Besides, no one knows I'm here."

Goode God in Hemel! Lena inched back, pointing at the door. "Get out."

"You're afraid of me?" Cornelis said in mocking irony. "What do you think I would do to you?"

Fear took shape, replacing reason. There they stood: Cornelis blocking the door to the world, Lena three paces from the classroom. *The classroom!* She backed up slowly, hoping he would not notice.

He did, and shifted toward her.

She sucked in a ragged breath as the space between them diminished. Wind blew through the belfry, sending an eerie bell-echo across the countryside.

Surely if I rang the school bell at this hour, someone would come! She flushed as she realized his eyes had followed hers to the rope hanging in the corner.

"You'd ring the bell like an alarm? Oh, Lena, I'm not dangerous." Like vacuity after a lightning strike, tension reverberated in the corridor.

He reached out; she inhaled sharply.

He grasped her arms, halting her escape. She trembled at his touch.

"Please don't be afraid of me, Lena. We should be friends—not enemies."

"Is this how it was for Brigetta?" The question shrieked inside her head. She looked down in horror at Cornelis' hands on her body. She twisted, but couldn't shake him loose. Heat radiating off his hands moved through the fabric of her dress and imprinted her like a branding iron.

From nowhere came Bartel's awe-struck description of the man who held her prisoner: *"He's like Charles Atlas!"* She was mortified by the whimper escaping her lips on the wings of knowledge that she was no match for Cornelis.

Cornelis' breath bathed her face. Frantic, she forced her eyes open as if to end the nightmare. Each ridge, each line, each curve shaping the structure of his face was as close as her own breath.

His voice pulsed in her ear. "You want to know what happened in the closet? I held Brigetta in my arms like this," he pulled her against him, trapping her.

As surely as Maas traps rabbits in a snare.

"No! Stop!" Her shuddering form melded against the contours of his body. Something akin to a consuming fire surged within her.

A frantic cry rose as she thrust her arms between them and pushed. "Stop!?" she sobbed. Forming fists; she pounded his chest. "Did Brigetta beg for mercy while you ravaged her?"

He shook her gently—but she was too frantic to realize he intended no physical harm. "Shhh-shhh-shhh," he whispered against her hair. "A kiss was all I wanted that day, right or wrong." His hands slid along Lena's arms, gripped her shoulders, brushed her neck.

She froze, imagining strangulation.

He cupped her face.

She whimpered, seeing faces she loved flash by.

His thumbs traveled her cheeks with a gentleness that scared Lena as much as had his fierce embrace.

Slowly, he lowered his lips to hers in a kiss that lingered only for a moment in physical contact, but set itself indelibly in two minds. "A kiss like this, Lena," he whispered hoarsely. "A sweet bond between a man and a woman. Perhaps the kiss I gave Brigetta was given in lust, but it rose out of one-sided love."

Lena's only response was a strangled wail. Her knees gave way even as her mind shouted, *"Stand firm!"*

Cornelis caught her.

Against her will, she wilted, letting his strength compensate for her weakness—though there was not one part of his body she dared touch. His unyielding embrace brought her cheek to rest against his chest. She felt a tremor ripple through his arms. She tilted her head enough to see his face.

His eyes were closed; his jaw twitched. His heart pounded in her ear. *Like a watermelon in a wagon bumping down a washboard road*, she thought inanely. Panic battled unsettling passions. A tumult of questions—none completely formed, but still terrifying—bombarded her.

Cornelis' ragged voice broke through her turmoil. "Surely you know more of the facts of life than to believe a kiss creates a child! Tell me the ways of a man with a woman aren't so incomprehensible that—"

He taunts me now? "I saw Brigetta's dishevelment."

He released her so quickly, she almost stumbled.

"Why did you come tonight? To buy my silence with a kiss?" Her fist bruised her lips like an eraser removing an error.

He laughed harshly. "I didn't come here tonight intending to kiss you, any more than I intended to kiss Brigetta that day."

"In both situations, you revealed yourself to be a man without restraint or regard for propriety." She glared across the abyss between them. To her shame, she saw only his mouth. She moistened her own lips with the tip of her tongue, cringing when he smiled knowingly.

"My older brother married the girl I had secretly thought would be mine someday. Was I wrong to hug and kiss her?" He shrugged. "I admit I made a bad decision."

"You are a despicable cad." *How sad my first kiss is from a man who is hardly the substance of my girlhood dreams.*

"Have you never heard of forgiveness?" he jeered.

"Have you never heard of repentance?" she snapped.

"You're incapable of a rational discussion. It makes me wonder about what kind of a teacher you are."

"Go away!" she ordered in blind fury.

"Oh, I'm leaving, but I have two questions: Now that you've had a chance to dump all your burdens on me, what do you plan to do next?"

"What happens next does not lie on my doorstep. You have confessed to no one, have you?"

"Doing so would only open old wounds. I have suffered enough . . ." he held up cautionary hands, ". . . I know, I meant we have all suffered enough. Nothing will change; thus nothing is to be gained. Let it go."

"If you cling to claims of innocence, nothing can change. What am I going to do, you ask? I don't plan to live in silence for ten more years."

"So you resort to threats? After all these years, you suddenly decide to levy a damning, unfounded accusation against the father of two of your students." He laughed contemptuously. "Look before you leap into that hole, Miss Stryker." He sneered her name and smirked when she blushed.

"You can no longer plead ignorance." Her words plunged like spring floods over an earthen dam. "I am not so much the innocent as to believe a kiss is all you inflicted on Brigetta. Can you honestly say there is no chance you created a child within Brigetta that day?"

His lips tightened as if pulled by an invisible cord. "I don't need to answer that question from you. If Bram asked, I'd understand. If Brigetta asked, it could suggest your suspicions are correct. Coming from you, the question smacks of wanting to hear a juicy tale."

"What if Bram or Brigetta did ask? Would you be honest? What lies would you tell Gustave?"

"Do you intend to tell-all after so many years?"

"Is that your second question?" she fired back.

"No, the second question is far more current than your conjectures. Are you able to teach my daughters without retaliation against them?"

Her nostrils flared. "You have my word—and my word, I remind you, is trusted in this community—that your daughters are receiving fair and kind treatment, and a good education. Surely, there has been nothing thus far to make you doubt that."

"If I suspect anything less, I will face you before the school board and provide facts to prove you are unfit for the classroom."

"You're chasing smoke if you hope to protect your girls from your past. Where there is smoke, there is fire. Be careful you and they don't get burned."

Loathing smoldered in his eyes; rage fanned it to a blaze. Without a word, he spun on his heel and left the schoolhouse. She lurched to the door, clutched the doorknob with both hands, and planted her feet against the base of the door. Unconsciously, she counted footsteps until she knew he was off the stoop.

All sounds halted. *He's standing there, waiting. Will he come back?*

Fumbling in the darkness, she managed to slide the lock into place. A satisfying *click* echoed in the silence. She heard Cornelis harsh laugh and flushed, realizing that he, too, had heard the *click*.

She held her breath and listened to gravel crunching beneath each footfall as her nemesis strode toward his car. She heard him open, then slam the door. It seemed an eternity until the engine roared.

Only after she was certain he was gone did she sink onto the rug pile inside the entry and stubbornly fight against tears. Finally, she forced herself to move into the classroom, closing the door between it and the entryway. Midst the familiar trappings of her everyday world, she shook as a mirage of horror took shape.

Sharp reality intruded with the return of mechanical noises outside the schoolhouse. *Oh, no! He came back!* She froze. *Footsteps.* She bit her lip and tasted blood. The outer door rattled. She yelped. A sharp knock; another shake.

She searched frantically for a weapon, racing to grab the fire-poker from behind the stove. She moved stealthily to one side of the inner door; the poker bumped her leg. Aghast, she looked at the wrought-iron tool in her hand. *Would I really attack him with this?*

A second knock, then came a worried voice. "Lena, are you all right? Gustave, the door's locked!"

Lena raced out to the entry. Fumbling, she slid the lock free and thrust open the door.

Hanna staggered backwards. Steadying her, Gustave exclaimed, "What a crazy night! Cornelis e nearly blew us off the road when we passed him. Have you seen him?"

"Whatever would he be doing here?" Lena hedged.

"Perhaps paying a pretty lady a social call?" Hanna teased in a singsong voice.

A muffled cry thundered in Lena's head. "Your purse is still right where you left it," she said woodenly.

Hanna sailed inside; but Gustave stared at Lena.

She dropped her eyes first.

"What's wrong, Lena?" he asked.

"I wasn't honest with you; Cornelis was here. We had . . . words."

"And you locked the door after him, and now answered the door brandishing a poker?" Gustave's eyebrows arrowed. "Did he . . . ?" The thought springing to mind was too bizarre to allow expression.

Lena grimaced, quickly moving the poker behind her back. "I, uh, I might have overreacted, but . . ."

"Did he threaten you?" Gustave persisted, trying to keep alarm and skepticism from his tone.

Lena's head bobbed between denial and admission until she felt dizzy. "Not an actual threat. He thought I should have squelched something the Huitink sisters said in church several weeks ago."

"Ready!" Hanna caroled as she returned, swinging her purse by its handle. "What every society woman carries . . ." Her gaze dropped to the poker. "Unless she prefers *wrought-iron* . . . Lena! What's going on?" Her eyes darted between her husband and sister.

"When I heard you arrive, I assumed it was him."

"And you were ready to hit him with a poker?" Hanna snatched the intended weapon from Lena's hand. "You could have killed him!"

True . . . and tempting. Lena shrugged. "Like I said, we had words."

Hanna twisted her lips. "Must have been harsh words. What did he do that elicits *this*," she dangled the poker like a putrid bandage, "from an intelligent, peace-loving, and kindhearted schoolteacher?"

In the blink of an eye, Lena considered alternatives, but opted for truth. "He kissed me," she said numbly.

Gustave stared. *Cornelis and Lena kissed?*

One syllable bore the weight of Hanna's hope and astonishment. "Oh!"

"It was more to silence me, than romantic. If you don't mind, I'd rather not discuss this. I'll see you Friday night, Gustave?"

He nodded, glad to have something to latch on to—even Lena's brush-off since it allowed him to give a normal response. "I'll be here."

Hanna returned the poker to its stand by the stove and, carrying her purse, followed Gustave outside. All the way to the automobile, she shot looks back to where Lena stood, framed by the doorway.

Dutchville's scattered lights came into view before either occupant of the Ford spoke. Then Hanna said, "Something's fishy, Gustave."

"You may be right."

"You know I am. Why would Cornelis want, or need, to silence Lena?"

"I have no idea. Shall I pay him a visit? I do feel a certain responsibility for Lena's protection."

"Lena would never forgive you. No; whatever will be, will be.

He chuckled. "Sage advice from a Dominie's wife who itches to shake the truth out of her maiden sister about a particular *swave* and *deboner* widower!" He drove into the buggy barn and steered the Ford into the stall next to Storm.

Hanna leaned against the nearest post, pondering life's vagaries, while Gustave replenished Storm's oats and shut the barndoor. Their arms linked, they walked toward the house.

Suddenly, the tugged his sleeve and skidded to a stop. "With Brigetta married to Bram, if Lena married Cornelis, Brigetta would be both Lena's niece and sister-in-law! Isn't that an odd thought?"

"It's 'putting the cart before the horse,' my dear!"

✱ ✱ ✱

Monday, October 21 ◆ Even though the teacher at the Dutch Valley School was a bundle of nerves, the schoolhouse echoed all day with singing. What had originated as an idea to please Saartje for her birthday, served to shelve haunting thoughts of a kiss and lift

Lena's spirits from the doldrums that Cornelis' denials and actions had inflicted upon her.

The students were delighted to sing counting songs and call it arithmetic. Songs that spelled out words were interspersed with songs about places (which they located on the map) to replace spelling and geography lessons for the day. Patriotic songs—Dutch and American—became their study of history.

At recess, Lena herded everyone out to the cloakroom and sang merrily as she distributed each sweater, jacket or cap to its owner: "Button up your overcoat . . ." She snapped her fingers. The children spilled onto the playground sounding like a castanet choir as the students picked up the beat.

Lena sipped hot water to sooth her throat. She leaned on the windowsill, observing the playground. Elsje and Saartje held the ends of a jump rope for the third-grade girls. The older boys practiced standing broad jumps.

By the pump, the first- and second-graders—*Ah, there's Wim*, Lena noted—surrounded Janneken. Lena watched the children attempt something Janneken demonstrated. As she moved down the line, Wim stomped his feet in frustration. The girls seemed to do better with the task, so Janneken returned to Wim. Lena leaned forward, now fully engaged.

"He's trying to snap his fingers!" she chortled. "Janneken is teaching the younger ones how to do it!" Then, a look of surprised joy on Wim's face bugled his success. Janneken grinned and hugged him.

After recess, Lena challenged the children to think of a song to match each month, January to December. When the list was complete, they sang their way through the year, hitting the familiar holidays' songs with particular gusto.

The afternoon was devoted to story-songs, and Lena started it all when she threw back her head and sent her voice to the farthest corners: "In the center of a valley, dwelt a maiden all divine . . ." Fancy footwork danced her over to Elsje; together they swooped around the perimeter of the room.

Returning Elsje to her desk, Lena glided to the piano in time to plink out the notes for ". . . and her name was Clementine!" She spun around on the swiveling piano stool. "Sing along!"

Sixteen loud voices joined in on ". . . and her shoes were number nine . . ."

Lena linked Liesbeth's hand with Maartje'. She then moved along the rows, pulling the remaining students from their seats to form a line that connected hand-to-hand.

The entire group swayed and sang, "Oh my darling, oh my darling, oh my darling Clementine, you are lost and gone forever, dreadful sorry, Clementine!"

"Your turn, Saartje! The next verse is about ducks."

To Lena's delight, Saartje kicked off her *klompen*, climbed on her desk seat and struck a pose. When she finished the verse, she pulled Janneken up. Using the aisle as their stage, they acted out ". . . stubbed her toe against a sliver, fell into the raging brine . . ."

"Do you know what falsetto means?" Lena asked. "No? Well ..." She demonstrated on the refrain while Wim plugged his ears.

The song had enough verses to try out stately and somber, plaintive, and even a pinched-nose-whiney version the boys loved. Lena adopted a melodramatic pose and pulled out all the stops on an operatic rendition that made the students howl.

Humming, or whistling while they skipped around the room, and even a tonette concert followed until Lena said, "We must sing the last verse with proper solemnity." She whipped out a hanky, wiped invisible tears from her eyes, and faked a sob for ". . . sadly calling, and her voice was like a chime . . ."

As if cued, the clock stuck the quarter hour. Everyone giggled, but kept singing, ". . . but alas, he was no swimmer so he lost his Clementine." The singers blubbered to the end, then finished the song-fest with "Happy Birthday" to Saartje as she brought out a chocolate layer cake.

While they ate, Lena talked about music. "No matter if you are happy, sad, feeling silly—there's always some type of song to match your feelings. Music also helps us memorize things, like the alphabet and counting tunes we sang. Some songs remind us of important historical events in our country, or special moments in our lives. I dare say, for the rest of our lives if we hear someone whistle 'Clementine,' we will think about today."

"I know I will," Saartje said dreamily.

Lena smiled. "Fill your lives with music. Hum when you do chores, or whistle while you walk to school, or make up special songs of your own. Today's lesson is to keep a song in your heart and sing it. You're dismissed, songbird choir!"

"We'll work extra hard, Miss Stryker, to make up the lessons we skipped," Saartje vowed at the door as she threw her arms around Lena. "I'll see to it that no one ruins our special days," she added fiercely.

"We may have skipped some classes, but we learned valuable things today—how to enjoy life is a very important lesson." *And, how a day of singing keeps dark thoughts at bay is another*, she mused, beginning her evening duties.

Part Three

Thursday, October 24 ◆ After Monday's musical extravaganza, the students applied themselves with admirable tenacity, though whether of their own initiative or at Saartje's insistence Lena did not know. When she reviewed the week on Thursday evening, she discovered all lessons were on target.

A roaring fire staved off the chill creeping into the schoolhouse through invisible crevices. Lena pulled on an extra pair of stockings and dragged her rocker out next to the stove, along with her knitting. "Sanna will appreciate new mittens because Minnesota must be as cold as Iowa!" She selected purple yarn from her basket and picked appropriate knitting needles.

With the rocker creaking comfortingly along with the crackling fire, Lena listened to the radio program that floated across the partition from her room. She tapped her foot to a song, smiled at the silliness of a program, and kept her needles flying. When the schoolroom clock struck seven, she heard a somber voice begin the newscast:

> "Heading the news this evening is a report on a terrifying day for investors. Beginning this morning, nearly thirteen million—not the usual four million—shares changed hands today. Panic reigned when the New York Stock Exchange's tickertape machine fell behind by an hour-and-a-half, leaving investors madly scrambling to sell their investments even without

knowledge of current prices. Mob-strength
crowds gathered outside exchanges and
brokerages in all major cities. Police were
dispatched to insure peace. At noon, the
Chicago and Buffalo Stock Exchanges closed."

Lena dropped her knitting to her lap, oblivious to
the needle that slithered to the floor and left a stitch
hanging. The voice continued:

"Following a meeting involving key leaders in
finance and banking, a senior partner at a leading
institution spoke with reporters, and I quote
from that interview, in part: 'There has been a
little distress selling on the Stock Exchange due
to a technical condition of the market. Things
are susceptible to betterment.' End quote."

"What does this mean?" Lena scrambled to her feet
and nearly tripped over her yarn basket as she raced to
the teacherage doorway as if being closer to the radio
would change what she heard. But there was only
more news that fueled more questions:

"The market rallied some after that, but today
true recovery was launched at 1:30 PM when the
NYSE vice-president walked onto the exchange
floor and asked for the latest bid on US Steel.
Upon hearing it was one-hundred and ninety-
five, he ordered ten-thousand shares at two-
hundred-and-five, and made similar orders for
over a dozen additional stocks."

Lena fervently wished she had a way to get to
Dutchville other than the bicycle stowed in the rafters

of the girls' outhouse. If the tires still had air in them, she'd gladly pull the bicycle down and ride against the wind to talk to someone and calm her unnamed fears . . . fears that grew when the newscaster continued:

> "In a related story, confirmed sources report nearly a dozen well-known speculators have committed suicide, though their identity is being withheld, pending notification of relatives."

A wordless sound spilled past Lena's lips. *Whatever is happening is grim, indeed, for people to take their own lives!* She did not begin to understand stocks, preferring to keep her savings in a simple account at the Dutchville bank. *That's a safe place, isn't it?*

She resumed knitting and kept the radio on well past her normal bedtime, but heard only the same news retold every half hour until the story seemed branded on her mind. There was trouble, and panic, and people who knew about things Lena did not understand could not agree on what the future held.

Untangling a strand of yarn, Lena said with false confidence, "Such troubles affect big cities, not Iowa."

✱ ✱ ✱

Friday, October 25 ◆ Lena's confusion was nothing compared to the children's muddled thoughts the next day. They had overheard just enough news and adult conversations to be concerned, but understood too little to believe anything happening could affect them. In this, they were similar to their teacher.

Depending on which reports the adults believed, some told tales of doom and gloom, others insisted on seeing the rainbow in every oily puddle. The adults' limited and pooled knowledge created a murky muddle of misinformation that was reflected in the students' comments.

A restlessness ran through the classroom all day. Lena chalked it up to the spillover of adult-concerns into a child's world. She tried to infuse an element of peace into their lives—and, in turn, her own—if only for the hours that the students were under her care.

All good things end, and so it was on this unsettling day, Lena turned the final page of "The Enchanted Castle." She paused to look at her audience, then said, "We've reached the last sentence, which says, 'It is all very well for all of them to pretend that the whole of this story is my own invention: facts are facts, and you can't explain them away.' The End."

Setting the book aside, she picked up another. "On Monday, I will begin this book, titled 'Tales Told in Holland.' One story is 'The Lady of Stavoren: A Tale from the Province of Friesland.' I think it will make a lovely play for our Christmas Program."

"Is it the one about a ruby ring?" Janneken asked.

Lena tapped her index finger against her lips in the classic "*Shush!*" signal. "Yes, but say no more! I will read the tale twice. On Monday, I'll let you to sit back and enjoy the story. Tuesday, I'll read it again and we'll think how we could act it out for the program. It will take work and creativity. Now, you're dismissed."

Cornelis arrived—by now, Lena recognized the sound of his automobile, even without the horn. He tapped lightly on the doorframe. "Lena?" he said in a neutral tone.

Startled, Lena looked up from retying Liesbeth's hair ribbons for her trip home. "Yes?"

"Gustave asked me to drive a ride to town. He was called to the bank to help calm folks, and I need to go back to town since Yzaak has much on his mind today with—" The slamming door interrupted him.

Two miniature whirlwinds bounded into the room and skirted past Cornelis' legs. "Miss Stryker!" Antje exclaimed.

"Tante Lena!" Maartje interrupted. "I mean, Miss Stryker! We have the best news! Father says you can ride with us when he takes us home, and he will drive you to town."

Cornelis' smile didn't reach his eyes. "Can you go now? Gustave won't be free until much later."

"What's happening?" Lena asked, sensing Cornelis had left much unsaid, even as dread at sharing an automobile with him surged.

"There is quite a crowd outside the bank. Mathijs van Steenwyk needed Gustave's help."

The bank? A crowd requiring Gustave's calming influence? In Iowa?

Riding along the roads leading to the de Boer farm, Maartje and Antje kept up a steady stream of conversation, which Lena appreciated since sitting within such a confined space and so close to Cornelis rendered her incapable of breathing enough to sustain life, let alone speak.

They pulled into the driveway. Lena opened the door and stumbled out as if fleeing a rabid animal, ostensibly to allow Maartje to exit the back seat.

Cornelis let Antje exit through his door and lingered outside the automobile, one foot propped on the running board. The girls raced up the walkway to Rebecca's arms.

Lena sagged against the automobile and sucked in air, releasing it only to inhale again. *Keep breathing: in-and-out . . . in-and-out.*

"Hello, Lena." Rebecca sent a questioning glance at the teacher who had yet to say a word.

"Hello, Rebecca." Her tone was sounded strangled.

"I may be late tonight, Mother," Cornelis called out. "I'll explain later. Dominie asked me to give Lena a ride to town since he is occupied elsewhere."

Rebecca nodded. "Your father was in town earlier today, so I understand. I heard from Hanna where Gustave is," she said cryptically.

Lena caught Cornelis' terse nod at his mother. As she turned away, her gaze fell upon the backseat. With lips clamped, she climbed into Maartje's space.

An odd sound rumbled in Cornelis' throat. Bending, he looked over the seatback, his gaze reflecting both ridicule and astonishment. "What are you doing? Sit in front!"

"I'm more comfortable here," she said primly.

"What will people think, seeing you back there?"

"That I am a woman of propriety?" she suggested haughtily.

He snorted. "More like one of questionable mental stability. You're the most confoundedly annoying woman I've ever met!"

"I imagine when someone who's accustomed to women swooning over him meets someone who finds nothing about him attractive, it must be annoying."

He pounded the car's roof, slid into his seat, and closed the door with unnecessary force. Several parts of the automobile rattled in rebuke. He gripped the steering wheel and stared across its arc at the peaceful world beyond. "I suppose this is how you punish me for kissing you?"

Lena stared out her window in silence.

Dour-faced, Cornelis shifted into gear and turned the Tudor Sedan toward the road. He enjoyed a moment's satisfaction when Lena grabbed the front seat to keep her balance on his intentionally wild turn. They passed no one on the way to town. No one saw Lena behaving in a seemly manner, but no one would have noticed her in the front seat, either.

The Dutchville Reformed Church's steeple was in view before Cornelis spoke. "What you consider righteous behavior, I call mule-headed." He braked sharply on the street in front of the parsonage. The pulsating engine echoed the pent-up tension between driver and passenger.

"Thank you for helping Gustave by giving me a ride to town," she said coolly and stepped out. "Now, if you will retrieve my satchel and box from the boot, you can be on your way."

Bitterness coated his words: "Before anyone sees that Miss Purity has tainted her image by riding with the depraved Cornelis de Boer?"

"Despite our earlier conversation, there is no proof you've tried to make things right. If anything, you compounded your indiscretions. Therefore, I want as little to do with you as possible."

"I hope you need not ever again endure something so repulsive." The tone was even, the words mocking.

"Thank you." Head held high, she took her satchel from his hand and headed for the walk.

"Oh!" She halted midway and turned, startled to see him staring at her. "Are you aware Bram and Brigetta are coming home for Christmas? You know what I expect to happen then."

His glare was akin to loathing as he roared away, coming dangerously close to taking out a fencepost.

Lena stomped up the parsonage steps and paused, one hand on the doorknob. "He left my box in the road? What an insufferable man!" She slid her satchel inside the entryway, and stomped back to retrieve her box of school papers from where it sat . . . mere inches from a horse's recent deposit.

When it became apparent Gustave would not be home, Hanna set a plate aside to reheat for him. She and Lena ate, but hardly tasted their supper.

As seven o'clock passed, the sisters emptied Lena's box on the dining room table and worked together to grade papers and organize them for easy redistribution.

Nine o'clock swallowed up eight o'clock; through it all, they talked, though solving nothing.

Hanna knew only a few more details about the numbing news of the stock market than Lena did, both women having heard essentially the same radio broadcasts, but being in town gave Hanna a front row seat on the effects of the crisis. "People gathered outside the bank in the middle of the night on Thursday. The constable scared me when he pounded on the door and asked Gustave to come. He said that by four in the morning, Friday, people had already been in line for several hours."

"Whatever for?" Lena asked. "I'm shocked that sensible Dutchmen would behave so rashly."

Hanna looked grim. "I wish we knew more than such scant details. The constable offered Gustave a ride, but Gustave said no. He dressed and took off immediately with only a cold meat roll in his pocket. He came home for lunch and slept about half an hour and then went right back to the bank."

"Who are these people, acting so out-of-character?"

"Farmers, shopkeepers. Normal folks." She shrugged wearily and massaged her neck. "The group is large and determined to withdraw their money—something Mathijs van Steenwyk is trying to prevent. The crowd got angry. Someone pitched a rock and broke a window. That's when and why they sent for Gustave. He came home at noon and said Mathijs might close the bank."

Aghast, Lena asked, "Can he do that?"

"Who knows? Mathijs made an announcement from the bank steps. Something about how each bank customer could withdraw up to ten percent of whatever was on their account.

"That seems fair to me," Lena said.

"It does, but men got belligerent and threatened him with bodily harm."

Gustave returned just after ten o'clock, weary and chilled. Hanna reheated his supper while he washed up. Water glistened on his beard and eyebrows when he came into the kitchen.

He filled a fork with food and dropped it to his plate without taking a bite. He picked up the coffee cup as if to drink it, but instead cradled it in both hands, inhaling the aroma and steam.

"Eat, Gustave," Hanna urged gently. "You've had so little food today."

He nodded and picked up his fork. He may have gained sustenance from his meal, but he was numb to pleasure or displeasure in what filled his stomach.

Finally, he pushed back and tilted his head to rest on his shoulders. "I'm saddened to learn how many families in our community have borrowed heavily. Some have mortgaged their homes and could face ruin if they are unable to repay their debts. Debt is a tempting mistress, but a fearsome landlord."

Lena shook her head in disbelief. "Throwing rocks at the bank's windows is hardly the appropriate response to the institution that holds our money and grants loans to so businesses and individuals!"

"People are afraid if the bank keeps their money and uses it to pay against loans, they'll be left destitute. We've become a country of people who want what we want when we want it. And it's been too easy to buy on the easy-payment plan. Now, banks may call in those loans—especially if their own loans from larger institutions are recalled. It's complicated, and made more so by conflicting reports from those with far more knowledgeable than I possess."

Hanna set the murky darkness in the bottom of her cup swirling with a rhythmic hand motion. "Causing a ruckus does not make anything better."

"You speak words of wisdom, my dear—words, I am afraid, no one in that mob today was willing or able to hear, no matter who said them."

"Let's go up to bed, Gustave," Hanna said gently. "Let me rub your back until you fall asleep."

"I should take a rain-check for some time when I am not ready to fall asleep in my supper. Your act of kindness may not last three minutes, tired as I am."

Lena cleared the table, leaving Gustave's dishes to soak. She wandered the house, pondering what he'd said. She thought of Cornelis' pitch to her students, suggesting their fathers could get loans to buy new cars. Then she thought of Cornelis' own flashy vehicle. *Is it truly his, or does the bank own it?*

Questions roamed like vagabonds. Lena needed something more pleasant to occupy her thoughts, so she went into the sewing room, found a hunk of yardage purchased long ago, and chose a pinafore pattern young Brigetta had always liked. It was easy to make one in Sanna's size that matched the pattern.

Two more dresses were cut out before Lena halted, scissors in hand. *Why am I making dresses for Cornelis' daughters?* She knew why: It was the girls' Tante Lena, not their father's archenemy, who sewed to survive a night in which she could not sleep.

❋ ❋ ❋

Saturday, October 26 ◆ Sitting down to an early breakfast of oatmeal porridge and bacon, Gustave looked at Lena as she slid a cup of coffee into place above his knife. "In all that happened yesterday, I neglected to apologize for leaving you in the lurch at school. I presume Cornelis followed through on his promise to me?"

"Yes," Lena said guardedly, "he did."

"Cornelis was on the bank crowd's fringe. I didn't want him to sully his name by getting caught up in the fracas, so I drafted him as your driver."

Lena bit back a snort that went unnoticed.

Gustave continued, "I likely needn't have worried; I assume he was there looking for Yzaak Baumgartner."

"Did he find him?" Hanna asked.

"Yes; I overheard them talking. Yzaak was taking note of who was part of the mob scene. Many in the crowd bought automobiles on credit. Yzaak gets his money up-front for each purchase, but he's worried about future sales, if loans stop. Anyway, I overheard Cornelis and Yzaak mention working late last night to know where they stand with inventory and orders.

Cornelis said he'd pick up his daughters, and return to town, so I asked him to deliver you home."

"I'm glad you didn't leave those who needed you far more than I. In the future, it won't harm me to stay at school. I have sufficient provisions, and plenty to entertain myself."

"I wish there were a way to let you know. I worried that you would think something had happened to me or Hanna that prevented us coming."

Lena laughed hollowly. "One improvement at a time at the school. First, electricity; then, a telephone!"

Gustave drank the last of his coffee and said, "Now I must retire to my study and give serious thought to what I will say to my congregation tomorrow. These are troubled times that will affect us all, whether or not we were among those gathered at the bank."

The women listened to his belabored footfalls on the stairs. When they heard the familiar creak that indicated he knelt beside his desk, as he always did before beginning his sermon preparation, Lena said, "Gustave has a kind heart—full of compassion."

Hanna nodded. "He seems to sense when people are hurting—and knows how to ease their pain. The same is true of you, Lena."

"No, not me," Lena protested quickly. "Of late, I sense an alarming hardheartedness in myself. Yes, I see pain in others, but rather than try to ease their hurts, I compound them. Too often, I lash out— causing more grief, even though I usually regret it instantly. I lack Gustave's gentleness."

"Perhaps you do not see kindness in yourself, but others do. Rebecca is so grateful for all you've done for Antje and Maartje. She said when Cornelis and the girls first returned, all she saw was sorrow in him, and fear and confusion in the girls. But, with you as their teacher, the girls are healing inside which helps Cornelis handle his grief, too."

Lena shut her eyes against a looming image of one stiff-necked and pompous schoolteacher riding in the backseat of an automobile driven by the father of two of her students. He'd acted not for improper reasons, but had simply transported her from the schoolhouse to the parsonage. *No ulterior motives. No inappropriate actions. Nothing but a gentlemanly gesture.*

"Hanna, last night when Cornelis brought me here, I treated him disrespectfully."

"How so?"

"I refused to sit with him in the front seat, after we left the girls at the farm."

Hanna examined her fingernails. "I see; but on the way to the farm, you sat in the front seat?"

Lena nodded. "I had no choice; the girls were already in the back seat when I came out of the school. There did not seem any alternative at that point. But coming from the farm in to town, there was. So I sat in the back seat rather than give any hint of impropriety to anyone who might see us."

"Lena, my dear! Do you honestly think anyone would consider it improper for you to accept a ride from him? Especially given the easily proven reason behind such an offer? One ride is all it was! Not a private dinner or Sunday afternoon ride in the country—neither of which is scandalous, by the way. It was a trip from school to farm—with two chaperones!—and then to town in broad daylight."

"Chaperones? Hardly. The girls were thrilled I was sitting in the front seat; I heard their whispers. They will probably tell their friends and, after Gerolt's tirade over my teaching English names, this is dreadful."

"No one else complained about the name exercise, did they?" Hanna asked practically.

"No," Lena admitted.

Hanna cocked her head. "Was it because Cornelis kissed you that you felt you should sit in back?"

Lena nodded. She was misery personified.

"Oh, sweet sister! A kiss is not such a bad thing."

"It was not a kiss given because he feels fondly toward me. It was meant to silence and shame me."

"Why would he want to do either?"

Tears burned behind Lena's eyes. "Cornelis fears I will tell what I know . . . something dreadful . . . from long ago. The story is not mine to tell, but it is behind Cornelis' kiss."

Hanna inhaled sharply. *"Perhaps, but something in you changes at the mention of his name. Even now, your face flames like a sunburn, as if you picked strawberries without wearing a bonnet!"*

When Lena added nothing to her choppy explanation, Hanna finally pushed back her chair. "Did you say you plan to bake bread today?"

"Yes; I thought I'd make four wheat loaves, and a batch of oatmeal rolls. What will you do?"

"I'll make apple pie. It cheers Gustave, and he needs cheering." She looked sideways at Lena. *"The same goes for you, dear Lena—although I doubt pie will help."*

❋ ❋ ❋

Sunday, October 27 ♦ A somber congregation gathered in the sanctuary of the Dutchville Reformed Church. Distressed, fearful, nervous, confused, sad— men and women, young and old, all came seeking answers to life's tough questions after several unsettling days.

News of the market had seemed better on Saturday, but nerves were still on edge. Allowing confidence to creep into the soul seemed risky.

Gustave looked out over the people gathered. *I have nothing to give them, no wisdom of my own. But thanks be to God, I am not without words to speak.*

He smoothed a page in the pulpit Bible. "Find comfort and instruction, my friends, in the readings for the thirtieth Sunday in Ordinary Time this Lord's Day, October twenty-seven, nineteen-hundred and twenty-nine, selected from the ninetieth *Psalmen*:

> "Lord, thou hast been our dwelling place in all generations. Before the mountains were brought forth ... from everlasting to everlasting, thou art God ... For a thousand years in thy sight are but as yesterday when it is past, and as a watch in the night ... Teach us to number our days, that we may apply our

hearts unto wisdom . . . Let the beauty of the Lord our God be upon us, and establish thou the work of our hands . . ."

Closing the large pulpit Bible, he pushed his glasses into position to look out at the pews. He leaned forward, atypically resting one arm on the lectern. "God's Word reaches across the ages. David's cries are no different than our own, and God's presence in David's life is no less powerful and comforting in his hard times than God's abiding presence is in our lives today. Almighty God was, is, and always will be our dwelling place . . ."

Despite her better judgment, Lena had sat again with the Huitink sisters, which put her directly in line with Cornelis' russet-hued head. She forced her attention to shift from the de Boer's pew to the pulpit.

Gustave's voice was a soothing balm coating a burn. His words brought hope and comfort to troubled hearts, including Lena's. She had few financial worries, having borrowed nothing, and possessing only a small, respectable savings account—but her troubled spirit was sorely in need of solace and she found it in the pew at the Dutchville Reformed Church.

"Our New Testament reading this morning comes from the Apostle Paul's first epistle to the Thessalonians, chapter two," Gustave was saying when Lena's attention returned to the pulpit. "When Paul writes 'But we were gentle among you, even as a nurse cherisheth her children . . . because you were dear unto us,' the image he conveys is one of a mother or anyone entrusted with the care of a child tending them lovingly, soothing their worries."

Lena's eyes drifted to Antje sitting quietly to Cornelis' left and to Maartje leaning against his right shoulder. *Motherless children.*

The congregation soaked up consolation like a desert opening itself to a spring shower. Nothing changed in their situations that hour, but burdens lightened as hope lifted its petals to the sunlight of God's Word.

"God's discipline may seem harsh. As every parent knows, love is also shown when we correct a child who goes astray. The writer of this Scripture says, '. . . because you were dear to us.' We are dear to the Heavenly Father. He provides daily bread. He longs to teach us to number our days aright, and to guide us to the place where we can say we have applied our hearts unto wisdom . . ."

Lena rose to her feet belatedly to join the congregation in singing the *Psalmen* that had been the focus of Gustave's sermon.

While others around her took courage from the opening stanza, Lena made the final verse her heart's prayer:

> *"En de liefelijkheid des Heeren, onzes Gods; zij over ons; en bevestig Gij het werk onzer handen over ons, ja, het werk onzer handen, bevestig dat: . . ."*

"Establish Thou the work of my hands," Lena whispered in her pew. "And let my heart know what You want my hands to be doing to please You."

* * *

Monday, October 28 ◆ Playground chatter was at an all-time fevered pitch. Hardly a student roamed who didn't have an episode from the weekend to report. If a given account suffered from inadequate drama, another student was eager to correct the deficit.

"That's nothing!" Lena heard Maas boast, and she watched with rising curiosity, the human hedge around Raimund shift to encircle Maas with his promises of more and better and bigger excitement. "One rock hit the safe and busted it wide open and money flew out!" His chest inflated as his news garnered gasps.

"Children!" Lena called out firmly, already striding toward them. "Since I know you were in school, not outside the bank on Friday, it would be wise for you to refrain from telling any stories."

"But my father says—" Maas protested feebly.

"Your father told me at church yesterday that he cared for a sick cow all day Friday," Lena said firmly.

"Well, he was gonna go to town, if the cow hadn't took sick," Maas said, looking even more defeated as his audience lost interest in him and his punctured-by-truth tall tales.

Lena sighed and shook her head ruefully. *Mondays!* She blew one sharp blast on her whistle. Heads turned toward her in surprise since it was not yet eight o'clock, and the last to arrive still held their lunch pails. "Put your buckets on the stoop, Lucas and Liesbeth. Hurry! Form a line by the pump and wait for my whistle, and then run around the fence!"

The race took the focus off storytelling, as Lena had hoped it would. Suddenly, the real challenge of passing a classmate on an open stretch surpassed the contest of topping a rumor. They tromped inside and conducted opening exercises in a circle at the front of the room. "Where is Janneken?" Lena wondered aloud as she did a quick nose count around the circle.

"Maybe a skunk sprayed her in the face, and she's vomiting," Raimund suggested.

"Maybe she fell out of a tree and broke both her arms and legs," Bartel said. The twins nodded at each other solemnly. "Plus, she's vomiting," Bartel added, not wanting to negate his brother's contribution.

"I'm sure Janneken arrive soon," Lena said. "Now, we will sing 'America, the Beautiful' and, by the time we finish, perhaps she will arrive."

But that did not happen.

Throughout the morning, each time responsiveness to lessons lagged, Lena moved silently, appearing beside a desk to redirect its occupant's attention. While investors across the country struggled with financial woes, students at Dutch Valley School tackled long division and diagramed sentences and memorized poems. By noon, their teacher was exhausted.

After lunch, Lena divided the students into two camps and launched a spelling bee. This being the first-graders' introduction to what was always a favorite activity, she let them each compete in the first round with words guaranteed to offer success, despite their limited vocabulary this early in the year.

For round two, she seated them near her with sheets of paper on which she drew four columns. Knowing they could not yet read their classmates' names, Lena quickly sketched twelve objects—thimble, leaf, apple, cat, shoe, hat, mitten, fork, chair, bed, bird, rake—on twelve scraps of paper. These she pinned to the other students' chests.

While the older students refreshed themselves at the water cooler, she drew those same objects—four on each first-grader's list—at the top of the columns. "Maartje, see the pine tree on the paper on Jaap's chest? When he spells a word correctly, put a chicken scratch in the column with a pine tree at the top. That is what each of you will do during our drill: match the pictures and pay close attention."

For the first few words, she aided the score-keepers, "Wim, find the column with the teapot to give Adda her point." Soon they followed along, doing so proudly each time Lena told the speller, "Correct."

As promised, the afternoon Storytime offered the first reading from the new book. "This story is one your grandparents may have heard from their parents long ago in the Old Country. It is titled 'The Lady of Stavoren: A Tale from the Province of Friesland.' Remember: Today, you listen; tomorrow, I'll give you different instructions when we read it again."

Lena assumed different voices for different characters, capably infusing mood and drama into words on a page. Usually, she stayed focused on the story, but when she read the Lady's order to the old sea captain: ". . . bring me the most precious thing in the world . . ." her mind wandered briefly, though her lips stayed true to the story. *What is precious? Peace? A reputation?*

She paused to turn a page. As she read the words ". . . many of the merchants lost everything . . ." terrifying sounds from outside the schoolhouse simultaneously drowned out her voice. An almost human cry rose above the harsh mechanical sounds, followed by the bleating horn so familiar to all.

One split second of eerie calm, then Wim shot up and ran to the door. The others were close behind.

"Freek!"

Lena knew she never forget his desperate shriek.

The little boy sobbed all the way to the road where the golden-haired dog lay trapped beneath the front tire on the driver's side of Cornelis' automobile.

Cornelis burst from the automobile in time to grab the boy and hold him tightly. Wim flailed at Cornelis' chest, and twisted in his arms until he faced away from Cornelis. Gulping sobs, the small boy reached helplessly toward the motionless form of his dog, struggling to push himself free from his captor.

"Oh, Wim," Cornelis choked out, "I . . ."

"Give Wim to me," Lena commanded, appearing at Cornelis' side. Tenderly, she led the boy a few paces away from the heart-rending scene. Turning him away from the scene, she anchored him, her arms forming an X across his chest. But he twisted around—needing to see, desperate to know.

Placing both hands on the bonnet, Cornelis braced himself and pushed against the automobile until it rolled backward. The front end lifted slightly and then leveled off as the tire moved off the lifeless body.

Despite this show of strength, no one whispered *"Told you he's as strong as Charles Atlas!"*

"Wake up, Freek!" Wim pleaded from the safety of Lena's arms. "He ain't moving, Miss Stryker. Mister de Boer killed Freek!"

"Shhh-shhh-shhh." Lena's eyes fogged over as Wim's despairing sobs penetrated her heart.

At last, Wim sagged against Lena's shoulder, too spent to cry any more. But weeping broke out around the tight circle of students as they realized what they witnessed. Cornelis bent beside the dog.

Wim broke free from Lena's arms and fell to his knees between Cornelis and Freek. He attempted to shove Cornelis aside and buried his face in Freek's fur. The boy's body trembled as he resigned himself to the truth.

Jaap had the presence of mind to run for a burlap bag, shaking it free of debris as he returned. Cornelis lifted the dog into the bag Jaap held open for him. Wim looked up at Cornelis. "Don't cover his nose," he pleaded. "Freek hates to have his nose covered."

Cornelis shot a questioning look at Lena. She could only nod; tears clumped in her throat. Carefully, Cornelis folded the bag back to free Freek's face. Then he lifted the bag into his arms and rose from his crouch. *"Now what?"* his haggard glance asked Lena.

She shook herself mentally and took charge. "Wim, Mister de Boer is going to drive you and Freek home. Freek will ride in the boot ... on a soft rug," she added quickly, noting Wim's dismay. Without waiting to be asked, Jaap ran to get a rug from the entryway. "Sit in the front seat, Wim" Lena said. "Antje and Maartje will stay here until their father returns."

Wim nodded dully and climbed in.

Lucas took charge of opening the boot—a skill he had gained during Cornelis' frequent demonstrations of the vehicle's features.

Jaap placed the rug in the center of the boot.

Cornelis placed his sad burden on it, taking care not to cover Freek's face, although seeing it was nearly his undoing. He carefully closed the boot and returned to the driver's side.

"Stay here at the schoolhouse with Miss Stryker; I'll come back for you," he told his daughters.

Slowly man, boy and their regrettable cargo moved along the dusty road. All eyes followed the vehicle until it was out of sight.

"Is Freek really dead, Miss Stryker?" Liesbeth asked tremulously. "Maybe he's just sleeping?"

Lena swallowed a lump the size of the burlap bag riding toward the Wynkoop farm. "No, he died, dear."

"He's a really good dog," Sterre said fervently. "He doesn't scare me anymore."

"Wim will be very sad," Elsje murmured to no one in particular. "Freek has walked him to school and home again every day."

Lena inhaled sharply, hearing her own voice make that very promise to Wim: "*You will always have a friend along for the walk home . . .*"

"That's right, Elsje. We'll have to be very kind and understanding. We will miss Freek; Sterre's right: he was a good dog. I think you had all better head home now, or your families will worry. Antje and Maartje, will you help me take down the flag while we wait for your father to return?"

Raimund tugged Lena's skirt. "Mister de Boer didn't mean to do it! You saw how he pushed that heavy automobile. If he meant to kill something, he wouldn't have done that, would he?" Fear shone from his dark eyes as his words tumbled past trembling lips.

"*It's hard to learn a hero is human, isn't it, Raimund?*" Lena thought sadly. "No; Mister de Boer didn't mean to hit Freek. It was an accident. He is sad, too."

In their usual groupings, but with none of their usual frolicking, the students left the schoolyard. "Thanks for helping, Jaap," Lena told the shy boy.

"I hope Wim gets another dog someday as nice as Freek," he said gruffly, giving undue attention to tying his lunch bucket to the handlebars before riding off. As Lena stared after him, the bicycle swerved when he lifted one forearm and swiped it across his eyes. Then he pedaled all the harder.

Antje's voice drew Lena's attention. "If Wim gets another dog, would he name it Freek, Miss Stryker?"

"Hmm? Oh . . . would he name a new dog Freek? I don't know, Antje. Why do you ask?"

"Father said if we ever get another Mother we could call her Mother, so I wondered."

Another mother? "Yes, well." Lena swallowed hard. "As for Wim . . . that is something we just do not know," she said lamely. To break the awkwardness, she suggested, "Would you like to help me straighten the bookshelf?"

Cornelis returned half an hour later, looking grim. "Thank you for keeping the girls, Lena," he said as his daughters scurried out to the waiting automobile. "Have you been listening to the radio?"

"No." Sarcasm abruptly replaced sadness. "Until the shocking ending to the school day, I was busy teaching. Then, suddenly I was thrust into the role of explaining the hard facts of life to innocent children."

He flushed, but didn't retort. Instead, he closed his eyes. His first words rode a sigh. "Things are not good in our country; in fact, it's so bad that when Freek jumped out of the ditch, I was thinking about what I'd heard on the radio. Next thing I knew—"

Lena wasn't about to let this become a 'poor-me' lament for Cornelis. "I'm not the one who needs to hear your excuses. How's Wim?" she asked curtly.

Cornelis jerked, as if having forgotten he was not alone. "Uh, fine. I mean, he will be okay. His mother . . . I mean, no one blamed me."

"Oh, sure! Who could blame Golden-Boy Cornelis de Boer for any tragedy he brought into their life? Even Raimund seems hesitant to admit Dutchville's *Charles Atlas* is capable of anything as ignoble as killing a young boy's dog. I hope you offered the Wynkoop family more sincere sympathy than the dollop of 'Everything will be fine' that qualifies as an apology in your book."

His voice cut like a razor. "I explained to Hilde Wynkoop; she assured me there are no hard feelings. Accidents happen—her words; not mine. Why do you turn this into a vendetta against me? Can't you accept I'm not a hardhearted bloke who kills puppies? I liked Freek; I looked forward to having him jump in the front seat every morning. It sounds crazy, but in some ways, Freek understood me better than humans seem to. I told him things I have no one else to tell."

"Maybe you should get a dog because when other families hear how you killed Wim's pet with your automobile, emotions may rise high and automobile sales may sink low," she snapped. "Mark this day well, Cornelis. It's the day you tumbled off the pedestal my students have allowed you to occupy since the first day of school. You can judge what's going on in other homes by your girls' report on today to your parents."

He glowered, clenching and unclenching his fists. "Has no one ever told you that you have an odd way of bringing comfort to the hurting?" The schoolhouse door slammed shut behind him, rattling both the windows and Lena's loose grasp on composure.

All evening, the day's events taunted Lena. Sights and sounds mingled until she couldn't concentrate. She kept hearing, "*. . . odd way . . . comfort to the hurting . . .*" She longed to silence that voice.

Seeking a distraction, she turned on the radio, hoping to enjoy a music program while she embroidered an apron. But there was no music, only solemn voices with serious news.

No sooner did the first crackle come across the airwaves than she recalled Cornelis' words: "... *things are not good.*" The faceless voice that filled Lena's room gave credence to Cornelis' claim:

> "Since September, the markets lost forty percent in value, but today will be marked as an even darker day in stock-market history. Bankers withheld any comments until after markets closed but their words were not optimistic.
>
> Volume levels are very high at just over nine million shares as speculators begin to realize no one can save the market. They are left with slim hopes the damage will not be too severe.
>
> One week ago, investors learned volume was high at over six million shares and the ticker tape fell seriously behind, forcing people to sell blindly. Today, the stock market dropped thirteen percent leading experts to fear ..."

She turned off the radio. Each phrase faded slowly: "... *darker ... no one can save ... slim hopes ... sell blindly ... fear ...*" until silence reigned: a silence Lena could not stand any more than the unsettling news of a country in distress.

Restlessly, she lit the gas light fixtures along the classroom walls to disperse more gloom than a lantern could accomplish, and then walked to the piano.

Songs moved off the pile of sheet music as she worked her way through them, setting aside titles that did not dispel her inner turmoil. If a tune was upbeat, Lena played it with frenzied attention to notes on the page. If it echoed in her heart, she played it twice.

In the world beyond Dutch Valley School, investors faced the same grim reality as the schoolteacher who banged out melodies in the night.

Yet, sometimes, even loud music cannot drown out the heart's cries.

✴ ✴ ✴

Tuesday, October 29 ♦ Cornelis brought Antje and Maartje to school early, arriving before any other children. His face evidenced a long night of little rest.

"I hope it's not too disruptive, Lena, but I told the girls they could sit inside and read quietly, unless you would rather they play outside."

"No, it's too chilly, even dressed as warmly as they are. They'll be fine in here."

He embraced his daughters and rose slowly as they headed for the bookcase. "I did not want to be here, the first day after Freek . . ." He cleared his throat. "I thought it'd be harder on the students to see me . . ."

"I'm not sure if that demonstrates compassion or cowardice on your part, but I'll give compassion the benefit of the doubt," Lena said coolly. "I appreciate what you did for Wim—taking him and Freek home, I mean. I'm sorry for what I said yesterday afternoon. It was mean-spirited, in light of how I know you didn't purposely hit Freek."

"I deserved it. If I drove a horse and buggy, Freek would still be alive because the horse would have shied. But I drive an automobile and I was not paying attention. Wim lost his dog because of me."

"I listened to the radio last night, Cornelis. At least until the news became too upsetting. I don't pretend to understand what's going on, but is Dutchville really at risk for all that people fear?"

"No place will escape; our country faces hard times. I just pray . . ."

"What do you pray?" Lena asked without animosity.

He exhaled a lungful of air in one forceful burst, shaking his head ruefully.

"What is it?"

"What I was going to say verifies every blasted thing you believe about me. What I pray is this that no more bad things happen in my life. I'm a selfish lout."

"You are probably no different than most people," Lena admitted slowly. "Except for Gustave, I know of no one who honestly puts his fellowman before himself when push comes to shove."

"Watch it, Lena—that sounds softhearted. Next thing you know, you'll be thinking I am an okay fellow." He buttoned his overcoat beneath his chin and cocked an eyebrow. "Can't have that, now, can we?"

He lifted his cap in a mock salute and drove away.

Shivering, Lena was surprised to see that she had followed him out to the stoop; she hurried back inside to where the de Boer girls sat, heads bent together, as they examined the illustrations in a simple book of fairytales. "That's a pretty queen, Antje—read this one to us," Maartje said.

Janneken and Wim were absent when morning exercises began. Even with fourteen seats filled, the empty seats loomed like caverns. "Does anyone know if Janneken is ill? It's unusual for her two miss two days in a row," Lena said.

"My father said at supper last night that Mister De Groot didn't come to the meeting at the creamery yesterday," Lucas offered. "Maybe the whole family is sick. Or maybe they're still harvesting."

Lena nodded vaguely. *I had hoped Janneken would be here—I planned today's opening exercises with her sensitivity to yesterday's sadness in mind.*

"Today, I'll reading our morning *Psalmen* instead of us singing it. Then, I'll teach you a song Dominie Ter Hoorn taught his daughter Brigetta—my niece—when she was a child."

After the Bible reading, Lena opened a songbook to a marked page and turned it around so the students could see the illustration. "On dangerous rocky points in bodies of water, people build lighthouses. They are tall, narrow buildings with lanterns on top to guide ships to safety during storms or at night. A lighthouse keeper climbs up and keeps the windows clean and the light glowing. It's a very important job; if the light doesn't shine, boats can crash into the rocks."

She raised the map to reveal words on the blackboard, returned to the piano, and sang:

"Do not wait until some deed of greatness you
    may do.
Do not wait to shed your light afar.
To the many duties ever near you now be true—
and brighten the corner where you are.
Brighten the corner where you are,
brighten the corner where you are.
Someone far from harbor you may guide across
    the bar,
so, brighten the corner where you are."

She accompanied their singing the simple melody,
and then said, "I traced an outline of a lighthouse on
the paper taped to the window. Today, the first- and
second graders will color the picture for Art Class.
We'll leave it on the window for a while because seeing
it reminds us to help others. The rest of you may copy
the song's words in your penmanship notebooks."

Every family had listened to the same newscasts
Lena had heard. Every household was numbed by the
news and, if Cornelis' words were true, affected in
inevitable ways. The country was caught up in a storm
of confusion—and while Freek's death was a minor
event in the big picture, for the students at Dutch
Valley School it would be linked forever with the
nation's distresses.

Not only had the students witnessed a tragedy, they
now realized their hero was a mere mortal with feet of
clay. Cornelis was strong enough to push his
automobile off Freek's lifeless body, but powerless to
undo the damage done in the blink of an eye.

At recess, there were no feats of strength, no stretching or twisting of young boys' bodies. First one, and then another boy pulled out the inevitable yo-yo from his pocket and entertained himself with Rock-the-Cradle or Loop-the-Loop.

In the back corner of the schoolyard, Saartje and Elsje played a game of horseshoes. The clang of metal meeting metal made a jarring backdrop to the desultory conversations around the grounds.

Katrien wandered over to Lena where she pushed Liesbeth and Maartje in the swings. "Miss Stryker, when we do penmanship today, I'll write the song like you said to do, but may I also write a note to Wim?"

Noting the girl's somber expression, Lena said gently, "That's a lovely idea; others may wish to do the same. Copying the song can be tomorrow's project."

"Perhaps Mister de Boer could take them all to Wim's house for us. He goes by there, he said . . ." Teacher and student fell silent, each remembering the conversation in which Cornelis had first allowed Freek to ride home with him, since he drove by the Wynkoop farm each morning on his way to town.

"We'll write the notes and find a way to get them to Wim," Lena promised.

The students seemed eager to express their sympathy in some tangible way. Lena distributed note cards, and older students helped the younger ones spell words. Walking around the room, Lena saw a drawing of over-sized blue tears running down ruddy cheeks on a girl who looked a lot like Adda, the artist of that card. Sterre drew a bright yellow dog chasing a stick beneath a rainbow. Mass depicted a tail-wagging dog drinking from the pump. Saartje labored over a poem. Each child seemed to have captured some way of letting let Wim know they shared his loss. Pride swelled Lena's heart as she picked up her own pen:

Dear Wim, Freek was a smart dog. He made us happy. We will all miss him. Thank you for sharing your dog with us.
Love, Miss Stryker

She asked Jaap to make a butcher-paper envelope large enough to hold the students' notes and drawings and, when the paste was dry, added her note, also.

With messages completed, lessons resumed. The various activities created an accompanying hum that blocked out the world. The usual drone of voices in the reading circle and rustle of turning pages and scratching pencils at the desks stopped abruptly when the door opened. Gustave stood in the doorway and met Lena's eye gravely. "I am sorry to interrupt. Lena, may I speak to you in private?"

She felt a chill move through her body that had nothing to do with the autumn breeze blowing a dried leaf into the classroom past Gustave's trousers. "Yes; certainly. Continue your work, children." She moved quickly to the door. Gustave retreated into the entryway; she followed and closed the door behind them. "What is it?" She searched his face for a reason behind this unprecedented midmorning visit. She saw no answers, only a weary man struggling with emotion.

"Frans De Groot is . . . he took his own life."

Lena swayed, the world swirling around her. *Frans? What of Betje and Janneken?*

She heard a sharp cry and wondered how the children inside the classroom could have heard Gustave's low voice, then realized the sound rose from within herself, not from beyond the closed door.

"Surely, there is some mistake."

He shook his head. "No, he hung himself in the barn early yesterday morning. Koenraadt appeared to work, as he and Frans had arranged last week, and he found Betje and Janneken attempting to get Frans down . . ." He closed his eyes briefly. "Sadly, no; it is true—I have just come from their farm."

Lena pressed knuckles against her lips. "*No!*" her spirit cried out, but she blocked any sound's exit.

"He left a note; he'd mortgaged the farm heavily through banks in Dutchville, Le Mars, and Sioux City in order to offset more loans than Betje realized he had taken out; she knew only of one. The recent news scared him when he realized all those loans will likely be called in and he had no way to repay them."

Lena closed her eyes and saw Janneken's graceful movements around the playground as clearly as if the girl was out there. She recalled the first day of school: "*. . . a book every week . . . four-line poems . . . watercolors . . . butterfly collection.*" *What will become of this waiflike child?*

Lena gripped Gustave's forearm to steady herself. "What should I do?" She nodded at the closed door separating them from the students.

"Those with whom I have talked—including several School Board members—asked if I would talk briefly with the students, unless you wish to do so. Afterwards, they thought you should dismiss school for the rest of the day."

She nodded numbly and reached for the doorknob, only to halt and choke out, "I don't trust myself to speak, yet, Gustave, so if you would help me . . . ."

"I will. Be as strong as you are able, but don't be afraid to show your feelings. Would you like me to tell the children, or stand nearby while you do so?"

"You tell them. Thank you, Gustave. The students are already upset . . . Cornelis' ran over Freek with the automobile yesterday, and now this. I know a dead dog is nothing compared to this tragedy, but they are so young . . . so defenseless in the face of life's blows."

"In all that has happened, I forgot about Freek. Cornelis told me of the accident earlier today when we met at the Post Office. He seemed understandably upset." Gustave's sigh came from deep within him. "Well, shall we?" He motioned toward the door.

All eyes followed the path Lena and Gustave took to the space between the teacher's desk and the reading circle.

Lena cleared her throat. "Dominie Ter Hoorn has sad news, children." She walked to the blackboard. Leaning against it, she managed a neutral expression, despite wishing she could sob.

Gustave quickly scanned the room, taking in each frightened expression. "As you know, Janneken is not in school because her father has died." His voice was soothing. "We know it will be hard to concentrate, so we're dismissing school. Let's keep Janneken and her mother in our prayers, and Wim who, like you, is sad about losing Freek yesterday."

How can the children comprehend all that has happened? I am years older, with more life experience than they have had, yet I struggle with such senseless events. Lena jerked, realizing Gustave was silent.

All waited for something from her—but she had nothing to offer. *How can I be numb from the news, but still feel inner pain?* "You are dismissed . . . Yes, Elsje?"

"Will we will have school tomorrow?"

"I imagine so. If there is any change, we'll call everyone." Then she remembered Maartje's birthday. Juxtaposed against everything that was wrong in the world, the plans seemed frivolous and sacrilegious. *Do we cancel?* Originally, she'd hoped to make one little girl's special day a little brighter. Now, she realized every student needed a reprieve, however momentary, from deep sorrow and pervasive confusion.

She hugged each child tightly as they left, acutely aware of the two who were not there—Wim desperately in need of a hug, and Janneken facing so many unanswered questions, a hug was inadequate.

The schoolhouse was eerily still, the playground nearly empty. Lena joined Gustave outside where he stood near the stoop with words of comfort for each departing child. "I feel drained, and can only imagine how you must feel," Lena said.

He looked toward the swings where only Antje and Maartje remained. Lena's heart ached for them. They, of all the students, knew some of what Janneken felt— and were likely reliving their own tragedy. As they walked toward the girls, Antje called out, "Should we walk home, Miss Stryker?"

Gustave replied before Lena could speak, "No, I'll give you a ride home; you may climb in the backseat."

Lena said, "When you get home, your grandmother can call Baumgartner Motors to let your father know you're home."

Gustave turned to Lena and said softly, "Come to town; you should be with people tonight—not alone. Gather what you need; I'll come back for you after I've taken the girls home—and bring you back tomorrow."

Lena nodded gratefully. "I appreciate that, but no need for you to retrace your steps. I can be ready in minutes. If you bank the fire, I'll collect what I need."

"Miss Stryker?" Maartje's soft voice halted Lena's progress; she turned. The girls leaned against the Ford, clutching each other's hands as they had on the threshold the first day of school.

"Yes, dear?"

"Will Janneken go live with her grandparents like Antje and I did when our mother died?"

Lena reeled, mindful of the myriad layers of grief the question revealed. She shot a pleading look for help at Gustave, yet moved quickly to the girls. Kneeling before them, she took their hands in her own. "We don't know what will happen, but

Janneken's mother loves her very much, just like your father loves you; she'll take good care of Janneken."

"Janneken must be very sad." Memories of loss filled Antje's eyes. Tears fell, each etched a tragic story's path along her cheeks.

Janneken's memories will include horrors not even imagined by these two precious young girls. She gulped back tears, knowing she had to be strong. *"Oh, God, why do You allow so much pain?"* Lena gathered them in a tight hug and kissed their heads. "Wait in the car," she said gently. "We'll be out soon."

Lena extinguished the lamps, and put the children's note cards to Wim on top of the box of frosted doughnuts she had made for Maartje's birthday. *I can easily make another batch, and these will make a nice gift for Wim and his family.* After a quick stop in the teacherage, she was ready to close the big door: an odd feeling, since it was not yet lunchtime.

It was a quiet trip to the de Boer farm. The smell of doughnuts filled the automobile until Lena felt she needed to explain. "Maartje, I made doughnuts as a special treat for your birthday, but I am going to give this box to Wim's family. I will make more tonight and we will celebrate your special day one day late."

Maartje's nod set her curls bobbing. "It will be like having two birthdays." She craned her neck to get a better look at the box on Lena's lap. "I'm glad you will give those doughnuts to Wim. Maybe he won't be so sad about Freek if he has a whole box of doughnuts to eat."

Lena smiled. "I'm sure he'll share with his family. Can you imagine how sick he would get if he ate a whole box of doughnuts?"

Antje leaned forward. "When our—" she shot a quick glance at her sister, "I mean, before we came to live here, a lady who lived by us gave us a big cake, and Maartje and I ate too much and we got real sick."

Maartje said firmly, "I don't ever want to taste that kind of cake again! What was it called, Antje?"

"Cocoa-something, but not good like hot chocolate. There were lots of little icky white things all over it."

"Coconut?" Lena shared an amused glance with Gustave who was enjoying the respite from sorrow the conversation offered. *He would love to be able to talk like this with Sanna*, Lena thought. *Sadness plagues the world.*

"That stuff was in the cake and in the frosting." Antje shuddered.

"Tell Wim not to eat too many doughnuts," Maartje said. "Otherwise he'll get sick and then he won't like doughnuts anymore."

Rebecca, having heard their arrival, waited inside the doorway. Gustave conducted a brief conversation with her on the porch while the girls headed for the warm kitchen.

From the front seat of Gustave's Ford, Lena recognized the look of shock on Rebecca's face as companion to the feelings that pressed against her own heart like boulders. The two women locked gazes while Gustave returned to the driver's seat. "We'll stop at Wynkoop's?" he asked.

"Yes, please. It is not just doughnuts; the children wrote cards to Wim. I had planned to ask Cornelis to deliver them in the morning, but it's better if I do it since I have this opportunity. If Wim had been at school today, he'd know about Frans. While you talk to Hilde, I'll tell Wim so he knows what the other children heard. Please tell Hilde what I'm doing."

As expected, Hilde had not yet heard, though Dries was in town and would likely hurry home when he learned of Frans' death. Gustave talked quietly with her in the front hallway while Lena went to see Wim in the kitchen where Hilda had said he was drying dishes.

When the boy saw his teacher, he dropped the dishtowel and ran to fling his arms around her. She hugged him tightly. "Your classmates and I are all very sad about Freek, Wim. They all wrote notes that your mother can read to you later on. And I brought something to let you know how sorry I am that this happened."

Wim's lower lip trembled. "I will miss you, Miss Stryker, but I'm not coming back to school, not ever again. I don't want to see the road where Freek got hit, or the places where Freek and I played."

Lena's mind raced for words of comfort. "That will be true for a while, Wim, but not forever. I promise." *Right; just like I promised he'd always have a companion on the way home?* She opened the box.

"See these doughnuts, Wim? If they were the only doughnuts you ever ate, doughnuts would always remind you of Freek. But I want to tell you something important: Your best memories of him aren't wrapped up inside doughnuts. The best ones are in your heart. When you come back to school, we'll have more doughnuts to celebrate Maartje's birthday. Those doughnuts will remind you of Maartje, not Freek."

Wim frowned. "I don't think so."

"I know it is true," Lena said firmly. "The same is true for when you see the playground. Yes, out there in the grass and dirt is where Freek ran and jumped and chased sticks—but the playground is also where you hit the ball so far that everyone cheered. Remember that day?"

Somber eyes blinked at her. "Uh-huh."

"And the pump, where you taught Freek to drink? That's also where Lucas pumped the handle so fast that water gushed out and splashed all over Jaap's shoe. Remember how everyone laughed really hard at the whooshing noises when he walked?"

Wim nodded and grinned, whispering *"Whoosh!"*

"Sad things can have good parts. The saddest part about Freek is how he died, but there were so many happy parts. Freek helped Liesbeth and Sterre get over being afraid of dogs—that's one good part."

"Yeah; he wasn't nothing to be scared of."

"Remember how Freek jumped into Mister de Boer's car and looked like he was driving it? That made us all laugh, didn't it?"

A smile flickered. "He was a great dog."

"The best, the smartest, the finest dog I have ever known. When you come back to school, you can help us all remember what a great dog Freek was. Your classmates are sad, too."

"They are?"

"They loved Freek. Don't eat too many doughnuts now—share them with your family. When Maartje passes around the box, you can take a doughnut and think 'Happy Birthday, Maartje!' not sad thoughts."

"I'll come back to school, but I don't want to talk about Freek right away," Wim warned.

"That's fine; the others will understand. But now, Wim, I need to explain why I am at your house in the middle of the school day. Dominie Ter Hoorn came out to the school to tell us that Janneken's father died. Everyone feels very sad about Freek, and now we also feel very sad for Janneken and her mother."

Wim looked up in horror. "Did Mister de Boer run over Janneken's father, too?"

"No," Lena said quickly. *Hilde can tell him more, if she wishes.* "Janneken will probably miss several days of school, but eventually, she'll come back. And when she does, she may not want to talk about her father— just like you don't want to talk about Freek. But even when we are sad, we still have to keep on doing the things that need to be done. Do you understand?"

Wim stared at his hands. He pressed his thumb carefully against his middle finger and slid it off. A satisfying *Snap!* rang out. He looked up at Lena. "Janneken taught me how to do this," he said sadly. "Her father taught her how. She's probably going to be very sad every time she snaps her fingers, isn't she?"

"Perhaps. But she might think about how happy you were when she taught you how to do it, too." She let that sink in before saying, "How about if you and I share a doughnut? I'll close my eyes and let you divide it. Then I'll play 'Which hand?' with you."

Wim peered into the box and selected what he deemed was the biggest of the lot. Lena covered her eyes, peeking only when he gasped and giggled and said nervously, "Uh-oh!"

She heard Hilde and Gustave arrive, but kept her eyes covered when Wim called, "Look what happened when I divided a doughnut! Miss Stryker is gonna pick hands!" He shielded what Lena's knew were two disproportionate pieces so his mother could see.

Gustave's hearty laugh rolled over them like a salve. "Well, Wim, let's see which hand she picks!"

Using knowledge she had gained from cheating, Lena pretended to ponder her decision. "Let me think . . . I'm right-handed, so I pick your right hand."

Wim brought his hands around front and giggled at Lena's mock gasp of dismay. "It just happened, Miss Stryker—I tried to break it exactly in half, honest!"

Lena reached for her piece and swallowed it in one gulp. "Good, because this is as much doughnut as I could possibly eat!"

Wim dissolved and sagged against her, giggling even harder as pieces of his larger portion dropped around him like birdseed. Not one adult complained. After all, what's a bit of clean-up compared to a boy who has found a morsel of joy in his troubled world?

Navigating the familiar road back to town, Gustave said, "Hilde will talk with Wim about Frans between now and school tomorrow. She greatly appreciated you telling him, initially."

Lena nodded, and they rode is silence until she said, "Janneken is a kind child—for all her dreaminess, she touches the other students in immeasurable ways. They were stunned the first day of school to hear the de Boer girls' mother had died—and they never knew Juanita. But everyone knew Frans."

"Not to demean Freek's death, but it seems as if God, in His mercy, allowed that to precede Frans' death. Such news is never easy, but in a way, the dog's death prepared them."

"It is almost too much, too soon, though," Lena mused. "The children are confused by their parents' distresses over the stock market, and then Freek, and now Frans. I don't know if I am up to the task of guiding them through all this."

"Your own grief will make you sensitive to their needs. I'm confident the routine of schoolwork and the day-to-day activities will be their haven in a world gone crazy. Especially Janneken, when she returns."

"I heard on the radio about suicides in far-away places, but I never thought such would cross our lives. How sad Frans could see no way out but to take his life and leave a wide swathe of unanswered questions."

"That's a dilemma I face as I prepare the sermon for his funeral," Gustave said grimly.

"When will the service be?"

"Perhaps Sunday afternoon."

"You carry a far heavier load than I do, Gustave."

"Each person's load is of equal weight—different sizes, perhaps, but of equal weight. God shares our burdens, and carries the heavier portion unless we insist we're able to do it alone."

She sensed he was reminding himself of this truth.

Hanna waited on the porch. Her arms stretched first to Lena, then Gustave who followed. "I'm glad you came home, Lena. This is no time to be alone. Gustave, there are notes on the telephone table, but first comes lunch. Your day will only get busier."

Lunch was interrupted several times by calls and knocks on the parsonage door. Each time, Hanna returned Gustave's plate of *hachee* to the warming oven.

The sisters retreated to the comfort of baking. The steady actions of their tasks, and the oven's warmth each time they checked a cake they would deliver to the De Groot home, and the incongruously cheerful splatters of doughnuts frying in the cast-iron pan provided a cocoon around them.

Plans for Maartje's birthday celebration weighed heavily on Lena's mind. "Her first birthday without her mother simply must have pleasant memories," Lena told Hanna as she boxed doughnuts. "But I can just hear Gerolt Hazenbroek ranting about how this is the time when children should learn, not laugh."

"Gerolt could surprise you, Lena," Gustave advised, overhearing their talk as he passed through the kitchen bearing an armload of firewood. "Children are not merely little adults—they don't view things with the same outlook. I say, go ahead with your plans and let me handle Gerolt, if needs be. Like I said, the episodes of today may have depleted his vexation."

A stream of troubled visitors dropped by the parsonage. Frightened voices on the other end of telephone calls asked, "May I speak to the Dominie?" With fears fueling questions the everyday world could not answer, the parsonage became a beacon of hope— a lighthouse for the distressed.

They kept the coffee pot bubbling and the cookie plate filled. "All who come must feel welcomed." Hanna refilled the cream pitcher and checked the sugar bowl before making another trip to the parlor.

Low voices rumbled like night trains, Gustave's never losing its steadiness. When the visitor was a man, he guided him into the parlor. When a wife came along, he called out, "Hanna, please bring coffee," to signal that a woman needed her comfort.

Buggies and automobiles parked beneath trees, or lined the roadside as their passengers waited for the parsonage door to open and close. When one seeker of comfort left, another dark-cloaked figure would move swiftly across the lawn and lift the doorknocker. Each time, Gustave welcomed them with, "Come in," showing none of his weariness as he laid a gentle hand on yet another stooped shoulder.

Lena alternately paced the kitchen floor and made trips to supplement refreshments in the parlor. *What Gustave brings to others and me, I can give to my students: a place of calmness midst life's storms.* Guiltily, she brushed aside nagging thoughts of Cornelis' grief and troubles. Although she knew Juanita's death must seem even more poignant now, Cornelis' attempt to procure her silence with a kiss only magnified the offense of his refusal to make things right.

The sympathy she was unwilling to extend to Cornelis, she lavished on parsonage visitors. Bleak faces and sagging posture revealed churning depths of inner tumult. Guests unknowingly called upon the same phrases the previous visitor had used: ". . . such a senseless tragedy . . ." and ". . . if I'd known, I could have . . ." and "Why would Frans do such a thing?"

Gustave's repeated words rang true each time: ". . . God in His wisdom . . . we are not to blame . . . reach out to others at times like this . . ."

Lena carefully put cups of steaming coffee or rich Dutch cocoa into shaking hands.

Hanna doled out her own handkerchiefs when tears rolled down chalk-white cheeks.

Gustave ended each brief visit or telephone call with a prayer to match each person's needs, always including the same verse from his favorite *Psalmen:* "God is our refuge and strength, a very present help in time of trouble."

About eleven o'clock, while Hanna and Lena washed the last cups and saucers, Gustave came to the kitchen waving a package. "Here is today's Sioux City newspaper, just thrown off the late train. Cornelis brought it by on his way home."

Lena glanced at the clock. *He is just going home?*

Gustave adjusted his eyeglasses, flicked the paper open, raised it, and read aloud:

"Thursday, a record of nearly thirteen million shares were traded. Ticker tape fell behind one-and-a-half hours. Today, a new record of over sixteen million shares was traded, causing the ticker tape to fall behind by over two hours. Following yesterday's thirteen-percent loss, today the market suffered a staggering twelve-percent loss."

He lowered the newspaper and looked at them. "This is not good." Clearing his throat, he continued:

"Top bankers met twice today about the market, first at noon and again this evening. Rumors abound that bankers are selling stocks rather than stabilizing the market. There are no positive remarks about the future, only fears from coast-to-coast.

A report from Seattle, Washington, indicates bedlam in brokerage houses there today as the greatest avalanche of security selling in our country's history was launched on New York exchanges. We can say, unequivocally, the stock market has crashed, leaving many trapped in the invisible, deadly rubble."

Dying coals crackled in the kitchen stove—the only sound, for the moment. Gustave carefully removed his glasses, and absentmindedly wiped them with his handkerchief. When he finally spoke, his voice trembled from exhaustion and grief. "It was mostly townsfolk who came here today."

"I noticed that, too," Hanna said.

"They're concerned, but I worry about the farmers. They must be reminded no situation is so bleak the light of God's love cannot shine into it. Tomorrow morning, Lena, after I take you to school, I'll visit farming families in the congregation. We must not lose another who feels so overwhelmed by life that they see suicide as the only way to escape difficulties."

"At school tomorrow, Gustave, what do I do? Should I stop the children from discussing what they overheard at home from adults, or on the radio? If some parents haven't mentioned the hanging, I don't want the children learning about it at school."

Gustave's chin sank against his chest. He puffed out his cheeks, reminding both women of how wind fills pillowcases on the clothesline. Exhaling with quiet pops, he stared unseeing into space.

Finally, he said, "You know children—they kneel by heating grates or hide behind doors to hear what parents whisper. They hear more than their parents imagine. I doubt there will be many, if any, who do not know about the tragedy."

Hanna said, "Farm children are usually aware that death is a part of life; they've watched their fathers butcher animals, and found dead birds and rabbits in the fields. But Freek's death made it more personal, and now Frans' death may make them afraid their fathers could die suddenly."

"I keep thinking of Antje and Maartje," Lena said. "Gustave, remember how they asked about what will happen to Janneken? To them, death means losing everything familiar."

He nodded. "The brutality surrounding Frans' death will haunt us for years to come. Children are bright, but intelligence and cunning are different from wisdom. That comes from life experiences. Wisdom is required to put tragedies in the right perspective. While you cannot rush your students into wisdom, you can offer comfort and stability to counter fears."

Lena said, "I dread facing Janneken's empty desk."

Hanna offered, "I could come with you to school tomorrow. You've said Janneken is such a help with the younger students, so I could take her place for one day, at least."

"I would love to have your help, but you will be busy enough here. I will be fine—it's the unknown that makes me nervous. And I am no different in that than any other American, right, Gustave?"

"Sad to say, but true. We are a nation made up of states where towns and families are in chaos. But I hope to encourage those whose turmoil is on the personal level to reach out for help. No one should feel alone."

Hanna smiled fondly at her husband. "I hear a sermon in the making. Your congregation will know you speak from your heart and your own experiences."

The God of Hope had sustained Gustave during my dark years of depression.

Gustave grasped Hanna's hand with his left hand and Lena's with his right. "We were never alone. See this?" He raised their joined hands in a triangle hovering inches above the table.

"We must remember: the three of us have God in the center. This . . ." he tightened his grip on each hand, "this is what I want for others: someone reaching back when they are reaching out. It's not that Betje wasn't a good wife to Frans, but sometimes a family needs a Lena."

The telephone rang in the hallway. Motioning for the women to stay seated, Gustave rose to answer it.

It was close to midnight when he finally extinguished the lights and Hanna dried the last dish. "Good night," they called to Lena who was dumping dishwater over the porch railing. Wearily, the Dominie climbed the steps, followed by his equally tired wife.

Hanging dishtowels to dry above the kitchen stove, Lena heard their voices fade, the sound replaced by the creaks and moans of an old house as the Ter Hoorns moved around their bedroom.

Lena pulled out a kitchen chair and sank into the room's silence as if it were a featherbed. Without warning, a kaleidoscope of out-of-sequence events and sensations blew over her mind's surface like fish leaping from the shimmering Floyd River:

Frans up to bat at the September picnic.
Cornelis standing in the doorway the first day of school.
Freek lying beneath the tire.
Brigetta bursting from the closet.

That infernal honking horn!

Cornelis' lips brushing against hers.

Faceless newscasters with stock and bond reports.

Antje and Maartje's laughter over kittens.

Betje and Janneken.

Cornelis' arms pinning her against his chest.

Wim's wails of grief.

She thrust back her chair, gripping the table's edge. Gustave's words echoed in her mind: *"God is our refuge and strength—a very present help in time of trouble."*

It was not just the Word of the Lord to a farmer dreading bankruptcy, or to a wife fearing her husband's mental collapse, or to a businessman at risk of losing his livelihood. It was God's voice of comfort, renewing His promise to Lena Stryker's troubled spirit.

Although the fourteen words did not promise everything would work out fine, they were words of unshakeable certainty from the One who knows the beginning and the end.

❋ ❋ ❋

Wednesday, October 30 ♦ When Lena placed the box of doughnuts on the Ford's backseat, the moon still shared the firmament with a spray of morning stars. She climbed in next and Gustave, carefully holding a canvas bag.

"What's in there?" he asked.

"Milk; for cocoa. After seeing how much all our visitors appreciated our limited hospitality yesterday, I thought the children deserve the same. Something different to help them ease into the day."

They were content to let sounds from the engine and small rocks hitting the undercarriage take the place of conversation for the short trip. "Do you want to come to town again tonight, Lena?" Gustave asked as they approached the schoolhouse. "I can stop on my way home from farm visits to get you."

"I would welcome you, if for no other reason than to let you know how the day went. But I cannot say at this point what I will decide to do. I am sorry to be so vague. If you are able to come, fine—but, if you find yourself far away at the end of the day, don't make a special trip back for me."

Gustave insisted on rebuilding a fire in the stove for Lena. Briskly rubbing his hands in front of the first flames, he turned to find her staring at Janneken's desk. "You will find God's strength when you need it, Lena. When the time comes, you'll know what to say."

"Not that I doubt you, but I hope you're right. I'll think of you throughout the day. Godspeed as you go about your difficult task. Where will you go first?"

"Den Hartog's farm, then work my way toward town. I'm sure the menfolk are already in the barns, so I will not need to disturb the families. I hope to see you later today, Lena. God be with you."

Lena watched the Ford's headlights mark the road Gustave traveled to the farm where a large hardworking family lived. When she could no longer see the car's lights, she stepped back into the entryway.

Despite inner shivers, she stood statue-still. "For all my words to Wim about memories of places, I wonder how long it will be before I forget Cornelis' kiss in this place?" She shuddered and quickly entered the school.

It was just now about the time she usually would awaken, so she used the extra time to catch up on paperwork. Stretching, after a good hour's concentrated work, she remembered she had refused Hanna's offer of breakfast, so made a cup of tea and alternated sips of it with bites of bread, rotating in front of the stove to warm herself, front and back.

The sun crept across fields like a robber stealing a dark night and replacing it with a golden day. Lena opened Janneken's desk and looked at all that filled the girl's days: pencils, a tablet, a ruler, scissors, a half-done book report, a button, three links of a colored-paper chain. Her place in the McGuffey Reader was marked with a crocheted bookmark Lena had awarded her for a job well done when she had helped the twins understand nouns and pronouns.

Lena blinked back tears. *Janneken is music, dance, poetry, butterflies, kindness, and laughter. She embodies what I want for each of my students—I must help keep the music and poetry alive in her soul, though they may be dormant for a while.*

Another day was beginning—a gray day, as if heaven, too, were sad. Lena heard Midnight's steady hoof beats bringing the twins to school and had a moment of panic. *I wish I had not been so hasty to turn down Hanna's offer to spend the day with me!* she thought as she welcomed the boys.

But help arrived in unexpected form. Raimund interrupted his chatter to report from the window, "Wim's here! His mother's driving their buggy and there's something big in the back that's covered up. Let's go see, Bartel!" They raced to the cloakroom for their coats and then outside, buttoning as they ran.

Lena looked up when the door flew open minutes later and smiled at Hilde who followed close behind the twins. "Wim has brought a surprise!" Hilde said. "Raimund and Bartel will help carry it in, but I'd like you to come decide if you even want it."

"Hurry, Miss Stryker!" Bartel said. "It's huge!"

Lena quickly donned her cape and followed Hilde.

Wim looked from the twins circling the buggy to Lena. "Come and look, Miss Stryker! It's a box with a cover for our story rugs so they won't look messy in the entry. It's so heavy, we had to came in the buggy."

The twins strutted, chanting, "We're as strong as Charles Atlas! Nothing's too heavy for us!"

Lena marveled at a mother's wisdom for how to make a first trip without his dog bearable for her young son. "What a good idea, Wim! And what a sturdy box it is."

The women helped slide the box to the back of the buggy, but the twins insisted on carrying it inside. Wim ran ahead to open the door. "If you don't want it . . ." Hilde murmured as they followed closely.

"Of course, I want it; thank you for thinking of it." The look they shared spoke volumes. "How's Wim doing?"

"Better than I expected. My, how he loved that dog. Thank you for stopping by—I don't know what you said, but it helped."

"What all does he know about Frans?"

Hilde shook her head sadly. "Only what you told him: that he died. We didn't know how to explain it."

"Just to warn you, it is bound to come out at school." Lena halted, one hand on the doorknob. In the entryway, the boys talked excitedly as they stacked rugs in the box. "I won't bring it up, but I make no promises as to what the other children might say."

"I know," Hilde sighed. "Dries and I talked long into the night about that. I expect he'll come home with questions. Do you mind if I stay for the first hour to see how Wim does? If needs be, I could take him home with me."

"That's wonderful, Hilde. I welcome your company and help. I made hot chocolate this morning. If you serve it, it frees me. It's a cold morning, and . . ."

". . . and you have a warm heart," Hilde finished Lena's intended sentiment with her own words.

Hilde wasn't the only mother who came to school. Helena Beekman appeared, holding Liesbeth's hand; a somber Lucas followed close behind. When both children were in the cloakroom, Helena told Lena, "Liesbeth had nightmares, and Lucas is strangely silent. I hope you don't mind that I came today; I will be glad to help in any way I can."

"Thank you; please stay as long as you like," Lena said fervently. "Perhaps you could copy a geography test for the third graders? You can use Janneken's desk." *How good God is to find the perfect way to fill that empty desk today with a mother.*

Hans crossed the threshold behind his two granddaughters. "Cornelis had to go to work early, so I brought the girls. I'll bring in firewood before I leave."

Antje and Maartje slowed their pace when they noticed the two mothers. They looked to Lena for an explanation.

"Thank you, Hans, and good morning, girls. We have special visitors today. You know Wim's mother from Sunday School, and this is Liesbeth and Lucas' mother. They are going to help us today. In fact, Mrs. Wynkoop is getting ready to pour hot chocolate for everyone. Won't that taste good this morning?"

The firewood supply was already ample, but Hans' offer had little to do with necessity. It was his way of encouraging Lena and comforting students—not just the de Boer girls. He returned carrying an armload, then picked up the extra water bucket behind the stove and filled it at the pump. Finally, he waved to the women, hugged his granddaughters, patted Wim's shoulder, and left.

Despite the added interest of extra adults in the room, opening exercises were conducted with duller voices and less enthusiasm than Lena could remember. "We are all sad about Janneken losing her father. And we all miss Freek, don't we? The most important things we can do today and every day is do our lessons diligently, play hard at recess, and giggle if something strikes us funny. It will be good to sing and memorize and recite and learn."

"What if we're too sad to learn stuff?" Wim asked.

"Sometimes, we'll be sad and afraid; sometimes, we will laugh or tease. When we do that, it won't mean we've forgotten about what made us sad. I'm sad, too, but if we remember to treat each other kindly, we will discover the parts inside that hurt will begin to heal." It was a long speech—underscored by Wim voicing the question on the others' minds—but the students absorbed every word. Lessons began.

Hilde gathered cups and filled the teakettle. Wim watched his mother begin familiar tasks of washing dishes, then found his place in the McGuffey reader. Like Wim, Lena felt a burden lift. Comfort gained from having his mother close by was immeasurable to Wim and solace to his teacher. Hilde stayed until recess; Wim waved from the swings.

Lena listened to Antje and Sterre challenging each other with flash cards of new words. "Kind!" Antje's eyes sparkled when Sterre nodded and flipped the next card. "Kindly! And the next one is kindness!"

"You're supposed to wait 'til I show you the card," Sterre told her classmate crossly.

"But I know what it is," Antje protested, "so if I say it before you change the card, we'll get done faster!"

Sterre sighed dramatically, looking to Lena to settle the skirmish. When Sterre showed the next card and Antje snapped, "Kindness. Told you so!"

Lena flinched as her own advice to the students boomeranged back in rebuke for her treatment of Cornelis: *"treat each other kindly."*

His face scored her mind. *Kindness from me without repentance on his part would only make him believe I'm releasing him from his responsibility to set things right. I am fully within my rights to withhold kindness.* It sounded righteous, but didn't sit easily on her conscience.

Close to six o'clock, Gustave stopped by, as promised, but Lena elected to stay at school. Sensing how tired Gustave was, and hearing a succinct report on his journeys around the county, Lena gave him the empty milk bottles she had carried on her lap earlier that day, and sent him home to his waiting wife.

"It seems years since we rode through the gate this morning, Gustave," she said, clutching the shawl, which she'd grabbed to wear around her head and shoulders while she lingered outside to see him off.

"That it does." He gave way to a yawn. "Frans' funeral will be at three o'clock, Sunday. His sister and family arrived today, and Betje's brothers, their wives and children will come tonight. Visitation is at the house all day tomorrow, Saturday and Sunday until the service. If you need anything, send word with a parent tomorrow morning and ask them to call us."

"I'll be fine. Hanna and I can go see Betje and Janneken on Saturday. Please give these notes from the students to Janneken when you see her."

"I'll go there again in the morning. Neighbors are rallying 'round them, bringing in food and taking care of chores. Several men cleaned the barn before the extended family arrived; it was a gruesome task," Gustave said bleakly.

"Do you know, yet, when the funeral will be?"

"Betje wants only a graveside service; the date is not yet set."

"It seems callous to worry about such things now, but what's the news of the stock market?" Lena called out, before Gustave started the engine.

"I've heard only scattered bits and pieces throughout the day, but it's not good." With that dismal, but expected response, he drove away.

✷ ✷ ✷

Thursday, October 31 ✦ Hoots of laughter made Lena and the already gathered students look down the road. Coming from the opposite direction than their farm, the twins appeared on Midnight with raucous shouts that soon became recognizable words. "Look, everybody! We have six legs!"

To be sure, three legs were visible against Midnight's broad right side. "Raimund has both legs on one side. He's riding like a girl!" Lucas scoffed loudly as the horse turned into the schoolyard.

"Uh-uh!" protested Raimund, who wouldn't stand for being insulted. "Turn Midnight around, Bartel!" His twin brought the horse full circle to reveal three legs on the left side. The blanket usually thrown over Midnight while he grazed on wintry days was bunched between them, pushing Bartel closer to the steed's proud head and Raimund back toward the flicking tail.

Suddenly, the twins shouted in unison, "Now!" and both leaned away from the blanket.

The shapeless form moved, and a familiar head appeared.

"Wim!" Lena exclaimed as the boy's jubilant laughter rang out. She hurried to help him dismount.

"The twins came to get me! I wasn't scared, or nothing! We decided to play a trick on everyone. Did we fool you? Huh, did we?"

"You surely did!" Lena slapped Midnight's rump. Raimund waved his hat like a victory flag as horse and the two remaining riders rounded the schoolhouse to secure the horse where he would spend the day.

Lena listened to Wim's excited report, "They don't even live by me so, boy-oh-boy, I was surprised to see them waiting for me at the section corner!" She wondered how the usually self-involved twins had conceived of such a perfect idea.

Yesterday, Hilde's visit to school had offered comfort, but today's adventure truly helped Wim resume life without his dog. The twins' actions accomplished what she promised Wim could happen: happy memories built on the foundation of sad ones.

During noon recess, the students stopped their play and stared up the road. Like a herd of sheep, they moved along the fence following a black automobile they did not recognize. Lena waved at the driver and hurried to the driveway. A low hum moved through the children's ranks.

Lena called, "Hello, Mister Rankin!" and quickly sought out Saartje and Elsje, "You girls are in charge of the playground while I help our visitor. Back to your play, children, until I blow the whistle."

Obedience battled curiosity over the man in black pants, black coat with long tails and a bowler hat clamped on his head as if hoping to tame his wild shock of white hair. Games resumed, but there was a subtle shift of activities. Lena laughed outright when she caught a glimpse of the twins climbing a tree in hopes of seeing above the windows' curtains.

When Mister Rankin had brought in the last of his well-draped and secretively boxed supplies, Lena told him, "I'm so glad you were willing to come today. In light of what's going on in our country, it may seem frivolous to some to put on a show simply for pleasure."

The man shook his head vehemently as he took off his coat. "No! Children need to know hard times don't mean that good times must end."

He whistled tunelessly, setting up a folding table and covering it with a snowy white cloth, turning his back on Lena several times to fiddle with the billowy sleeves of his white shirt.

Myriad tools of Mister Rankin's trade piqued Lena's interest and she knew the children would thoroughly enjoy the next hour with the grandfatherly man. He removed a silver cloth with royal purple tassels from a suitcase, flicked it open to cover the table and its contents, and then lifted one corner to adjust a few items beneath the table.

"All's ready! Let the children in!"

Even before Lena's first blast on the whistle, the students came running because Maas (the self-appointed lookout) had called out, "Okay! The door's open!"

They filed in, all eyes on Mister Rankin who stood behind the table with its mysterious lumps and bumps. Bowing gallantly, the man peered out from beneath bushy eyebrows and said in a rumbling voice, "Hello, children! My name is Mister Rankin. Since this is a school day, we will do arithmetic problems for several hours. Is that all right with everyone?"

"No!" several students dared to respond.

"No? I thought children love arithmetic! Most bewildering!"

From the mysteriously draped table came the echo, "Most bewildering!"

Mister Rankin jumped two feet off the ground, landing lightly on his feet. Several children giggled. His hands were busy in his pockets. Out came three scarves. "How many scarves do I hold?"

He waved a red one. Answers rang out: "One!" A yellow one: "Two!" A blue one: "Three!"

"One, two, three," the echo said. Mister Rankin jumped again; his hat flew off. More children laughed outright as he glared at the draped table.

By now, the children were on the edges of their seats. Scarves disappeared, then reappeared. Mister

Rankin performed amazing jumps. One such leap sent all sorts of items bouncing out of his pocket when he landed: a comb, nails and screws, a spoon, a stubby pencil, a pretty stone.

As students scrambled to retrieve everything, he fussed while returning items one-by-one to his pocket, "I had a gold coin in my pocket. Does anyone see it?"

No gold coin was found. Jaap was drafted to check the pocket again, but found only a feather. "Where'd all that other stuff go?" he demanded.

"Most bewildering!" the children chanted. This time, the echo laughed.

Mister Rankin said, "Let's review what happened: I jumped in the air, everything flew out of my pocket, and we searched high and low—but no gold coin. It must still be in my pocket."

Jaap agreed to check again, but quickly pulled back, exclaiming, "Something's alive in there!"

Mister Rankin said, "Alive, you say?" He reached in and brought out a parrot. "Well, howdy-do to you, my feathered friend! How do you explain being in my pocket?"

Perched on Mister Rankin's index finger, the colorful bird stared intently around the room, then tilted his head and said, "Most bewildering!"

"My-oh-my, what have we here?" the magician asked, plucking at two brightly colored bands wound around the bird's legs.

"It's the scarves!" Katrien gasped.

"Young lady, may I ask you to see if this is true? If so, it would explain how a shivering parrot from the tropics of South America would not freeze to death on a chilly day in Iowa!" Katrien gingerly removed the yellow scarf that was wrapped around one foot, the blue scarf from the other. "But where's the red one?"

The parrot looked at Katrien, pivoted on his finger-perch, stuck his beak into the breast pocket of Mister Rankin's jacket and pulled out the red scarf. "One, two, three!" He flapped his wings excitedly as the red scarf floated to the floor.

"All scarves are accounted for, but we must find my coin!" Mister Rankin called for a yardstick and instructed Maas and Lucas to measure precisely three feet from the right front leg of the table. "Now, tap the cane on that exact spot three times." Lucas did so.

"Come in!" the parrot said.

Though all the children laughed, Wim's giggle lingered like an angel's song in Lena's ears.

Sterre and Antje correctly identified the disguised object on the table as a birdcage. Mister Rankin moved the parrot into the cage and covered it with the cloth again. "Help! Rescue me! It's dark in here!" the bird protested, much to the children's glee.

"Oh, hush!" Mister Rankin tapped the birdcage three times.

"Come in!" the parrot said.

The children's laughter surged, delighting Lena.

"Help! Most bewildering! One-two-three! It's dark in here!"

"Oh, forevermore," Mister Rankin sighed. "Young lady," he motioned to Giertje. "Will you please uncover the cage so we can continue our search for my gold coin without this racket?"

Lifting the cloth with one hand, Giertje gasped, "The bird is gone! But he left a feather!"

Mister Rankin paced and moaned, "Oh, woe is me! My gold coin is gone, and now my bird is missing, too!" He moved around the room, looking into, behind, and under anything he came to, all the time muttering, "Most bewildering!"

This time, no echo. The room was in an uproar as students suggested places to search. Mister Rankin added to the mayhem with his barking laugh and fussing over lost coins, birds, and disappearing scarves.

From her unobtrusive post at the back of the room, Lena watched the children behaving like children should. Gone, for the moment, were burdens too heavy for them to carry. Each child was stockpiling memories of something grand, mysterious, and exciting—even while the world outside their classroom struggled with reality.

If only Janneken could be part of this, Lena thought sadly.

Surrounded by sounds of delighted voices, Mister Rankin finally found the parrot sitting sedately on Lena's chair, where he had slyly placed the bird while passing by the desk. Scolding and fussing, Mister Rankin returned the parrot to its cage and continued to search for the coin.

He found pennies behind four children's ears, but then exclaimed, "I know what has happened! That pesky bird has taken my gold coin. But how will I ever learn where he has hidden it?"

Several children had ideas—like, letting the bird out the cage in hopes he'd led them to the hiding place—to which Mister Rankin protested, "If I set the bird free, I may lose both bird and coin. Hmm." He halted beside Maartje's desk and tapped his finger against his chin. "Perhaps if someone had something very special happen recently, we could trick the parrot to give her the gold coin for a present. But who could do that?"

Wide-eyed, Maartje gasped, "It was my birthday!"

"You don't say? What a perfect special event!" Mister Rankin guided Maartje to the table where he introduced her to the parrot as ". . . the birthday girl."

Maartje stared at the bird; it studied her with equal concentration. She shuddered. "I'm glad this isn't a chicken. I'm scared of them; they fly in my face!"

"He's locked securely in the cage," Mister Rankin assured her. "Quickly now: Ask the parrot where the coin is. If he tells you, you'll receive one of the scarves as your reward for helping me."

Closing her eyes as if preparing to make a wish, Maartje shivered excitedly and begged, "Please, pretty bird, where is the gold coin?"

The parrot lifted his left wing and stuck his head beneath it. When he repeated this with the right wing, he came out with the gold coin in his beak. He dropped the coin between the cage's bars and into Maartje's outstretched hand. "Happy birthday!"

"How did you know today is my birthday?" she demanded.

"Most bewildering!" the parrot replied.

Maartje chose the red scarf and each student received a colorful feather, which Mister Rankin assured them "the parrot will never miss." Everyone, including the magician and his parrot, enjoyed Maartje's birthday doughnuts.

Under ordinary circumstances, Lena would have wearied of hearing "Most bewildering!" for the rest of the afternoon, but these were hardly ordinary circumstances.

Wim was first in line at the door after dismissal. "Whenever I eat doughnuts from now on, Miss Stryker, I have three things to remember: Freek, Maartje's birthday, and Mister Rankin."

"All fine things," she said with a smile and tugged his cap a little lower over his ears. "Don't forget, everyone," she said a little louder before opening the door, "there is no school tomorrow because of harvest. Be careful when you're helping your parents!"

"Wait up, Wim," Bartel called. "We'll give you a ride back to the section corner, if you'd like."

"Okay, but I don't want that stinky blanket over my head!" Wim warned, running after the twins.

❋ ❋ ❋

Monday, November 4 ♦ Janneken returned to school the following week. It was a brisk morning but the children seemed content to remain outside. Lena moved among them, filling her lungs with clean crisp air and lingering close to Janneken.

None of the children seemed to know what to say to their classmate, but most greeted her, if only to mumble something unintelligible.

Only Wim hung back, finally coming close enough to bump her arm. "Hey, Janneken." He pulled off his mitten. "Got sumpthin to show ya. I practiced every day. Look!" Pressing his thumb and middle finger together, he snapped them in a perfect *Swuppp!* "I can do it with both hands," he boasted, and proved it. His mittens fell unheeded to the ground.

Janneken tucked her mittens into her armpits. Boy and girl looked at each other, positioned their fingers and snapped a four-beat impromptu concert. Wim grinned hesitatingly; Janneken smiled faintly. In that moment, a bond both unique and mutual formed.

"Can you teach me how to whistle without spitting?" Wim asked hopefully.

She shrugged. "I guess so. After school today, I'll go with you as far as the section corner and we can practice while we walk."

Wim nodded. "I could meet you there tomorrow morning, too," he suggested hesitantly.

"Sure," she repeated. Without another word, both turned away.

A snap of a finger, a spit-free whistle, companions for a lonely trip. Lena raised the whistle to her lips. *Such is the stuff and substance of comfort.*

The continuing sounds of late harvest in nearby fields droned on like a distant beehive. Inside the schoolroom, Lena's students divided fractions, or practiced Palmer-method writing, or learned about clouds, or conjugated verbs.

Outside for morning recess, each student visibly inhaled heady aromas of dark and pungent loamy soil. Back inside, dance without music began. As if choreographed to do so, they moved easily from games to classes, gliding from the reading circle to the globe, from the blackboard to the bookshelf, and from desk to desk with changing partners.

For everyone at Dutch Valley School, life seemed about as good as anyone could expect.

✸ ✸ ✸

Tuesday, November 12 ◆ The morning passed quickly. "Miss Stryker?" Giertje spoke in a trembling whisper as the children collected their lunches from the cloakroom and prepared to eat them at their desks. "I'm, uh, too warm in here. May I please eat my lunch in the cloakroom? It's cooler there."

Lena automatically touched Giertje's forehead. "You don't feel warm. Do you think you might be getting sick?"

"Oh, no!" the girl said quickly. "I'm just too warm. Please?" she pleaded. "I won't leave a mess. I'll come right back to my desk as soon as I finish my lunch."

Giertje was clearly lying, though Lena could not imagine why. She granted permission for the strange request. "Get a rug from Wim's box in the entryway, or take a chair from the reading circle. It's much too cold for you to sit on the floor."

The girl nodded and heaved a sigh Lena could only interpret as relief. Lena opened her own lunch.

Then she remembered the penny missing from Liesbeth's pocket. *Oh dear; I hope Giertje has no such intentions.* Suddenly, she no longer felt hungry and set aside her own lunch.

Raimund said, "Look, everyone. I'm a chipmunk!" and stuffed half of a hard-boiled egg into each cheek. The students' howls of laughter covered Lena's purposeful footsteps.

She paused outside the cloakroom, her heart beating erratically. *I don't like spying on my students, but I also don't like if my students engage in activities that require me to spy*, she thought grimly.

Ducking her head into the cloakroom, she asked lightly, "Are you freezing in here?"

Seated on a chair she had pushed up against the wall (*Opposite the coats,* Lena noted) Giertje quickly stuffed something into her mouth. Like Raimund, she, too, resembled a chipmunk—but without his appreciative audience. Wild-eyed, she bent over the remainder of her lunch on her lap and pulled up the hem of her dress to form a protective bowl.

It was an absurd moment: a panicky student facing a bewildered teacher. Neither knew what to do. Time stalled in Dutch Valley School's cloakroom.

Unable to speak around her mouthful, Giertje tried to chew enough to swallow, but it was a futile effort.

She was clearly stymied, and Lena was even more baffled.

"What's going on, Giertje?" Lena tried to infuse kindness into the inquiry, but it still sounded abrupt.

Something went down Giertje's throat the wrong way, making her cough. She tried to cover her mouth, but one hand was not adequate to hold her shirt.

Speechless, Lena stared as a biscuit rolled from the girl's lap. A sheet of waxed paper floated to the floor.

Giertje gave in to despair; her shoulders heaved. A frantic cry erupted, spewing the mouthful she had tried to conceal.

Lena looked to where one biscuit lay surrounded by the debris of another half-chewed plain baking powder biscuit: the sum total of Giertje's lunch.

The girl slid to the floor, grabbed blindly, gathering and stuffing the dregs of lunch back into her pail.

Lena knelt beside the girl. "Please tell me what's wrong, Giertje. Maybe I can help."

She expected a report of a mother feeling poorly, a distinct possibility since Lena knew Sytje's third child would arrive before spring. *Or maybe Giertje's brother Jeroen is in some sort of trouble in high school . . . ?*

"Please don't tell anyone," Giertje pleaded.

Startled, Lena exclaimed, "About spitting out your lunch? Of course not! It was an accident."

"No; about this." Giertje pointed to the bucket now containing only a dry biscuit and a handful of crumbs. She busily brushed the remaining crumbs onto the waxed paper.

Lena stared at the bucket and gripped the empty chair to steady herself. *No!* She did not want to further embarrass the girl, and certainly did not want to pry, but something must be said or her silence could be misconstrued.

She said the first thing that came to her mind, hoping against hope it would not offend. "I truly love a baking powder biscuit." Licking her lips, as if tasting such a treasure, she added, "Mmm-mmm-*mmm!*"

Giertje looked up, astonished. "You do?"

"I do, but I have no way of making them here at the schoolhouse. Seeing yours makes me very hungry for one! Well, let's get the broom and dustpan; you can sweep the cloakroom today."

All afternoon, Lena conducted the usual lessons with one distinct difference. She now wondered what clues she might have missed in each student. She feared Giertje's shame in having only two dry biscuits to tide her over may not be the only such occurrence.

Daily radio broadcasts told of businesses and farmers threatened with foreclosure. Newspapers carried somber stories of declining fortunes. But somehow, she'd believed frugal and thrifty Dutchmen were immune. *Apparently not. Oh, how naïve I am.*

That evening, she pondered how to help without adding to Giertje's embarrassment. She wished she could deliver a basket from her own amply supplied larder to the Ten Broek home. *Maybe on the pretense of Sytje's pregnancy? But still, that would not be an easy thing to do without wounding their already bruised pride even more.*

❋ ❋ ❋

Wednesday, November 13 ◆ The next day, Lena and Giertje each privately dreaded lunch as much as the others anticipated it. When the clock struck twelve Lena still hadn't determined what to do.

One thing was certain. She wouldn't allow a little girl to retreat to the cloakroom every day for the unforeseeable future.

Winging it, she said dramatically, "I have a craving for a baking powder biscuit that won't quit! If anyone in this room has one, I'd gladly trade a cookie for it."

Giertje's eyes popped open. Slowly, she raised her hand, lowered it, and raised it again. "Uh . . . I do, Miss Stryker."

Lena exclaimed delightedly, "I know a teacher is not supposed to have favorites, but Giertje Ten Broek, I believe I will make an exception today—at least until I've devoured every crumb of your wonderful biscuit!"

"Man-oh-man," Bartel moaned. "I wish our mom had put baking powder biscuits in our lunch. Now Giertje gets one of Miss Stryker's cookies!"

Suddenly, Giertje's treasure-trove of two biscuits was the envy of the other students—none of whom, thankfully, noticed when nothing else emerged from the girl's lunch bucket. Lena brought a knife and butter from the teacherage and, chatting merrily to divert attention, sliced open and buttered both biscuits before exchanging a cookie for one. Giertje ate her generously buttered biscuit in silence, and savored every morsel of an oatmeal-raisin cookie.

Lena started paying attention to the student lunches that day and, noting that, while none was as obviously dismal a situation as evidenced in Giertje's bucket, there were subtle changes. *I simply must do something—and without delay.*

"May I have your attention, please?" Her voice halted the chatter. "Tomorrow, we will do something different and fun for lunch! I discovered I have a surplus of vegetables and they are getting overripe because I didn't store them properly."

Seeing confused expressions, she crossed her fingers behind her back against that fib. "What you may each bring is a bowl and a spoon—nothing else. I'll make a big pot of soup to use my vegetables and I would love to share it with you. So, don't bring a packed lunch—just dishes with which to eat soup!"

She thought of the loaded pantry shelves at the parsonage, an entire wall of canned meats, vegetables, and fruits. Sometimes it was more than would be used over an entire winter before the next year's garden began producing daily bounty.

Was Sytje Ten Broek unable to garden this summer because of her pregnancy? It was one more mystery Lena did not understand in a world gone awry.

✽ ✽ ✽

Thursday, November 14 ◆ After opening exercises, Lena lined up potatoes, carrots and onions—thankful no one noticed that they were hardly in withering condition. She provided sharp knives, a cutting board, pints of string beans and peas, and packets of herbs.

Preparing the ingredients for lunch became a lesson in measurements as she directed the younger ones to record precisely how much the older ones cut and diced.

"If this turns out to be the best soup we've ever tasted, we'll have a recipe!" she announced cheerfully.

Having thoroughly cleaned her largest bucket the night before, Lena sent Lucas and Jaap out to fill it at the pump. They emptied it into the water cooler from which they would measure water for the recipe. The first item put into the bucket was four pints of canned chicken, which Elsje and Saartje had chopped into pieces. Seasoned with herbs, it simmered until morning recess—by then, everyone was salivating.

After recess, the remaining ingredients were added. "Our soup needs color. I know just the thing—stewed tomatoes!" Lena said and produced a jar.

Lena taste-tested the soup at noon and pronounced, "Lunchtime!" No one argued when she brought out a loaf of oatmeal bread and assigned Janneken to carefully divide it into sixteen chunks.

"Don't worry about slices," she advised. "Just make chunks so we don't end up with only crumbs."

Out from pails and buckets and Sterre's fancy basket came soup bowls and spoons. Lena ladled soup into waiting bowls and then distributed bread chunks all around, skipping herself without comment.

"This is the best soup I have ever tasted," Adda said fervently. Agreement swelled to the accompaniment of spoons clicking against bowls. Lena poured hot water into her dishpan and cut it with enough cold to prevent burns, added soap flakes and then had the students line up to wash, rinse and dry their bowls and spoons before packing them away.

"That was really good soup, Miss Stryker," Giertje said at the door that afternoon.

"I thought so, too." Watching the girl walk way, into lengthening shadows, Lena vowed silently, *"Somehow, some way, I am going to make sure you have more than baking powder biscuits, my dear."*

Since the soup had depleted Lena's stockpile of vegetables for the week, and cut into her supply of canned goods, she sat down to a meager supper of cheese, crackers, and applesauce. But her heart was lighter than it had been since she found Giertje in the cloakroom.

The next day, Lena was still undecided as to how to feed a child without drawing undue attention to her. *I hate to think of Giertje going home hungry with Saturday and Sunday looming ahead—and who knows how little food in the house.*

Morose over her inability to solve the problem, Lena took her seat in the center of the reading circle while the third graders gathered around her and opened their history books.

Giertje read first. "Johnny Appleseed traveled the American wilderness planting apple seeds . . ."

"Stop!" Lena laughed at the astonishment in her students' faces. "No, you've done nothing wrong, Giertje; I just had an idea."

She nearly tripped over her own *klompen* in her haste to retrieve four apples from the teacherage.

Back at the reading circle, she distributed them, saying merrily, "We cannot read about Johnny Appleseed without enjoying an apple! You eat, and I'll tell you more about the man than is covered in your history book. By the time your apples are gone, you'll be even more interested in the story we're about to read. Johnny Appleseed's real name was John Chapman; he was born in Massachusetts . . ."

Third graders chomped on apples from the parsonage tree while Lena chatted. When they were ready to toss the cores, they first counted and separated the seeds. "If we planted these, would we get apple trees?" Maas asked.

"We would, but it would take a long time. For now, we'll save the seeds and research how to plant them— and decide where to do so."

Giertje resumed reading. "Johnny Appleseed dreamed of a land where apple trees blossomed everywhere and where no one was hungry. A kind and gentle man, he slept outdoors and walked barefoot around the country planting apple seeds everywhere he went . . ."

At the lesson's end, Lena's eyes followed Giertje back to her seat. *One day down; one day in which I was able to supplement one student's meager lunch . . . but I cannot imagine how she will handle noon recess today.*

When noon arrived, the answer to Lena's troubling question came from, of all things, Sterre's complaint.

"I just got to the best part of the story! Why didn't lunch time come when I wanted to quit studying geography?"

Lena could have hugged Sterre. "Why, I do believe we can help you with one part of your problem, Sterre! Listen, everyone: Today for lunch, you can each get a rug from Wim's special box and put it anyplace you would like to sit. Then, get your lunches and the storybook you've been reading and enjoy a reading lunch! Sit with friends, or find a corner by yourself if you do not want to be disturbed."

Giertje planted her rug in the front beneath the flag, and sat down with her lunch bucket and a well-worn copy of "Honey Bunch: Just a Little Girl," which girls had loved ever since the series began in 1923. With the book balanced on her upraised knees, no one could see what went into her mouth.

Elsje seemed more interested in what the younger girl was reading than what was in Giertje's lunch. "That's a good book! And if you like it, I have two more like it at home I'll loan you."

Within minutes, everyone had settled in for a half-hour of time to read without quizzes or recitations expected—and it was a half-hour of privacy for a young girl who, once again, had only biscuits for lunch.

When school was dismissed that day, several other parents beside Cornelis arrived to collect their children. Ruud Van der Voort and Teunis Vande Veer greeted each other and then talked with Cornelis while Sterre, the twins and Antje and Maartje donned coats.

Before Teunis headed out to hitch Midnight to the buggy along with the younger restless horse that had brought him to the school, he slowed in the doorway. "I'll send one of the boys in with a package from Mirjam that I forgot it in the buggy, Lena."

"Glad Teunis mentioned that." Ruud brought out a potato and onion from his pockets. "Here, Lena; Geesje sent these to you. We didn't know what you were up to, telling the children to only bring bowls and spoons yesterday. But last night when Sterre told us about the soup, Geesje figured your larder could use replenishing."

"Please thank your wife for me, Ruud. Making soup was a way to have arithmetic be fun—and it gave us a hot meal on a chilly day." She put the potatoes on her desk, very glad Giertje had already left for the day.

Despite conversations with fathers and departing students, Lena was keenly aware of Cornelis. His presence filled her senses. Her cheeks recalled the rasp of his roughened tweed overcoat. His laugh played in her mind like a song she could not silence. The scent of his tobacco, when he passed her desk, took up residence in her nostrils. She drank from the dipper and tasted lips that lied, accused, denied, and did battle with her strongly held opinions and beliefs.

"The temperature's dropping," Cornelis said, making small talk with other fathers. "Wouldn't be surprised but what we get a storm out of this."

"How will that automobile of yours manage when the snow is up to the running boards?" Ruud asked.

Cornelis chuckled. "Guess we'll find out when the time comes!"

"A horse . . . well, as you know, a horse either steps higher, or knows enough to refuse to budge an inch out of the barn," Ruud joked.

"That's what they call horse sense," Cornelis said with an amiable grin. "Say, Lena, is Gustave coming for you tonight?"

She halted in her superfluous straightening of papers on her desk. Her heart was in her throat as she answered quickly, "Oh, yes. And he'll be here soon. I need to collect my things so I don't keep him waiting."

"Too bad there's no telephone at the school, or we could save him a trip. I need to take the girls in to town to try on their new *klompen* before heading home, so we could've driven you home."

Antje and Maartje looked at each other. "Our shoes are ready?" Antje asked excitedly and danced around, holding hands with Maartje as both girls sang an impromptu melody. "We are little Dutch girls, getting *klompen*, little Dutch girls, getting *klompen* . . ."

He grinned. "Not 'getting,' not yet. The wooden shoemaker needs to check the fit before you begin walking in them."

Lena shared none of the girls' enthusiasm for this important step in embracing all-things-Dutch, which was a shock as she realized that somewhere, deep within her, she had envisioned a day when the unrepentant Cornelis gathered his lovely daughters and returned to Chicago. *Klompen? Now they'll never leave.*

What happened to two little girls who told me they hated wooden shoes because they are noisy?

Other fathers left, but Cornelis dawdled. He unbuttoned his coat and pulled his scarf out from around his neck and dropped his cap on Antje's desk while he wandered aimlessly around the room.

His presence was, well, a presence behind her as she wrote the maxim for Monday's theme on the board. It was only when she turned around and faced Cornelis' scorching gaze that she glanced back at what she had written: *Two wrongs don't make a right.*

"Do you ever give up?" he demanded in a blistering timbre. His confrontive spark ignited her defensive ember. Instantly flames consumed the fragile straws of civility that had linked them since the entryway kiss.

She stormed across the room and thrust the paper from which she had taken the six words that had incited an inferno between man and woman. "See for yourself. This is next in the assignments I planned last summer, long before you arrived. Last week was 'A rolling stone gathers no moss.' Next week will be 'A penny saved is a penny earned.' Just because you're in the room when I write this adage, don't assume—"

She halted her tirade, belatedly aware of four dark eyes darting between father and teacher.

Cornelis turned abruptly. "Come along, girls."

"Goodbye, Miss Stryker." Antje looked worried, but her voice trilled in its usual lilt as she bobbed along behind Cornelis. He had already pushed Maartje out the door.

Through the window, Lena watched their progress across ice-crusted gravel. Cornelis' breath hung like white clouds; the girls' exhalations formed meringue-tufts dotting the air.

She craned her neck when his broad shoulders abruptly disappeared on the far side of the automobile. Just as she feared he had fallen, the unsettlingly familiar russet head of hair reappeared as a hatless head. Lena glanced at a man's hat on Antje's desk.

She didn't breathe as Cornelis swung his right arm in a mighty arc and lifted his left leg at the second an ice-packed snowball shot through the air. She flinched as if the *Splat!* on the fence post had hit her. She recognized the surging emotions behind his powerful swing which sent that snowball flying. Last Autumn, she had missed the same post when Cornelis made her so angry she aimed a stone at it. As she watched him clap his hands to remove loose snow, it occurred to her that she brought out the same frustrations in him that he did in her.

She grabbed his hat, ran out, crossed an icy patch without mishap, and flung open the passenger door. "You forgot this, and I did *not* want you returning to get it." She tossed the hat on the seat and shut the car door with more force than necessary, then skidded along the precarious journey back to the stoop.

Cornelis hit the horn with a long, startling blast, which effectively gave him the last word in the latest of an agonizing series of futile encounters between the Unrepentant and the Unforgiving.

"Christmas is coming, Cornelis, and if you were still a child, *Sinterklaas* would give you only coal in your *klompen*," she muttered.

She slammed the schoolhouse door behind her and stomped her foot, wishing it was Cornelis' leather shoes, not merely a wooden floor. "You better decide what you're going to say when you face Bram and Brigetta."

✸ ✸ ✸

Tuesday, November 19 ♦ Lena met Gustave at the schoolhouse door when he brought the pumpkin bars Hanna had baked that morning for Elsje's birthday treat. During Art Class, while other students cut snowflakes to decorate the classroom, Elsje had the enviable privilege of painting seasonal designs on the windows. Then, Lena let her skip geography; instead, she blissfully created a beautiful wintry landscape in one window, and a manger scene in another.

"You are a good artist, Elsje," Lena praised. "Your artwork is a fine addition to our program decorations."

"This is the best birthday present you could ever give me, Miss Stryker!" Elsje enthused. "Last summer, I asked Father if I could paint a mural on the side of our barn, but he said, 'Absolutely not!' So these windows are the largest pictures I've ever made!"

Lena envisioned Gerolt Hazenbroek's dismay at the thought of owning a barn adorned with art. "Then you must sign your work, Elsje! Put your name in the lower right-hand corner. That's what artists do. Then everyone will know who did this impressive work."

Elsje joyful face gave way to Gerolt's scowl in Lena's mind. *"So there, Gerolt—you may not recognize talent when it scoots up your supper table, but, I will see to it that Elsje gets the message that her work is appreciated."*

❋ ❋ ❋

Wednesday, November 20 ◆ To have two birthdays close together always presented a challenge; this year was no different. Next came Lucas' birthday, and Lena noticed him observing the preceding day's festivities for Elsje, albeit with guarded anticipation. All the students knew something singular would happen for their birthdays, but each one was kept in suspense as to when and what it would be.

To show too much interest in his special day posed a dilemma for Lucas—he had invested too much effort this year in being bored to suddenly lurch into unbridled excitement. But there was something appealing about being King of the Hill for one day.

In planning Lucas' event, Lena was a woman with a mission. When the day arrived, she was on pins and needles, worrying that perhaps in her zeal to dethrone Cornelis, she'd missed the point of pleasing (or, at least, surprising) the honoree of the day. The burning question was: *Will Lucas be disappointed?*

The students' continuing interest in Cornelis had waned for a while after Freek's accident, but Cornelis still consumed far too much of the six boys' adulation as far as Lena was concerned. She determined to set examples of true heroes before them—beginning with Lucas' birthday event.

After the September picnic's ballgame, she vowed to herself, "There will be no more events featuring Cornelis de Boer's muscular physique." From then on, she set about planning programs for the remaining boys' birthdays that highlighted true accomplishments, not physical appearance.

Today, she welcomed the children with a nervous jitter underlying every action. She dodged questions about why the Storytime stool was already positioned at the front of the classroom, and conducted opening exercises as usual, even though she caught more students eyeing the stool than the flag they saluted during the Pledge of Allegiance.

This is it, she told herself. "As you all know, today is Lucas' special day.! Happy birthday, Lucas!" The boy grudgingly allowed happiness to nudge his usual jaded attitude aside when the students sang to him. Then Lena said, "If you will open your desks, you'll each find a card that explains your first assignment today."

She watched Lucas' hope for grandiose events deflate when he pulled out what seemed to be a blank piece of stiff paper. All around the room, children discovered the same thing. "There's nothing written on mine, Miss Stryker, and nothing on Raimund's neither," Bartel said.

"Are you sure?" Lena asked, faking puzzlement.

"Positive," Raimund agreed. "Me and Bartel both got blank papers."

"Me, too; lots of us did," Jaap said, hiking himself up from his desk to peer at other desks.

'Well, someone would disagree with you," Lena said with a laugh. She walked back to the teacherage and opened the door. "Come on out, please!"

A massive German Shepherd appeared in the doorway, followed by a stoop-shouldered man who held a stiff U-shaped handle connected to the dog's body harness. They moved between the back wall and the stove, turned at the bookcase, passed the windows, rounded the bend in front of the teacher's desk, dodged the reading chairs, and came to a standstill slightly off-center beneath the unsmiling George Washington's picture hanging above the blackboard.

The dog stood at attention. The man's hands followed the form of the handle along the dog's spine until he reached the fitted body harness, which he exchanged for a leather leash.

The man gave a German command in a low voice and the dog led him to the Storytime stool. With confident hands, the man assessed the height of the stool and determined it had a solid back and four legs joined by crossbars before he sat down.

He spoke a command; the dog moved between his master's legs and sat. Still holding the leash, the man put his hands on his knees. Sixty seconds had passed since Lena had opened the teacherage door: a minute in which sixteen students' eyes and bodies had moved only to follow the man and his dog's path.

"Good morning, students of Dutch Valley School," the man said in a pleasant voice. "My name is Sam Green and this is my friend, King. Miss Stryker and I met at the State Fair many years ago. She has been friends with my wife and me and King ever since, so if I slip and call her Lena, that is why."

Sam Green would need to call Lena 'Humpty Dumpty,' or break out in hives, or stick carrots up his nose before the students would have thought twice. Their attention was firmly planted on King—that handsome, intelligent, and focused canine who eyed them with detached interest, but was fully engaged any time Sam Green so much as shifted a muscle.

Lena spoke from the back of the room, where she sat in her sewing rocker: "Mister Green, perhaps you can answer the children's concern. I gave them cards this morning, which they insist are blank. Would you be so kind as to examine their cards? All sixteen of my students are here today, and they are sitting in four rows of four desks each."

Sam Green seemed unfazed by what the students deemed insensitivity on her part, at least if their looks of dismay over Lena's seemingly cavalier attitude toward a man's now-obvious disability were any indication. She could almost read their thoughts: *"He's blind, Miss Stryker! He can't see our cards!"*

"I'm willing to help in any way I can." Sam said cheerfully and shifted off the stool, reaching for King's harness leash. "But first, I have an important word of instruction to the students. King is friendly and loves children, but when I hold this handle," he tapped the firm U-shaped leash sticking up in the air, "King is working; his attention is on our surroundings. So, please do not pet him. If you do, it could mean disaster for him and me." All around the room, eyes widened.

"When I remove this lead, he is off-duty. When that happens, he will love to meet and greet everyone. Now! Let me examine the baffling cards Miss Stryker mentioned." He hooked the leather leash back on the harness and reached for the hard-form leash.

Sixteen students waited in silence, watching King and Sam Green move confidently to the front desk closest to the door. King stood at attention while Sam held out his hand to Liesbeth. That little girl, whose nose was about level with King's muzzle, scooted to the far side of her desk and pushed the card along the desktop within range of Sam's searching fingers.

He picked it up and ran his fingers over its surface. "Hello, Liesbeth! How do you like first grade?"

The timid girl gasped and looked from the man who smiled pleasantly beside her desk to the dog who seemed an even larger presence. "Fine," she managed, too concerned about King to marvel at the mystery of being known.

Sam spoke a German word; King moved to the next desk. Katrien was ready and thrust her card into Sam's outstretched hand. "Good morning, Katrien. Ho-ho; you're a third-grader!" The girl nodded and blurted, "Yes," as she realized, to her embarrassment, that a nod was worthless.

Maas' hand darted out to touch King's head, but remembered Sam's warning and pulled back. Once again, Sam held the card and he knew name and grade. It happened again with Jaap. He crossed the aisle and King halted by Lucas' desk. "Hello, Lucas. It seems that not only are you in sixth grade, but this is a special day for you. Happy Birthday, young man!"

He nudged King with his knee. King barked.

Sam chuckled. "He's not musical, like your friends, but that's 'Happy birthday' in dog language!"

On and on it went, Sam reaching for cards, correctly identifying each student—even the twins, whom strangers could rarely tell apart—finishing with their respective grade in school. Wim had volunteered, "I had a dog named Freek—he died."

Sam nodded sympathetically. "I had a dog before King, and he died, too. I'll never forget Buster; he was a good dog—but so is King."

Maartje dropped her card in her haste to put it in Sam's hand. She gingerly ducked between her seat and the massive dog to grab it off the floor. When she came up, her expression was one of shuddering disgust. "Tell your dog to put his tongue back in his mouth. He drooled on my head!"

Sam Green laughed heartily. "That would be a new command for King, Maartje! He knows hundreds of commands, but 'don't drool' isn't on the list."

At last he reached Antje's desk. He tossed out the details of her name and grade, returned her card and signaled King to return to the Storytime stool.

With King between his knees, Sam said, "Let's review. The first row to my left is Liesbeth, Katrien,

Maas and Jaap, behind which Miss Stryker leisurely rocks."

All heads turned.

Lena smiled serenely and kept rocking.

Sam grinned. ""The second row is Wim, Adda, Raimund, and today's honored student: Lucas. At the back of the next row we have Elsje, who is quite warm sitting by the stove this morning. Then, Bartel and Giertje, with Maartje in front. The fourth row has Antje nearest me—she's probably like to exchange places with Elsje until she warms up! Sterre and Janneken are next, with Saartje by the water cooler."

"How do you know Miss Stryker is rocking?" Jaap challenged.

"The same way I know that Saartje sits near the water cooler," Sam replied and tapped his ears. "I hear the floor creaking very rhythmically—the way a rocker sounds on a wooden floor, and I pay attention to the direction her voice comes from. If someone looks beneath the water cooler, they'll find a puddle growing bigger drop by drop, perhaps beneath the dipper I heard Miss Stryker use a moment ago."

Saartje slid out of her seat and examined the floor beneath the dipper. "He's right! There's a puddle under the dipper!"

"How did you know I am cold?" Antje asked.

"Ah, dear child, when you handed me your card, your fingers were cold, and Elsje's hand was warm."

"How'd you know all that stuff you said about us?" Wim demanded, voicing the question on every mind.

But before Sam Green could respond, Raimund blurted, "My card has bumps on it!" In every row, students picked up the cards last held by the intriguing Mister Green and examined them with the same intensity employed by government officials suspecting counterfeit money.

Affirmations rang out. Sixteen sets of eyes moved from the previously dismissed, now-absorbing, cards to the unassuming man on the Storytime stool with his attentive canine attendant seated between his knees.

"I best explain it with a story. When I was in first grade, my family had a farm on the Nebraska border near Sioux City. I was healthy until I turned five; then I got rheumatic fever and lost my sight. My parents enrolled me in a school for the blind in Sioux City. My school was similar to yours, with two differences. The students brought dogs like King to school, and we learned to read using Braille!"

"What's Braille?" Jaap asked.

"Your cards are an example; they have your names and grades punched in precise bumps. Those marks told me what I need to know. The rest was up to me, since I did not keep the cards. I memorized your names and where you sit. A blind person benefits from a sharp memory and the ability to pay attention."

"But how did our names get on the cards?" Katrien demanded.

"Your teacher helped me! Last evening, I came on the train from the school for the blind I attended, and where I am now a teacher. Miss Stryker and I sat at the parsonage table in Dutchville while I used special equipment, which you'll see soon, to stamp details on the cards. This morning, Dominie Ter Hoorn gave Miss Stryker, King, and me a ride to school. Before I answer Jaap's question more fully, Miss Stryker, could we possibly enjoy your peanut butter cookies?"

Lena laughed. "Did you steal a sample when you were hiding in the teacherage this morning?"

"No; I was in the parsonage kitchen when those cookies came out of the oven, and then they rode with us to school!" While all munched Lucas' favorite treat, Sam began the educational part of his presentation. "One hundred years ago, Louis Braille created a system based on a two-by-three-inch grid of six dots arranged in different patterns . . ."

By the end of the morning, Sam had explained the Braille alphabet and given each child a chance to use his Braille machine to press out a simple Christmas greeting on a card they would finish in Art Class.

At last, Sam removed King's harness, releasing him from duty so the children could pet him while he told about learning to work with his first seeing-eye dog, and answered questions about training canine helpers.

Putting King back to work, Sam demonstrated basic commands and signals he used while working with King during a typical day. He also described what it was like for students who lived at a boarding school for the blind.

Before Gustave arrived to drive Sam and King back to the train station, each student received a card with

Braille symbols for the alphabet so they could read special cards Sam assured them would come from students at the School for the Blind.

The rest of the day, the children talked about King, Sam, and Braille. Not surprisingly, at recess the younger students designated half their number to be seeing-eye dogs who were commanded to guide their masters and mistresses around the playground.

Despite accusations, it was unlikely seeing-eye-Wim intended to run scarf-blinded-Katrien into the pump. Nor, when Maas gave a command, did clear-sighted-Adda purposely put him between two swings, where vision-impaired-Maas unwittingly grabbed two chains, and sat without a seat under him. It was innocent fun.

❋ ❋ ❋

Friday, November 22 ♦ Thanksgiving decorations seemed to fill every available inch in the classroom. Each grade's history books covered some portion of the account of the pilgrims, Indians and Plymouth Rock. Since the students kept an ear tuned to other grades' lessons, by the time Friday rolled around, even the youngest students knew important dates, and Captain Miles Standish's role in the first Thanksgiving.

Lena's eyes moved up and down the rows of desks as Jaap read aloud to the whole group, ". . . declared a national holiday by President Abraham Lincoln during a very difficult time in our country's history . . ."

Janneken, Antje and Maartje, Giertje, and even Wim all face a difficult holiday this year, as do many other families, even those who have not lost a loved one.

"You read very well, Jaap," Lena praised. "Who knows what the 'difficult time in our country's history' refers to?" One hand shot up. "Saartje?"

"The Civil War."

"That's correct. Many families sent their boys off to war, so there was much sadness in many homes, both in the North and the South. But President Abraham Lincoln knew that our nation had much for which we could be thankful. What are you thankful for?"

"Pretty clothes," Sterre piped up and caressed the soft yarn of the new sweater her grandmother Van der Voort had knitted for her.

"I'm thankful my brother didn't wear out his pants before he outgrew them." Jaap got a laugh—but one of agreement, not derision, since almost everyone in the room (except Sterre) wore hand-me-downs. "They don't have holes in 'em, so I don't care if they aren't pretty." His disgusted look was wasted on Sterre who was still busy admiring her finery.

Elsje said, "I'm thankful for a warm house."

Others added ideas of family, friends, and food. When a natural ebb came, Lena asked, "Has anyone noticed a common thing in what you've mentioned?" Only the snapping logs in the stove could be heard for a moment; then one hand waved wildly in the air.

"Yes, Wim?"

He said in a rush, "The twins are thankful for Midnight, but I don't have a horse, so I said I'm thankful for my mother." He shot a worried glance at the de Boer sisters. "But Antje's thankful for her cats, and Maartje's thankful for their grandmother. It's all different stuff, huh?"

Out of the mouths of babes. "You're right, Wim. There's a saying that goes 'One man's trash is another man's treasure.' It means what's very important to one person may not be important at all to someone else."

"Like the Lady of Stavoren?" Janneken asked.

"Exactly. What's the most precious thing in the world? The answer is whatever you are most thankful for this Thanksgiving."

"I'm thankful for you, Miss Stryker," Janneken said.

"What are you thankful for, Miss Stryker?" Liesbeth asked as Lena struggled to control her emotions.

"I have a list of names: your names are part of it. You sixteen children are all very precious to me." Blinking fast, she motioned toward the blackboard. "Elsje has written the words to a song for us to sing."

It was a very good thing Lena knew the tune because she could not see a single note of the musical score resting on the piano. As the students sang with simple beauty, she thought her heart would take wing:

"Now thank we all our God, with heart and
 hands and voices,
Who wondrous things has done, in Whom
 this world rejoices;
Who from our mothers' arms has blessed us
 on our way
With countless gifts of love, and still is ours
 today."

314 • Hadley Hoover

Afterwards, Antje whispered, "Miss Stryker, what does the part about 'our mothers' arms' mean?"

Lena lifted a curl that had crept inside the girl's collar and coiled it around her finger, buying time to consider her answer. "Your mother loved you and held you, and when you think about her, you can still feel her hugs, can't you?"

Antje nodded solemnly.

"We're thankful to God for those memories, but mostly because it's how He loves us, too. He gives us countless gifts, like a mother's love, that last forever."

"I like this song. May I please copy it for my penmanship lesson?"

Lena nodded. "Would you like to have a special piece of paper I have been saving for just such an occasion?" Seeing a nod, she took a single sheet of lavender stationery with a bouquet of violets in one corner and gold-edged scallops from her desk.

Antje blinked. "It's beautiful, Miss Stryker! I'll write ever so carefully."

"I know you will. Move a chair from the reading circle close to the black board and write it on regular paper first. Then go back to your desk and copy on the pretty paper."

Antje nodded and walked away. She found her tablet, placed the lavender paper in the center of her desktop and hissed at Maartje, "Don't let anyone ruin this paper!"

During the time it took Antje to copy the words, Maartje accomplished nothing with her own studies.

Dutifully, she stared at the paper on Antje's desk, glaring at anyone who walked by, as if such activity put her charge in peril. She reprimanded Maas—seated two rows away—for coughing without covering his mouth. "You spit all over the air and your nasty spit-stuff could have ruined my sister's special paper!"

When Antje finally returned to her desk, Maartje collapsed with a sigh. "I'm never gonna keep watch on sumpthin important again! You never asked me if I had to use the outhouse—I coulda wet my pants, watching your paper!"

"You didn't, though, did you? Wet your pants, I mean," she whispered, horrified.

"No, but I could-a," the younger girl huffed. "May I watch you write on that pretty paper?"

"No. You might jiggle my arm or something. It has to be perfect, Maartje!"

"Is it what you are most thankful for, Antje?"

She nodded solemnly. "It's my new most precious thing."

Observing the scene from her desk, Lena prayed: "*Lord, is it wrong for me to love those little girls so much? Why must their blasted father frustrate me so much?*"

That evening, she was still under the spell of the day as she and Hanna dawdled over supper dishes. "You seem happy . . . in a quiet way," Hanna said, up to her elbows in suds.

"That phrase, 'quiet way,' describes my mood perfectly," Lena agreed. Starting with Jaap's reading, she told Hanna about the day's unusual twist, finishing with the admission, "I used to think Wim was my pet student but, fond as I am of him, Antje and Maartje hold special places in my heart. Partly because of their situation, but more because they remind me of us as young sisters."

Hanna nodded. "Through thick and thin, I know I can always count on you. That's what I would have said if I had been in your classroom today telling what I'm thankful for."

Lena's mouth dropped open. "But what about Gustave . . . and Brigetta, and Sanna!"

"Oh, they are high on the list, but I've loved you even longer than Gustave. There's very little that you and I don't share; you know me inside-out." She tipped her head to look over the top of her glasses. "Hmm, silly me. I thought by now you'd have assured me that I'm on the top on your list!" she teased.

Lena flushed. "You are; I was just thinking, that's all . . . of course, you're right at the top."

"You hesitate to put me at the top of your list! I relinquish the honor *only* if it's Brigetta's place'!"

"Don't be a goose. I love you both."

"You have that look about you again."

"What look?"

"The one that means you're thinking about something private. That look."

Lena started to shake her head, but halted. "Well . . . everyone has things—oh, forevermore! If I told you every single thought I had, we would just sit in the parlor thinking-and-saying, thinking-and-saying!"

They laughed, but Hanna didn't give up: "Are you ever going to tell me about what's been on your mind ever since school started?"

"Hmm," Lena murmured vaguely, meaning anything and revealing nothing. "Hopefully someone else will do what he is supposed to do and I will not need to tell you a thing."

She said 'he' which must mean Cornelis. But whatever did he do to her that she cannot tell her own sister? Hanna gave her undivided attention to scouring a stain off a kettle. Fifteen years' worth of scrubbing hadn't removed the stain. *"Oh, Lord, I wish life were simpler to figure out!"*

Lena hung wet dishtowels to dry by the stove. "Do you know much about the Ten Broek's situation, what with the problems with the banks, and all that?"

"I know of nothing specific regarding them. Why do you ask?"

"Based on Giertje's lunches—and her embarrassment over them—I worry things are not going well." Lena recounted the cloakroom incident and subsequent temporary solutions, ending with a deep sigh. "I don't know what to do. If I slip Giertje food too often, it will draw unwanted attention to her. Yet, the only other solutions seem either to feed them all, which I can hardly do every day, or coming up with Johnny Appleseed–type ideas, which tax my brain!"

Hanna refilled the teakettle and set it on the stove. "As Gustave says, things are critical in our country and not likely to improve any time soon. My heart goes out to Giertje. If we could figure out a way to give that family food in a manner that allows them to keep their dignity.''

"It's not long since summer. Our garden produced so much that I erroneously assumed it was a good year for everyone. And they live on a farm, which usually means readily available meats and poultry, fruit trees and a garden. But Giertje's biscuit was dry, as if even their milk cow ran dry.''

"Whose milk cow ran dry?'' Gustave asked from the kitchen door.

"Oh, good; you're here, Gustave! Come and sit down. Lena, repeat what you just told me.'' Hanna reached for the coffee pot and cups.

Somber and silent, Gustave listened. Halfway through Lena's account, he reached into his pocket and pulled out his pipe, packing tobacco into it while Hanna interjected comments throughout Lena's story.

"This sheds light on a peculiar situation from earlier this week,'' he said. "I met Leendert driving his truck down the road.''

"When was this?'' Lena asked.

"It must have been on Monday. In my mirror, I noticed a box with chickens fall off after he turned a corner, so I turned around and honked to stop him. His truck was overloaded with two cows tied near the front, several hogs crated at the back, and maybe a dozen boxes of chicken lashed to the sides.''

"My goodness! That's quite a load!'' Hanna said.

"I said the same, but he got agitated. He mentioned Sioux City, so I assumed he was selling the livestock.''

"Were they milk-cows?" Lena asked.

"I don't recall; I was busy helping him rope the box of chickens on more securely. And then he took off."

The three sat glumly contemplating a husband and father's efforts to get money to pay debts, even at the price of taking food from his family's mouths. "What can we do, Gustave?" Hanna asked at last.

"We don't have much money either, but perhaps we . . . ah-ha! You know, I've been meaning to tear out a stall in the buggy barn to make more room for the Ford. I'm so busy lately, I could honestly use help— and hire Leendert."

Hanna nodded with relief. "Yes! Lena and I were thinking of ways to get food to the family, but your idea helps them hold their heads high."

Gustave nodded. "Perhaps he will refuse payment. That's happened before when I have asked for help from parishioners. But if I handle it right, he may accept a fair sum. I wonder how he's gotten into the financial mess we suspect. He has a large farm, and has seemed successful, and is well respected in the community. Though, none of that excludes having difficulties."

"I've never been happier to live a simple life than I am now," Lena said fervently. "I wonder if Cornelis somehow talked Leendert into buying an automobile he could not afford."

"That would be an expense, but hardly enough to throw a farmer into ruin. Speaking of Cornelis, have you talked to him lately, Lena?" Gustave asked.

"No . . . well, only at school when he comes and goes." A blush tinted her cheeks. "Why do you ask?"

"I talked with him at Vander Molen's store the other day and he mentioned something about maybe not being around for Christmas. That's too bad because I know Hans and Rebecca have thought the girls would love to meet Sanna."

"That dirty rat!" Lena slapped her hand on the table. The salt and pepper shakers jumped and toppled, sprinkling black and white specks together like soot on snow.

Gustave and Hanna stared in undisguised shock. "Lena!" Hanna gasped. "What on earth is wrong between you and Cornelis? He is practically family, yet you act as if he were a criminal!"

"He is, in my book," Lena said. "He committed a crime against two families and I gave him an ultimatum. Either he confesses by Christmas, or I'll speak up. That coward! That unspeakable, low-down, miserable wretch."

"That's a strong indictment, Lena, without solid proof," Gustave said gently.

Refusing to recant, Lena only said, "Cornelis has hemmed and hawed and delayed and denied, and now he's running again. I hope he points his nose at the Missouri River, keeps on walking, and get swept away in the current! Now, if you'll excuse me, I have a great deal of work to do in my room."

The silence in the kitchen after she left was deafening. Neither Gustave nor Hanna moved for several minutes. "Do you have the slightest idea what she's talking about?" Gustave asked.

"Not a clue. She makes it sound as if Cornelis did something horrendous. Surely if that were true, we'd know . . . Right?"

"Would we?"

"Would Hans and Rebecca know what she means?"

"They've never indicated any such worries to me about Cornelis."

"They're good people, Gustave—our friends and Sanna's in-law's. I can't fathom anything as dastardly as what Lena hints at."

Gustave said ruefully, "It would explain Lena's odd behavior recently. We've commented on it, wondering if it were because of her stage of life. However, if she has kept a horrible secret involving Cornelis all these years, I imagine seeing him again would rattle her." He chuckled.

Hanna frowned. "I fail to see the humor."

He patted her hand. "I'm not laughing about the situation—but, you must admit, there is some humor to Cornelis thinking he can escape our Lena! Once she has spoken, she rarely changes her mind. She is the sweetest person on earth, unless something comes between her and those she holds dear."

Hanna's eyes sucked Gustave into their depths. "Of all Lena holds dear, Brigetta is the dearest."

Gustave's jaw tightened. "If Cornelis did anything to Brigetta, I do not hold much hope for his survival. Lena is like a mother in the wild, willing to take on even a grizzly bear to protect her young. If Cornelis did anything to Brigetta that Lena knows about, he would do well to run."

"And that's what he did," Hanna said thoughtfully. "He ran. And he stayed away from Dutchville for ten years. But now he's back . . . and Lena's bothered."

"God help us all. The only thing worthy of Lena's attitude is, well, to put it plainly: unthinkable. If anything like Cornelis rushing off, or Bram and Brigetta moving away happens again, God knows what the present holds for Cornelis."

Hanna suddenly noticed her self-inflicted pain. Red half-moon nail-shaped welts in her palms whitened when she unclenched her fists and flexed her fingers. *Brigetta is coming home and will find us at sixes-and-sevens and will not know why . . . or will she?* Her eyes leaped to the calendar on the kitchen wall; she did a quick mental calculation: *One month from tomorrow, Brigetta, Bram and Sanna will be at this table.*

She closed her eyes, and whispered, *"Dear God, please let it be a happy time for everyone."*

Upstairs in his study later, Gustave did battle with strong emotions he'd rarely allowed to reside in his soul. Pipe smoke circled his head as he let his mind float over past years.

He kicked off his shoes and pushed aside the commentaries, his Bible and a tablet of sermon notes. In the space available, he propped his feet on the open surface. The desk chair creaked as he leaned back, pushing it to its sharpest incline.

It was in this chair I sat with twelve-year-old Brigetta on my lap when she first told me of the changes that made her a woman. He examined the worn toes of his carpet slippers atop the desk.

I have knelt countless hours beside this desk, beseeching heaven for answers to my questions about why God seemed deaf to my prayers for Hanna during her deep depression. He pulled his feet back and stood.

He paced, aware it was audible to the women. *This room is directly above where Lena sleeps, or tosses, every night, knowing something so horrific she could not tell another soul.*

He moved to the window from which he could view the church's steeple. Moonlight behind it created a dark pyramid on the snow. *The wrath that has risen in me toward Cornelis, even without knowing the truth, frightens me. It is displeasing to God in any man, but an utter reproach in me: the man who purports to represent God to the people . . .*

Three somber adults gathered at the breakfast table on Saturday. Gustave conducted devotions without enthusiasm. His prayers lacked conviction that the gates of heaven were even open to petitions or praise.

After Gustave's "Amen," Lena said slowly, "I was wrong . . . to speak of things I promised Cornelis I wouldn't mention until he has done his part."

Hanna asked, "You mean, to make things right?"

Looking into space, Lena nodded. "I'm not sure things can ever be made right again, but he must try."

Gustave flashed back on his conversation with Lena about leopards changing their spots. *This has been on Lena's mind for a long time.*

"When you said he might not be here for Christmas," Lena continued, "I got upset because that's when I assumed he would . . . do what must be done. I spent a sleepless night, knowing what I said was dishonorable."

Hanna flashed back on their conversation about thick-and-thin. *Sad to say, Lena and I haven't shared everything, after all. The hardest burden of all that she carries, she has carried alone.*

"Thank you for not pressing me," Lena said. "And forgive me for what I said last evening. Please withhold your judgment of Cornelis until he has an opportunity to speak in his own defense."

"Everyone knows the saying about 'locking the barn door after the horse is stolen,' but I am not so sure you should carry all the guilt for speaking out of turn," Gustave said.

Lena's eye opened wide as she stared at him.

"If you confronted Cornelis and made a deal with him—which he is now reneging on—then, your accusations against him are justified. He is a rascal of the first order. I would like to the kind of man who can say, 'Let God deal with him,' but the human part of me wants revenge if he has injured those I love."

A chill descended, reaching even her bones. *What have I done?* "That's a dreadful way to live. Believe me: I know. I regret planting such feelings in you."

"If it were not for Cornelis, there would be no problem. Isn't that the way you see it?" he asked.

Lena nodded morosely, saying nothing.

He continued, "Don't assume guilt for things that are not of your doing."

"But I broke a promise."

"I know sin is sin," Hanna snorted, "but, in the scheme of things, how can breaking a promise possibly compare to . . . real sin?" That three-letter word hung like a three-thousand-pound boulder ready to crush the three seated at the kitchen table.

Hanna persisted, "It seems as silly to say the pain of a splinter is like the pain of a broken back. There are crimes parents punish their children for by making them sit in a corner, and then there are crimes people are imprisoned for committing."

Gustave felt less like a Dominie and more like a criminal himself that morning. He had no answers. Advent was not in his heart as he opened his sermon notes after breakfast.

Part Four

Tuesday Morning, November 26 • The students arrived with ice-caked scarves and mittens. Giddily, they caught snowflakes on their tongues, or thrust fistfuls of snow down classmates' collars.

Since the temperature had dropped and remained low for several days, Lena issued her annual warning about putting tongues on the pump. After morning recess, the clothesline that stretched wall-to-wall over the stove drooped with soggy mittens and scarves.

By noon recess, the snow had accumulated to depths that made walking difficult for the shorter students. In the afternoon, the wind picked up, forming drifts against the bushes and across the stoop. Lena sent Lucas out to shovel the drifts blocking the doors to both outhouses and he came back exhausted.

"Miss Stryker?" Raimund said. "Midnight is getting restless; he senses storms. Should we hang tarps on his shelter like Father did last year?"

"Yes, but be careful," Lena warned. "Lucas can get them down from the outhouse rafters, and help you hook them in place."

Hooks aplenty lined the rough frame that sheltered the water trough and the bales of hay Teunis Vande Veer stored there against such emergencies. The back wall of the lean-to supported the slanted roof that also rested on pillars in front. These features offered little protection against severe weather but, with canvas hung, even Midnight would have shelter.

Lucas checked and double-checked the tarps, and tightened the ropes that secured them to hooks and pillars before coming back inside with the twins. "Listen, boys," he said. "We gotta take care of the twins' horse. Whenever we go to the outhouse, poke holes in the ice on the water trough, okay? You can use a stick I put in the corner nearest the hay bales. If you can't get a hole big enough for Midnight to drink through, let me know and I'll go do it."

Lena smiled. *Lucas is rising to the occasion!* She kept watching the weather after classes resumed, wondering if—or when—parents would arrive to begin ferrying their children safely home.

After lunch, Lena joined the children outside for exercise and fresh air, but it wasn't long before the outdoors lost its charm. All trooped back into the schoolhouse, seeking warmth. That's when Lena knew there would be no afternoon excursions into the cold, either children setting off for home without their parents' knowledge, or even going to the outhouse by themselves.

Jaap put snow-filled buckets along the back wall—a necessary precaution when the stove burned so hot. Lucas hauled in extra firewood and stacked it neatly in the entry. Bartel brought in the ice-crusted stoop bench and put it near the stove to thaw; soon a puddle formed beneath it.

Nervous excitement permeated the schoolhouse. The first true snowstorm was underway! Since the children didn't sense Lena's anxiety, their exhilaration made the air sizzle like the condensation dripping off the stovepipe onto the hot shove. "Look!" Wim said, pointing at the window. "Elsje's picture is like the snow outside!"

They looked up in time to witness the wind gain strength and howl through invisible cracks. Within seconds, the still-life painting became an eerie match to the world beyond the shaking windowpane.

Fear was evident in each face. "What a noisy wind!" Lena forced a lighthearted tone. "Thanks to Lucas, there's plenty of wood inside to keep us warm. You'll all have rides home today!"

Liesbeth's lip quivered. "What if no one comes?"

"Anyone who doesn't have a ride gets to stay overnight with me! We'll all camp out in the schoolhouse! Oh my; look at the clock. It's time for afternoon classes to begin. Just because the wind blows, doesn't mean the fourth graders get out of taking their vocabulary test!"

Raimund and Bartel groaned an eight-note-scale groan in unison, as they always did when vocabulary tests were mentioned. Everyone replied, "Hush!" in a matching descending rebuke, like they always did when the twins groaned.

Lena knew she had missed the narrow window of time during which she could safely let any student head home. The storm was gaining intensity quickly. After getting the twins started on their quizzes, she gathered Lucas, Elsje, and Saartje around her desk on the pretense of giving their reading assignments.

She turned her back on the others who worked in small groups on a crossword puzzle and spoke softly. "It appears we will be staying at school tonight. I doubt any parents will attempt to come in this weather. I need your help to keep the others calm and busy. First, we'll make soup for supper."

"Where will we sleep?" Lucas asked nervously.

"Raimund brought in the rugs to make room for firewood in the entry, so they'll be our beds, and coats make good blankets. It will work out fine."

Elsje wrinkled her nose. "But what will we do? Do we have to do schoolwork all night?"

"Absolutely not! We'll dismiss school at the normal time. Before it gets dark, Lucas, I think we should tie a rope to the stoop's post and use it to guide us to the outhouses. There are ropes in the cloakroom storage closet. I am putting you in charge of tying together enough sections to reach that far."

Lucas voiced a lingering concern: "Do boys have to sleep with the girls?"

"We'll make sure it is all very respectable," Lena assured him. "How about if the boys camp in the cloakroom?" Nodding, he expelled a relieved sigh.

"Lucas and Jaap, you'll make alternate trips to escort the boys to the outhouse; Elsje and Saartje will do the same with the girls. No one goes out alone. We can make this a fun night, not a scary one."

After Storytime ended, Lena's usual "You are dismissed," earned none of the expected flurry of activity. Sixteen quiet students remained in their seats, unsure of what to do next. "Form a line around the walls," Lena said, her eyes twinkling. "It's time to walk home!" She laughed at their baffled expressions.

Whistling and swinging her arms, she led the pack around the room, conducting an endless stream of chatter. "What a pretty flower! Oh, look! That blackbird has a squirmy worm in his beak!" The second time around, she halted and spun on her heel. "On my left I see a weathervane with a big bird on top. Where am I?"

"On Wim's farm!" Janneken answered with a surprised giggle.

"Yes! You guessed correctly so it's your turn, Janneken, to take us on a walk. Give clues along the way to help us guess where we are when you stop."

This activity was a perfect match for Janneken's imagination. Lena moved out of line and watched the girl's face turn dreamy as she led her classmates around the room. She mimicked Lena's example, even the whistling. "Doesn't that cloud look like a hair ribbon? That pine tree is loaded with cones!" She stopped. "I see a white picket fence with ivy. Where am I?"

That took some thought because the farm belonged to a family without school-age children, but Maas knew: It was his grandparents' home.

On it went, down the line. A grove of willow trees, a windmill painted green, a tire swing, and the crooked elm—which Jaap pantomimed—all these descriptors helped the children identify landmarks. During the many journeys past the teacherage door, Lena half-listened to the students and half-conducted a mental review of her larder and linens.

Before she could begin to think of how to feed her charges, she must produce adequate entertainment for the hours until it could be deemed bedtime. *It will be early for some, late for others. The critical issue is the little ones missing the familiar routines. If they can get to sleep, the rest of the night will pass quickly.*

✹ ✹ ✹

Tuesday Evening, November 26 ◆ Darkness began to creep around the edges of Elsje's painted windows. Lena let the older girls light the wall lamps while she cleared her desk to use for activities. The four littlest girls moved chairs around the table the older boys had carried out from the teacherage.

Then Lena brought out her sewing basket. "Do you remember the leaf-house you made on the playground? Well, my niece, Brigetta used to make a button house during winter storms! This is the jar she used." She unscrewed the lid and poured out a colorful stream of buttons, which Antje began sorting.

Meanwhile, Lucas and Jaap called Maas, Wim, Raimund and Bartel away from tic-tac-toe on the blackboard for a game of dominoes. Elsje and Saartje, returning from outhouse trips with Janneken and the third-grade girls, were ready for a sedentary activity and all begin a jigsaw puzzle on Lena's desk.

With everyone engaged in activities, Lena took time to assess the contents of her hutch, and then put her water bucket on the stove to heat. The little girls were so busy finding all the black buttons for the outer walls and white buttons for windows and doors they barely noticed her watching over their shoulders.

"The pink buttons can be the kitchen," Liesbeth said. Smiling, Lena moved along to check the domino game. Wim struggled to keep up, but the other boys helped him, so she didn't interfere. The jigsaw puzzle was taking shape nicely. *All is well in the kingdom of The Little Old Woman Who Lived in a Shoe*, Lena thought with a wry grin. *Now, all I must do I is feed these children!*

She took vegetables from the flour bin, and selected pint-jars of string beans, stewed tomatoes, corn, and peas, and two pints of stewed beef. Even with the array before her, she feared soup was inadequate to feed sixteen hungry children. *What was I thinking? Marching them around the classroom created bigger appetites!* She was pondering how far a jar of jam could go on a loaf of bread when she heard a sound riding the wind.

She grabbed her coat and hurried through the room. "Everyone stay here; I heard something."

The students gathered near the door. "I hope it's our father, Lucas." Liesbeth crept close to her brother and reached for his hand. He took pity on his sister (perhaps because he wished for the same thing) and willingly held on.

"I bet it's our dad," Raimund said, "with Thunder and the buggy. Then we'll hook up Midnight and be home as fast as I can snap my fingers!"

Wim forgot about the storm and missing his parents and worrying about if he could sleep without the special blanket no one at school knew about. He positioned his fingers and let loose a satisfying *Swuppp!* That success made him look for Janneken. Her expression reminded him how his insides felt when he thought about Freek. *She hasn't got a father to come get her.* He elbowed his way to stand by her.

Janneken hesitated, but let him hold her hand.

Standing in the entryway's door, Lena squinted into blowing snow. Faint light through the transom above the classroom door did little to help her see. *Is someone fighting the wind, or is it my imagination?* A shape made slow progress from the road. "Hello!" The wind whipped her voice back to her. By now, Lena knew the sound she'd heard wasn't an automobile. *Machines can't compete with an Iowa blizzard, but this person is trying. Was it a cry for help that I heard?*

In the agonizing minutes during which the unknown person battled the driving snow, Lena grew progressively colder. When the silhouette was lost in the whirling gusts, she wondered if perhaps she had imagined sounds and sights. But then the figure lurched into view again, struggling to escape a drift.

"Move to your right!" Again, gale-force winds swallowed her words. She held the door open in hopes the light could guide him to warmth and safety. Lena thought of the meager supper and muttered as she shivered in the doorway, "Whoever he will need sustenance, which mean I need to stretch the soup."

Finally, the man reached the stoop. He stumbled, barely able to climb the single step. Clinging to the doorknob, Lena stretched and grabbed a snow-crusted sleeve. She pulled him forward, tapping strength she didn't know she had. Inside, he fell to his knees panting as shards of ice and snow fell off his coat—a coat Lena recognized beneath the frosting of snow.

"Cornelis!" she exclaimed, shocked at how this powerhouse of a man was taxed by his exertions. In the back of her mind, the horror of the storm dumped all its pieces into one ominous thought: *If Cornelis could barely make it, thank God I did not allow any of the children to leave the school!*

He finally pulled himself up off the floor, balancing against the wall and breathing hard. "It's bad out there." His words came in labored spurts.

"Come in by the stove." Lena kicked snow and ice off the threshold so she could close the door.

He rose slowly to follow her. Fourteen faces stared at what seemed an apparition, but Antje and Maartje squealed and raced to throw themselves at Cornelis. He tottered beneath their exuberance—a sign of utter exhaustion. Antje emerged with snow lodged in her dark curls like a misshapen hat.

Cornelis didn't downplay his ordeal. He supported Lena's earlier assurances that their families knew the children had remained at school. "Miss Stryker did the right thing to keep you here where you are safe and warm."

"Can we go home now?" Maartje asked anxiously.

"No, our automobile is stuck a mile away. The roads are drifted over. In the morning, I'll dig out."

"Will you stay here overnight, too?" Lucas asked.

"I have no choice," Cornelis said ruefully.

Dandy. Lena groaned inwardly. *Why is it Cornelis who beats unbeatable odds?* She immediately felt guilty. *Look at how fatigued he is. The only reason he was able to get here is because of his physical condition, and even that was nearly not enough.*

While Lena chopped vegetables at Lucas' desk, she listened to Cornelis' account, which she sensed was edited to avoid frightening the children: "When I started out, the storm wasn't bad in town yet. I hadn't gone far before I got stuck the first time when I misjudged a snowdrift. The wind still hadn't picked up, but by the time I passed Wynkoop's farm, it was a full-blown blizzard."

"You could have stopped at my house," Wim said.

"Yes, but I couldn't turn around because I couldn't tell what was road and what was ditch. So I kept going and got stuck two more times. When I passed the crooked elm tree, I decided to follow the fence and walk the rest of the way here. When I walked into the ditch to get to the fence, I sank up to my waist. But eventually I found the fence, stared walking, saw the lights, and here I am."

As he spoke, Cornelis removed soaked and dripping outer garments and footwear. Basking in the warmth, he rotated in front of the stove. Lena eyed his feet nervously. Something about seeing two vulnerable male feet sticking out of damp trousers seemed indecent . . . provocative . . . inappropriate for a single lady's view. *He can't spend the rest of the night walking around with bare feet!*

She disappeared into the teacherage where she opened the trunk and found long woolen stockings which she gave to Cornelis. Holding up a hand, he halted the twins' discussion of how long it would take to freeze fingers and toes and noses into black stumps certain to fall off. He sat on the stove-dried bench to pull them on. The heel of the stocking landed in the middle of his foot so he turned it around, which formed a puff like a blister on his instep. The children hooted.

He stuck out his feet. "Don't I look pretty?"

Before he could resume his story, Lena said, "Soup will be ready soon."

"That reminds me; I have something for you." Elsje had hung up his coat, so he padded off to the cloakroom in his ill-fitting socks, and returned with two paper bags. In one, was a quart jar of milk, in the other, a loaf of bread. "Yzaak gave me these in case I got stranded. I thought he was crazy, but I'm glad I took them—and that the milk bottle didn't leak!"

Lena felt a surprising rush of gratitude. First, that something worthwhile was added to their supplies and, second, for what seemed to be the first time she'd heard Cornelis admit someone else was right and he was wrong. "I have a quart of milk on my windowsill, so we have enough for breakfast."

Reality whispered, *"Cornelis will be sleeping here."*

Lena blanched and inhaled sharply.

If Cornelis noticed, he didn't react. While Lena blindly chopped the beef into smaller pieces, he roamed the room—admiring the button house, adding a piece to the jigsaw puzzle, and teaming up with Wim at the domino table.

Lena felt an unexpected spark of hope flicker and admitted that for her, like the children, Cornelis' presence held fears at bay. Another adult on-board lightened her burden of responsibility for the children. Such relief, however, felt as peculiar on her conscience as her stockings looked on Cornelis' feet.

Every bowl and cup was put into service for the younger children. Canning jars emerged from the dishpan for the others. "Get the meat and vegetables out with a fork," Lena said, "and drink the broth."

"Can we slurp?" Raimund asked with a grin.

Lena laughed. "Under such unusual conditions, I think slurping if it allowed!"

Cornelis cut the bread, and Elsje assumed butter-and-jam duties. With the students finally eating at their desks, Cornelis and Lena stood at the back of the room and sighed in unison. They shared an awkward smile and both spoke at once. "Go ahead," he said.

"I want to thank you for your help. What were you going to say?"

"Just that you should go ahead and eat. I see there's a little soup left."

"Oh. Well, that goes for both of us."

"Is there enough soup for two?"

"Yes; the only thing we're missing is dishes."

338 • Hadley Hoover

He peered into the soup bucket. "Do you have a saucepan?"

"Of course." She returned with it and her tooth-brushing mug.

He pulled out his jackknife. "I can use this."

"I'll slurp!" She smiled, and divided the remaining soup between the mug and pan, giving more to the pan. They ate standing up. Lena was still hungry when her portion was gone. She felt guilty, realizing Cornelis must be famished after all he'd been through.

"I saved the crusts for us." He handed her a thin piece, and chewed his slowly before tipping the saucepan to get the final swallow of soup.

They set up an assembly line, using the stoop-bench and the back desks so the children could wash and dry their own dishes. "It would have gone faster for us to do dishes," Cornelis murmured near Lena's ear.

"True," she whispered, "but it became twenty minutes of entertainment!"

Wet dishtowels joined Cornelis' socks and assorted mittens on the line over the stove, and then Lena brought out the cookie jar. There were oatmeal cookies for everyone, followed by a drink from the water cooler.

"Let's thank Miss Stryker for the delicious supper she made," Cornelis prompted, and led the chorus.

"Do you have any food left?" Bartel asked. Everyone laughed.

"Are you thinking about breakfast?" Lena teased.

"No," he protested, but his voice lacked conviction.

"We'll have oatmeal with raisins and, thanks to Mister de Boer, we have plenty of milk. I will soak beans overnight for lunch and, in the morning, add molasses and canned ham from the September picnic. Tomorrow, we'll eat breakfast, begin school, as usual, and wait to see what the day brings."

Bartel smacked his lips. "It was good ham, so I hope we're still here!"

Cornelis joined in the laughter. "Time to begin the outhouse trips." He exchanged Lena's stockings for his own—which had dried quite well—and pulled on his coat and overshoes. "I want to make sure we can get the doors open, so unless someone has a desperate need, I want you to wait inside until I return."

Wrapping a scarf around his neck Cornelis instructed the older students, "Start getting the others ready, but don't let them get too warm yet." Lena explained about the ropes tied between the post and outhouse doors. Cornelis nodded appreciatively and pulled on woolen mittens and headed off.

Back inside, he said, "Listen, everyone. Tonight, there's no girls' or boys' outhouses. Whichever one I tell you to go in, that's what you use. Once you're in there, do what you came to do, and then pound on the wall to let me know you're ready to come out. I'll be waiting between the outhouses. Understood?"

Two at a time, students and Cornelis left the safety of the schoolhouse and grabbed hold of the ropes. Soon all had visited one of the dark cold little houses. With the last students safely returned, he motioned for

Lena to come to the door, a place he had not left since the first trip to avoid tracking unnecessary snow inside. "You have a chamber pot, right?"

"Yes, but, it's . . ." She flushed.

"Go get it; we'll need it overnight. Now, it's your turn for the outhouse adventure. But hurry; the storm is worsening instead of improving."

Her mouth went dry, but her hands turned clammy. Even knowing a trip alone was ill advised, a trip to the outhouse with Cornelis was not something she had considered. She hurried to the teacherage and was back in an instant. She paused to say, "Children, I'm putting Elsje and Saartje in charge."

The minute the door opened, the world condensed to one man, one woman and a wildly swinging chamber pot against the elements. "Where do you think you're going?" Cornelis demanded as Lena shot past him.

"The outhouse," she shouted, grabbing a rope and bracing herself against a nasty snow-packed gust.

"Get back here! We go together, or not at all. I've made the round-trip nine times and it's no walk in the park."

He gripped her hand so tightly, she could no more escape without losing her mitten than fly to the moon. Glaring at each other (no easy feat with ice crystals forming on eyelashes) they stomped down the steps as if each wished the other's face were beneath their feet.

They rounded the corner and the sheer force of the wind nearly lifted Lena off the ground. Between the unpredictable snow depths and the fact that earlier paths were already obliterated, she wondered how the little ones had managed.

As if reading her mind, Cornelis shouted, "I carried all but the five oldest. If you don't quit be so independent, I can pick you up, and haul you, too!"

Never! But then she sank into a drift, the action pulling her hand free of Cornelis—a move he deemed more rebellion against him touching her. He shook her as if in reprimand, but she was scared enough to admit it felt good to be in the care of someone bigger and stronger than herself. *Even Cornelis . . .*

She lifted one foot, and sunk in deeper with the other; she toppled sideways. He grabbed for her, but the crusty snow gave way, making her tilt precariously in the opposite direction.

Cornelis yelled near her ear, "I told you to stop fighting me! You can't possibly be hoping I'll kiss you again."

Any kind thoughts she'd entertained toward Cornelis bolted. She bristled and swatted at his arm. "You idiot! I'm not fighting—I stumbled! As for kissing, hens will grow teeth before that happens again." She thrust her nose in the air, which sent a shower of snow swirling into her scarf. Plunging ahead, she kept one hand on her rope with the chamber pot banging against her hip, and the other firmly in Cornelis' unyielding grip.

After what seemed an interminable distance and time, they reached the outhouses. Cornelis dragged girls' outhouse door open, forming a fan-shaped design in the glistening snow. The wind buffeted the door, but Cornelis held firm and warned, "Don't start back without me, you hear?"

"Aren't you going to warn me about putting my tongue on the door handle?" she snapped.

She sensed it was a good thing she couldn't hear Cornelis' reply. Inside the outhouse, she dumped the chamber pot to avoid kicking it over. That accomplished, she seated herself on what felt like an ice-fishing hole on the Floyd River.

"Yikes!" she yelped, leaping up. She thought a moment, and then arranged her mitten as a barrier between bare skin and cold wood. *Hope I don't lose them down the hole!*

An outhouse in a blizzard was about as dark and unwelcoming a place as Lena could imagine. "Those poor little ones must have been terrified out here," she murmured while the wind's almost human voice howled all around.

Aware this was possibly her only moment of privacy for the next twelve hours, she closed her eyes. Her mind filled with images of Cornelis finding his way from the stranded automobile to the school . . . Cornelis standing bare-footed beside the stove, revealing a second toe slightly longer than his great toe . . . Cornelis carrying children between school and outhouses repeatedly, without complaint . . .

"*I can pick you up and haul you . . .*" Her eyes popped open. *That will not happen. Cornelis will not gain points for rescuing me! It's enough that he appeared tonight to help the children. The children! They're probably frantic with worry!*

The door shook beneath an urgent pounding. "Have you fallen in?" Cornelis shouted inches away from where Lena sat with her bloomers around her ankles.

Hastily, she finished her business, collected her mittens, and pulled herself together. The instant she lifted the latch, he pulled the door open and grabbed the chamber pot.

She eyed the rope, wishing she could use it to flail him after such a disrespectful question. Instead, she opted to grasp hold of it, though any meekness Cornelis inferred from that action was faked.

Off they went, Cornelis firmly gripping Lena's arm above the elbow as they trudged at a pace more suited to his long legs' gait than what her frozen appendages could manage with dignity. Reaching the stoop, they kicked away the accumulated snow. So much snow falling so rapidly did not bode well for rescue.

The relative silence of the entryway was a blessing as the door separated them, at last, from the wind. They stomped their feet and—after a moment's hesitation—brushed snow off each other's backs and shoulders before stepping into the classroom. Elsje and Saartje had organized a game of Simon-Says.

Inside the schoolhouse, peace reigned.

That peace was not mirrored in Lena's soul.

She had to wait a full ten minutes before her frustrations with Cornelis simmered down enough to allow rational thought. *Hoping for a kiss, indeed—if he even so much as puckers up after eating a pickle, I will slap him!* Her stomach growled. *We're all hungry. Would the children consider watermelon pickles an acceptable bedtime treat?* She looked at the clock. *Only seven o'clock? For all that's happened, it should be midnight!*

Saartje showed wisdom beyond her years (or perhaps it was merely hope that equaled in the heart of every other female within twenty miles of Cornelis). She brought the game to an end with, "Simon says, 'Everyone gather around Mister de Boer for a story!' as soon as he gets dry socks on again!"

Cornelis traded socks, and accepted the book Antje handed him. Leaning against the wall, he began to read. The students settled in, some lying on their stomachs with chins resting on crossed arms, others lying on their backs using their arms for pillows, others sitting cross-legged facing the storyteller.

Lena fled to the teacherage, telling herself it was to contemplate bedding—not to avoid Cornelis. *My bed pillow, a throw-pillow. Two linen sheets, two flannel sheets already on the bed. Three pillowcases, a feed sack, an afghan, two quilts, one comforter . . . not much, for eighteen.*

Cornelis' voice wafted over the partition that divided the classroom from the teacherage as he ended one story and began another.

She almost hated to interrupt, but knew it would take some time to get everyone settled. She made piles of linens, and then slipped into the cloakroom where she spread the storage closet curtain across the floor as a barrier between the chill air seeping through floorboards and the boys' rugs. Hearing Cornelis say, ". . . and everyone lived happily ever after," she quickly finished her task.

"Thank you, Mister de Boer," she said, coming into view. "Perhaps you could read another story before we turn down the lights. Now, we must make up beds. The boys will be in the cloakroom and the girls can—"

"Excuse me," Cornelis interrupted, "but I think it would be better for all of us to be together in the classroom where it is warmest."

Lena hated to admit it, but he was right. Privacy would hardly be an issue tonight with everyone sleeping fully clothed. There was comfort in a larger group. "In that case, the boys will be one side of the stove and the girls on the other."

"The chamber pot will be in the teacherage," Cornelis said, addressing another issue that, in the confusion, Lena hadn't considered. "If you need to use it during the night, remember: A closed door means the room is occupied."

"Liesbeth and Sterre, after Mister de Boer and Lucas bring out the mattress from my bed, you two can share it, lying end-to-end. Antje and Maartje, you may bring out the braided rug by my bed to sleep on." With careful positioning of rugs, two children could share most pieces of bedding. Pillows were distributed fairly based on Cornelis' system of, "I'm thinking of a number between one and fifty . . ."

Cornelis took down the storage closet curtain in the cloakroom and helped the boys arrange their rugs on it. Coats became blankets; hats, mittens, and scarves filled the pillowcases and feed sack, leaving bare pillows for other heads. The silliness of watermelon pickles at bedtime eased the awkwardness of boys and girls bedding down in one room.

If she had remembered they were Cornelis' favorite (a detail he didn't miss, smacking the very lips she was desperately trying to forget) pickles may have eased, rather than magnified, a certain single schoolteacher's discomfort, too.

❋ ❋ ❋

Tuesday Night, November 26 ◆ Finally, the schoolroom grew quiet. Because of using the mattress, two rugs remained: one on the boys' side where Cornelis would sleep; one on the girls' side for Lena.

Cornelis added another log to the fire. Lena put the water bucket that Lucas had filled with snow to melt on the stove for the next morning's oatmeal, and got beans soaking in another. Cornelis extinguished the wall lamps. He left the lamp on Lena's desk burning, but turned the wick low.

In the shadows, his voice was soothing. "Even if you're not tired, close your eyes and rest. Instead of reading another story, I'll sing to you. Miss Stryker and I will stay awake until we know everyone is asleep. And even then, if you wake up and are afraid, come wake us up. Miss Stryker will sleep beside her desk, and I will be near the entryway door."

That news was enough to calm even the most fearful child who fervently believed not one fearsome thing could get past Mister de Boer.

Cornelis carried his and Lena's rugs to the blackboard where he folded them to cushion the floor. He motioned for her to join him. Standing in the back of the room, she debated retreating to the teacherage. *To do what? Sit alone in the darkness? No, I need to be out here for the girls' sake.*

She stepped out of her *klompen* and padded silently across the bed-strewn floor to where Cornelis awaited her. She pointedly moved her rug a few inches farther away from his. Once she was settled, he began to sing.

The sheer splendor of his voice stunned her. It had been years since she had heard the de Boer family sing together. In the months since school began, she had often marveled at Antje and Maartje's abilities. Tonight, Cornelis' unaccompanied voice wrapped itself around simple songs and infused them with comfort.

For Lena, the sound muted every harsh word that had ever crossed his lips. It fogged every harbored grudge. By the third song, she could have forgiven him everything as long as he kept on singing.

She leaned her head against the wall and closed her eyes and let Cornelis' velvet voice take her to places she craved, but had never been: places where life was always sweet, places where happiness reigned . . . places where there was no stock market crash . . . no killed puppies . . . no missing mothers or fathers . . . no blizzards putting her at such close proximity to a man who set her self-control tottering with one kiss, and now nearly finished the job with songs in the night.

She jolted back to consciousness when Cornelis' whispered, "Are you awake?"

Her nod bounced against the wall. If she had not been able to see the shadow of his hand lying lightly on hers, she may have deemed it a dream.

He began to hum, his voice bridging the gap between silence and song so gently even the lightest sleeper did not startle. Lena leaned against the wall and let the music wash over her again. Humming shifted to singing ... songs as soothing as lullabies, each one chosen from what Lena suspected was the repertoire Antje and Maartje knew well.

Sleep overtook her senses. *"Move your rug and lie down."* But the mind is a funny thing; it picks and chooses what it wishes to hear and ignores the rest.

To Lena's mortification, she roused enough to discover her mind hadn't only embraced the idea of lying down, but her head rested on Cornelis' shoulder.

She scrambled to move away, rising too fast and at the wrong angle, which meant she banged her head on the chalk tray. The sharp pain was a welcome sensation because it offered something on which to concentrate besides her indiscretion.

Cornelis tugged her back down and whispered. "You've had a busy day. Put your head on my lap, if you'd like."

Horror rose like bile in her throat. She couldn't have been more shocked if he'd suggested she undress.

"Several children are restless," Cornelis whispered. "Janneken has yet to settle in, and Maas is still awake, I'm sure. If I know Antje, she is trying to hold out to hear the last song. We'd better stay here, because once we go to bed, we will be out like lights."

Lena offered hesitantly, "I'll stay awake; you must be exhausted."

"I should have listened to Yzaak today, but if I had, you would be alone with the children."

"It is good to have you here tonight."

He poked her lightly with his elbow. "Hard for you to admit, isn't it?"

Muffled sounds drew their attention to Janneken. The girl sat up and looked around the room. She wended her way to the teacherage and closed the door.

"How is she doing?" Cornelis asked.

"Janneken is a loner so it is hard to see much difference, but she and Wim have formed a solid friendship."

After Janneken returned, Lena tiptoed through the room, bending to cover a shoulder, or move a shoe out of her path. Maas now breathed steadily. The boys snored and snuffled, deep in sleep. Several girls tossed, but no eyes stared back at her. Except for Janneken, Cornelis' calming voice had sent them all to dreamland. The blizzard was the least of her worries.

Lena extinguished the lamp on her desk and paused there until her eyes adjusted. Finding nothing else to do, she returned to Cornelis.

"Everything okay?"

She nodded. They stared into the darkness, each succumbing to private thoughts and exhaustion. A surprising calm passed over Lena—such serenity that Cornelis' quiet voice startled her. "I wrote two letters. One to Bram, one to Brigetta."

Her throat constricted. "I see," she managed.

"I apologized, and said we must talk at Christmas."

Gustave's kitchen announcement sizzled in her mind. "I thought you were going to . . ." she tempered the accusatory "run" she'd almost said to the gentler wording of: "go away at Christmas."

If he wondered how she knew, he did not ask. "That was panic talking. I'll be here to meet first with Bram alone, then with him and Brigetta together."

The jolt of his words left Lena numb. Just as she'd not felt the release she hoped for when she first confronted Cornelis, she now felt none of the triumph a victor should feel. *He has satisfied my ultimatum, giving me nearly everything I wanted. In fact, his solution is better than speaking to everyone he had wronged . . . So where is the sense of freedom I should feel?*

He squeezed her hand. "Usually, I wish you would shut up, but your silence in unnerving."

"It took courage to write those letters, but a wound must be cleaned to heal without festering. Your letter is like a cleansing agent. I am . . ." she choked on the words *proud of you* and settled on "pleased."

"There's something you need to know." His lips hovered so close to her ear, she felt each word vibrate in her head as his warm breath on her skin wreaked havoc with her emotions. "I will talk to them about the past, but not to you. Can you accept that?"

She sucked in her breath. Despite his promises, she harbored a suspicion he'd leave vital stones unturned, and be amused that he had silenced her. *I was only a partial witness to what happened in 1919. I fume over his lack of repentance, but can I learn to forgive?*

I believe you wrote the letters," she said slowly, "but how will I know you have followed through on the rest? If I knew, I would give my word to never mention the past again."

"Fair enough." He stretched far above his head and yawned. "Do you realize what has happened here tonight, Lena? We managed to have one conversation without attacking each other."

"That's probably due more to sixteen students within hearing distance than any credit to us," she admitted with a crooked grin. "We were at each other's throats like alley cats on the way to the outhouse. I'll gladly bury the hatchet, Cornelis, but please don't renege on your promises."

Cornelis leaned forward, supporting his knees in the crooks of his elbows. He stared at his stockinged feet with their soles pressed together. When he spoke, his words were surprisingly impersonal. "Are you warm enough? The fire is going down, but to stoke it now would wake everyone."

"I'm fine, and the children have enough covers."

He sprang to his feet with the ease of a twenty-nine-year-old man in perfect condition. His feet, planted inches apart, formed a narrow V through which gray light from the window shadowed her face. Lena struggled to rise, all too aware her forty-six-year-old body was no match for his suppleness. He reached out slowly, as if afraid she' reject his offer of help to rise—which she nearly did.

Cornelis didn't release her hand; rather, he sought the other one. "Can we be friends, Lena?" he asked. He swung their hands between them.

He tugged her hands in a silent reminder of the unanswered question: *"Friends?"*

She nodded.

Moonlight reflecting on the snowy world outside marked the path of his smile. He dropped a slow kiss on her forehead, then lifted her hand and rubbed each knuckle along the stubble on his chin. Abruptly, he released her hand, picked up his rug, and walked towards the sleeping boys.

Clutching her rug, Lena shuffled across the floor to her desk. She lowered her body to the rug, pulled her coat off the desk chair and settled it over her body. Turning to one side, she hugged her knees against her chest with one arm, bent the other to form a pillow, and stared into the shadowy room.

From a corner, a child's muffled voice sounded as if rising from a bad dream's depths. Others stirred. Cornelis hummed, filling the ears of those in need of comfort but not disrupting those already asleep.

Lena closed her eyes and floated above slumber's cottony fields like a dandelion's white heads blown free. Her last coherent thought before sleep claimed her was, *I could listen to him sing forever.*

Lying by the entryway's door, Cornelis couldn't sleep. It mattered little that he was on a rug in Dutch Valley School, not at home in bed. His night-musings since the September day he first laid eyes on Lena Stryker again made no sense.

Everything about her drove him to distraction: her flashes of anger . . . her high-and-mighty demands . . . the full-scale laugh that lit up her eyes until their cornflower blue took his breath away . . . her gentleness with his daughters . . . the stubborn set of her jaw . . . the curve of her cheeks . . . the wild-flower taste of her lips . . . the way she could spit tacks one minute and tease the next.

At least, after he talked to Bram and Brigetta he could put Lena out of his mind. Once he wiped clean the slate of past transgressions, she'd revert to being his daughters' teacher; nothing more. The only reason he kissed her the first time was to put her in her place.

And tonight's kiss? It was to celebrate an unemotional conversation; a "thank-you" gesture, that's all it was. His last coherent thought before sleep claimed him was: *I are a fool if I believe that.*

✳ ✳ ✳

Wednesday, November 22 ✦ The whisper was faint. "Lena?"

She jolted awake, her heart pounded, fragments of an odd dream lingered. "Wh-wha-what is it?" she stammered.

"I emptied the ashes, and poked the remaining coals into flames with the kindling that's left . I'm going to clear a path to the outhouses, and then I'll bring in more wood. It's not quite six o'clock, but the children are beginning to stir."

She lifted her head and rubbed her eyes. Sixteen mounds lay unmoving; fire crackled in the stove; Cornelis wore a scarf draped around his neck. "You did all that without me hearing you?" she whispered.

"It's not because I'm quiet; you sleep like a log!" Cornelis helped her rise, then picked up her rug.

In the early morning light, the classroom lacked the charm of the night before—it now looked like the aftermath of a disaster. She stretched beneath her coat-covering. "I'll start breakfast. Once everyone wakes up, it will be chaos. Lucky you, getting to shovel and enjoy a bright and peaceful world!"

"I can do oatmeal, if you'd rather change places," he teased. "Oh, and you should comb your hair!"

She swatted at him on her way to the teacherage. One look in her mirror was enough to startle anyone. "Hopefully I haven't looked like this since I came in from the outhouse last night!" she muttered and brushed her hair vigorously, pinning it up in a high twist.

With neither the time nor sufficient privacy sufficient to allow her to change clothes, she carried breakfast supplies out to the classroom.

While Cornelis checked the fire to ensure it wouldn't go out, the students awakened one by one.

Some moaned and rolled over, covering their heads; others sat up and took stock of their surroundings.

Satisfied the fire would keep going, Cornelis dressed for outdoors. The blast of cold air coming from beneath the entryway door when he left was enough to roust the last remaining sleepers.

"Good morning, everyone!" Lena caroled as she measured oatmeal and salt.

Adda woke up cheerful and energetic, hopping rug-to-rug as if each bed was part of a game of hopscotch. Finally, Lena assigned her the task of stirring raisins and brown sugar into the oatmeal. That freed Lena to prepare for lunch. Others helped dissemble beds and return items of outerwear used as bedding to the appropriate hooks in the cloakroom.

Wim scratched an opening in the ice crystals on one window with his fingernail and offered a running commentary. "Mister de Boer is chopping a hole for Midnight to get water. Now he's pitching hay."

Cornelis returned wearing a shroud of cold air and announced the path to the girls' outhouse was open. "Everyone uses it until I get the drift in front of the other one cleared." With the new day's calm weather, it was deemed safe for the older students to take over Cornelis' escort duties.

"Are you going to help Miss Stryker teach us today, Mister de Boer?" Raimund asked after breakfast.

"I'd much rather teach than shovel my automobile out of the drift that has now likely covered the bonnet! Which reminds me: I know the snowdrift going from the ground to the roof of Midnight's shed looks like it'd be fun to climb, but I don't want anyone trying it. It's too risky; dangerous, even."

Lucas and Jaap restocked the wood box with dry wood from the entry, refilled buckets with snow to melt near the stove, and then helped Cornelis shovel. Meanwhile, the others took turns washing breakfast dishes and reorganizing the room back to normal. School began on time.

After opening exercises, Cornelis pulled Lena aside. "If I get dug out and the engine starts, I need to drive somewhere. The logical place is back to town. Wherever I land, I'll call the other parents to let them know all is well. It's possible someone will make it out here by noon, but if not, will you be okay?"

"Of course. My main concern is food, but I'll add rice to stretch the beans and ham for lunch. If supper is needed, there's canned fruit and eight eggs. Hard-boiled, that would give each child half an egg. Oh, and enough popcorn for several batches. It's not much, but better than nothing."

"I'm not sure when I'll be back to pick up the girls."

"They'll be fine. Who will come for Janneken?" She looked at the girl bent over her geography book.

"Her nearest neighbor is Jillis Van Leuven. He'll come for Saartje; I'll have him work it out so Betje doesn't attempt the trip."

He hunkered down between his daughters' desks and conducted a quiet conversation. They nodded; he kissed them. Antje hugged him, but Maartje flung her arms around his neck and kissed him six times—on his forehead and nose, each cheek, the lips and chin.

Cornelis rose and cleared his throat, the tear-choked sound hinting that what Lena suspected was true: Juanita's love shone through Maartje's playful kisses.

Unexpected emotion filled Lena's throat and eyes as she bent to help Maas.

The sun rose, cloaking the earth in satiny snow like a bridal gown studded with pearls. Each student returned squinting from the outhouse. Light filtered through Elsje's painted windows in dazzling beauty.

"I'm glad Elsje's pictures are big, or we'd all need blinders like what Midnight wears!" someone said.

The first parent arrived after the lunch of beans mixed with ham and rice. Dries Wynkoop appeared in the doorway, his arrival announced happily by Wim who had scratched a peephole in the painted windows when approaching sounds outside the confines of the classroom offered hope of rescue.

When the door opened, Wim looked up from the floor where he sat pulling on his overshoes. He jumped to his feet and buried his face in his father's familiar woolen jacket. Dries patted the boy's shoulder and grinned at Lena. "Everything all right here?"

"We'll be glad to see our families, but worked out."

"Cornelis got word to everyone." Dries looked into fifteen expectant faces. "I wish I could help more of you get home, but roads are under drifts as high as a horse's head. I followed Cornelis' path to our house to get here; I'm sure glad he shoveled what he did!"

He reached into his deep pockets. "Hilde sent these. Wim gets his at home." He handed Lena two brown bags.

While Wim and his father headed home, Lena distributed *broedertjes* all around; there was even one for her. The sweet muffins were a welcome reminder a familiar world awaited them beyond the snowbound schoolhouse's walls.

After Dries & Wim Wynkoop's departure, Lena struggled to keep things scholarly and resorted to the all-time solution: a big group activity. With the Christmas program fast approaching, a rehearsal would help pass the time and engage everyone.

Fathers appeared, and students disappeared. Those that remained, carried on. Midafternoon, Hans arrived and told Lena that Cornelis had reached town safely. Her relief felt like finally being able to rise to the surface of the gravel pit's pool and breathe again.

When Teunis Vande Veer came, Ruud Van der Voort lingered to help him shovel a path from Midnight's stall to the road, knowing Teunis had already cleared many drifts from his far corner of the county just to reach the school.

Then, Lena stood alone in the quiet schoolroom. Echoes of children's voices raised in laughter, teasing, excited conversation mingled with a niggling memory of one soft voice whispering, "...*friends*...?"

Assuming the road would be clear for Gustave to arrive at his usual time, Lena quickly packed her satchel and stacked the used linens. Piling canning jars and tins into a box, she marveled, "If it were not for the teacherage, we'd have had nothing to eat!" She shut the doors on the nearly empty hutch.

All the way to town, she regaled Gustave with tales of the adventures. He laughed and commiserated, taking note of the smile couching each word.

As Gustave's headlights pierced the growing darkness, out on the farm in Rebecca's kitchen, Antje begged to help prepare their early supper, insisting that Hans play a game with Maartje in the parlor while she and her grandmother worked together.

Midst helping Rebecca pare carrots and potatoes, Antje confided, "Grandmother, last night while we slept on our rugs, Father kissed Tante Lena!"

Rebecca squeezed a potato so hard it slithered from her hand and skated across the kitchen floor. "Oh!" Her thoughts raced, she longed to pump the little girl for details, but feared doing so could come back to haunt her. *Children often imagine what they wish to be true,* she reminded herself. "Have you told anyone else about this?"

Antje shook her head. "Only you."

"Let's keep it our secret, okay?"

"It's a good secret, isn't it?" Antje said, crinkling her nose.

"Hmm," Rebecca said noncommittally, though her heart raced.

In town, after a good evening together around the supper table and assembling a jigsaw puzzle in the parlor, Lena pleaded tiredness and disappeared into her bedroom at the foot of the steps. Snow on the parsonage lawn shimmered beneath the starry sky as Gustave and Hanna made their rounds, preparing the house for the night.

Snuggling beneath their down comforter, the Dominie pulled his wife close and posed a question that had been pushing against the surface of his subconscious ever since the ride home from the schoolhouse. "Did it seem to you that Lena was particularly happy tonight?"

Hanna's responding nod bumped against Gustave's chin. "She did. And I know why! Remember how I was on the telephone when you came in? It was Rebecca with a secret she could not contain. Right before she called, Antje had told her—well, you need the whole story! It seems Cornelis spent last night at the schoolhouse with Lena and the students. All very proper, of course."

"Of course. And?"

"Cornelis got snowbound at the school when he went to pick up the girls." As she shifted her body, Gustave felt the flutter of her eyelashes against his cheek. "Antje said Cornelis and Lena sat on rugs by the blackboard and 'talked for hours,' according to her version. She couldn't hear their words, but she said: 'Father kissed Tante Lena, Grandmother!' We heard stories galore of soup, dominoes, ropes, and wet mittens from my unusually happy sister, but the story of a kiss is one she neglected to tell us!"

"Well, well, well."

"Apparently, Lena has set aside whatever kept her in a dismal state of mind since school began. Funny how a kiss or two can wipe a woman's memory clean!"

"We should test that theory!" Gustave lowered his lips until they stilled his wife's whispers. "What do you think about Lena's storytelling gaps now?"

"Who?" Hanna murmured, and snuggled closer.

✱ ✱ ✱

Tuesday, December 10 ◆ Midafternoon, Lena walked nonchalantly to the window and then turned and winked at the twins. Raimund asked permission to go outside, and Bartel promptly waved his hand. Lena did not correct the other students' assumption the boys were visiting the outhouse.

They returned within seconds, followed by Teunis Vande Veer. "Look here, Maas!" Raimund crowed. "Our father brought your birthday surprise!"

Maas obviously did not view an old metal toolbox and lumpy knapsack as much of a birthday surprise, but he smiled politely.

Teunis made several trips out to his buggy and then motioned for everyone to gather around the hastily constructed table of boards and sawhorses. "One of the most important things a person can do is to create something beautiful. What I do to is provide houses where God's choir can live."

He withdrew several birdhouses from the knapsack and placed them in the center of the table. "There's enough wood for everyone to build one."

At this news, Maas perked up.

Two hours sped by as the students measured, sawed, sanded, and nailed. Some added dowels from which the birds could sit and sing; others nailed spools of different sizes like steps leading to the door.

Teunis helped Maas add two windows to his birdhouse because "Even birds like to look outside," Maas explained to Lena.

When each house was shingled and painted, it was carefully propped to dry on slats near the wall.

As they relaxed at their desks over apple fritters, Mister Vande Veer took his place on the Storytime stool and whistled birdcalls for them. Some, they identified readily; others stumped them. By the time the last crumb disappeared, each student could whistle at least one bird's language.

At day's end, Teunis said, "When you take your birdhouse home in a day or two, hang it in a place where birds can live safely and sing—and then, someday, make another house so they can invite a friend to live nearby."

Even when Cornelis arrived, Teunis Vande Veer retained honors as Man-of-the-Hour.

Mission accomplished, Lena gloated. *Maas had a good birthday, and the twins now know that though their father may not be Charles Atlas, he is someone humans and birds can laud.*

❋ ❋ ❋

Sunday, December 15 • The first hint of trouble came in church. Lena was bone-tired after weeks of intense efforts to prepare for the Dutch Valley School's Christmas program. Over the years, this program had stimulated increasing excitement in both participants and attendees.

This year the program promised to deliver far-and-beyond all expectations. *And for that, the credit is due to the de Boer girls' marvelous voices,* Lena admitted. Even at rehearsals, the music soared and the children's confident voices carried their perfectly memorized speaking parts to the farthest corners of the room.

What with parents creating costumes and building sets, it was difficult to keep the program a secret that only the students and teacher knew. When the crowd gathered tonight, they would enjoy an inspiring and entertaining program.

Sitting in church, Lena's spirit caught up with her body. All day Saturday, she had baked. A pesky burn on her left hand—shaped like a half-moon in the pouch between her thumb and index finger—was a stinging reminder that even routine tasks require full attention. *After the program tonight, things will get back to normal,* she vowed privately and swallowed a yawn.

Swallowing yawns made for tear-blurred eyes. But even through that veil, Lena noticed something was amiss as she took stock of her surroundings. Four rows ahead of Lena and the Huitink sisters, the de Boer pew was missing three-fifths of its usual occupants. Hans and Rebecca sat shoulder-to-shoulder; Cornelis, Antje, and Maartje were missing.

Lena pleaded, "*Oh dear God, don't let my best singers be sick!*" The service began, but Lena was too busy worrying and plotting to pay much attention. *If needs*

*be, on Antje's solo, the others can hum while they conduct stage
business behind her; that will increase the volume if her voice is
weakened by a cold. But Maartje simply must be able to sing!
She carries the townsfolk' song and no one else, not even Antje
can do it so well. Doggone it, I knew I shouldn't allow the
students to make snow angels last week. But it was a perfect
day, and childhood has so few winters . . .*

After church, Lena moved quickly to the end of her
pew. "Rebecca!" she called over Geesje Van der
Voort's shoulder, halting the fond mother's report on
how excited Sterre was about the upcoming program.
"If you'll excuse me, Geesje, I simply must speak with
Rebecca," and added with what she hoped was enough
fervor to pacify the woman, "Your daughter will be
quite the hit with her piano solo, I know."

Rebecca paused in the aisle at Lena's beckoning.
Both began to talk at once, and the older woman said,
"Go ahead. What I have to say is not good news, so
there's no rush."

"Oh dear; I hope your not-good-news is unrelated
to my frantic question: Where are Antje and Maartje?
Please tell me they aren't sick! I feel terrible about
letting the children make snow angels. I bundled them
up, but snow does creep into collars and up sleeves.
With the program tonight, I need those two angel
voices in perfect health!"

"Oh, it's not their health that is of concern; it's their
whereabouts. Cornelis took off with them yesterday
morning, and we assumed they had gone Christmas
shopping. When they didn't come up to the Big

House last night, Hans went over to the Little House and found a vague note from Cornelis on the kitchen table. On our way to church this morning, we saw his car at the train depot. To be safe, Lena, you should make other plans for the girls' parts, because it looks as if they will not be back in time."

Behind her, an eavesdropping Geesje Van der Voort said hopefully, "You know, Lena, if the de Boer girls are unable to participate, Sterre could take their parts. She knows them perfectly. She picks up things so quickly." Geesje's boasting shattered beneath Lena's steel-tipped glare.

Lena sank down on the nearest pew. People milled about, heading for the foyer, talking to friends—people whose lives had not disintegrated when they hit the brick wall of Cornelis' arrogant view of himself. Such a lofty perception allowed whatever he wanted (or thought he deserved) to have precedence over that others may need or desire.

He has run again. I bet he's laughing about suckering me into believing him. All his empty promises . . . Did he think maybe he should wait until after the program tonight to leave? No! All he cares about is the man he sees in the mirror.

Rebecca asked, "Can others take the girls' place if they are not back in time?"

Lena shook her head—not as in denial, but in shock to be perched on a crisis' precipice. "Rebecca, I could wring Cornelis' neck! He's the most thoughtless . . ." She struggled to stem a surge of bitterness. "Forgive me; you're his mother, and we're in church. Hanna,

Gustave and I will go out to the schoolhouse at four o'clock. If you hear anything before then, please call."

Lena dodged slower parishioners and made her way along the aisle. She bypassed Gustave and stepped outside. Cold air slapped her face and wrapped her skirts around her ankles, but she pulled her cape closer and scurried along the footpath leading to the parsonage.

Reaching the kitchen, she slammed pots and pans around, creating a din that muffled her outbursts: ". . . rotten, low-down . . ." *Crash!* ". . . miserable, selfish . . ." *Bang!* ". . . pig-headed . . ." *Boom!* Lena's supply of nasty names, always on the sparse side, soon ran thin. She spat out a word that had always struck her as vindictive: "Seersucker!"

When said at top pitch and accompanied by the satisfying *Clatter-clunk!* of kettles tumbling off their shelf, "Seersucker!" was the perfect cussword for a member of the Dominie's household.

The swinging door between kitchen and hallway bounced off both walls. Hanna grasped her sister's shoulders and shook her—hard. "Lena! What's going on? I could hear you halfway across the lawn! I come in the front door and what do I hear? You—the teacher of young children, and the Dominie's sister-in-law—caterwauling like an alley cat! What's wrong?"

A lid slipped from Lena's hand and struck the floor, rolling crazily toward the wall where it bounced back and rocked like a resounding cymbal. Hanna stretched out her foot and stomped on it.

Lena knelt to gather the pots and pans and lids into sets again, reserving the saucepan she had first sought, which had begun the whole cacophonic kitchen concert. "It was, uh, well, you know, I guess . . . uh, sorry."

Hanna rolled her eyes. "Well, that explains everything! Get yourself under control while I reassure our guests that—"

Lena shot up from her crouch, the abruptness silencing Hanna. She let loose a wild "*Arrgghh!*" more terrifying than the crashing pans.

"Hush!" Hanna hissed. and lunged for her again.

"What guests?" Lena demanded, twisting free of her sister's iron grip.

Hanna quickly blocked the closed door like a watchman standing guard. "The Huitink sisters."

"*Arrgghh!*" Lena yelped again. She grabbed Hanna's arm and pleaded, "I'll fix dinner, but you must excuse me from sitting at the table with those two old biddies. It is simply too much for me today. You have no idea!"

"I guess I don't," Hanna snapped. She moved close to Lena; her eyes narrowed. "You sit by these two women every Sunday for years, but refuse to sit across the table from them when they are guests in our home? The only reason I invited them is because I thought it would be something you'd enjoy—to help you relax before the afternoon's activities begin."

"You have no idea what—" Lena's wail ended, leaving Hanna hanging as to *what* was *what*.

"Hello," caroled two frail voices. Hanna and Lena whipped around to face Floris and Femmetje.

"May we help with preparations?" Femmetje asked in her bird-like twitter. "Your kind invitation at church this morning caught us by surprise, so we have come emptyhanded. The very least we can do is assist in the kitchen."

"We are so delighted to be invited to our Dominie's home!" Floris chirped. "It will go in our diaries as the highlight of the year! We have kept diaries since we were young girls. Oh, the stories they tell!" She fluttered her hands between her lips and her heart. "Gracious! Sister and I often say, 'We would do well to burn those before we pass on!' That's what we say, but we never do."

"Floris and I are so much alike, as are the two of you," Femmetje trilled. "Isn't it wonderful to have a sister? A dearer friend I've never had! Why, Floris knows my deepest thoughts."

The Huitink sisters were too busy cooing to notice their hostesses' radish-hued faces. Only Lena heard the burbling undertones in Hanna's quick reply. "There will be no helping in the parsonage kitchen! Already, Lena is experiencing butter-fingers over the thought of entertaining such fine cooks as you."

Firmly, she ushered them away. "The best place for us is in the parlor. We'll have a nice little visit until the Dominie comes home. I know he will want to hear all about your trip to your cousin's funeral in Pella, wasn't it?"

Only half-listening to her sister's running chatter, Lena opened the oven to check the roast. "Cornelis de Boer," she muttered, stepping back from the oven's blast of heat, "I hope someone, somewhere, someday, treats you as rotten as you treat others!"

By the time Gustave arrived home, Lena's mood was in storm-cloud stage. Her anger with Cornelis had transformed into utter despair as she realized that, within a matter of hours, she would welcome a crowd of parents and grandparents, neighbors and friends to a program that was missing its stars.

With Gustave on taking-care-of-guest duty, Hanna dashed into the kitchen, took a look around and started making a cream sauce for the peas. "Okay," she said as she stirred steadily, "what's your problem?"

Lena spread frosting. "Cornelis left town today—the day of the school Christmas program for which Antje and Maartje have key roles. She added caustically, "Did I mention he took the girls?"

"Lena!" Hanna's stern tone meant business.

"Don't try to scare me with that voice; I'm a teacher; I know all the tricks."

"Yes, and you know how to fix a problem. You're upset because Cornelis took the girls away? What if they had measles or pneumonia? You'd adjust the plans, right? Do the same now. It's not the end of the world; it's a bump on the road. Life goes on."

"Life goes on," Lena mocked. She concentrated on repairing the gouges in the cake where she'd wielded the knife with more frustration than finesse.

"Why are you really upset, Lena?" Hanna asked as she tasted the sauce and added pepper. "Don't forget, we are sisters and sisters are 'dearest friends'," she trilled in perfect imitation of Femmetje.

"Will you hush?" Lena grinned crookedly. "Why can't I ever get to have a tantrum? That's what makes me madder than ten wet hens. Just once—once, mind you!—I should be allowed to stomp around, throw things, and cuss a blue streak *and* then have people just step aside and say, 'Leave Lena alone; she's really upset. Something dreadful must be wrong!' Why does someone always try to talk me out of it, or scold me until I feel like an idiot?"

Hanna hooted. "Oh yes; I heard you cussing a blue streak, all right: *'Seersucker'!*" She fanned her cheeks. "Whoo-*eee*, sister! Let's see . . . what was it you wanted to happen? Oh, right." She backed toward the porch, her arms spread like shields. Scanning the kitchen, her eyes narrowed and then widened slowly.

Lena was mute and, for once, oblivious to frosting hardening in the bowl. Hanna waved her arms as if restraining a rampaging crowd on the porch. She planted her feet, assumed a fighter's stance, and growled, "Back off, I say. Leave this cussing, fuming woman alone. She's dreadfully upset. Ain't no telling what she'll do next. Danger lurks! Stand back!"

Gustave opened the swinging door with a bounce that he caught on the backswing. "I'm floundering in there! Please say dinner is almost ready," he pleaded. Then he noticed his wife—frozen in crouched-statue posture. His brow furrowed. "Everything all right out here?" he asked cautiously.

Hanna drew back her lips and snarled at him like a rabid dog. "Dandy."

Slowly, she rose and shook her shoulders like a caterpillar shrugging off the final inches of its cocoon. Reincarnated as the Dominie's sedate and lovely wife, Hanna cooed, "Never better. And you?"

Across the room, Lena gurgled. Her lips twitched. She burped out a chuckle, then let loose a loud laugh that, once started, didn't stop. She hiccupped, wiping tears away with her apron, and doubled over a chair's back while tears spurted down her cheeks. She pulled her apron over her head and howled a sound that hovered somewhere between pleasure and pain.

"What's wrong with her?" Gustave asked, glancing over his shoulder toward their guests. For once, he was grateful the Huitink sisters were deaf.

Hanna pursed her lips as her mind sifted out the most pertinent detail: "The de Boer girls will not be singing tonight in the school's program."

Wisely asking nothing more, he backed out of the kitchen. *I'll do better with Huitink sisters than Stryker sisters.* Pasting on a smile, he reentered the parlor.

"Have we ever told you the story of how our father came to Dutchville?" Floris asked eagerly.

"I'm not sure I recall all the details," Gustave hedged. *But, weighed against the kitchen drama?* He settled in to hear an unremarkable account in another lengthy telling that he knew well from past- and oft-repeated experience began: *"Our father was a poor but honest, hard-working, handsome, good Christian man . . ."*

Out in the kitchen, Hanna gave a mime's *"Calm-down, back-off!"* gesture to an invisible crowd, then grinned at Lena and crossed the kitchen to plant a noisy kiss on her sister's cheek that was rosy from unbridled laughter.

"Oh, Hanna, I don't know how or why you put up with me. Thank you."

"Putting up with you? That's not the problem. Understanding you? Now, that's enough to send me screaming from the room! Okay; what's left to do out here? Gustave is carrying on valiantly in there, but reinforcements are necessary."

Filling the gravy bowl, Lena said sadly, "The lies Cornelis told upset me the most. If he hadn't said he would be here for Christmas, I could have handled today's crisis better. But he lied and he took the girls!"

"Later," Hanna ordered. "Now it's pot roast and smiles. It's not Christmas yet. Later, I'll listen to the full story of Cornelis-the-low-down-lying-scoundrel; now we rescue the man who is saintly and not lying about floundering."

Stuffed to the gills with fine vittles and friendly chatter, the Huitink sisters finally finished dessert and coffee. Their ancient horse and equally antiquated buggy creaked down the driveway just in time for Hanna and Lena to race from the front door to the pantry, from where they loaded Gustave's arms with Saturday's baked goods. Jugs of cider and trays of cookies and currant bread filled the Ford's boot and shared half the back seat with Lena.

Arriving at school, they saw Dries Wynkoop had delivered the boards and sturdy wooden boxes he stored for the school. While they created benches, they tossed out ideas for how to handle the de Boer girls' absence. For one song, Sterre could take over. "Geesje will be thrilled!" Hanna said.

Lena rolled her eyes. "Sterre may know the words, but Maartje gave them life. The de Boer girls' voices are truly a gift from God." *Like their father's,* she admitted and slammed a mental door on such unnerving thoughts.

"Cornelis could be back in time," Hanna said.

Lena shook her head. "The station master told Hans they caught the East-bound train to Chicago. Even if he returned tonight, it will be too late."

"Lena," Gustave said, "the best thing for your peace of mind may be to recognize Cornelis for what he is. Some people make promises they think they can keep. When they don't, they fall back on a history of broken promises, after which, life always goes on. They tell themselves, 'It has in the past, it does in the present, and it will do so in the future.' That becomes their philosophy."

He ignored Lena's muttering and continued, "It makes it hard to live or work with people like that, or trust them. And that's difficult because so often they have jobs, like Cornelis does, where getting a skeptic to trust them is part and parcel of the job. This type of person learns early on how to work a crowd, please a customer, or sell himself as believable."

"That's Cornelis," Lena said miserably. "I knew it, yet I believed every word." *And, like a fool, each kiss.*

Families arrived, stomping off snow and exchanging cheerful greetings. Students gathered in the teacherage where Lena explained vaguely, "The de Boer girls have gone away with their father."

As she reassigned parts, she boldly assured those with adjusted roles, "You'll do fine; all will go well."

At seven o'clock, Lena looked out the teacherage door and whispered, "No empty seats!" She sounded a note on her pitch pipe and the students filed out, singing (to the tune of "Clementine," the ballad from Saartje's birthday) written they had written. "Long ago there lived a Lady in the Province of Friesland . . ."

Arriving at the front, they took their places on the set. Saartje, who would both narrate and sing, began the story, "The Lady of Stavoren was the richest and proudest of all the citizens of the great port city . . ."

Lucas, as the sea captain, wore what three people recognized as Gustave's old bathrobe. Lucas faced Elsje (her lacy dress was once Brigetta's bedroom curtains) and asked, "What did you say, My Lady?"

As the Lady of Stavoren, Elsje's response held all the haughtiness the role required: "You must bring me the most precious thing in the world." Her threat, that if the sea captain failed to meet her demands he would never again work in Stavoren, sounded so real that one grandmother in the audience gasped.

Lucas replied in his best sea captain voice, "I will do my best, my Lady." The twins, in (bedsheet) sailor suits, furiously rowed the seaworthy vessel (erstwhile, the parsonage copper washtub) to carry the captain to faraway lands.

The third-grade girls portrayed townsfolk who wondered, as months passed (Wim turned calendar pages) what precious thing the sea captain would find: "A pearl bigger than an egg?" or "Bolts of silk cloth?" or "Statues of finest marble?"

Saartje recited, "Each month the captain returned with treasures, only to be rejected and scorned by the Lady of Stavoren. Each time, he sailed again. Finally, he returned, confident he had achieved success."

"What have you brought for me?" the Lady of Stavoren asked.

"Wheat!" Lucas exclaimed. "My ship is filled with wheat! What is more precious than that which gives us our daily bread?"

"Wheat? Pour every grain into the harbor!"

"My Lady," the captain pleaded. "This is wheat enough to feed our city! Give it to the poor and needy! Someday you could be in need and . . ."

"In need?" Elsje shrieked. She pulled a ruby ring from her finger and flung it into the harbor. "This ring will come back to me before I am ever in need!"

"And so," Saartje narrated, "the sea captain did as the Lady ordered and sailed away, never to return."

Antje, as the Lady of Stavoren's maid, was to have sung a poignant song of how someone with everything anyone could want could not appreciate it. Sterre managed the song quite well and the audience never knew it was not all it could have been.

Gaiety emerged as the play continued. Lena's teacherage dishes filled the table for a grand feast (consisting of painted papier-mâché food made in Art Class) that the Lady of Stavoren hosted for the richest merchants. Katrien, as chief cook, set a roasted fish before the Lady of Stavoren who noticed something in the fish's mouth as she carved. She drew forth the ruby ring, much to the diners' fearful shock.

Saartje narrated, "It was not long before fishermen noticed a sandbar blocking the harbor's mouth. The discarded wheat had sprouted and grown, catching sand that once drifted freely. Soon, ships couldn't enter the harbor. Fortunes were lost. Merchants—including The Lady of Stavoren—lost everything."

"Look into Your Heart," the townsfolk' song (written by Janneken as a poem and scored by Hanna on the parsonage piano) which should have been the de Boer girls' duet. Janneken sang words mirroring the sadness of those brought to ruin when the Lady of Stavoren failed to recognize what was truly precious.

As the play ended, the applause required several bows, and an encore of "Look into Your Heart," which the students sang a cappella. Still in costume, the actors headed for the table that was loaded with Hanna and Lena's baked goods and supplemented by mothers who couldn't stop talking about Lena housing and feeding their children during the blizzard.

She wanted to shout, *"Enough talk of the blizzard! That is one night that should never have happened—and one I hope to forget."* Instead, she kept an eye on the door. But it never opened to admit a rogue father or his daughters who were denied their place in the limelight (*Well, okay; the gaslight*) because of his broken promises.

◆ ◆ ◆

Wednesday, December 18 ◆ "I didn't realize you were bringing a partner." Lena cast an icy glance at Cornelis who stood behind Ruben De Jong.

Her nerves hummed like a taut violin string as she watched the men construct a simple stage, hang a curtain, and remove two puppets from a box. They talked idly, but Ruben kept one eye on Lena, much as he would a bull ramming a barnyard fence.

Leaving Cornelis to finish the tasks, Adda's father approached Lena. "Cornelis is new to puppetry, so today's skit will be fairly simple. But he's pleased to be here since this is in honor of Antje's birthday."

It was all Lena could do to keep from snapping, *"It would've been nice had he been as concerned about the program."* She recalled Antje and Maartje's happy voices when they returned with stories about a train trip.

That news paled, however, when Antje and Maartje realized they had missed the highlight of the year. Sterre's boasting of her role in the Christmas program's success had pushed Antje to tears. Maartje's lip had trembled, though she put on a good front. "Me and Antje, we don't care! We have a secret 'bout where we went that we can't tell a single soul!"

What stuck in Lena's craw was how easily Cornelis had ensnared his daughters with the lure of secrets. And here he was, acting as if he were God's gift to mankind just because he'd connived with Ruben to be part of the show. Lena's fury rose like steam from a boiling pot. But she could hardly argue with a father providing a surprise for his daughter's birthday. "I'm sure the children will enjoy the program." Grudgingly, she set her frustrations aside. *This is a special event for the children; don't let your grievances against Cornelis spoil it.*

When the students came in red-cheeked and smelling of crisp winter air, the puppeteers were hidden from view. After Lena's brief introduction, Ruben's voice intoned, "And now, back from their world-wide tour of famous theaters where they have performed for Kings and Queens, please welcome the stars of our show: Pop and Bob."

"Welcome, Pop and Bob!"

The little red velvet curtain opened jerkily. Two hand puppets waddled into view from opposite sides of the miniscule stage. They bowed to each other and then to the audience.

Raimund whistled shrilly with two fingers between his teeth while the others clapped.

One puppet wore a straw hat atop matted hair, and a flannel shirt that was buttoned wrong. A sign around his neck read "**pop**" in lower-case letters.

The other puppet sported blue suspenders over a bright green shirt. He was completely bald, and had a prominent nose. The sign around his neck said "**bob**."

The puppets shook fingerless hands and slapped each other's rag-stuffed shoulders repeatedly before remembering they had an audience.

"We are Pop and Bob." Pop made great show of straightening the sign around his neck. "I am . . ." he looked down at his sign. "Hmm, that's strange. I thought my name was Pop . . . But my sign says '**dod**,' so I guess I'm Dod."

"What kind of a name is "Dod,' you silly goose?" Bob-the-puppet asked disdainfully. "You're Pop; it's what your sign says: I can read it clearly."

"Are you telling me I need eyeglasses? My sign says '**d-o-d**' as plain as the nose on your face, which is very plain to see because it's so large."

Bob sighed. "Your name is Pop and, as you can see from my sign, I'm . . ." he scratched his head, "I guess I'm Gog. How very odd; I thought I was Bob."

"No, my friend, the sign says 'Bob.' You're luckier than I am. I'm stuck with a name like Dod for life."

Bob was still muttering to himself, "Why would my sign say '**gog**' if my name is Bob? Surely my mother did not name me Gog! Ah-ha! Perhaps we are too close to the problem to see things clearly."

He stuck his head around the red curtain. "Hey, little boy in the front row, tell me what my sign says."

"Bob," Wim answered.

Pop slapped Bob's arm and hooted, "Told you so!"

Bob protested, "I know what I see!" But other students confirmed that Pop was Pop, and Bob was Bob—according to the signs they wore.

Both puppets paced the miniscule stage, scratching their heads, knocking into each other with each passing, and muttering. Then Pop raised his hands and cheered. "I know! We must create a test to see if our audience can read! Usher, please distribute cards to the audience." While Lena played the role of usher, the puppets resumed pacing their confining stage.

"Children, may I have your attention?" Bob said. "Boys, please write **p-o-p** on your cards. Girls, please write 'b-o-b.' We will solve our dilemma soon!"

Pencils scratched. Bob asked, "Boys, what do your cards say?"

"Pop!" six boys responded.

"Well done! Now, girls?" Bob prompted.

"Bob!" ten voices chorused.

"Ah-ha! Okay, Bob! Now, we can *finally* sing the songs which have entertained kings and queens around the world," Pop said grandly.

"That's why we came," Bob agreed, "but the mix-up with our names has me quite upset. If only I could understand what has happened. Why is it when you looked at your name sign, you saw '**dod**,' not Pop and when I looked at mine, I saw '**gog**,' not Bob?"

"Ask that little girl in the front seat by the window," Pop suggested. "She looks very smart."

Antje burst from her seat to kneel beside the puppet stage. "Pop is '**dod**, upside-down,' and Bob is '**gog**,' upside-down! See?" She demonstrated with her card, and Bob and Pop gushed their profuse thanks.

"How about that? My name truly is Pop, and Bob really is Bob!" Pop slapped his forehead incredulously. "Bob, we should sing a song to celebrate learning an important lesson," he suggested.

"What lesson is that?" asked Bob.

"Why, that not everything is as it seems! I thought my sign had the wrong name and you thought—"

"Please don't mention all that confusion again!" Bob pleaded, clutching his stuffed head with fingerless hands. "Let's sing a song to chase troubles away."

They dramatically flung signs over their shoulders.

Then Pop warbled off-key to the familiar tune of London Bridge, "Things may not be what you see, what you see, what you see. Things may not be what you see—upside-down!"

"That's the worst song I have ever heard!" Bob scoffed.

Pop waggled a stuffed finger at him. "Perhaps what you think is the worst song is really a gem! It may not be what you first think it is!"

Bob snorted. "Maybe it would sound better if our audience sang along with us."

They did, and it sounded fine.

Since Bob-the-Puppet has the de Boer family's musical talents at his disposal, why wouldn't it? Lena's conscience not only pricked her, it stung. *Things may not be what they seem? Once again, Cornelis twists everything so that he looks good.* She stalked into the teacherage to bring out spice cake, imagining how good it would feel to heave it at Cornelis.

"Please stay to share our treat," she said more to Ruben than to Cornelis (who seemed amused by her discomfiture). Him, ignored.

When Cornelis returned later that afternoon to pick up Antje and Maartje, the students swarmed around him, most still wearing their 'pop' or 'bob' signs. Lena's temper smoldered while she buttoned jackets and tucked scarves into collars. *How dare he presume just because of a silly puppet song I'll let him off the hook for his many—and multiplying--offenses?*

"Cornelis?" she called from the stoop. "Perhaps you could borrow the puppets to put on a program for Bram and Brigetta. They'd enjoy hearing your view on dealing with life's pesky problem of what's really true."

He sucked in his cheeks. Then, he mouthed words Lena suspected were inappropriate for children to hear, and stared at her with the single-minded focus of a hunter staring down a gun's barrel.

Children trampled the gently falling snow, aiming snowballs at each other. Their light-hearted laugher seemed at distinct odds with the antagonism volleying between Lena and Cornelis.

For one fleeting moment, Lena wondered if she had gone too far. *Do I really want to wreck the holy season with the facts of how our families fell apart?* She suddenly feared what it could do to Christmas if he confessed then.

Warming herself by the stove, she thought, *The puppets were right: I got tricked into believing the lies of a kiss—things may not be what I see. I seriously doubt Cornelis intends to talk to his brother or Brigetta—or, that he sent the letters he claims he wrote. It's true: things may not be as they seem . . . I don't know what to believe.*

✹ ✹ ✹

Monday, December 23 ◆ Six adults and two children waited with others who lined the Dutchville station's platform. The first whistle blew, announcing the arrival of the Westbound train. Antje and Maartje jumped up and down, tugging on their father's hands.

Wrapped in muffs and hooded capes, Hanna and Rebeca chatted merrily. Each word sent up a puff like smoke signaling joyful messages. Gustave and Hans stood close by, stomping their feet to keep warm as they laughed and talked.

Propelled under Antje and Maartje's steam, Cornelis dodged clusters of Dutchville citizens also awaiting the arriving passengers. He allowed his daughters to guide him to where they'd decided the coach car would stop. No one noticed Lena's quiet distraction. She flitted between Hanna and Rebecca and Gustave and Hans, unable to stand still and unwilling to be near Cornelis.

At last the train came into view, arriving with so much noise that conversation on the platform became impossible. Cornelis grasped his daughters' hands—two small ones in each of his—and twirled them until their feet left the platform and they circled like a Maypole. Their lips opened wide in joyful shouts. When he slowed and they landed back on earth, the girls continued to spin dizzily, laughing even harder.

The railroad cars twisted and turned, their couplers protesting, on the final curves. Lena shot a quick glance at Cornelis, finding his face impassive and his posture rigid. *I'm not hiding a secret, yet my stomach is in knots. I can't imagine how he must feel, knowing that within minutes he comes face-to-face with his past.*

The crowd surged along the platform. Brakes screeched and a coal-smoke stench filled the air. The conductor swung off the train and positioned a three-step stool beneath the door.

After a seemingly endless delay, Brigetta's voice called, "Mama! Papa! Tante Lena!"

The next moments were blissful confusion.

Bags tumbled to the ground; hugs became more important than luggage. The others disembarking needed room, so bags, boxes, and bodies performed a shuffling dance. Lingering hugs and overflowing laughter mingled with excited questions and joyous greetings.

Brigetta's arms gathered Lena into a crushing embrace. She released her only when Bram demanded his turn. Lena bent to smother Sanna in kisses, lifting her high in the air until Gustave snatched her into his embrace.

Midst the commotion, Cornelis stood aside—a detail that only Lena noted, until Bram looked over the heads of their assemblage and extended a hand to him.

Time slid into soundless slow motion.

The two brothers' hands joined; each man drew the other into an embrace with his free arm. From her place behind Bram, Brigetta watched the men rock in place. When they separated, she moved in quickly and wrapped her arms around Cornelis. "How's my favorite brother-in-law?"

Hearing that, Lena felt her world tilt on its axis, sending her skittering to a cave where echoes haunt and images' sharp lines blur.

From within that hollow place, she heard Hans hoot, "Don't get puffed up, son! You're the only brother-in-law she has!"

Cornelis grinned awkwardly. He dropped his eyes to where Antje and Maartje dodged luggage and played ring-around-the-rosy with Sanna, much to her delight. "Annie!" the little girl said. She tugged Antje's coat. Then: "Mary!" She poked Maartje's stomach. All three girls giggled.

"That's one smart little girl," Rebecca exclaimed. "She already knows her cousins' names and which is which!"

Antje and Maartje initiated an impromptu game with Sanna while Hans and Gustave gathered luggage. Lena stared. *Such instant familiarity and ease for children just meeting one another. Oh, to be a child!*

The group walked to the waiting automobiles that would ferry them to the parsonage for their first meal together. Gustave and Hans grabbed luggage and took the lead, the three girls skipping along. Two mothers claimed Brigetta and Bram.

That left Cornelis and Lena on an island of disconcerting isolation in the chaotic excitement. She broke free of his gaze and hurried to link arms with Brigetta, leaving Cornelis to bring up the rear alone.

When the luggage was loaded into two vehicles, Cornelis suggested, "Mother and Father and the three girls can ride with me, and the others can go with Gustave."

From the center of the back seat, there wasn't much for Lena to see other than the Tudor Sedan ahead of them. Closing her eyes didn't stop the silent movie playing in her mind.

Try as she would to concentrate on the lively conversation between the other occupants of the humble Ford, she could only think about two curious occurrences on the railway platform: *How is it that a two-year-old knows which cousin is which? And how can Brigetta hug Cornelis without cringing?*

In the parsonage that bright and cold December day, what would become the routine for Bram and Brigetta's visit began. The girls played with Brigetta's childhood toys, the women worked and laughed in the steamy kitchen, and the men talked and smoked in the parlor. Brigetta moved back into her familiar role with ease—only Lena seemed on pins and needles as they prepared supper.

With all the boards added, the dining room table easily accommodated eleven. Hands joined around the table as Gustave offered the opening prayer of thanksgiving. Lena, seated between Sanna and Brigetta, suffered an internal tug-of-war between happiness and fear. She looked up after the "Amen" to meet Cornelis' eyes and knew he was engaged in a similar battle.

Cornelis accepted the dish of Lena's watermelon pickles and took three—then asked for it again, pronouncing them, "... still the best I have ever tasted; no offense, Mother!" Lena flushed as her pickles continued around the table.

"Sauerkraut!" Bram chortled and put the bowl right on his plate. "All mine!" he announced with a firmness and diction no doubt learned from Sanna.

Above the din of voices and silverware on china, came Maartje's question, "Did you find my dolly under your piano, Aunt Brigetta?"

Real life became still life in the parsonage dining room. Gustave froze, holding the meat platter midair. Rebecca halted a question to Sanna mid-word. Lena nearly dropped her water glass. All eyes moved from Maartje to Brigetta. She looked at Cornelis for an agonizing moment, then softly said, "Yes, I did, sweet girl; your doll is in my suitcase."

"Dolly!" Sanna giggled. "Dolly under piano!"

"That's right!" Maartje joined Sanna's laughter. "You put it there when we sang at—" She slapped a hand against her lips and looked guiltily at Cornelis. "I'm sorry, Father," she whispered tremulously.

Cornelis motioned to Maartje with one finger: *"Come here."* Her chest visibly shuddered beneath the napkin tucked into her collar. Slowly, she pushed back her chair and walked behind chairs to where her father sat beside her white-faced sister.

Pulling Maartje close to him with one arm, Cornelis nuzzled her hair with his chin. "It's okay, Mary-girl.

We don't need to keep that secret anymore." His voice carried like smoke in the wind to every ear at the table.

Still holding Maartje, Cornelis cleared his throat and ran his fingers through his hair. "Last Saturday, the girls and I caught the morning train to Rochester. There was something I needed to do. I'm sorry the girls missed the school Christmas program, Lena, but I wanted them with me. It was important that I made things right with Bram and Brigetta before Christmas. I didn't want to ruin this visit by delaying a face-to-face apology."

Turning to Lena, he added softly, "I had a promise to keep."

Lena gripped the seat of her chair as the earth quaked beneath her.

Cornelis continued, "Ten years ago, I destroyed a relationship with my brother and sister-in-law. My actions brought grief and separation to our families, for which I ask forgiveness. Bram, Brigetta and I have agreed to put the past behind us and move on."

Gustave cleared his throat. "Brigetta?"

Panic shaded Brigetta's face. "Yes, Papa?"

"Do you agree with Cornelis? That all is well between you?"

She hesitated only a second. "Yes, Papa."

Gustave turned to Bram who studied his water glass. "Do you agree?"

"Yes. I've missed my brother. This year, Christmas is truly happy."

Every adult expelled a breath, like a choir picking up a song at the director's cue. The children's happy chatter became the orchestra's accompaniment. Bass and tenor mingled blended with soprano and alto, and a song was born. A joyous song with only one noncompliant member of the chorus: Lena, who watched in disbelief as two families simply heard Cornelis' apology, accepted Bram and Brigetta's assurances, and picked up their parts in the harmony.

No song played in Lena's soul. Above the din of goodwill around her, Cornelis' words in the dark, blizzardy night rang out: "... *it will not include you* ..."

Sitting in the parsonage dining room while love and laughter swept years of heartache away, Lena sagged under the ramifications of her promise: "... *I give you my word, I will never mention the past again.*"

Like Cornelis, she had a promise to keep—a promise she had doubted would be required of her. Unlike him, she wasn't sure she could honor her promise, after all.

❋ ❋ ❋

Tuesday, December 24 ◆ Lena awakened before dawn, no more rested than a hen can be after a fox has circled the coop all night. She dressed quickly and checked Sanna who slept in Brigetta's old child's bed set up in Gustave's study.

She smiled at the child sprawled across the covers, her curls flung every-which-way over the pillowcase, except for the one stuck to her cheek. Easing Sanna back under the blankets, Lena crept back downstairs.

She'd hoped Sanna would awaken and sit in the kitchen like Brigetta used to do during breakfast preparations. But it had been a late night and the little girl needed her rest, what with everything this day would hold.

Pannekoeken. Apple and berry; appropriately festive fare. With batter mixed and in pans, Lena poured a cup of coffee and rested her feet on the chair opposite her. She didn't want to taint the day's joys with unsettling thoughts, but couldn't block one troubling question: *Did Brigetta tell Bram the whole story, or does his forgiveness cover an abridged version of what really happened?*

She dropped her feet to the floor with a dull thud and gathered ingredients to make syrup. As she stirred the thickening mixture, she heard footsteps on the stairs and waited, spoon in hand, while the sugary liquid bubbled.

The swinging doors opened and Brigetta, wrapped in a dressing gown, burst through. "Tante Lena! You've made pannekoeken! I make pannekoeken, but mine never turn out as good as yours."

"Do you open the oven to peek?" Lena teased.

"Of course not!" Brigetta said in mock horror. "You taught me better than that!" She strolled around the kitchen, touching the enamel top of the stove, running her finger around the curves of the new gas refrigerator's door, tapping the hook where, for years, her sweater had hung.

She caught Lena watching her and grinned. "Home," she said succinctly. Opening the cupboard, she selected a cup, moved to the stove to pour coffee into it, and refilled Lena's cup. "Come; sit with me for a bit—like we used to do."

Lena nodded, not surprised at all that their wishes coincided. "Sanna was sound asleep when I checked. She's a beautiful child."

"Yes; I limit myself to three compliments a day!"

Her laugh erased the years for Lena until she would not have been surprised to look up and see that Brigetta was wearing braids again. "It is wonderful to have you here. We have quite a list of activities planned for your short visit. Sanna will sleep the whole way home! By the way, may I assist in paying for the tickets? I've saved funds for special things."

"No, we bought them with money we'd put away before the stock market's troubles. If not, we would have been tempted to stay home. But then Cornelis came to see us, and that made me doubly glad we were able to come home. Aren't his daughters delightful?"

"I love them dearly," Lena was able to say honestly. She waited, hardly daring to breathe, in hopes Brigetta would mention Cornelis again—anything to give her an opening.

"I wish we could have met Juanita, but when we look at the girls, we can see she must have been a beautiful woman."

A sound in the hallway brought Hanna to the doorway holding Sanna. "Look who I found awake in her bed!" *It won't be easy to have a private conversation this week,* Lena thought, but smiled to hide her irritability.

The four females sat around the table drinking coffee, with milk in a cup for Sanna. She made them laugh when she blew across the cup's surface and said, "Good coffee, Tante Lena!" in perfect imitation of her mother.

"We'll have lunch today and supper tomorrow at the farm," Hanna said. "Since you are staying here, we'll share you with Hans and Rebecca on Thursday. But, we get you back on Friday until the train leaves!"

"Tonight is special, though. It involves *klompen* in the parlor." Lena pointedly looked over Sanna's head.

"Sanna knows about **S-i-n-t-e-r-k-l-a-a-s**," Brigetta spelled, though her daughter was too busy licking the cup's rim, like a kitten lapping milk, to have noticed if the caped man himself had entered the room.

Hanna watched her granddaughter's antics with amusement. "I can see you in Sanna, Brigetta. I wonder if Rebecca sees Bram in her, too? Perhaps if you ever have a little boy, he will look like Bram so we can claim Sanna for the Ter Hoorn side and the de Boer clan can claim him!"

Only Lena understood Brigetta's facial expression as she said briskly, "Well, there's only one little girl at our house, so both families can claim her. Sanna, let's go wake up your Papa for breakfast!" She scooped up her little girl and left the kitchen.

"Isn't Sanna a precious angel?" When Hanna got no response, she looked up and mistook her sister's expression for tiredness. "Oh, Lena, I'm sorry! Here I am, sitting around like royalty, and you've been working like a slave." She began to set six places at the table.

Which de Boer brother would a little boy resemble? With no answers, Lena, once again, shut a mental door. But this time, that invisible closure separated her from a future whose unguarded edge seemed riskier than the past's.

After lunch, both families skated on the Floyd River. Between supper and the Candlelight Christmas Eve service, Hans, Bram and Cornelis, transformed into *Sinterklaas* and his two helpers.

Their sleigh circled close enough to Rebecca's back porch for *Sinterklaas* to toss wrapped candies to the three excited children. Everyone trooped into town where *Sinterklaas* had miraculously filled three sets of *klompen* with good things.

Lena slipped away to finish supper preparations while the others lingered in the parlor. She had much on her mind, so was caught off-guard when Brigetta joined her. "Something smells so good, Tante Lena!"

"Just *stamppot*," she said with forced lightness.

Brigetta lifted a lid and inhaled blissfully, then opened a drawer and counted out sufficient silverware. Clutching a handful of forks, she said, "Tante Lena, we're not having time to talk, you and I, like old times."

Old times? Which old times? Before or after our lives fell apart? "Yes, well . . ."

Brigetta leaned against Lena's back. "I'm so happy, Tante Lena! I wish we lived closer to Dutchville . . .

what am I saying? I wish we lived here all the time! But Bram has a very good job. With things in such upheaval in our country, that isn't something to take lightly."

"It's not as if we can't travel to see each other."

"Exactly. But I want you to know I have a good life—a husband who loves me, a beautiful daughter, a fine home, friends, and a wonderful family here."

"I'm glad that's true and you recognize it, as such," Lena said. "Now, child, we must get this supper to the table while it is still Christmas Eve."

"Happy Christmas, Tante Lena," she said softly.

A nod was all Lena trusted in response—anything else would have betrayed the agony in her soul.

❋ ❋ ❋

Saturday, December 28 ◆ All too soon, it was Saturday. Two vehicles made a somber pilgrimage to the railway station. Sanna looked at her cousins as they all huddled together on a bench inside the station, making their legs swing in unison. "My dolly under bed," she said matter-of-factly.

"What?" six adults exclaimed.

Maartje grinned and put her arm protectively around Sanna. "Did you put her there on purpose?" she asked, their noses mere inches apart.

When Sanna nodded happily, Brigetta knelt beside her. "But she's your favorite dolly, Sanna!"

She giggled. "Annie and Mary bring her to me?"

Brigetta shot a look at Bram over their daughter's head. "You've had fun with your cousins, haven't you? Maybe they can come see us next summer." She rose from her crouch to ask Hanna, "Will you mail the doll to us, Mama?"

Gustave laughed outright. "I know that look in your mother's eye. She thinks delivery in person is a better idea!"

The train steamed into sight, overloading the senses the closer it came. Farewells sprouted from the deep loam of the visit like tulip bulbs thrusting through spring's cold soil, offering hope with a twinge of sadness at the brevity of their blooms' life.

"I wish they lived in Dutchville," wailed Maartje.

Her father held her close and let her sob.

Lena turned away, recalling too well the sensation of Cornelis' shoulder beneath her own cheek. Sitting alone in the back seat of Gustave's Ford, she looked out the window at the bleak winter day. Tears pooled and rolled down her cheeks. Hanna, getting no answer to a question which Lena had not even heard, turned. "I miss them, too," she said softly.

A tear touched Lena's lips. Swiping it away with her muff, she merely nodded as if in agreement. But the Brigetta whom Lena missed was a far different Brigetta than the one Hanna missed. It seemed improbable the Brigetta whom Lena mourned would ever be seen again.

Innocence, once destroyed, cannot be resurrected.

Part Five

Thursday, January 2, 1930 ◆ There had been some debate about whether to recommence school after the holiday vacation; only two days remained in that week. But, with farm-families' hopes for early planting, it was deemed necessary to get in as many days as possible before spring arrived.

Spring seemed remote to the sixteen students and their teacher as all gathered at Dutch Valley School two days into the new year: 1930.

The country had celebrated Christmas and New Years with cautious optimism. Decorations had been hung in defiance of dreariness; carols had been sung loudly to drown out haunting worries; good cheer had been shared cautiously as if, drop-by-drop, it might disappear, never to be seen again.

Underlying all the festivities was a sense of uncertainty. Surely a new decade would shake off the doom and gloom of the past three months and put its foot forward in confidence. But the first steps of the new year were shaky, at best.

Rumors abounded. Some became fact. As the 1928 Republican presidential nominee Herbert Hoover had promised, "We are nearer to the final triumph over poverty than ever before in the history of any land."

His election seemed to ensure prosperity. *A pipe dream*, Lena thought, overhearing her students speak of pending hardships. No child should need to know or understand bankruptcy, foreclosure, unemployment; it was hard enough for adults to handle.

If required to put a name to her emotional state, she would have said "Numb." She was numbed by the country's unsolvable troubles, numbed by the depth and breadth of the students' needs, and numbed by the supposed resolution of her problems with Cornelis.

She missed feeling alive; she even missed heart-pounding fear and blood-rushing anger. Christmas had been a season fraught with conflicting emotions that should never have occupied space in her heart and mind. Earth's troubles had edged Heaven's joys out of first place.

The first students to arrive on Thursday helped Lena pack away Christmas decorations that would serve another year. By the time everyone had arrived, the room seemed frightfully bare—a feeling Lena easily identified because it resided in her heart.

Saying goodbye to Brigetta and Bram and Sanna had been wrenching. But the cavity in Lena's heart ached for more. She had envisioned Brigetta taking her aside for a heart-to-heart. *"I am happy, Tante Lena"* did not fill the bill.

It took all her will power for Lena to infuse any enthusiasm into geography and history and word drills. If it had not meant disappointing the one student who so desperately needed joy in her life, Lena would have been tempted to downplay the next birthday event.

Janneken's summer birthday granted her a half-year celebration. The fact that time fell when Lena did not feel like celebrating, didn't allow her to wallow in the mire of grim thoughts.

If everything fell into place (which required gambling on the weather) Janneken's birthday surprise would be a treat for all. In preparation, Lena wrote and sealed notes which she sent home with the students to their parents.

Earlier than the first-arrival, Hans brought several toboggans from his barn and hidden them behind the outhouses. He then returned home to collect and deliver his unsuspecting granddaughters to school.

At morning recess, Lena hauled out the sleds. Everyone rose to her challenge of loading each one with snow. They accepted her vague reasoning of the need to clear the approach from the road to the schoolyard as adequate rationale for their efforts, and turned it all into a game.

After more of the same during the noon hour and afternoon recess, there were plenty of wet mittens and rosy cheeks in evidence of the effort required to form mounds of snow like beaver huts on the playground. Lena pronounced their work a success. All that exercise stimulated their minds and the children fell back into the habits of schoolwork with greater ease than did their teacher.

At day's end, the children headed home bearing Lena's special notes to their parents. Only Antje and Maartje remained in the schoolhouse.

When it became obvious that Cornelis was late, they began a game of Chinese checkers. Lena busied herself with small tasks: tightening the clothesline above the stove, trimming dead leaves off the ivy on her desk, refilling glue pots. "I hear Father's car!" Maartje said abruptly.

"I only have three more marbles! Can't we finish our game?" Antje pouted.

Hearing Cornelis enter, Lena looked up to explain why the girls were not ready. But an eerie chill stifled the words when she saw his ashen face.

"I need to talk to you," he said woodenly, swaying in the doorway.

She motioned to the desks. He lurched across the floor as if buffeted by a strong wind, and collapsed on a seat. His shoulders sagged in mute misery.

Lena shot a quick glance at the girls. The sound of one marble marching home was followed by Antje's squeal of joy. "I won! Father, I won!"

"I didn't lose, I just didn't win first," Maartje said, giddily redefining defeat.

"The story of my life." Cornelis' voice held a bitter, chilling timbre.

Thinking fast, Lena said, "Girls, I need your help. Come with me." Back in the teacherage, she put cups and a jar of dried beans on the table. "Divide the beans so each cup has the same number."

In the classroom, Cornelis had not moved. He looked up, seemingly unaware she had stood beside him for several moments. "Yzaak has let me go," he said in a voice as lusterless as a long-buried silver spoon.

"Let you go," Lena repeated, stunned.

"No one is buying automobiles. In fact, some want to sell their cars back to him at the price they paid," he said with a harsh laugh. "Yzaak has no further need for an employee. It was a shock, but no surprise."

"When did you find out?"

"This morning, before I took off my coat. He said, 'I'm sorry, Cornelis, but there's not enough income to support both of us. I have to let you go.' Then he handed me a dollar bill. All I could think was, if there's not enough income, why give me a dollar?"

"What will you do?"

He seemed to age before her eyes. "That's what I've pondered all day. When I was out West, before I married Juanita, I met a fellow who worked in lumbering up on California's Northern coast. He warned me: 'It's hard and dangerous work.' But he also said a fellow like me would make good money."

Knowing that sounds carried over the partition, and hearing the girls counting beans on the other side, Lena kept her voice low. "You would take the girls to California on such a whim? What are you thinking, Cornelis? Can't you help stay here and your father on the farm? The girls are settling in here. They have their grandparents, and friends at school and church."

"No, they'll stay here, at least until I get settled. But I must go. The only reason I felt I could live at home was if I were bringing in money from a job away from the farm. Things are tight and getting tighter, even for farmers who have long thought they were immune to city folks' problems. If I get a lumber job, I can send good money home to help my parents survive."

"But what about the girls?" Lena choked out.

"They were my first thought after Yzaak told me. I have yet to tell my parents, but I know they'll be willing and happy to keep the girls until the end of the school year."

"But what if you go all the way to California and there's no job, after all?"

"Lumbering is not a job just anyone can do. That's in my favor."

Lena reached blindly and lowered herself to Liesbeth's desk. With her palm pressed against her ear to support her head, she heard sounds like the ocean's voice in a seashell that young Brigetta had treasured. *Perhaps a seashell from California*, she thought inanely.

"The beans are almost gone, Tante Lena," Antje called.

"That's fine," Lena responded dully.

Cornelis leaned forward and clasped her shoulders. "Lena, look at me." She turned her head; his fingers were so close she could see every downy hair, every line and pore. "My daughters love you. Knowing you'll be part of their lives in my absence makes it possible for me to even consider leaving."

"I love them, too, but their love for you is overwhelming." His hand's warmth penetrated her clothing and skin until she felt him in her bones. "When will you leave?"

"Tomorrow. On the train."

She swallowed hard. "So soon?"

"Nothing is gained by delaying. A job could be lost if I am not there to claim it. And, a quick departure is easier on everyone than prolonged farewells. Yzaak says he'll pick up my automobile from the depot and attempt to sell it. He'll give whatever he receives to Father without taking his cut, out of respect for my work. But even so, I don't expect it will be much—not these days."

"The girls will miss you." Slim comfort, but his was a brave decision without a certain outcome, and he still had to face his family's shock. "I'll do my best to make the time you're gone as bearable as possible for Antje and Maartje."

He relaxed somewhat, but his visage still revealed a tormented soul. "It's not as if I won't return. I'm glad we had Christmas together. Yzaak was kind to delay his news until afterwards."

"Was Christmas a happy time for you?"

"Perhaps 'happy' is too strong a word. But it was a good time in that the girls now know their aunt, uncle, and cousin. And they have pleasant memories of their first Christmas without Juanita."

He reached out and tucked a wandering curl behind Lena's ear. The tenderness of that gesture rattled the lock on a slammed door: the door to a forty-six-year-old woman's perplexed heart.

She bolted from Liesbeth's desk and stood in the aisle waiting for the blood to cease pounding through her veins, searching for something—anything—to shift the focus. "I'm concerned that you're making a very long trip with no assurance of employment at the other end."

"I've always been able to get work, Lena." It was empty assurance.

"But to make such a move on such a slender thread as one conversation, years ago, and with a man you really don't know?"

"I figure the trees are still there. Even the stock market cannot change that. And people still build homes, so someone must do the work of getting lumber from the forest to the mills."

Each word sat in Lena's mind like a cracked egg. One false move would leave a mess, so she barely lifted her feet, and moved with purposeful care as she followed an aimless path around the classroom. Cornelis would soon be gone but, in ways she had never imagined, they were linked even in his absence.

The girls skipped into the room; their laughter swelled like water coming to a boil. Cornelis and Lena's eyes met and held for an agonizing moment.

She read sadness and worry in his and wished she could know the future.

He read despondency and loss in hers and wished he could cling to the present.

Cornelis waited by the door as Lena tied scarves and fastened buttons. "Father, do your tongue-click for that song about buttoning our coats," Maartje pleaded. She tugged Lena's skirt. "Listen, Tante Lena!"

He obliged his daughter's simple request, and began the staccato pulse of tongue-against-teeth to the rhythm for "*Button up your overcoat . . .*" that mimicked the sound of a squirrel cracking nuts. Lena's mind shouted the words, right up to the phrase that choked her: "*. . . you belong to me . . .*"

He held out his hand. A fluttery heartbeat later, Lena took it, leaning heavily on him as she rose from her crouch.

"You belong to me!" Antje chirped merrily and flung her arms around Lena's waist. She followed Maartje out the door and called back, "Come on, Father!"

The schoolroom door closed. Cornelis still held Lena's hand. "A kiss for luck?" he asked hoarsely.

If he were a soldier going to war, I wouldn't deny him. What he faces is as fearsome as any battlefront. She nodded jerkily.

He drew her close and kissed her forehead, then each cheek, then her nose and, next, her chin. After an excruciating pause, his lips brushed hers with a touch like a raindrop. He pulled her against his chest.

It was neither his nor her heartbeats filling her ears. It was Cornelis tongue-clicking the rhythm to "*. . . take good care of yourself . . .*" while his strong arms held her for a moment.

He released her and left without a word.

Like the fabled lad Pieter at Holland's dike, holding back an ocean with his tiny finger, she pressed a fist against her lips until the last sound from the Tudor Sedan faded. Wails springing from her core released a flood of tears that would have swamped an entire country had she been that fearless young Dutch boy.

She made a supper she could barely swallow. Finally, she turned from staring, unseeing, out the window to face the student's assignments awaiting her attention. Eventually, she finished her tasks and brought out her rocker and sewing basket, pulled up close to the stove and propped her feet on its ledge.

Hoping to lose herself in a routing task, she snapped an embroidery hoop around a faint pattern ironed on crisp linen. But as the minutes dragged toward bedtime, her mind couldn't dismiss events of the past two weeks.

She felt like the cloth in her hoop: stabbed with sharp needles, and yet waiting for more. *And Cornelis is always there to give more . . . more grief, more confusion, more frustration . . . more questions I will never have answered.*

❊ ❊ ❊

Friday, January 3 ◆ When Lena awakened, she immediately sensed a difference in the temperature. Though still not warm by a long shot, the air did not paralyze when she stuck her foot out from beneath the covers in search of her slippers.

On a day when she should have felt happy about a break in the weather, she could barely find the energy to write assignments on the board.

A somber Antje and tearful Maartje arrived in Hans' buggy. He accompanied the girls into the school and handed Lena a note. She opened it while he lingered as if waiting for a reply. She unfolded the plain paper:

Lena: By the time you read this, I'll have caught the early train for California. Wish me luck, and take good care of yourself and my girls. Cornelis.

She looked up. Hans' expression was one of grim resignation—that of a man who has loved and lost before and gone on living, one day at a time. "I'll come for the girls at four," he said, and left.

The paper in Lena's pocket alternately felt like lead or hot coals for the rest of the day. She didn't look at it, but the day's classes held subtle reminders, making her their prisoner—

In Reading: *by the time you read this* . . .

In Geography: *the early train for California* . . .

In Music: *take good care of yourself* . . .

When the fifth graders pulled down the United States map and quizzed each other on mountain ranges, Antje crept up to the front of the room (noticed, but unstopped by Lena) and asked quietly, "Which place is California?"

Janneken pointed to a long golden strip near the map's edge. "Here."

Antje tilted her head. "Is California farther away than Chicago?"

Lucas tapped Iowa. "Here's where we live, here's Chicago. California is lots farther away than Chicago." He spanned the distances with his hand. "California is as far as you can go from Iowa without falling into the ocean!"

Neither de Boer girl had yet spoken of their father's departure, but something in Antje's expression must have tugged at Janneken's heart. "Miss Stryker, when Lucas and I are done with our geography lesson, may I please help the second graders with their word drill?"

"Yes; now is a good time." With Antje and Sterre busy working with Janneken, Lena gathered Elsje, Saartje, Lucas and Jaap around her desk and took them into her confidence about Janneken's birthday surprise.

The morning dragged along. Lena caught students eyeing the clock, waiting for her to dismiss them for recess. She marshaled all her will power and carried on with what had long been planned to lighten Janneken's heart—but now, with the heaviness inside her, almost seemed too frivolous to accomplish.

Before she announced recess, she moved to the window. "I guess it wasn't such a good idea, after all, to drag all that snow over here," she said as students collected near the windows from which they could view the mounds.

"We could smooth it out for you," Lucas offered, right on cue.

Lena protested, "But that's so much work."

"Not if we flatten the mounds in the middle and leave the edges in heaps," Saartje said, biting back a grin. "The little kids could play King-on-the-Mountain and we big kids can stomp the snow flat in the center."

And so it was that Janneken dreamily kicked snow around, lost in her own world and totally oblivious to her teacher and classmates' schemes. The younger children tumbled and jumped, cheerfully creating chaos from carefully mounded snow.

By the end of the day, all but one hill had been flattened. Lena smiled when Lucas and Jaap nodded at each other and sauntered to the playground. Within minutes, the job was done and the boys headed home.

"We survived one day," Lena murmured with relief as she waved to Antje and Maartje who stared at the world from Hans' buggy—looking more like expatriates leaving the homeland than children going home to loving grandparents. She didn't envy Hans and Rebecca the dismal months ahead of comforting them.

As they had promised, Gustave and Hanna arrived to help smooth the surface of the playground's rectangle now enclosed in knee-high walls of packed snow. In the lengthening shadows, Lena threw herself into the work, grateful for anything that kept her from thinking about Cornelis on a train heading West.

She tried to convince herself her sorrow was for Antje and Maartje, but she knew that, while true, it was not the whole truth. Like Antje, her heart had split wide open at Lucas' words: "... *California is as far as you can go from Iowa* ..."

✹ ✹ ✹

Monday, January 6 ✦ Lena looked out the classroom window to survey a perfectly suitable surface for her intended surprise. Sunday afternoon's relative warmth had helped, and the overnight freeze had finished the job.

As arranged, Lena gave Saartje and Elsje a special signal when she usually would have announced recess. The two girls moved to Janneken's desk and led that bewildered girl to the front of the classroom. They each took an elbow and, grinning, lifted her up on the Storytime stool. Clutching a lumpy bag, Lucas came forward and looking like *Sinterklaas* about to bestow gifts on all good children.

"Do you know what today is, Janneken?" Lena asked.

The girl glanced at the blackboard, "Monday, January six."

"True, which means today is your half-year birthday celebration!"

The students broke into song while Elsje and Saartje knelt to exchange Janneken's *klompen* for shoes and skates that emerged from Lucas' burlap bag. With wooden runner guards in place, Janneken clomped after Elsje and Saartje who led the way to the window and pushed aside a curtain.

Janneken released a rapturous "Oh!" and turned beaming eyes to Lena. "We made a skating rink! I dearly love to skate!"

"I know you do, dear," Lena said and hummed a familiar skating melody as she pulled a box out from beneath her desk.

"How did these get here?" Wim demanded as she handed him his new Christmas skates.

"Your mother brought them to church yesterday for me and hoped you would not look for them in the afternoon! Well, what do you know?" she said merrily. "Here's a pair of skates labeled with Adda's name, and another with Bartel's . . ."

Soon everyone had had their own skating shoes and skates. All had been brought to church, on the sly the previous Sunday, by each student's parents who responded to Lena's sealed notes of instruction—and managed to keep the secret from their offspring.

It was perfect skating weather and the thrill of a private rink was exciting. Skates etched the ice. Voices rang out joyously. At the end of recess, no one wanted to come inside. Only the allure of frosted angel food cake muted their moans.

❋ ❋ ❋

Between the students' scheming for ways to get their work done more quickly so they could have prolonged skating times, and the underlying sadness camped in Lena's soul, and her increased watchfulness over Antje and Maartje, Lena nearly missed something that changed the course of the school year.

It happened one day when she was giving Lucas and Janneken an oral quiz incorporating speech, geography and history. It was Janneken's turn, and Lena asked, "In what state is Yosemite located?"

"Colorado?" Over Janneken's tentative answer (which would have lost points for geography and speech) Lena heard a whispered, "California."

Lena looked out across the four rows of desks. Everyone attended to their own lessons, with one exception: Bartel seemed too intent on looking busy.

"No credit for that question," Lena told the fifth graders. "Name at least three documents important to the formation of our country." Surreptitiously, she watched Bartel, but called on Janneken.

Gun-shy now, the girl answered hesitantly, "Uh, Declaration of Independence and, uh, the United States Constitution, and, oh! The Pledge of Allegiance," she ended in a rush.

Lena said, "The Pledge of Allegiance is incorrect, Janneken, and you lose one point for poor diction. Lucas, you may continue."

"She took the easy ones," he grumbled. "Okay. Bill of Rights, and, uh, Magna Carta, and, uh, and . . ."

This time the whispered response clearly came from Bartel. "The English Bill of Rights, The Mayflower Compact, and The Articles of Confederation."

Feeling the weight of eyes turned in his direction, Bartel turned red. "Sorry," he mumbled, sinking lower in his seat.

Lena pursed her lips and nodded toward the empty chair beside Lucas. "Bartel, please join us."

Fright kicked Bartel's nervousness aside. "Should I bring my book with me?" His voice wobbled.

"That won't be necessary." When Bartel slid into the designated chair, all pencils ceased their scratches, all pages stopped turning, and all recitations halted across the room.

Lena said casually, "Bartel, if I asked Lucas and Janneken to name important people from the American Revolution, what names could they give?"

He closed his eyes and rolled his head back on his shoulders. "They'd get lots of points if they picked King George, Lord Cornwallis, uh, John and Samuel Adams, and Paul Revere——he's awfully exciting . . . and Benjamin Franklin; I really like him—and George Washington and Thomas Jefferson . . . oh, and there's Patrick Henry, too."

Janneken said defensively, "Bartel has no business looking at my history book! He does that, you know! When he's supposed to be reading his own stuff, he sneaks it out of my desk while I help the little kids."

Tattling felt good, Lena could tell. It was refreshing to see a spark of life from Janneken. Thus, Lena would have let it go without reprimand, anyway, had not the information gained been so jarring.

"Is that true, Bartel? You've been reading the fifth-grade history book?"

Bartel sank lower in his chair. His chin bumped against his chest; he couldn't meet Lena's eye.

"Excuse me, Miss Stryker?" Raimund blurted. His twin was in impending danger—time for a rescue, even at risk of losing a recess for interrupting lessons.

"Yes, Raimund?" Lena acknowledged, continuing to watch Bartel.

"Bartel ain't the only one who does stuff like that. I saw Katrien looking at our spelling words one time. And once, Jaap said Elsje's dumb because he knows her science questions better than she does!"

Gasping, Elsje pitched forward, fists ready to punch. "You little sneak!" she hissed at Jaap who cowered beyond the stove to escape his irate accuser. She flopped back in her desk; Saartje reached across the aisle with aa comforting shoulder pat.

A tumbling log inside the stove echoed like gunshot, but even more startling to each student was what Lena didn't do—that being, reprimand anyone— and what she did do. From between the bookends on her desk, she selected the book every Dutch Valley School student recognized as the teacher's enviable source of every lesson plan, every quiz, and each question on every test.

She opened the book and flipped pages slowly. Then, her glance scanned the room, dropped back to the big book, then traveled up-and-down each aisle.

"I'll ask a series of questions. Anyone who knows the answer may raise a hand. This won't be graded— think of it as a practice test."

For the next half hour, questions and answers flew:

. . . "What is the difference between latitude and longitude?"

. . . "What is one word in which the letter Y holds the place of a vowel?"

. . . "Which thirteen states border Canada?"

. . . "What is five-sixteenths multiplied by nine-twelfths?"

. . . "What are the original colonies?"

On-and-on it went, until Lena leaned back.

Students eyed each other nervously. In the eerie stillness, Maas whispered, "If you'd kept your mouth shut, Bartel, we wouldn't be in trouble."

Lena rose to perch on the corner of her desk. "No one is in trouble."

An audible sigh of relief swept over the rows.

"Why did you ask all those questions, Miss Stryker? I didn't know hardly any of the answers," Wim said.

"Ah, but the ones you knew were very interesting. You see, I didn't ask a single question from first-grade lessons—yet, each first grader correctly answered several second- and third-grade level questions."

"Does she mean we're smart?" Bartel asked in a stage whisper.

Lena bit back a smile, but ignored his question. "My experiment, of asking you these questions, tells me everyone is working above grade-level in at least one subject. You've learned by listening to other students recite, and by reading more difficult books during reading time. This means all of you may be ready for more difficult work in some subjects."

After the groans faded, Bartel asked, "Miss Stryker, you mean it's okay if we listen to other grades?"

"It's nothing we can stop, given our close quarters! Enjoy the rest of the day, because from now on it will be work, work, work," she growled playfully.

The students groaned.

Miss Stryker smiled.

Lena worked late, preparing tests. When she sank into bed, her last thought was Saartje's whispered confidence at dismissal; it made a short night and aching fingers worth it. "Miss Stryker, school's fun!"

❋ ❋ ❋

Postmark: Mendocino

Dear Lena,

I enclosed this note to you in a letter to my parents and daughters. At what address do you wish to receive mail in the future?

I arrived in California and secured a room over a laundry in the village of Mendocino. By asking around, I found the man I talked to years back. He hired me as a tree feller. At present, it's raining heavily and mudslides keep the crew from working. As soon as we can get into the woods, I'll join them. Until then, I'll install a stove in the laundry in exchange for a month's rent until I get paid.

The trip here was uneventful, except the train got stuck at Donner Pass. That delayed us 1 day, but we arrived without accident or injury. The men from the crew who I've met seem like a silent, sullen lot. Hearing from you would keep my spirits up.

Cornelis

❋ ❋ ❋

Thursday, January 16 ◆ Doc Draayer's scheduled appearance at Dutch Valley School fell on a day so frigid, snow sounded like crushed glass beneath Lena's feet when she helped him carry his supplies inside.

He quickly spread out an array of objects. Lena knew his presentation would delight the twins, whose interest in all things gory and gruesome showed no signs of waning.

"You're Raimund and Bartel's birthday surprise, but also the science lesson for all grades," she explained.

As per Lena's request, the doctor was prepared to conduct the opening exercises. "For You created my inmost being; You knit me together in my mother's womb. I praise you because I am fearfully and wonderfully made," he read from Psalm 139, which led perfectly into all he packed into the next hour.

By the time he left, the blackboard was filled with drawings and names of body parts. To the twins' delight, they had seen and touched "real bones" from a human skeleton. And each student understood how their body's joints and muscles worked, and knew how to tie a tourniquet.

The children deemed the visit a raging success, and Lena added another chicken-scratch to her mental list of "Ways to Show Brawn Isn't Everything—Brains Are Important, Too."

❋ ❋ ❋

Postmark: Dutchville

Cornelis,

Antje brought your note to school. That's a satisfactory means of delivering any future letters. She told us about a seagull on your windowsill. Including a feather made the story even more real. Maartje reported on the Chinese lady who owns the laundry. We made a geography lesson out of the resulting discussion on the distance between California and China!

I don't understand a tree feller's job, but it sounds ominous. I assume it involves huge trees crashing to the ground and, hopefully, missing the man wielding the ax. Be careful; your daughters need you. Lena.

❋ ❋ ❋

Friday, January 17 ◆ While Hanna and Lena prepared supper, Gustave offered grim news. "Betje De Groot got a letter from the Dutchville bank today saying they will foreclose on the farm if she cannot pay off Frans' loan within sixty days."

"Mathijs would do such a thing?" Lena gasped.

"I understand both sides, though I'm not in total sympathy with either one. In Mathijs' defense—"

Lena snorted.

"No, hear me out," Gustave said. "His name is on the letter, but his hands are tied. He must answer to the government for defaulted loans, or he could lose the bank. As for Betje, she is at the bank's mercy—which doesn't allow her to get away without paying debts, despite her widowhood. Frans borrowed excessively, and not only from the Dutchville bank."

"But if she kept the farm, and if she hired help and if she had a good crop next year, she could pay back the loans," Hanna protested.

"Those are big if's—all, I fear, have little hope of becoming reality. What Betje needs, she is unlikely to find in sixty days, given the local-area population: that being a husband. But even just a benefactor to provide financial assistance would be welcome."

"She has family in Pella; perhaps she'll move there." Lena hated to think of losing Janneken. "Frans took a coward's way out."

"We can't judge motives. Maybe he thought leaving Betje dealing with his suicide was easier than facing the shame of losing her family's farm."

Supper was a somber affair. Still subdued, Lena and Hanna did dishes. But even with the De Groot's tragedies looming large, Lena had something else on her mind. "I received a note from Cornelis."

Hanna dropped silverware into the rinse water. "I know; Rebecca told me."

"Wh-wh-why did she feel the need to mention such a thing?" Lena stuttered.

Hanna grinned mischievously. "Perhaps because of what Antje told her after the blizzard, about Cornelis staying at the school that night?"

Lena turned as pink as the roses on the plate she busied herself in polishing to a high sheen. "He was a great help to me . . . and the children."

"I'm sure seeing Cornelis de Boer kiss Miss Stryker gave the children a great sense of calm!" She dove to rescue the plate that Lena nearly dropped.

"*Goede God in Hemel!* Do all the children know?"

"About the kiss? No. Antje heard Cornelis and you whispering, but not what was said. Rebecca told her the kiss is to remain their secret."

Lena moaned, "I'll never be able to face Rebecca again—or the girls, for surely Antje told her sister!"

"Nonsense; you did nothing unseemly. Surprising, perhaps, but not forbidden. So, what did your beau's letter say?"

"Hanna! Hush! Cornelis is not a beau; he wrote out of concern about how his daughters are handling his absence."

"I see." Hanna wrung out the dishrag. "And the kiss fits in . . . how?"

"Not at all, nor does the letter," Lena admitted. "I don't plan to correspond with him, yet he asks where I want to receive personal mail. I might as well tell you, Hanna: He kissed me again, the night before he left. But that was just for luck."

"Hmm; only for luck? I hope you told him to send future letters in care of the parsonage. Because the minute a letter from California arrives, I will personally whisk it out to Dutch Valley School, rain or shine, hail or snow!"

"I told him it's fine to send any future notes through the girls."

Hanna's eyebrows shot up like arrows leaving a bow. "What were you thinking? You trust two curious children to deliver notes declaring their father's undying love for you?"

"Questions about Antje's difficulties with arithmetic are more likely than declarations of undying love."

Hanna smirked. "The man kissed you, Lena. We're up to three times, by my count. When your lips met, did he say, 'Oh, Lena! You are as perfect as the times-four multiplication table to me!'?"

Despite her discomfort in this conversation, Lena had to muzzle a chortle. "The kisses meant nothing, and changed nothing. Actually, the last time was six kisses—a family tradition."

Hanna watched Lena's finger trail along her forehead, across her cheeks and nose, then pause on her lips before brushing her chin. "Am I right to believe your harsh feelings toward Cornelis have softened, maybe even melted away, since Christmas?"

"Cornelis talked to Bram and Brigetta, but it doesn't erase our age difference. Nor does it change the fact that if I entertain romantic feelings toward Cornelis—which I don't—Brigetta would be deeply hurt."

"Dear, silly, clueless Lena! She'd be thrilled you fell in love with someone who loves you, too."

"Trust me, she may have forgiven Cornelis on one level, but she . . ." She clamped her lips into a rigid line, and heard Hanna sigh. "I'm not playing coy. My reticence is because I'm keeping my word to Cornelis."

"I want a sister with fewer scruples and secrets than you!" Hanna complained mildly.

"Oh, what I wouldn't give to be that sister for you."

✳ ✳ ✳

Postmark: Mendocino

Dear Lena,

Time drags in the evenings. Writing letters is a far more appealing activity than spending money I don't have to go drink with people I don't admire. My room is sparsely furnished, but provides all I need: bed, a shelf with hook, table, chair, cupboard. My suitcase under my bed holds my private things (a thief wouldn't look there!).

I have now worked 5 days as a tree feller. Our crew is typical in size and duties. Another man and I saw an undercut into a tree trunk to control the direction of the fall, and use axes to knock out the undercut and drive wedges. This controls the direction the tree will fall with the least amount of damage to it and the forest around it.

Two more men are buckers. They trim the tops, limbs, and branches and cut ("buck") the logs into useable lengths. Two others fasten chains around the logs so they can be dragged or floated down-river to the mill.

I've never worked as hard, not even during harvest. But I'm grateful for a job when many are without. Please write soon! Cornelis.

✳ ✳ ✳

Postmark: Dutchville

Cornelis,

Hopefully, you received my earlier letter. In your latest you describe your crew's duties. It occurs to me you downplay the danger in your job—which makes me wonder, what happened to the tree feller whom you replaced?

I happily report Antje has mastered the multiplication tables through the fives. She prefers words to numbers. Maartje storms through books like a hurricane. When I told her that, she wanted to read about hurricanes. Thankfully, I found a book that covered such, so I assigned Lucas to write a description of a hurricane in words at her level. Two birds struck with one stone, since it made him think, too.

I imagine you must get quite soiled, felling trees—especially after a heavy rain. How fortunate to live above a laundry! What types of trees do you cut down? On 2nd thought, don't tell me, tell your daughters. It can be a project for them to learn more about trees.

Lena

✹ ✹ ✹

Postmark: Mendocino

Dear Lena,

Did I see a hint of concern regarding my safety? Teasing aside, I do appreciate your concern. The man I replaced died on the job, but caused his own tragedy, coming to work drunk. I don't invest money in hangovers for don't worry.

My physical strength is put to the test daily, as is my mind. It often requires logic and quick thinking to do the job well and safely. I entertain the crew by singing! The rhythm of a song aids our work.

Please put the enclosed dollar toward future birthday treats. My daughters dearly love sweets, which may be why they love you.

As ever, Cornelis.

✹ ✹ ✹

Friday, February 14 ◆ Valentine boxes decorated with lacy trim, ribbons, and colorful papers lined the classroom windowsills. Girls' boxes featured hearts; boys preferred Cupid shooting deadly-looking arrows. Lena's over-sized, heart-shaped red-frosted sugar cookies interested the boys; the girls relished everything about the day.

Since making cards and decorating boxes had occupied several recess periods on cold days, there were few surprises except for the sentiments expressed in the children's cards.

The day was similar to each preceding Valentine's Day in Lena's years of teaching. Similar, that is, except for one startling discovery in the Valentine box on the corner of the teacher's desk. The pretty card's envelope was addressed to Miss Lena Stryker. The fancy valentine inside the envelope read Be Mine on the front side and Lots of Love, Cornelis de Boer on the back.

The writing suspiciously resembled Antje's, right down to disproportionate curves on the upper-case B's.

* * *

Postmark: Mendocino

Dear Lena,

I don't know which more enchanted my daughters about Adda's birthday surprise: your cherry pie, or Stereopticon Day. Maartje wondered if Yosemite is outside my window.

"I saw a picture of it on the starobteacan about California," she wrote. (It took 3 cross-outs before she settled on the spelling of the that tricky word!)

Truth is, from my window I look out across several roofs and a muddy road! But in the near distance (two streets away) I see the Pacific Ocean.

Waves crash and tides roll. I find the whitecaps endlessly fascinating. Whales spout, fish leap, sea lions stretch on the rocks and honk as if for joy. Even if I'm tired after a day in the forest, the Headlands draw me out for a stroll along the headlands nearly every evening.

I wish you could be here to see what I see. As always, Cornelis

* * *

Postmark: Dutchville

Dear Cornelis,

Thanks for faithfully writing to your daughters. You do well, finding things of interest.

After Antje received the letter with the picture you sketched of sea lions cavorting on the rocks, Katrien said, "I wish my father would go to California so I could get such exciting letters!"

It's bone-chilling cold here. You smell ocean breezes and the forest, I smell potatoes baking on the stove!

Students bring half-baked potatoes to warm their hands on the way to school, which then finish baking on the stove for lunch.

All of the children find your stories of logging the redwood forests very exciting. They asked me if the wood is truly red. I suspect it is, but perhaps you could enclose a splinter in a letter to your daughters.

What I see out the parsonage window this afternoon is a gray sky heralding yet another snowfall. Not nearly as delightful as your view.

I'll walk (and be watching for ice, not mud as you face!) to the Post Office. Then, Gustave will take me back to school.

Lena

✸ ✸ ✸

Postmark: Mendocino

Dear Lena,

Another week passed. Another paycheck puts me closer to coming home. Reading between the lines of Father and Mother's letters, I suspect the money I send them is sometimes all the cash they have. Other years they have sold livestock for winter income, but few are buying, and those few are not paying much.

I chuckled reading Antje's account of Liesbeth's birthday. Molasses cookies were a hit and merited a drawing of how big they were! It was my girls' first encounter with stilts ("I won't join the circus if I have to walk on wobbly sticks!") To which I say, "Whew!"

The box of molasses cookies you sent to me not only gave me a chance to taste the treats Maartje praised so highly, but provided pleasant lunches this week. I am eating the last morsels as I write to you, so my thoughts are sweet.

Always, Cornelis

✹ ✹ ✹

Postmark: Rochester, Minnesota

Dear Tante Lena,

I know you still harbor hard feelings toward Cornelis. Perhaps if we'd talked at Christmas,

I could have helped you understand how I can forgive him. In 1919, we left Dutchville because we feared Cornelis fathered the child I carried. To give up a baby was the hardest thing we'll ever do, but we didn't see how we could raise a child born of such awful memories.

Those were dark days. Then came Sanna and, with her, more unanswered questions about who and how and why, but also much joy!

Cornelis says (and we believe him) that while his actions toward me were inappropriate, he did not father the child I bore. It was bittersweet to see the cousins playing together and realize there's a little boy living with another family.

I pray you can forgive Cornelis soon. Life is too short to waste on hatred.

Lovingly, Brigetta

✸ ✸ ✸

Postmark: Dutchville

Dear Brigetta,

Thank you for your letter even though I am sure it was difficult to write as it for me to read about the sad times you and Bram have weathered. As Cornelis pointed out quite firmly, I was least affected by the events that fateful day. I was afraid for you—even though I didn't know the full story.

My anger with Cornelis has haunted me. I should find it easier to forgive than you did but, I confess, I do not. Because of his actions, two families suffered separation and the tragic loss of a son, a grandson, a nephew, and a cousin.

I take your words to heart, but can make no promises. You are a far better person than I am.

Love, Tante Lena

❋ ❋ ❋

Postmark: Dutchville

Dear Cornelis,

Soon I'll take another letter to the Post Office to mail, so I might as well take 2. The other letter is my response to Brigetta's in which she told me of your conversation in Rochester before Christmas. She wrote solely of her own volition; I honored my promise to you.

Brigetta assures me she and Bram accept your account of what happened. So much sadness, it seems too much to bear, but her forgiveness seems true and complete.

One day I was about to scold Maas for wandering around the room when I saw his meandering's purpose was to take him past Antje's desk! I remembered her Valentine for him was especially pretty. Have I missed symptoms of young love?

Maartje, on the other hand, told Wim flat-out one day, "Wim, I love you and I'm gonna marry you, so don't forget." His response? "Okay; I won't."

Next Wednesday is Katrien's birthday. We'll have an indoor picnic, complete with "ants and spiders" that Hanna and I will make from raisins and nuts. Maybe your daughters will not recognize the hairy legs as coconut! Gustave constructed a fine target for a beanbag toss and has contributed gunnysacks for a three-legged race. Without Hanna and Gustave's help, I fear life at Dutch Valley School would be just pencils and books.

Lena

❋ ❋ ❋

Postmark: Mendocino

Dear Lena,

Sometimes, it seems like just yesterday since I last saw you. Those days, work keeps me too busy to think. Other times, it seems I've been here forever. Those days (like today) I'm sick of living in one room all alone, and tired of the smells and noise from the laundry below.

Then, I look up and see the picture of my girls and realize the reason I'm here is to secure their future. It's just that the future seems awfully far away, much like the horizon.

The horizon is an amazing thing. I have never thought much about it until coming here where it seems more obvious when not blocked from view by buildings (as in Chicago) or by Iowa's cornfields.

Seeing the sun rise and set over the ocean is breathtaking. One coarse man on the crew walked back to town with me last night. The sun was setting and we both stopped in our tracks. An apricot line blended sky with sea like a kaleidoscope. The sky turned lavender, quickly adding the vivid orange of a pumpkin. Last came a rosy film over water and clouds; the edge of the earth seemed to suck the sun under its lip.

When I turned to look at Hank, he held his hat over his heart, as if the flag were passing by. We walked the rest of the way without a word, and only waved our hats when parting.

Thinking of you, Cornelis

✹ ✹ ✹

Postmark: Dutchville

Dear Cornelis,

This envelope is thicker than usual because I enclose notes the students wrote in response to your thoughtful gifts for each of them. If redwood splinters are that you stand there when they fall—be careful!

The letters were first a penmanship
exercise (hence my red marks) but the
sentiments remain the same, regardless of
whether Lucas writes with total disregard
for commas, or the twins' excessive use of
exclamation points makes reading their
notes mentally exhausting.

There's no need to return them. The
students have seen my comments, and I
have recorded the grades.
Lena

* * *

Postmark: Mendocino

Dear Lena,

I'm thinking ahead to summer. I miss my
daughters, but cannot give up the money this
job provides. My idea is for them to come
here. A woman from the village can care for
them while I work.

I'll send funds for the girls and Mother's
train fare. If the visit goes well, the girls will
stay and go to school in Mendocino in
September.

My landlord says the largest of the four
rooms above the laundry is available at the
end of April. It will provide space for the
girls' bed, so I'll gladly pay extra.

Thank you for your letters; they make home seem not so far away.

As always, Cornelis.

❈ ❈ ❈

Monday, March 31 ◆ The last day of March tried, and succeeded, to preempt April's showers. Rain washed winter from the earth. A downpour started in the night and continued throughout the next morning.

Instead of sopping mittens, it was wet socks that now dripped above the Dutch Valley School's wood-burning stove. There would be no morning recess, not with barefooted children and mud puddles galore from the persistent showers.

Lena put a kettle of water on to boil and made weak tea and honey for everyone to sip while she abruptly shifted Storytime to midmorning. "If the weather clears, I will give you a longer afternoon recess. Meanwhile, we will all drink honey-tea while I read."

Even before lunchtime, it sounded like everyone was sniffling. Lena ripped soft cloths from her ragbag into sixteen pieces. "If you feel a sneeze coming on, or if you cough, or if your nose drips, use this cloth!"

Lena was at the blackboard helping Jaap and Janneken diagram sentences when her chalk went wild on the object-of-the-preposition line. A sneeze rivaling any student's prior eruption exploded from her. Without time to grab her handkerchief, Lena employed her skirt to trap the spray.

"Excuse me!" She belatedly scrambled to retrieve the hanky that was halfway up her sleeve.

Wim giggled, "I saw your knees when you lifted your skirt, Miss Stryker!"

The day slogged along as if it, also, had a stuffy head.

At three o'clock, Lena asked, "How many came on your own today?" Hands rose, including Antje and Maartje's. "Well, since it is not raining now, I think you should start for home. The rest of you may play games or read until your rides arrive."

One by one, the children donned coats and galoshes, gathered umbrellas and lunch pails, and headed home. Three students remained: Sterre, Maas, and Katrien, but their parents arrived promptly at four o'clock.

"You don't look well, Lena!" Cokkie said, seemingly unaware her daughter's appearance was no better than the flushed teacher's.

At Cokkie's bidding, the other parents still there divided the list of school families so everyone would know school was cancelled the next day.

Alone at last, Lena built up the fire to last into the evening. Now, she would welcome the fever that had increasingly plagued her during the day. Instead, she shivered by the stove. She felt foolish doing so, but decided a nap before supper was in order and headed for her bed. The next thing she knew, she had jolted awake, believing someone had called her name.

Despite thinking it had been a dream, she croaked, "In here," then tried again, louder. "In here."

The teacherage door burst open, admitting Hanna. "Oh, Lena! Cokkie called to say you looked like death warmed-over, but the fact you're in bed at six o'clock is even more alarming. Get up; we'll take you home so we can care for you properly."

Lena had no say in the matter—not that she fussed. Gustave tended the fire and Hanna wrapped Lena in quilts until only her eyes were visible, then rushed her from the bed to the Ford. "Faster!" she ordered when Gustave seemed content with a decent speed.

"I'm not dying, Hanna." Lena protested, but her voice feebly supported her claim. "It's merely a spring cold. I don't have time to be sick. One day off, and then it's back to school." Her words were lost to a cough she smothered with a corner of her quilted-cocoon.

Tuesday was a blur. Lena slept most of the day, wakening only to think, *I'm so glad I didn't have to teach today, feeling this rotten.*

Hanna appeared regularly with soup and tea. Midday, she announced that she had called each student's home to ensure no one had mistakenly gone to school. "They're all as sick as you are, so I told them, no school tomorrow either."

"You can't do that," Lena protested.

"Well, I did. Go back to sleep. Maybe there will be school on Thursday."

Wednesday morning, Hanna appeared in Lena's room with tea, custard, dry toast, and what even Lena (in her fuzzy-headed state) couldn't deny was a curious facial expression. After fussing around for a while—shifting a pillow, adjusting a curtain, she sat on the foot of the bed and stared at her patient intently, opening and closing her mouth without speaking.

Lena finally set her cup down in exasperation. "What is it? You obviously have something to say, so spit it out! Why are you staring at me like that? Oh, no! You didn't cancel school for tomorrow, too, did you? I'm feeling better; I'll be fine by then."

"What? Oh, no; it's nothing." Hanna reached for the tray and set it on the dresser and returned to her place at the foot of Lena's bed. Even after Lena scooted back under the covers and closed her eyes, Hanna didn't leave.

"Unless you have something to say, I'll take a nap now," Lena said pointedly.

"Did you dream last night?"

"Dream? Not that I recall. I rarely dream or, I should say, I rarely remember dreams. Let me sleep some more, and if I have a dream, I'll try to remember enough of it to tell you," she croaked.

Hanna didn't move. Instead, she twisted a yarn tie on the patchwork quilt around her finger and asked casually, "Do you remember calling out last night, and that I came in here?"

"What? No, of course not. Obviously, you're the one who's dreaming!"

"No, I have a witness. Gustave and I heard you call out Cornelis' name and say, 'I'm sorry!' and sob as if your heart was breaking."

"Don't be ridiculous! I rarely even think about Cornelis, so why would I dream about him?"

Hanna arched an eyebrow, unfurled her legs and stood. "Be that as it may, the man you rarely think about," she paused to wink, "thinks about you." She dropped an envelope with a familiar postmark on Lena's chest, and left the bedroom.

Lena held the envelope for a long time before tucking it, unopened, under her pillow. She closed her eyes. *Talking in my sleep? Calling for Cornelis? Sobbing?*

"Hanna?" Hoping for (and getting) no response from the hallway, she retrieved the envelope, opened the flap, and extracted a single sheet of paper.

✸ ✸ ✸

Postmark: Mendocino

Dear Lena,

The tone of your last letter was cool, as if in hearing the truth from Brigetta, you shut me out. I realize it would've been better for all 4 of us to talk. Secrets left a wall between us that I find distressing.

I told Bram and Brigetta the ugly truth. Shameful on my part and without provocation on Brigetta's, my actions in 1919 could not have created a child. We wept over all that has transpired, and we can now be friends again, though I do not deserve it.

I accept full responsibility for heartache and damage I caused. Please accept my

apology, Lena. Oh, how I wish words could erase the past and all its trials, anguish, and sin. I pray God and you can forgive me.
Humbly, Cornelis

✻ ✻ ✻

Postmark: Dutchville

Dear, Cornelis,

School is closed for several days due to a common cold. By common I mean shared, as well as the usual meaning of nothing spectacular. A spring cold is dreadful, with the constant sniffles, frequent sneezes, and too many runny noses. We resume classes tomorrow and I hope all will return greatly improved.

I accept your apology and agree with your sentiments. "If only" is a heavy burden. Accepting means I must work to forgive you. I believe you, and continue to pray for forgiveness on my part to follow and sustain that belief.

Lena

✻ ✻ ✻

Postmark: Mendocino

Dear Lena,

A day when there was no school produced 4 wonderful letters for me. Yours brought great joy. I hate being at odds with you and pray we can soon find total peace. Antje and Maartje wrote detailed reports of playing with paper dolls in their sickbeds. Mother spoiled them with custard 3 times!

The 4th Dutchville letter was a surprise. Betje De Groot wrote about visiting me here. She faces a different life without Frans and contemplates leaving Iowa to begin anew where folks don't know her story. She asked how one goes about getting housing here, if a seamstress would find work easily, etc. I tried to answer her questions, but said it's best is to see for herself. I'd hate to encourage her to make a wrong decision.

Lena, you are such a treasure to all your students' families. Betje mentions how Janneken will miss you if they move here. I trust you've recovered completely by the time you read this. People count on you!

All my best, Cornelis

✸ ✸ ✸

Postmark: Mendocino

Dear Lena,

Things have progressed quickly since I last wrote. My letter to Betje encouraged her to check out the situation here. When she learned from Mother and Father that Antje and Maartje will join me this summer, she offered to escort them, leaving Dutchville

May 31. This is a wonderful solution to the dilemma of how to get the girls out here because June is busy for Mother and Father. Please make sure my daughters don't let their studies slide in their excitement!

As always, Cornelis

* * *

Postmark: Dutchville

Dear Cornelis,

I wondered what Betje plans to do. I understand staying here is difficult, but I wonder at the wisdom of her going so far from friends and family. She has relatives in Pella—much like you moving here where family can help.

We had a treasure hunt for Giertje's birthday. Gustave, Hanna, and I devised clues. Hanna threatened to never speak to me again if I ever do another treasure hunt! But I noticed she gave extra care to decorating sugar cookies, so I don't worry too much!

Spring is finally here. We're all waiting for the tulips, and lilac bushes are sprouting leaves. Every day without a fire in the classroom stove is a delight. Soon, I'll open the windows to let the breezes in— and then we'll know winter is past. I envy you being able to escape much of the dreariest times.

Lena

✳ ✳ ✳

Postmark: Mendocino

Dear Lena,

What a surprise to receive the reports on logging! My crew was amazed that Iowa students are so interested in our work and do good research. The men are not much for writing, so extend thanks to the children on their behalf.

Yes, I'll remind Betje during her time here that relatives make a transition easier. Pella is far enough away from Dutchville that she should not feel as if everyone is staring at her and thinking of how Frans died.

If you notice a difference in my writing, my fingers are calloused from working with timber. It makes holding a pen awkward. I'm very aware I'm writing to a teacher who evaluates penmanship!

Speaking of evaluations, the crew boss (a gruff, burly man) surprised me last week when he yelled, "Take it easy, or you'll kill the best tree feller I ever had!" A backwards compliment is better than none, so, here's mine for you: when lilacs come to mind, I think of you, and I'm mighty fond of lilacs.

Cornelis

✳ ✳ ✳

Friday, May 2 ♦ Storm pranced through the gate, gleeful to be out midst the heady smells of the plowed fields around the schoolhouse. As was Lena who waited on the schoolhouse stoop.

"Hanna!" she exclaimed as the sole occupant of the buggy tied the reins loosely around the hitching post.

"Your chariot awaits, Miss Stryker!"

"Where's Gustave?"

"I'll ignore that inhospitable welcome for your sister who has set aside chopping onions to come pick you up! Gustave's working on his sermon, so I'm here. Besides, I wanted to rush this letter that arrived today out to you. It can't even wait until you get to town! If only the Post Office delivered mail to the schoolhouse. But," she added impishly, "if it did, I wouldn't be able to keep my eye on you!" Grinning, she waggled an envelope before Lena's face.

Like a bull lunging at a red flag, Lena grabbed for it but Hanna raced away. The women chased each other around the schoolhouse, ducked between the swings, laughing the whole way. Gasping for air, Lena caught Hanna by the pump and snatched the letter.

"Is this the sixty-first letter?" Hanna asked impishly.

"Don't be silly," Lena scolded. Joy brightened her eyes, illuminating her feeble denial. "It's only been eighteen." Belatedly, she snapped her jaw shut.

"Eighteen! My, that's amazing, especially since Cornelis has only been gone . . . let's see, what is it? Sixteen weeks?"

"Something like that," Lena murmured vaguely, determined to give no clue to the undeniable fact that every day upon awakening her first thought was to add one more day to the increasingly depressing total. *February 1: thirty days . . . March 15: seventy-two days . . . Today: one hundred and twenty days . . .*

"And how many letters has he received from you?" Hanna teased in a singsong voice as they climbed into the buggy.

"I answer each letter he sends. It's the mannerly thing to do."

"Cornelis is fortunate that his daughters' teacher respects etiquette!"

Leaving the schoolyard, Lena gave undue attention to a split-rail fence around a pasture. "Hanna, you need to know something. Cornelis is looking forward to Betje De Groot's visit when school is out. She and Janneken will accompany Antje and Maartje to California. He seems pleased—excited, actually—to see her. I'll discourage further correspondence with him."

Hanna jerked toward Lena so suddenly that Storm veered to the right in response to a swift tug on the reins, requiring a hasty correction. "Betje? Why is she going there? Cornelis never showed the slightest interest in her, did he?"

"Not that I knew. But you must admit, they have much in common. Both have daughters, both have lost spouses, both are . . . young." That final word filled her throat, choking further speech.

"Oh, Lena—" Hanna began, only to be cut off.

"Please don't be kind to me, or I'll blubber all the way to town."

"All along, you've protested that Cornelis means nothing to you . . . but, maybe, just maybe . . . does he hold a place in your heart?"

"No! Don't be silly. I'm just overwrought because I don't think that Betje, I mean, I think Cornelis is . . . well, there are the girls to consider too, and Janneken is . . . well, you know what I mean."

"Of course," Hanna lied blatantly.

Lena burst into tears. "It's frustrating and difficult to communicate through letters. I see the girls every day and can't help but think of Cornelis—I mean, how much he's missing by being . . . so far *awaaaay*!"

Hanna yanked the reins purposely this time. Storm stopped in the middle of the road as his mistress gathered her weeping sister into her arms and murmured wordless, but comforting sounds. They clung to each other; tears flowed and soaked both sisters' shoulders.

"We need to keep going; Gustave will be waiting for his supper," Lena finally said, releasing another body-shaking sob that ended in a hiccup. She attempted a smile that not only lacked joy, but faded so quickly it could almost have been a facial tic.

Hanna ran her knuckles across Lena's cheek in a comforting gesture that sprang from their childhood. "He knows where the kitchen is," she quipped, but nonetheless, she flicked the reins.

Faithful, patient Storm swished his tail and carried two women and their buggy-load of thoughts, sorrows, dreams and prayers safely home.

❋ ❋ ❋

Sunday, May 4 ◆ Lena looked across the aisle of the Dutchville Reformed Church and took notice of the delicate bone structure in Betje De Groot's face. In profile, her nose followed a graceful line to her lips. Her chin showed strength of character.

Her unwrinkled skin and brown hair with its healthy shine belied her recent tragedies. Her posture spoke of youthful resilience, not a middle-aged teacher's exhaustion.

As if all that were not depressing enough, Betje's spring coat's complicated sleeves and perfectly set collar showcased her skills as a seamstress in a tasteful manner. A well-behaved Janneken sat beside Betje, proving Betje's skills as a mother. Seeing all this did nothing to alleviate Lena's depression.

Gustave began the invocation. Lena sat down, though all around her—including the Huitink sisters— stood. She closed her eyes, but it was more an action of shutting a door on the past than reverence in the present. Then the organ filled the sanctuary with soaring notes of opening anthem.

Seeing Lena, Floris Huitink asked solicitously, "Do you feel faint?"

Lena shook her head. The spinster sisters watched her like hawks on a fence around a chicken coop. Lena wrote on her tablet: *I'm fine. Don't worry.*

Floris showed the tablet to Femmetje, both women seemed disappointed in Lena's assurance of good health. Despite appearing to give Gustave her full attention, Lena knew part of her heart was sweeping up the dust of a dream.

＊ ＊ ＊

Postmark: Dutchville

Dear Cornelis,

I'm relieved Betje will accompany Antje & Maartje to California. She is a fine woman & a good mother. Her skills with a needle are unsurpassed. Unless Mendocino is overrun with seamstresses, she'll earn a fine living & provide a valuable service there. Janneken is a fine child—a good companion for the girls.

Next week is Wim's birthday. Hanna and I spent Saturday morning making gingerbread men & one gingerbread dog. Why a dog? I asked the Vet to bring cats and dogs to show the students how he cares for small animals. Doctor Vander Zwaag mentioned his visit to the school to Dries Wynkoop when he was caring for a sick hog.

One thing led to another, so Dries & Hilde will be in attendance when the Vet presents Wim with a puppy & a dog-cookie!

I know you are counting the days until you see Antje & Maartje again. Anytime someone pulls down the map, Maartje announces, "See that gold thing by the blue water? That's California where our father works very, very hard!"

I know you'll help Janneken find the gold in her new experience, too. She does fine in school, but needs cheering. You will provide a happy summer for her & Betje.

All the best to you, Lena

※ ※ ※

Friday, May 30 ♦ The schoolyard was awash in vehicles. The children clutched report cards and bid farewell to classmates. Except for Janneken, Antje, and Maartje, the students would all see each other at church or on rainy days when farm children could play together.

Lena accepted parents' thanks, hugged the children, laughed at jokes and stories, and mutely counted the minutes until she could be alone with her thoughts. Thoughts submerged for many days now shouted inside her head: *In a few days, Cornelis welcomes Antje, Maartje, Janneken . . . and Betje.*

Try as she might, Lena could not block out Betje. The young widow glowed as she talked to other parents, telling Martina Hazenbroek, "It's a long trip, but with Cornelis to welcome us, everything won't seem foreign!"

Then she gushed to Magda De Jong, "Cornelis has written several times, telling me what to expect for weather. My goodness, to think of living in a place where winter means rain, not snow!"

Lena trembled. *Of course, Cornelis continues to write to Betje. Why didn't I expect it? But, why is she talking about winter? It's only May!*

That evening, the Dutchville train depot platform rumbled beneath dozens of feet as the Westbound train approached. Hanna tucked her arm through Lena's as if afraid her sister would bolt, despite a stern supper-table speech after Lena said she wasn't going to the station.

"Oh, Lena, it will crush Antje and Maartje if you don't see them off!" Hanna exclaimed.

At the depot, words gushed from Lena. Even Hans and Rebecca had less to say than she did. Or perhaps it was only because she gave no one else much of an opportunity to speak.

"Be sure to tell your father you got the highest penmanship grade, Antje!" and "Maartje, remember to sound out new words you see on signs or storefronts or in newspapers!" and "Janneken, you'll be able to paint a watercolor of the ocean!" and "I'm sure Cornelis will be so happy to see a familiar face, Betje, he'll talk your ear off!"

No one was more relieved than Lena when the conductor called "All aboard!"

Rebecca and Hanna thrust boxes into Betje's hands, midst laughter.

"Is it cold chicken and biscuits, Rebecca?" Hanna asked, grinning.

Rebecca asked, "And yours is hardboiled eggs and apples?" Hanna nodded.

Lena stepped forward to place her box in Betje's loaded arms. Midst laughter as Betje transferred one box to Janneken and another to Antje, Lena said, "My box contains lemonade, watermelon pickles . . ."

"Those pickles are Father's favorite!" Antje shouted out above the din.

Lena wished Betje was not standing so close.

She continued quickly to cover her confusion: "And oatmeal cookies—which could be breakfast—slices of pound cake, and dried-beef or cheese sandwiches."

"My goodness," Betje said. "We won't even have time to look out the windows with so much to eat! I can't thank you enough."

After hugs all around, the travelers entered the passenger car. Much handwaving ensued until Lena thought, *Will the train never leave?*

It soon did. The train's mournful voice announced its approach to Dutch Corners' crossing. The whistle grew fainter. In the Ford's backseat, Lena covered her ears, resting her elbows on her knees.

Tears dropped and formed cloud-shapes on her skirt. Arriving at the parsonage, she passed through the kitchen without slowing, and closed her bedroom door softly.

An hour later, Hanna rapped lightly, then peeked in the doorway. Lena was asleep. Her tear-stained cheeks offered testimony to the fact that even teachers have been known to lie about affairs of the heart.

❋ ❋ ❋

Postmark: Mendocino

Dear Miss Stryker, Father and Tante Betje have gone for a walk but we can see them from the window so we are not afraid in our room. That's what our house is here—just a room. There is a big bed for us girls and one little bed for Tante Betje. Father sleeps downstairs in the laundry. Isn't that funny? He and Tante Betje whisper until we fall asleep. I liked the train ride. The ocean is very big. Love, Antje

■

Dear Tante Lena, California is not gold like on the map. Janneken helps us spell and reads to us. I want to live on a train. Father has 4 chairs and a barrel to sit on. He has a beard now. I love you! XXOO Maartje

■

Dear Miss Stryker, I am having a wonderful time. Uncle Cornelis gave me a journal (that's what you call a blank book) when he met us at the train. He had flowers for Mother, and a basket of fruit for all of us, and dolls for Antje and Maartje. We had a picnic by the ocean today. Thank you for giving me my very own copy of "The Secret Garden." Love, Janneken

■

Dear Lena and Hanna: We had a safe and wonderful trip. We had plenty of food, thanks

to you and Rebecca. We even arrived here with some to share with Cornelis. He has a small, but serviceable room and is working hard and making good money. Next week, he'll introduce me to the woman in the village who sews for townsfolk. Meanwhile, I'll sew doll clothes for the girls and hunt for durable cloth to make trousers for Cornelis. The ones he brought with him are nearly in tatters from working in the woods. Sincerely, Betje

■

Dear Lena,

Thanks for the pickles! Antje and Maartje seem to have grown several inches, but it could be my imagination. It's wonderful to have Betje here—without her and Janneken, the girls would face lonely hours. They became good friends on the trip out here. Thanks for your kindnesses to my girls. Enjoy a restful summer!

Cornelis

✱ ✱ ✱

Thursday, June 19 ◆ "Just watching you, Lena, makes me tired," Hanna protested. "Stop long enough to enjoy a glass of iced tea with me."

Lena kept digging. "A garden won't plant itself."

"True, but between laundry, gardening, painting the pantry, and washing windows, you've been a whirlwind." She led Lena to a bench by the garden.

They sipped, content to sit without talking until their glasses were nearly empty. Then Hanna said, "I bought stamps when I mailed our letters to Brigetta." Getting no response, she added pointedly, "In case you need a stamp."

"I won't need stamps anytime soon."

"You won't answer Cornelis' last two letters?"

"I didn't know you kept track," Lena said coolly.

"Don't get your dander up. I just know how much a letter means to Brigetta. The same must be true for Cornelis and the girls. Won't they think it odd if they write to you, but receive no reply?"

"Answering too promptly gives a wrong impression. Don't worry; I'll write to the girls and Janneken. They're my main concern. Now, I need help to haul away the rocks that surfaced in the garden over the winter."

"I'd rather get rid of the rocks in your head."

Lena wisely let it pass.

❋ ❋ ❋

Postmark: Dutchville

Dear Janneken, Antje, and Maartje,

You have been in California for 6 weeks! I enjoyed your stories of collecting shells and driftwood to put on the windowsill.

Janneken, your mother is very clever to make matching dresses from feed sacks for the 3 of you. Antje and Maartje, I'm sure

your father appreciates the notes you hide
in his lunch bag as much as the good food
Betje packs for him each day.
  How nice to have a buggy-ride to see
lumbering. Now you've seen redwoods!
Love, Miss Stryker

Lena called up the staircase. "Hanna, are your letters to California and Minnesota done? If we don't leave for the depot now, we'll miss the train."

The sisters hurried along the street, waving to neighbors on their porches. They chatted briefly with the stationmaster who added Lena's letter to the mailbag awaiting the Westbound train. "The Eastbound train coming in heads North from here, so this Rochester letter goes out first, but the Westbound train is due within the hour."

Lena only half-listened, distracted by something farther down the platform. "Look, Hanna—there's Jillis Van Leuven!" She hurried over to greet Saartje's father.

"Hello, Lena," Jillis greeted her. "What brings you to the depot tonight?"

She laughed. "That's my question for you! Why aren't you in the field?"

"Just being neighborly. He pulled out his pocket watch. "And here comes the train now, right on schedule."

Conversation became impossible, so Lena waved and walked back to Hanna. Meeting a train was as much entertainment as anything awaiting them at home, so they lingered and watched passengers climb down the steps to stretch their legs. Luggage, boxes and mailbags passed between the baggage car and the platform.

The conductor appeared in the coach-car's doorway and gave a signal. With an ear-splitting *Hiss!* the train moved out of the station.

Hanna grabbed Lena's arm. "Lena, look!" She pointed toward Jillis Van Leuven. The man had bent to pick up two satchels and, as Hanna and Lena watched, he smiled at the owners of those bags: Betje and Janneken De Groot.

A gargling sound bubbled from Lena's lips.

"Did you know they were coming home?" Hanna called over her shoulder, already moving toward the threesome.

Lena darted after Hanna and clutched her sleeve. "Wait! They haven't seen us yet. Let them leave with Jillis . . . surely, he needs to get back to his fieldwork."

"That's rude and unkind, Lena! We saw Betje and Janneken off to California, so why not welcome them home?"

"But what if they're not returning here to stay?"

"That's what we'll find out," Hanna said practically. She shrugged off Lena's restraining hand and hurried along the platform, calling out, "Betje!"

Betje halted. Janneken squealed, racing to fling her arms around Lena who was ten steps back. "Miss Stryker! How did you know we were on this train?"

"I didn't know." *Have truer words ever been spoken?*

For someone who should have had stories galore about her time in California, Betje seemed inordinately disinclined to talk. She barely managed greetings, let alone details of any adventures.

That suited Lena just fine.

She and Hanna watched Jillis load the satchels into his truck and drive away with Janneken seated between him and Betje.

"Well, forevermore," Hanna murmured.

Back at the parsonage, Lena retreated to her room. When footsteps stilled overhead, she pulled a satin-covered box from her bottom dresser drawer.

Out on the De Groot farm, hope wavered. Betje perched on a porch railing and watched the moon stencil patterns on the clouds, remembering moonbeams floating on an ocean's face.

In the Dominie's bedroom, hope danced. Lying beside a gently snoring Gustave, Hanna fell asleep with her fingers crossed.

Above the laundry in Mendocino, hope struggled. With his legs propped up on the windowsill while his girls slept nearby, Cornelis stared out into the darkness to where the ocean rocked with mysteries of the ages—and wished he knew the answer to even one.

And in Lena's bedroom, Hope breathed its last.

Lena undid the ribbon around a stack of twenty-two envelopes, read each letter again, and then padded out to the kitchen, dumped the lot into the stove, and lit a match. As Hope turned to ash, she went to bed.

❋ ❋ ❋

Monday, July 14 ✦ "Mercy, Lena! What's keeping you so occupied? You haven't made a peep for hours!"

"Lesson plans. The summer is half over and I still have much to do before I will be ready to face the children."

Hanna thumbed the stack of arithmetic quizzes had completed. "Which grade is this?"

"Second."

"But, there are only two sets . . . ?"

"Of course; that is all that's needed: one is for Liesbeth, the other set is for Wim."

"What about Maartje?"

"That is a California teacher's concern."

Hanna pursed her lips and then said softly, "You don't know that they won't return to your classroom."

"Nor do I know it's not true. It's a waste of time and materials to create assignments that will not be used."

Leaving the room, Hanna whispered a plea: "Heavenly Father, it requires Divine wisdom, not my all-too-human intervention to fix this situation. I humbly ask You: please do whatever it takes . . . and help me wait patiently for—and accept—whatever Your answer will be."

❋ ❋ ❋

Postmark: Mendocino

Dear Lena,

I hesitate to write to you in my current state of mind. Depressed best describes it.

Today, I received a letter from Betje said that while she and Janneken thoroughly enjoyed their time here, she feels "making such a move is improper outside the bonds of holy matrimony."

Betje added that she isn't hinting for a proposal because, while I was "a gentleman" to her, she sensed that I "lack the feelings of love for her that should precede the God-pleasing marital union of man and woman."

If I loved her, she'd consider moving here as my wife. Since I didn't appear interested, she will not return, not even to make her own way in a place that needs her skills.

So, that's it. Having barely survived the 3 weeks since Betje and Janneken left, the girls have grown far too somber and I've become much too testy.

After Betje and Janneken's departure, I hired a young woman to care for Antje and Maartje. They, however, hated her and (I suspect) irritated her until she abruptly quit 3 days ago, taking with her the pint jar I used for tea in my lunches—the final insult!

It breaks my heart to walk along Main Street each evening and see my daughters hanging over the windowsill, waiting for me.

Forgive me for writing such a long, gloomy letter. Things will improve once we become accustomed to life on our own under less-than-ideal conditions.

Cornelis

＊ ＊ ＊

Postmark: Dutchville

Dear Antje and Maartje,

I'm proud of you for the nicely written letters I have received! Antje, you did a good job on making paragraphs. Maartje, you have a fine start on cursive writing, thanks to Antje and Janneken's help. I'm glad you like the booties and nightcaps I knitted for your dolls.

You mentioned trying to think of games to pass the time. Ask your father to save a piece of butcher paper so you can make a checkerboard. Draw it like the one you used at school (8 squares by 8 squares). Use small stones and beans for pieces. School starts soon; then you'll be busy all day! Give each other hugs from someone who loves you very much. Who is that? Your Tante Lena!

＊ ＊ ＊

Monday, August 11 ◆ Lena accepted a Western Union telegram from the messenger who tipped his hat, leaped off the front porch, and hopped back on his bicycle. The intended recipient was clear:

Miss Lena Stryker

She pulled out the thin paper and read silently. The words blurred in her trembling hand.

Escort girls home? Wire intent. Cornelis

Hearing the bell, Hanna had made it to the sewing room window in time to see the uniformed messenger riding away. She sent a query down the stairwell, "A telegram?" She raced down when Lena's only response was no answer at all, just a helpless squeak.

Lena released the wrinkled paper to her sister's outstretched hand. Hanna read the words aloud, her eyes opening wider with each one. She ended with a whoop and swept Lena into a joyful dance.

Lena pulled away and gripped Hanna's forearm. "Stop it! This is *not* a good thing! Whatever is he thinking, to send such an incriminating message to a single lady. It's inappropriate and . . . crude!"

She the telegram from Hanna. "This proves I'm wise to be rid of him. A true gentleman would never ask a single lady to come cross-country." she sniffed.

Rid of him? Hanna thought, but only said, "Way-back-when, Gustave sent a telegram, and you came to Dutchville! This time, it appears the sender has more romantic interests in a certain single lady than your proper brother-in-law did!"

"Hanna, you're ignoring important details." Lena sank to the bottom step as she ticked them off on her fingers while Hanna smirked.

"One: Brigetta and Bram have forgiven Cornelis; I haven't. Two: I'm forty-seven—too old to gallivant all over just because a thirty-year-old man beckons.

459 • Unguarded Edge

Three: Rebecca should go. Four: How do I complete my lesson plans if I traipse off to California?"

Hanna nudged Lena to one side of the step and joined her, holding up four fingers of her own. "One: Don't punish Antje and Maartje for whatever you have against their father. Two: Ninety-nine would be too old to escort two young girls across the country; forty-seven is hardly doddering! Three: If Cornelis wanted Rebecca, he'd ask. Four: The pressing task remaining is Antje and Maartje's lessons; if you don't go to California, the work wasted.

Grinning, she waggled her fingers under Lena's nose. "My points are better than your puny ones!"

Shocked, Lena leaped up. "You think I should go?"

"You're an idiot if you don't—and quickly! What time is it?"

Lena checked her lapel watch. "Quarter past four."

"Plenty of time to get you on the evening train."

"What?" Lena squawked.

Hanna sighed, "Lena, Lena, dear-dear Lena! Let me spell it out. Cornelis thinks highly of you; maybe even fondly. It appears he's in love with you, but I won't push past fondly because it might give you apoplexy!"

"But," Lena blurted, "he loved everything about having Betje there. Antje said they whispered at night." Tears welled up as she remembered the blizzard. "If he were as fond of me as you seem to believe, would he whisper with Betje?"

Hanna snorted. "What are they going to do but whisper? The room where the girls sleep—where

Betje and Cornelis would go one walks and leave their daughters alone—is probably no bigger than a postage stamp! They likely share news from home or talk about where Betje can buy thread."

Lena blinked. Never had she envisioned the scene in such unromantic terms; to her, the scene matched one blizzardy night in the schoolhouse. *Perhaps Cornelis had said, "Can you mend socks?" instead of "Sweet Betje, you are so dear to me!"*

She burst out laughing, but then her face crumpled and she hiccupped through laugh-studded tears. "Oh, Hanna, I don't love Cornelis, but I'd like to be his friend. If you think it's proper, I'll go as a friend, and for the girls. But leaving today is impossible! The bank isn't open—"

Hanna interrupted, "We'll rob the sugar bowl. You bathe. I'll pack food, and get a satchel from the attic."

When Lena emerged from her bath with dripping hair and glowing cheeks, Hanna was pouring chilled tea into a fruit jar. "The box has buns with ham, Gouda cheese, or apple butter; there are carrot sticks; apples; almond patties, and a pint of your watermelon pickles—save them for Cornelis in case his heart still runs through the melon patch!"

Lena flushed. "More than I need, but I'll arrive bearing gifts. Oh, my; this makes it seem real."

"It is real; a real adventure. You don't have to come back madly in love with Cornelis, Lena; you're going for the girls. Just accept anything else as God's blessing, including seeing the ocean and redwoods!"

Lena stood with Gustave and Hanna on the railway platform, comforted by their unwavering strength. In her satchel, was money from the sugar bowl and Gustave's wallet that was left after buying her ticket, and a volume of romantic poetry Hanna had not-so-innocently selected from the parsonage bookshelf.

Lena felt so nauseous by the time the train pulled into the station, she could barely move. Hanna tugged her toward the coach car and pushed her up the steps. "She's fine," she assured the worried conductor.

"We'll send a telegram to let Cornelis you're on your way," Gustave shouted above the din.

Soaking up Gustave and Hanna's encouraging smiles, Lena waved until she could see only the tip of the Dutchville depot's chimney.

As the train picked up speed, so did doubts the past two hours of activity had forced into retreat. "What on earth am I doing?" she asked her reflection in the window. *A telegram changed my life thirty years ago—will another do the same now?*

She rested an elbow on the seat's arm and balanced her chin on a trembling hand.

A woman across the aisle asked, "How far are you going, Miss?"

"To the edge of the world," Lena said softly. "The very edge.

❖ ❖ ❖

Late August ❖ "Gerolt, if Lena were not planning to return in time for school to start, she'd have let you know. If she's not back in time, Hanna is prepared to

462 ◆ Hadley Hoover

assume responsibility for the interim. Her express purpose in going is to escort the de Boer girls home."

Gustave tried to end the phone conversation, which was going nowhere because Gerolt wasn't listening to reason—if he was listening at all.

Gustave hung up the telephone and rejoined Hanna in the parlor. "Gerolt worries too much," he said with a prolonged sigh. "But I wish we knew what Lena is thinking, waiting so long," he added, picking up his paper. "Why can't she send Gerolt a telegram?"

Hanna smiled placidly. "God knows the future." She copied a third-grade geography lesson for Antje.

A week later, Antje and Maartje leaped off the train into Hans' waiting arms. He staggered slightly and Gustave braced him from behind. "Grandfather! You got Father's telegram! We're back in time for school!" Antje said. "We're going to live with you again!"

"Father's coming home for Christmas!" Maartje exclaimed.

"Let me take a good look at you, " Hans said with a rolling laugh. "The best part of the summer is seeing you girls come off that train!"

"I've been counting the hours ever since Rebecca let us know to meet this train!" Hanna kissed Lena on both cheeks. "You look happy!" she added, before releasing her to Gustave's welcoming arms.

After a bath and supper, Lena found Hanna and Gustave on the porch. She stepped through a moonbeam to join them. Talk was desultory, which suited Lena.

Her mind was floating on ocean breezes that carried the call of a gull like the songs of a lover. Cornfields and mosquitoes seemed almost foreign.

Gustave asked about redwoods.

Lena recalled removing redwood splinters from Cornelis' hands.

Hanna mentioned lesson plans.

Lena thought of Antje's voice behind her and Cornelis as they traveled a country road in a borrowed automobile. *"If you don't remember your sums, Maartje, you can't be in second grade!"*

And she heard Maartje's airy retort. *"If Tante Lena married Father, she'd be our mother. Our mother wouldn't care if I didn't know my sums!"*

Gustave mused about oceans.

Lena saw two intertwined hearts drawn on the sand below Mendocino's cliffs. She described whitecaps, tides, sea caves, and slapping waves, but heard Cornelis asking, *"Whose names do I write in the hearts, Lena?"*

Gustave excused himself to finish his sermon preparations; Hanna patted the vacated spot on the porch swing; Lena left her chair and took his place.

Hanna turned sideways. "Your stories answer many questions, but I still have one: Has Lena Stryker learned to love Cornelis de Boer?"

Lena thought of how Cornelis and Mendocino, equally unforgettable, had joined forces in a full-fledged campaign with that very purpose.

Night birds called. The porch-swing creaked.

Hanna's question hovered, awaiting an answer.

Lena stared up at the stars, then closed her eyes—still able to see their reflection on the ocean's rippling surface. *"Diamonds for my lady,"* Cornelis' voice whispered in her memory.

Her lips felt Cornelis' soul-mining kisses transform all rational thoughts into feathers in the wind as they walked, hand-in-hand, along the Headlands.

While the girls played nearby, weaving necklaces from coastal wildflowers, their sweet voices turned Janneken's song from the Christmas play—"*. . . look into your heart . . .*"—into a serenade wafting across rocks and waters to find a home in the hearts of one man and one woman searching for what is most precious.

Hanna's question hummed, needing an answer.

Did I learn to love Cornelis? Lena reached for Hanna's hand and linked their fingers. She pushed one foot against the porch floor to set the swing moving again. "Not love. Not yet. But I learned not to hate him."

And Hanna smiled.